Jeff Stone

Rec'd
21 February 1979

from

Publisher's Central
Bureau

# The
# Ringway
# Virus

# *The Ringway Virus*

## RUSSELL FOREMAN

Little, Brown and Company • Boston • Toronto

FIRST AMERICAN EDITION

T 07/77

LIBRARY OF CONGRESS CATALOGING IN PUBLICATION DATA

Foreman, Russell.
  The Ringway virus.

  I. Title.
PZ4.F7185Ri3  [PR9619.3.F56]  823  77–6244
ISBN 0–316–28920–5


Designed by Susan Windheim

*Published simultaneously in Canada*
*by Little, Brown & Company (Canada) Limited*

PRINTED IN THE UNITED STATES OF AMERICA

*To Victoria and Keith Shipton*

The plague not only depopulates and
kills, it gnaws the moral stamina
and frequently destroys it entirely . . .
Times of plague are always those in
which the bestial and diabolical
side of human nature gains the upper
hand. Nor is it necessary to be
superstitious or even pious to look
upon great plagues as a conflict of
the terrestrial forces with the
development of mankind . . .

— BARTHOLD GEORG NIEBUHR, 1816

# The
# Ringway
# Virus

# 1 ∿∿∿∿∿∿∿∿∿∿∿∿∿∿∿∿∿∿∿∿∿∿∿

The pilot glimpsed the rain forest through a gap in the cloud directly below and ahead of the airplane. His right hand leaped to the throttles. He pushed on full emergency power and pulled back on the control column. Rain streamed against the aircraft as it lurched upward, buffeted by the violent ground turbulence. Lightning flashed and fixed the treetops in an eerie glare. The pilot still had the control column back when the aircraft flew into the forest. For a few seconds it planed, as if upon a green, heaving ocean — then the fuselage snapped in two.

Elizabeth Reece was seated in the back of the cabin. One moment she was looking at the lighted NO SMOKING — FASTEN SEAT BELT sign on the bulkhead, wishing for a cigarette because she was frightened, the next she heard a harsh rumbling below her and was jolted hard against her belt: it felt as if she were being dragged across a mammoth corrugated washboard. Then she was pitched violently onto her right shoulder, and pain shot through it. A sickening, wrenching freedom followed, then she felt a lashing at her body as if she were being whipped. When she again became aware of herself she realized that rain was pounding down on her, rain heavier than she had ever known, that spouted and gushed about her with such intensity that her first clear thought was that she would be drowned.

Elizabeth found she was enmeshed in a tangle of vine and creeper, which she'd brought down in her fall through the trees. Under her lay the softness of decayed leaves and branches, ferns, and the roots of the great creepers that climbed the trees in search of light. The air smelled dank and sour-sweet. The buttressed roots of the jungle trees stood high about her, flanges glistening beneath the cascading water.

Slowly, tearing at the vines that bound her, Elizabeth struggled to her knees. Arms free, she pulled at her hair, drawing it from her face. The rain stung her eyes and blinded her. She felt no pain, only the numbing pounding of the water. Three times she tried before she could get to her feet; then she stumbled about, her senses dulled by shock and the drumming of the rain against her scalp. Her dress was torn and gaped open at the front and kept sliding off her shoulder, pinioning her right arm. Her teeth began to chatter. Appalled by the density of the jungle that shut her in, she stopped moving, clung to a vine, and stared about her helplessly.

It was then that she saw the torn remains of a jacket: blue, with silver buttons, it was hanging in a tangle of smashed branches about twelve feet above the ground. Under it lay the stewardess, her body horribly contorted and naked except for a few strands of cloth that still clung to her.

Elizabeth pushed through the vines to the girl and knelt beside her. The skin was already cold and waxy pale in the rain. Elizabeth remembered the pilots, because she had seen the girl with one of them at the airport in Manila and had wondered if there was anything between them. Where were the pilots? And the other passengers? Was she the only one alive? She turned from the girl and saw that it was growing dark, as long streamers of cloud moved across the sun. Suddenly lightning flashed and thunder clapped so close that the jungle seemed to jump under its impact. Afterward, she couldn't remember leaving the girl, but the thought that she might be the only one alive drove her on, sobbing with fear. Ooze squelched between her toes and sometimes rose above her ankles; she was repelled by the slippery decay of the jungle floor.

The rain stopped as if a tap had been turned off, and at once a great silence grew in the forest. Only slowly did she begin to hear the drip from the trees and the run of the water that coursed on the sloping ground. Then thunder rumbled farther away, and gradually the call of birds unknown to her started up. With the end of the rain the jungle became hotter.

She all but stepped on Lewis. Her first thought was that he, too, was dead. She dropped to her knees and touched him, a big man in the remains of a light blue suit. His skin felt faintly warm. She put her ear to his chest and heard the unmistakable throb of life. Frantically she began to tear at the creepers and vines that wrapped him. A gold watch glinted on his wrist, and she saw that the sweep second hand was still moving.

His voice startled her. "Jesus . . ." he said softly.

She bent closer, staring at him. He was a man of about fifty, his hair beginning to go gray; there was a cut over his left eye and his lip was split, blood showing on well-cared-for teeth. She realized then that this was the American who'd been sitting across the aisle from her, a confident, evidently important man, looked after carefully by the stewardess. Before they had landed at Biak, the pilot had come back into the cabin and asked him if he would like to come forward to the flight deck. He had thanked the pilot, but said no. She remembered that he'd spent much of the time from Manila reading papers that he took from an expensive briefcase.

When she began to pull at the creepers again, she saw the blood on his trousers. His eyes flickered and opened, but he did not seem to see her. Then he said, "Stop it, will you?"

"But I've got to get these vines off you. Your leg is twisted." She stared at him helplessly. He was a very big man. "If only I had a knife," she muttered to herself as she turned back to look at the mass of vine wrapped about his legs.

That he seemed to understand. His right arm moved, groping for his pocket.

"Have you got one?" she asked.

His eyes flickered again and then closed. For a moment he continued to grope; then his hand stopped moving and his body became limp.

"I'll get it," she said, and, wriggling her arm through the vines, managed to find the pocket.

He nodded. Now he began to focus better, to watch her, to

[5]

remember her as the tall, good-looking Englishwoman of about thirty-five with the straw-colored hair, aloof, yet polite, showing a kind of English distrust of strangers. Her hair hung in damp cords about her shoulders, her dress stuck to her skin, and where the bodice was ripped the tight fullness of a white brassiere showed. Aided by the knife, she hacked and pulled at the vines. She stopped suddenly at the sight of so much blood.

"I guess it's broken," he said. He stared away from her, straight out across the ground, not wanting to see her face nor his legs. She didn't speak. A wave of helplessness swept over her that he sensed. "Any of the others around?" he asked, turning his head and looking up at her.

"I've only seen the stewardess."

"She okay?"

"No," she said softly.

He looked past her, his eyes moving about, taking in the denseness of the jungle.

"Do you know where we are?" she asked.

He grunted. "No. Unless you call somewhere between Biak and Port Moresby knowing where you are." Then he looked back at her. "What's the time?"

She leaned across him and looked at his watch. "Just after three o'clock."

"That's no help." As he spoke, blood ran from his lip. "The guy was lost. We might be anywhere."

"I'd better look at your leg."

He didn't seem to hear her. "We're going . . ." he said weakly. "We're going to need shelter."

"Your leg is twisted. It must be broken. There's a lot of blood."

"Forget it."

"But," she began.

"I said *forget* it." He made the effort to summon authority. "Now let me think. We've got to get a shelter rigged. Or you've got to. I'm no use."

"You mean branches and things?"

He took almost a minute to get up the energy to answer her. "Or," he said, "maybe part of the airplane."

"I don't know where that is."

[6]

"You've not found any of the others?"

"Only the stewardess."

"You call out?" He screwed up his eyes, trying to focus them on her.

"No."

"Try it."

She called several times, and they waited, listening, but no answer came.

"Better get going," he said finally. "I guess we're like grandma's tooth — on our own." He paused, overcome by the effort of speaking. Then he said, "Get this jacket off me and tear it into little strips. You'd better tie them to the trees as you go. Otherwise you'll never find your way back."

"I can't do that," she said quickly.

"You'll have to," he said.

"I mean, I can't take your coat. You're hurt. You should be kept as warm as possible."

"For Christ's sake. This is New Guinea. Night falls mighty quick here." The effort of explanation drained him. "Do as I say, will you? What's . . . what's your name?"

"Elizabeth Reece."

"Steve Lewis. Now," he said, as though this exchange of names had sponged out her objections, "help me get this coat off." He tried to move but fell limp again.

"I'm not going to," she said stubbornly. "You must be suffering from shock, so you've got to be kept warm. I know — I can tear up my dress."

"Okay," he said wearily. "If that's what you want."

The sodden dress clung to her. Then it tangled in her hair, but finally she got it off.

"You lost your shoes," he said. "Take mine, they'll be better than bare feet."

She said nothing, and he watched her as she crouched down and picked up the dress and began tearing at it.

"You English?" he said.

She looked up quickly, nodded, and said yes.

"What part?"

"London." She gave a small sideways snap of her head, a char-

[7]

acteristic movement to flick her hair back onto her shoulders, then she bent again to the cloth. When she had finished, he said, "Now tuck those bits of cloth into the top of your pants, so you'll have your hands free. Tie the strips onto bushes at about eye level. And listen, make sure you can always see the last one when you tie on the next. Got that?"

"But I don't like leaving you," she said.

"You've got to. For both our sakes. Rig some kind of a shelter." He wanted to add more, but the effort was too great; his eyes closed, and she thought he'd lost consciousness. She felt his pulse; it was weak but steady enough.

She had taken about half a dozen steps from him when her fear of the jungle and her loneliness in it overwhelmed her. She stopped and looked back at him. He was so still and gray that he might have been dead. Slowly she came back and dropped onto her knees beside him again.

His eyelids flickered but didn't quite open.

"I'm frightened," she said softly.

For a moment she thought he hadn't heard her. And she was half-pleased that this might have been so because she felt suddenly ashamed. Then his eyes opened. "Sure," he said. "So am I. Anybody says he isn't would be a fool. And a liar. I can't go. Shelter. You hear me?" He looked up at her.

"I hear you."

"Then find . . . the airplane. You've got," he added, "gray eyes . . . good eyes."

The daring of despair forced her away. She had no idea in which direction she ought to go. For all she knew she was going in a circle, but she kept telling herself she must do as he said and tie on the strips of her dress. And find the aircraft. Part of her fear was because of the way in which the jungle suddenly revealed its horrors. She had tied on about a dozen of her markers when she almost stepped on the body of a woman, crumpled, part buried. Ants were already swarming over it. When she was past it she stood for some minutes trying to compose herself, fighting the need to turn back.

She saw the first signs of the crash in broken branches hanging high above her, her eye caught by one that swung in the wind.

Then she saw trees with branches splintered off, and shredded leaves and vines beginning to litter the ground, greening its brown darkness. Quite suddenly she was in an open space, heavy with the stench of kerosene. Here the rain forest looked as if it had been cleared with one slice of a giant scythe. At the end of the cut was the machine, an appalling confusion of crumpled metal and snapped-off trees.

The aircraft had slewed to the right, its starboard wing torn off by a great anisoptera tree. One side had been ripped open. Forward, the wreck was buried in a tangle of vegetation, but aft of the wing the fuselage gaped where the end had been broken away.

She approached slowly, terrified of what she might find. Some yards away she stopped and called. No one answered. For minutes she stood there, fighting for the courage to enter. Twice she moved toward the open end of the fuselage; twice she drew back. Suppose, she thought, they were not all dead in there? Perhaps someone was alive, horribly injured. What should she do? She wouldn't be able to desert him. Besides, she had that man back there, with his broken leg and God only knew what else wrong with him. For the first time she thought of Steve as a person, not merely as another survivor, but as someone she already felt responsible for and therefore someone from whom she drew sustenance. Dear God, she prayed, let them all be dead — and then she felt shame at the thought.

On shaking legs she reached the opening and peered in. Many of the seats had been torn from their fastenings where parts of the floor had been crushed in. A tangle of seats, ripped cabin lining, hand baggage, and bodies was piled against the port side of the cabin and against the forward bulkhead. It was hotter in here, and already flies were settling.

Horror would have driven her from the wreck but for Steve's insistence that she make some kind of shelter for the night. Her eye fell on a strip of the plastic fabric to the left of the center lighting panel. A good part of this was intact. She wondered if she could get it down. She pulled at it, saw it was attached to a frame, and, tugging, found it was held by clips that came undone easily enough. She worked her way forward, pulling down the lining. It took her some time, but she finally undid it all and dragged it out of the airplane. She followed the scraps of material back to Steve.

"You've moved," she said when she got down beside him again. "You've moved your leg." She looked from his bloodied trousers up to his face.

"I feel okay," he said, then looked past her to where she'd dropped the piece of cabin lining.

"Let me look at your leg," she said.

"Looking's not going to make it any better. Let's see what you got." Speaking, even moving his head, seemed to be an effort.

"I could bandage it," she said, staring at the bloodied trousers. "And make a splint for it. We can't just leave it like that."

"In the old days at sea, they borrowed the carpenter's saw and got a cauldron of pitch boiling." -

She gave a tiny chuckle, the merest catch in her throat, as characteristic as that sideways snap of her head.

"Let's see what you got for a tent," he went on, shifting his gaze to look past her again.

"I didn't get enough for a tent. Now." She hesitated, then said as firmly as she could, for she was very frightened of what she was going to find, "I'm going to cut off your trouser leg."

It was worse than she had expected. The bone had come raggedly through the flesh, and from knee to ankle the leg was torn and swollen.

"I'd rather not look at it," he said.

She had no idea what she ought to do with it. Except that it would need splinting. And bandaging. Perhaps, she thought, staring at it, she ought to do that first. The bone looked whiter, smoother — except for its ragged end — than she had expected. "I'll have to tie it up," she said. "To keep the dirt out."

"I said you could look. That's all."

"I still have some of my dress left," she said. "I can use that for a bandage. Please, if I'm going to be of any use to you, you must let me help you."

He opened his mouth to object but then closed it. Pain came in waves, and he had the feeling that it would submerge him. He didn't always see her clearly; her handsome, intelligent face kept

[10]

slipping out of focus, as did her gray eyes, large and very much afraid.

By tearing and cutting with the knife around the hem of what was left of her skirt, she achieved a fair length of bandage. Darkness was coming quickly, the air heavy and damp. Several times Steve winced as she worked, and once he cried out so loudly that she stopped.

"Jesus," he groaned, clutching at his face with one hand while he thrust out the other to restrain her. Finally he said, very weakly, "Okay, go on with it." Her hands were shaking and bloodied when she finished and stood up.

For minutes he lay utterly still. Then he opened his eyes, looked up at her, and said, "Let's see if what you brought will cover us."

She wondered why she hadn't thought of another piece to go under them. She stumbled about in the dusk, and it was almost completely dark when she finally let herself down beside him.

The night was an agony, spent drifting between a shivering awareness of her body and sleep tormented by dreams that ended in a sudden, appalled wakefulness. Steve appeared to be in a coma much of the night. A heavy dew fell. She could hear it dripping from the trees onto the cloth that barely covered them. The creepers under them did not stop the dampness rising from the ground. She must have slept at last, for she woke into full daylight, with shafts of sun striking down through the canopy above. Birds filled the air with strange cries. The heat came quickly, causing a thin mist to rise from the jungle bed. Daylight brought another face of the jungle: brilliant greens set against an intense, brooding darkness. Now the dank, sour-sweet smell was stronger. She saw fungus and flowers, and a great butterfly that went wobbling by, jeweled wings caught for an instant in a shaft of sunlight. All around her was a pulsing and vivid life, mysterious and forbidding.

She turned and saw that Steve's eyes were open.

"Tropic Hilton," he said weakly. "Jungle safari. Glorious Technicolor. Air conditioning. Finest room service in the world. Not to mention the beautiful girl I slept with."

As she got to her feet, night thoughts of rescue returned to her as if they'd been part of some suddenly remembered dream, and she said, "They will come looking for us, won't they?"

"Sure they will. Just as soon as we're overdue. They'll be at it now."

"How will they find us?"

"They'll see the crash. The pilot will have filed a flight plan. Air Control will know our course to Moresby."

"But you said we must have been off course to fly into these mountains."

"Did I?"

She didn't have the heart to say yes; he seemed so anxious to do what he could to comfort her, and this touched her. "There's the radio, too," he went on. "They probably have got a fix on that. The pilot may have been talking to Moresby when we crashed. Don't worry about us not being found, honey. It's only a matter of time. Now listen," he went on, strengthening a little, anxious to change the subject, "why don't you go off and see what else you can locate? Look for the galley that was in the back of the airplane. Somewhere near the tail."

"I don't think I saw any of that at all."

"Go find the main part of the airplane again. See if you can't find the galley. But don't forget to tie those bits of your dress onto the trees as you go."

"Don't you want to — to relieve yourself?"

"Are you English so damned polite?" He smiled. "Sure I want to relieve myself, but see if you can't find any food from that galley. I want to be alive when they find us. Say, is there any water about here?"

"It can't be very far off. I heard it when I went to the crash."

"Maybe you can find one of those plastic cups in the galley."

Soon, in sunlight slanting down onto it, the crashed aircraft looked even more terrible than it had the night before. She stood at the beginning of the great scythe's sweep and with her back to the wreck began to move forward, pulling the little streamers from her waistband and tying them on as she went. Birds screeched and called. The ground underfoot was firmer now, and though the jungle was no less dense she felt she was making a quicker way through it. But it was all very strange and new and

[12]

frightening. Her way was mostly downhill. Occasionally a breeze touched her skin with its coolness.

She had tied on some dozen strips of cloth and was putting another about a vine stem when, out of the corner of her eye, she caught the faintest movement. She spun about and at first could see nothing. Then, because of some difference in its surface, she saw that a large looped object little more than an arm's length off was no part of a tree or vine or fern. Her heart stopped beating, her mouth fell open, and she stood paralyzed by fright. It was some minutes before she was able to search about for the last strip of cloth she'd tied, and when she came again to the place where she'd seen the snake there was no sign of it.

She was surprised to see how cleanly the aft part of the airplane had been broken off. The baggage compartment had been torn open, the elevators were gone, as was most of the rudder, but the galley was more or less intact. She got a carton of single portions of sugar, four bottles of whiskey from a mess of broken bottles in a compartment reeking with the smell of the spirit, a can of instant coffee, a bottle of aspirin, a box of teabags, and four trays of sandwiches, each square in a plastic wrapping. She also found an open packet of paper napkins, a bottle of air-sickness medicine, and a packet of sanitary napkins. She found plastic plates, saucers and cups, and three stainless steel kitchen knives. She also found a plastic sack and the waterproof bags supplied to airsick passengers. She put her finds into these and began to make her way back to Steve.

A dozen yards from the wreck a slip of paper caught her eye. She stopped, mechanically reading it: Passenger Terminal Fee (International) Valid For only one departure from the Manila International Airport. Pursuant to Section 1, Part V of CAA Administrative Order No. 4 Series . . . Near it a postcard glinted. The caption read: The Rice Terrace of the Philippines, 8th Wonder of the World. She turned away quickly because she had seen the postcard before, having bought one at the little shop in the Bayview Hotel in Manila and sent it to Julian, plastered with big bright stamps.

Because they had no solid food in them, the whiskey took effect quickly. Steve said they must ration the sandwiches, but as she was burning more energy, he insisted she have a whole round. He had half. They were ham and, because of the sealed wrapping, still good.

As she helped him up under the shoulders so he could drink, she said, "I had a terrible fright. I saw a snake."

"I forgot to warn you about those."

"I almost put my hand on it." She shuddered at the thought. "It was in a tree."

"Green? With cream or white markings?"

"Yes."

"Looped in a strange way, with its head over the middle loop, about seven, eight feet long?"

"God knows how long it was, but it was looped."

"Papuan tree python."

"Do you know about snakes?"

"A little. It's a very beautiful snake, rare in captivity. Though I saw it at the London zoo once. It has greatly enlarged front teeth to help it catch moving things."

"Don't tell me any more," she said.

"Better you know, honey."

They were silent, looking at one another. "It's what you don't know that scares you," he said. "Unless you're gutless. Which you are not."

"I'm just plain frightened."

"So," he said, "who isn't? Imagine what one hell of a thing it'd be, if we had to live our lives through knowing just what a painful end was in store for us. You know something else," he went on. "I'm trying to figure out who you are. They told me in Manila, but I'm damned if I can remember what?"

"Your lip is bleeding," she said.

"When I talk. Otherwise I feel just fine. How do you feel this morning?"

"I'm half naked. I'm covered with mud. My legs and arms are all scratches. My hair is a hopeless tangle and I've no comb. How do you think I feel?"

"You look just fine to me." He smiled at her. "I mean it: just fine. I figure I'm a very lucky man. Why, you could have been some whiskery old guy with a wooden leg, a glass eye, no teeth,

[*14*]

and bad breath. Anyway, what are you complaining about — do I look as if I'd come straight out of Brooks Brothers?"

For moments their eyes met. Then she said, "I think I'm lucky too."

"Did I tell you you had nice gray eyes?"

"I'm going to get more water," she said, getting to her feet.

He was going to pay her another small compliment, but as she moved away there was in the small, defiant snap of her head a gesture that revealed how close she was to losing control. Silent, he watched her pass out of sight, admiring her legs and back. Then his eyes returned to the denseness of the leaf canopy above him. He *was* lucky, he thought; she was a fine, fine woman. And she was game; come to think of it, she was gamer than most. It wasn't ignorance that let her go off into the jungle like that; she was far too intelligent not to realize how dangerous it could be. The problem, he told himself, would be in being able to go on encouraging her, returning the help she gave him. And that, he decided, would largely lie in his ability to keep from her his fear that, untreated, his wound was a mortal one. Septicemia was the danger; he had no illusions about how quickly an untreated wound would go septic under these conditions. The pain came at him in waves. He lay very still, telling himself that with her he must keep silent about his fears, especially his fears about their not being found . . .

She came back, interrupting his thoughts. As she dropped down beside him, she noticed that he looked grayer. She prepared the coffee and held him while he drank. "You put a lot of sugar in," he said, looking up at her.

"Strength," she said.

"You a doctor, or something?" He stared at her. "I sure wish I could remember what they said about you, something important."

"As soon as you've had this, I'm going to splint your leg." She stopped as his head dropped to the cup again. The memory of what lay under that blood-soaked bandage appalled her; how should she go about it? Did she have to draw the ends of the broken bone together? The thought of her inadequacy struck her like a physical blow. She winced, thinking of what she must attempt.

"Now don't be scared," he said kindly, lifting his head from the cup. "You can do it just fine. First go get two good, strong sticks as straight as you can find. I guess you put one down one side of the leg, one down the other. Then you bandage them. Then," he added weakly, "I guess we just hope."

The first stick she found easily enough. She brought it back and he approved of its strength and straightness, so she cut it to the length he said with one of the knives she had found in the wreck of the galley. Then she went off for the other stick.

This was harder to find. She wandered about, pushing her way between the vines and creepers and bushes, and then realized that she had forgotten to tie on the strips of cloth that would lead her back to him. Instantly, panic rose in her. Then she got some control and told herself that she must try to stay calm. She began to breathe more quickly, standing still and looking about her, consciously trying to calm herself; then she shouted his name, once, twice, three times, and stood listening, cocking her head, turning it this way and that, but there was no answering call.

This puzzled her, because she didn't think she could be so very far from him. Surely, she told herself, the forest must show some signs of her having passed through it. She thought she saw a tree she'd passed. But then she wasn't sure. Suddenly every part of the jungle began to look like every other part. Again panic pricked her and this time grew, so she began to move more quickly, her breath coming faster and faster. She got caught in a creeper and stumbled, then her hand slipped on a branch that whipped back and cut her across the mouth. She cried out, put her hands to her face, and slowly subsided onto her knees, overwhelmed by the danger of her situation and the stupidity that had brought her to it.

She was still on her knees when she felt herself grasped from behind. She had an instant's glimpse of a hand before it was clamped over her mouth and a warm, animal, oily smell flooded her nostrils, nauseating her.

She struggled to rise but other hands held her. She tried to bite the hand over her mouth, and as she did there slid into her vision the shapes of small, dark men, grotesquely decorated, crouched low, coming quickly toward her.

# 2 ∿∿∿∿∿∿∿∿∿∿∿∿∿∿∿∿∿∿∿

Percy Lambert banged the front door of his seventy-thousand-pound house off the King's Road, Chelsea, crossed the entrance hall with its candy-striped wallpaper, and started up the stairs to the first floor, calling his wife.

"Nell, where the 'ell are you?"

"I'm in the barf. Getting ready early, like you said to on the phone."

He went quickly through their bedroom, where the bathroom door was ajar. Nelly was standing knee-high in a sea of bubbles, soaping herself. The room was thick with the scent of jasmine.

"How's tricks, love?" He grinned at her; flattish-faced, square-headed, he was a long-bodied, short-legged man of forty, dressed in an expensive suit and wearing a heavy gold signet ring.

"What's all this about some special dinner tonight?" Nell did not stop working at herself with the soap. "Bein' a bit secretive about it, aren't you?" She dropped the soap and reached for the shower hose. She turned it on and, after satisfying herself that the temperature of the water was right, sprayed it first under each armpit and then into her crotch.

He watched her as she moved the spray about. He was grinning at her, enjoying watching what she was doing.

[17]

"We *are* pleased with ourselves tonight, aren't we?" She spoke looking down at the spray.

"Just wait till I fill you in on the beautiful details. Where's Barby?"

Still she didn't look up. "Nanny's got her in the bath."

As he moved from the doorway she called after him, "Don't you forget you said on the phone we was to be ready early tonight!" Then she settled down among the sea of jasmine-scented suds again, enjoying their warm softness, looking forward to the evening to come, content that he was home.

He ran up the stairs two at a time and pushed open the door to the nursery bathroom. "Hey, Barby," he called. The child's back was to him. She spun around quickly, a sharp-eyed, five-year-old elfin face grinning at him.

"Ooh, Daddy, we went to the park today because it wasn't so cold, and at the Round Pond we saw lots of yachts, beautiful yachts, all sailing about on it. Didn't we, Marilyn?"

Lambert pushed the door fully open and said good-evening to the girl beside the bath. She said, "Evening, Mr. Lambert." And then, "I do wish you wouldn't open that door so wide, Mr. Lambert. There's a horrible draft comes in when you do that. I don't want her to catch cold." Marilyn Petworth was a good-looking girl of twenty-six, big-bosomed, in a blue and white pin-striped uniform. She had been Barbara's nanny for two years.

"Tyrannized by women, that's what I am," Lambert said cheerfully. He winked at Marilyn, called to Barbara that he'd come and say good-night to her before he went out, and went down to the living room. He opened the bar recessed into the wall and poured himself a brandy and soda. Then he went to the door and shouted up the stairs. "You got a drink, Nell?"

"I'll have a Campari soda," she called back.

When he brought the drinks to their bedroom he put hers on the glass-topped dressing table and stood watching her. She was sitting on a lavender stool drawing on tights. There was a pertness about her, a London cockney sharpness even in the way she moved. He crossed to her and kissed her on the top of the head. She looked up, pleased. "Coo," she said, "what's all that for?" He took a cigarette from a gold case and snapped a lighter to it.

"How'd you like to go to Australia, love?" he said through the smoke. "Take a trip out there, eh, an' see that brother of yours?"

"I wouldn't mind." She stood up to pull her tights on. "Who'd you leave in charge?"

"No one."

"You gone mad or something?" She stopped moving and stared at him.

"What would you say if I told you we was thinking of selling out?"

"You've said that before." She went on pulling up her tights.

He sat on the edge of the bed and sipped his drink. "You remember, Nelly, when we got off the barrows and started in our first shop, we always said one day we'd sell out for a smashing good price. That we'd have a good time before we got too old to enjoy our money. That for us it wasn't to be no gold-plated wheelchairs. Eh? Remember that?"

She liked the way he always spoke of the business as something *we* had started — that first shop they'd bought, when he'd been behind the counter and she on the cash register. "For the first time in our business life, love, I've kept something from you. As a little surprise, like." He stopped there, smiling at her, enjoying her impatience.

"Value-Rite?" she said.

He nodded.

"I thought you said they was just nibbling."

"For the past month they've been more than just bloody well nibblin'. Remember how in the old days when we was on the barrows we used to go fishing sometimes on the Serpentine, ledgering, and one morning I hooked that big one . . ."

"That one got away. Besides, we don't go ledgerin' anymore. We're off the barrers too. Now, what about Value-Rite?"

"They've offered nine-fifty. I've told 'em we'll settle for nine-seventy-five."

"Is that a firm offer?"

"It is. And they'll come to our price, too, because we're frightening hell out of 'em with that new branch at the Angel."

"It's not a bad offer," she said after a moment. She was trying hard not to show it, but he saw she was impressed. She crossed to a drawer and pulled out a brassiere.

"It's a firm offer, Nelly." But he wasn't going to press her; he had too much respect for her business sense to try to influence her unduly. He watched her hook the bra behind her back. "I want your approval, though, you know."

He sat looking at her steadily, not smiling, waiting for her decision.

Finally she gave it. She wriggled the bra into place, settling it, then said, "If it's all right by you, Perce, then I suppose it's all right by me. Mind, at nine hundred and seventy-five thousand pounds though," she added. "Cash. No shares in somebody else's mistakes."

"That's my girl," he said quickly, beaming at her. "They think they're gettin' a bargain and I'm 'appy with nine seventy-five. Always good, you know, love, to let the other chap think he's on to a good thing."

"And so they are," she said sharply. She opened two doors and stood looking at a row of dresses. She found herself a little embarrassed, it had all come so suddenly.

"What I thought was this, love," he went on, talking to her back. "We'll sell up, see, and then we take a trip out there to Australia and 'ave a gander at Les and Myrtle and take a Captain Cook at the place. We might even find we like it. Les does. Lots of other people 'ave. It can't be all that bad. What do you say?"

"What about Barby?" She turned from the wardrobe with a green dress on a hanger.

"Well, she 'asn't started school yet. Not properly. We can bring Marilyn with us to look after 'er. She'll be no worry. And the change'll do 'er good," he added.

"There you go again, always runnin' down that child!" She didn't mean it and he knew it. She threw the hanger on the bed.

"I'm not running her down! All I mean is that she's been a bit seedy lately. You know that. She's never been what you'd call strong, and a trip out to Australia might knock some of the peakiness out of 'er."

"Well, I don't mind," she said.

"Funny, isn't it," he said that night as they lay together in the big bed, "how things go in fits and starts. Last month here we were with nothin' really big on, and now we've not only sold the business — at our price, too, mind — but we've decided to go to Australia."

"Not for good though, eh, Perce?" There was a trace of uncertainty in her voice as she snuggled up to him. She felt a little drunk; she'd had too much of Value-Rite's champagne.

"Not if you don't like it, love. But you'd like to see Les, wouldn't you? And that Aussie wife of his? I've been thinkin' — what say we go as far as New York by the boat? The sea voyage would be good for Barby — and from there we could fly the rest of the way. Eh?"

The next evening Percy was home early. With loving care he parked his cream Corniche. For Percy it was more than just a fine car, it was another way of telling the world that he had made it, succeeded where others had failed. Nelly was never quite as sure as Percy was. Six months after he'd bought the Corniche he'd been able to change its registration number, switch plates with an almost-new Rover he'd bought because it had the initials of his business followed by the digit 1 for its registration number.

"There's such a thing," Nell said sadly when she saw the new plate on the Corniche, "as what's called quiet good taste, Perce. Somehow, I thought we'd come a bit further than I see we 'ave."

"Well, it isn't as if it was me own initials," he said defensively.

"There is what's called ostentatious, Perce."

"Look, love, I know you don't like the mascot."

"A gold Silver Lady is bein' just silly. And that number plate lets everybody see how hard you're tryin'!"

Now, after Percy parked the Corniche, he locked it carefully, took one last lingering look at it, and hurried to the house.

"Nell," he shouted as he shut the front door behind him, "I got it all fixed." She was in the kitchen. "All Sir Garney, love." He kissed her. "I got it all deluxe. On the *QEII*. We're on what's called the signal deck, whatever the 'ell that is. An' we've got suites. Ours is the Trafalgar, best on the boat. We 'ave a week or so in New York and a week in Los Angeles. More if we want it. Then we fly on to Sydney."

"Don't everyone get sick in Los Angeles from the smog?"

"Barby wants to go to Disneyland, don't she? Now, tonight you better write off to Les and Myrtle. I've got all the main dates 'ere. And tomorrow you get off to Harrods and buy some new suitcases. We're away in two weeks!"

"Two weeks!" Nelly was horrified. This was almost as bad as selling the business. It was all very well to talk about selling out, to talk about going to Australia to see Les and Myrtle and their kids, but to actually *do* it all, from one day to the next . . .

"Well, what's the point," he asked her, "in 'angin' around 'ere, once we've made up our minds?"

"But 'ow'm I going to get all me new dresses an' things in that time?"

"Ah, you'll do it, Nelly girl, you always do."

"All very well for you men," she grumbled, but she was pleased nevertheless and began to feel a tiny stir of pleasant anticipation inside.

Two days before they were due to leave Southampton, Barbara complained of feeling tired.

"It's excitement, that's all," Percy said. "Once she gets to sea on the *QEII* she'll be a new girl. You see if she won't."

"Well, I don't like 'er always bein' tired like this," Nelly said. She sounded piqued, slightly resentful.

"She's not always bein' tired." Percy was jumping to Barbara's defense as much as he was justifying his faith in the benefits of the sea voyage.

"It's not the first time she's said she felt tired. And she's told Marilyn too," argued Nelly.

"Would you like me to fetch the doctor, love?"

"We'll see how she is in the mornin'." Nelly felt she had won her point. "Now you go up and have a talk to her. She's on her own."

"Where's Marilyn?"

"Gone to Folkestone to say good-bye to 'er mum. My God, if your 'ead wasn't screwed on you'd forget that too."

The next morning Barbara seemed better.

Marilyn returned. Lambert asked the Rolls-Royce agents to

send a man to drive them to Waterloo in the Corniche and then to garage the car while they were away. Their cabin in the *QEII* was filled with flowers, and Value-Rite had sent them champagne.

For Percy this was a voyage of fulfillment. At last he was beginning to reap some of the fruits of his labors. For the first time since he'd started on a barrow in Soho's Berwick Street Market at fourteen he felt he could afford to relax. It was a curious sensation, entirely unexpected. The ship ran sweetly with barely the suggestion of a roll. They dined in the Queen's Room and at the Queen's Grill (Percy made a joke about that which Nelly didn't quite like), and gave a party in the Q4 nightclub. As he went about making friends, showing off his expensively dressed wife, metaphorically, if not literally, clapping his new friends on the back, he often found himself smiling at the wonder and the pleasure of it all. This was living, he told Nelly. It had all been worthwhile.

The day before they were due in New York, Marilyn came in while they were having early morning tea in bed and told them that Barbara looked paler than usual and said she felt too tired to get up. Nelly put on her dressing gown and went to see her. Ten minutes later she was back. "I think we'd better have the doctor," she said to Percy as she closed the door behind her.

After breakfast the doctor saw Barbara and then asked Percy if he would come along to his office. Something in the doctor's manner struck a tiny dart of fear into Percy, reminding him of what he felt as a weakness in himself: not so much a fear of the unknown as a fear of being unable to fight the unknown, whatever that was, just because it *was* unknown. Percy had to be able to see all his problems laid out before him, as figures in a profit-and-loss account or as goods spread on a counter.

The doctor asked him to sit down and said, "Your wife tells me, Mr. Lambert, that your little girl has been getting tired, unusually tired, for some time now."

"Well, a bit tired, like, yes." Percy was on the defensive. "But that's nothing to worry about," he went on confidently. "She's always been a bit peaky, like. We thought this sea trip would do her good. She's been as right as rain up till this mornin'. But

[23]

what's up with her?" he added, as if the doctor should be telling *him* things, not the other way about.

"She may be anemic," the doctor said carefully.

"Ah, I see. Well then, she needs a good tonic. Drop o' port to make blood, eh? Needs buildin' up." Percy was determined to keep control over whatever might be wrong with Barbara. "You know what kids are like, they get a bit run down from time to time. Growing, an' all that. She's grown quite a bit lately, she 'as." She hadn't, but he didn't want the doctor to know that.

"I think," the doctor said slowly, "that you should take her to see a specialist, Mr. Lambert."

"Oh, I will," Percy said quickly. "When we get back to England I'll take her to the best chap in Harley Street. In the meantime, what about that tonic? Maybe she's not getting enough vitamins."

The doctor paused before answering, not because he was considering Percy's suggestion, but because he was wondering just how to put what he had to say. "When will you be back in England, Mr. Lambert?" he said finally, looking up from his blotter.

"Can't really say," said Percy almost offhandedly; he didn't really like this doctor; he didn't think he wasn't any good — he probably was, as good as the next one — but he didn't quite take to him, he seemed very much a person Percy couldn't control. All the same, better explain some more . . . "It's like this, y'see, we're, well, we're just starting on this trip."

"In that case . . ." The doctor paused, sensing the antipathy. "In that case, if you take my advice, Mr. Lambert —"

"Oh, I will," put in Percy quickly, anxiously expansive and genuinely determined not to let the doctor have the slightest doubt about his good intentions. "I'll do that orl right."

"Then," the doctor went on, "I wouldn't wait until you return to England. You must understand, Mr. Lambert, that here in this ship, well equipped as we are, there are certain testing facilities that we don't have, that no ship has."

"Testing facilities?" Percy looked puzzled.

"As I say, I think Barbara may be anemic. I'm sorry I can't be more positive, but if you take her to a good doctor ashore he can make tests and be more specific."

"Trouble is," Percy said gloomily, "I don't know any doctors ashore. In New York. Good or otherwise." He was annoyed because the doctor wouldn't say more.

The doctor made a gesture, brushing Percy's objection aside. "That can easily be fixed." He sat staring at Percy. "Mind, it won't be cheap," he added.

"The money's no object. It's not that. But we was goin' to have a few days sightseein', y'see. You don't think, do you, that she'd be well enough to wait until we got out to Australia, eh?"

The doctor was in no doubt at all. "Frankly, Mr. Lambert, if I were in your shoes I'd treat this as an emergency."

When Percy left the doctor he found Nelly still with Barbara. He called her into their stateroom.

"Where's the medicine?" she asked.

"There isn't any. Now let's sit down, love, and I'll tell you."

She listened without interruption. "So he thinks there's something really the matter with her, is that it?"

"Ah, you know what doctors are like." Percy wanted to hedge. "They're always a bit cagey. He says 'e can't tell, not here, not on the boat."

"Why can't he?" It was now Nelly's turn to be frustrated.

"Because 'e says he can't do the right tests and things. He's going to radio New York and make an appointment for us with some real good specialist. She'll be all right, old girl." He put his arm around her shoulders. "Maybe it's a blessing in disguise. They got some pretty  good doctors in New York, and Barby *has* been a bit peaky lately. You've said so yourself. He'll give her a good goin' over and soon 'ave 'er right as rain."

"We got some good doctors in London, too," Nelly answered. "We should've taken her to one of them before we ever left."

"Now don't you go blamin' yourself, Nell," he said firmly. "Barby was all right when we left, you know that. She wasn't as pale as she is now. This chap in New York'll soon put her right — you see if he don't."

Dr. Lucius Spellman was a small man with a round, smooth face who smiled at Barbara through bright rimless glasses. Barbara thought he was ever so kind and told Nelly that he hardly hurt her a bit. Two days after the visit, Spellman's secretary called Lambert at their hotel and asked if he would come to Dr. Spellman's office at eleven o'clock that morning.

"I suppose it'll be to pick up the prescription, now that he's found out what's wrong with her," Percy told Nelly, who was watching him anxiously as he put the telephone back on its cradle.

That morning, Spellman's smooth face and glasses seemed to Percy brighter and more polished than ever. There was a plastic folder in front of the doctor, and Percy saw Barbara's name on it, along with some smaller print at the bottom right-hand corner. Again that tiny dart of fear pricked him.

"Well, what's the verdict?" Percy began, determined to be cheerful.

"Mr. Lambert," Spellman said slowly, "in the course of my long medical experience I have had — unfortunately — to tell many parents what it is now my duty to tell you. The fact that I have had to do this often does not make it come any easier."

Percy tensed, his mouth opened, but the doctor put up his hand. "I have no desire to keep you in suspense any longer than is necessary, Mr. Lambert. It will be much kinder if I come directly to the point." He paused, then said, "Barbara has leukemia."

"Leukemia," said Percy, but he said it automatically, as if not properly understanding.

Spellman nodded. "You have heard of the disease?"

"Well, yes," Percy said. And nothing he'd heard of it had been good. But because he'd heard of it didn't mean that Barby had it. There must be some mistake, must be something else the matter with her. And he said so.

"I am sorry, Mr. Lambert, but there can't be any mistake. You do realize the seriousness of what I'm saying?"

"Well, I know leukemia's a serious thing, yes," Percy said, "'course I do, but the doctor on the boat thought she might be anemic. You're quite sure she just don't need a tonic like, need buildin' up a bit?"

Spellman shook his head and his glasses glinted.

Percy sat silent, digesting it all. Then hope flared. "But there's a cure for it, there must be!" He hadn't got where he had by accepting the inevitable without a fight.

[26]

Again Spellman's glasses glinted. "That, Mr. Lambert, is our difficulty."

"But you can do *somethin'* for her, can't you? I mean, lots of people have diseases you can't cure. Right? I know a chap who's got sugar diabetes, that sort of thing."

"Diabetes is something else, Mr. Lambert —"

"Well, I know that," Percy said stubbornly, "but what I'm saying is, you can surely give her somethin' for it, like?"

"Mr. Lambert, let me explain it a little more fully. Barbara has what we call acute lymphoblastic leukemia, and in recent years we have learned enough about this particular form of the disease to increase the average survival time from diagnosis from about three months to somewhere around three years. The treatment may or may not prolong Barbara's life — I wouldn't want to make any positive predictions — but one assurance I can give you is that almost certainly her suffering will be greatly reduced. And in medicine, Mr. Lambert, there is always that outside chance, let us call it, that some great advance may come along. Just because a disease is incurable doesn't mean it shouldn't be treated aggressively. One just never knows what is around the corner."

"While there's life there's 'ope," Percy said grimly.

"Why not indeed? I do not wish to raise excessive hopes in you, Mr. Lambert, but our most modern treatment of the particular kind of leukemia Barbara has means that about one percent of cases live for five years, some even a little longer."

Percy's eyes lit for an instant. "So she's maybe got more than five years?"

"I said one percent of cases, Mr. Lambert."

"Well then, how long has she got?"

"This is difficult to be precise about," Spellman said patiently. "And I do not wish to deceive you. If she's lucky, the treatment should give her about three years."

"And if she isn't treated?"

"Three months."

"Jesus," Percy said softly. Then, " 'Ow could she have got this?"

Spellman gave the slightest shrug. "Who can say, Mr. Lambert. Leukemia and other cancers are, after accidents, the most common cause of death among children between five and fourteen.

And deaths due to these causes have increased recently, almost certainly because of nuclear testing."

Shaken as he was by Spellman's death sentence for Barbara, it took a moment for the last part of what Spellman said to sink into Percy. "What did you say?" he asked. "D'you mean our Barby could've got it from these atomic bombs an' things?"

"I won't go so far as to say that, Mr. Lambert. But the scientific evidence we have here in the United States indicates that already at least one out of three children who died before their first birthdays in America in the 1960s may well have died as a result of nuclear testing." Dr. Spellman spoke as if he were delivering a scientific lecture. "The quite unexpected genetic effect of strontium 90 is now evident from the increase in infant mortality along the path of the fallout cloud from the atomic test at Alamogordo in New Mexico in 1945," he went on. "This is also backed by a detailed correlation of state-by-state infant mortality rates in excess of those expected with yearly changes in the amount of strontium 90 in milk. And it's not only atmospheric testing that increases these deaths. We now have evidence that the underground nuclear test in Nevada in December of 1970 brought about rises in child mortality rates in the neighboring states during the months following the test. We also know now that a similar pattern of infant deaths exists near nuclear reactors and nuclear fuel processing plants."

"We don't live near anyplace like that," Percy said.

"Mr. Lambert, I'm not suggesting Barbara has leukemia caused by fallout. But the French and Chinese are still conducting atmospheric tests, and we know just how dangerous these are. I am in touch with Australian doctors who are afraid that the recent French tests in the Pacific are responsible for the number of abnormal babies born in the nine months since radioactive iodine has been discovered in the Townsville milk supplies, that is in Queensland. It has been announced officially in Australia that since the French Pacific tests, concentrations of radioactive iodine have been found in six of the nine milk sources monitored by the Australian authorities. We just do not know what can happen, Mr. Lambert, when such incredibly dangerous substances are ingested in the normal diet.

"Here in America we now have documented evidence that fall-out appears to produce serious effects at a rate consistent with what might be expected from a study of the effects in children who were exposed to prenatal X rays."

He paused, suddenly struck by a thought. "Do you happen to know whether Mrs. Lambert was X-rayed while she was carrying Barbara?"

"Nelly never carried her," said Percy. "I should have told you, I suppose, but the question didn't come up and Barby doesn't know yet — though we're going to tell her when she grows up, of course. But Barby's not our kid, you see. We couldn't 'ave our own children. We tried all sorts of things, and the wife had a lot of women's trouble and I was tested and all that, but it was no go. So we adopted Barby. But do you mean she could have got this from 'er own mother if she was X-rayed when she was 'aving Barby?"

"It's certainly possible, though less likely in England, where the connection between X-ray pelvic examination and childhood leukemia was first discovered."

"But I don't even know who her mother was!"

"Heredity in itself is not a factor, Mr. Lambert. Put your mind at rest on that score. Barbara could just as likely have got it had Mrs. Lambert been her actual mother. Or even perhaps if her mother had contracted influenza during her pregnancy."

"The *flu*?"

"Scientists at Oxford have reported that leukemia appeared to be somewhat slightly more common among children whose mothers had contracted influenza. But there is no final proof of this yet; and who knows, the influenza virus might just be a factor in causing infantile leukemia. It is all very complicated — and often contradictory, Mr. Lambert."

Telling Nell was the hardest thing Percy had ever done. At first she refused to believe it. She clung to him, sobbing, then beat her fists against his chest, saying again and again that they would get another doctor, that this couldn't be right, it couldn't happen to Barby. Finally he quieted her. Then he rang room service for two double whiskeys. Calmly and patiently he made her see the uselessness of going to another doctor, of submitting Barby to another examination, troubling her unnecessarily.

"This chap Spellman's a real expert, love," he told her softly. " 'E's not just any ordinary doctor. 'E's a specialist. An' in a way, you see," he went on, "in a way we *'ave* got two opinions. That doctor on the boat must've 'ad a pretty good idea of what was the matter with our Barby, otherwise 'e wouldn't have sent us to this specialist chap. I worked that out comin' back here in the taxi. Of course, we mustn't let on to Barby that she's sick."

"We'll 'ave to tell Marilyn."

"I'll do that."

"What about the medicine?"

"Well, first she's got to 'ave a blood transfusion."

"What's that for?"

"Well, 'e said it was for the anemia —"

"*There!*" The word shot from Nelly. "That's what the doctor on the boat said, that she might be anemic."

"And so she is, love."

"But you said she'd got leukemia."

Percy sighed. Spellman had told him that most patients with leukemia needed blood transfusions to control the inevitable anemia that accompanied the disease. He tried to explain, ending, "Anyhow, love, that's what he said, and that's what she's going to have."

"What'll we do about Australia?"

" 'E said we'll 'ave to stay 'ere for a while when 'e starts the treatment and makes some more tests and gives the transfusions, and then we can go on. 'E'll give me a letter to take to the doctor out there."

"Which doctor?"

"One 'e said 'e'd put us on to in Sydney."

They were surprised at how easily they fell into a pattern of deception in front of Barbara. Marilyn knew more about the disease than Nelly, and she received the news with an appalled, stunned silence. "I don't want to sound cruel," Percy said to Nelly and Marilyn, "but I don't want none of you all of a sudden being ever so nice and kind to her. She's a clever little monkey; she knows there's somethin' up with 'er an' she'll be 'aving this transfusion and pills and all, and we don't want her gettin' any idea that she might be kind of interesting. Just try to go on as you've always been to 'er. The 'ardest time," he added, "will be *now*, when you go straight back to her. Just try not to look at 'er too 'ard, not for a bit, not until you get used to the idea of it. All right?"

Vividly, Percy remembered his first sight of certain, impending death. He'd been eleven, walking along Praed Street, and his father had said, "Now, when we gets in the 'orspital, if your Uncle Alf says anything 'bout Cup Final, talk to 'im as if 'e was goin' to be there. But he won't, see. You heard what yer ma said. Or better, don't say nothink. If Uncle Alf says anythin', leave it to me."

His father had touched his arm and led him in, and he'd not expected to see his uncle quite that funny color; he recalled that long-forgotten feeling of not being able to take his eyes off his uncle, as if he was about to swim the Channel or was the king, suddenly glimpsed driving by. Now, remembering, he knew his uncle was the first celebrity he'd ever seen — because he was going to die.

Whether it was due to the drug Spellman had prescribed they didn't know, but when the time came to leave New York, Barbara was brighter and stronger than she had been for some weeks past.

They loved California. They even found much to admire in Los Angeles. They thought Disneyland the most exciting experience they'd ever had. They went on a guided tour to see the homes of the movie stars in Beverly Hills: Marilyn thought this rather old hat, but Nelly and Percy enjoyed it hugely. They flew up to San Francisco and, though they loved the bay and the Golden Gate Bridge, found the town a bit stuffy after Los Angeles. Honolulu was entirely different from anything they had known or even imagined. They spent three days there and then flew on to Fiji, where the warm, wet heat hit them as they stepped onto the tarmac at Nadi. Nelly's brother, Les Robinson, was waiting for them at Kingsford-Smith Airport when they reached Sydney.

Les was two years older than Nell. There was still a lot of the cockney sharpness about him, though fifteen years in Australia and marriage to an Australian had stripped him of much of his Englishness. Proud of his rich brother-in-law, determined to make his sister's stay a memorable one, he had taken a three-week holiday from the plastics factory he had started thirteen years before. His natural inventiveness and his luck in finding a partner who was a fourth-generation Australian, as clever on the money side as on the engineering, had brought him prosperity. Myrtle, his wife, a Victorian from Bendigo, was a good-looking, slow-moving, biggish woman. The Robinsons had two children: Caroline, nine, and Betty, seven.

Myrtle and the children had not come to the airport. As Les's new Holden threaded its way through the traffic toward Neutral Bay, Nell got her first look at the brashness and the vigor of Sydney. She felt a little daunted at the thought of meeting her Australian sister-in-law. She need not have worried: the wariness was mutual. There was a moment of tenseness while Les rambled on with the introduction, and then Nell knew that they were going to get on well together.

For her own peace of mind, Nell's meeting with Myrtle could not have been more opportune. Anxious to show off his rich English relatives as soon as possible, Les had, as he put it, "invited a few of the mob round for tonight." A few of the mob turned out to be enough people to fill the road where the Robinsons lived with cars. Percy was in his element; this was even better than the QEII. In the warm summer's night the party overflowed into the garden, where the great dark bowl of the harbor below was a soft darkness peppered with lights. Guest after guest tried to make him see the shape in the constellation of the Southern Cross. It was when the visitors had started to thin out, when she was helping Myrtle stack the dishwasher, that Nelly screwed up her courage and told Myrtle about Barbara.

When the last car door had banged and driven off noisily into the early morning, Myrtle and Les came to Percy's and Nell's room. Les said quietly that Myrt had told him about Barbara. Percy said he was glad of that. "But now look, Les," he said, standing in his underpants, feeling the warm breeze as it billowed the curtains and passed on through the house, "now look . . ." He paused and drew his hand down over his face. "I know I've 'ad a

[32]

lot of this 'ere Sydney beer tonight — and pretty good it is too — but this ain't the beer talkin'. Nelly'll tell you that. I don't want you to think we're being cruel to Barby, but if we go showin' 'er all kinds of extra favors, I mean bein' extraspecially kind to 'er, like, she's goin' to wonder what's up, see? The great thing is to go on just as though she wasn't sick. That's what the doctor in New York said. And at the moment she doesn't look it, does she? The only difference between her and your kids right at this moment is that she gets more tired than they do. The best thing you can do is to go on with any plans you've made for us just as if you didn't know Barby was as sick as she is." He stopped speaking suddenly, feeling anguish hit him as a great wave strikes a beach, breaking onto it, sweeping far up it, burying all it touches.

The first week shot by. Taking Myrtle's old Holden as well as Les's new one, they went on picnics and ate at the tops of long beaches on which a big surf broke. Les taught Percy how to use a surf ski. They drove high into the Blue Mountains and sat at rustic tables eating steaks Les had grilled on a fire for which they all gathered sticks, drinking beer cold from the portable icebox and then boiling the billy, surrounded by the vastness of range after range of mountains, blue and purple in the transparent heat. They went to Circular Quay and took the ferry to Manly. They drove out to Middle Harbor and on to Ku-ring-gai Chase and Bobbin Head, and one day they went south to La Perouse where the explorer had landed and stood on the little bit of land there that belongs to France by gift of the Australian government. Another day they drove around Botany Bay to the spot where Captain Cook had landed. The Londoners loved it all, the more so as Barbara seemed to be thriving; her eyes grew brighter and the sun darkened her skin. Watching Barbara running down a beach with her cousins, Nelly had to pinch herself to believe in the agony of the loss to come. Mrytle said nothing to Nelly, but to Les one night she wondered aloud if that doctor in New York might not be wrong.

For their second week Les had the use of a property belonging to his partner Dick Hathaway. "She's a nice place quite a way from here," he told Percy and Nell. "Down near the Victorian border. In the Alps. Wallanulla's the name of it. Dick's only too pleased to let us have it, and you'll see a bit of the real Aussie bush. We'll take the two cars."

"And we won't hurry," said Myrtle in her slow way. "My word, we won't. There's plenty to see on the way. We'll just stop whenever we feel like it."

"What about school for your kids?" said Percy.

"They break up Friday," said Myrtle.

"You're in Australia now," Les grinned. "Out here the kids have their long holiday over Christmas. This was Myrt's idea," he went on. He was proud of her, his big country-girl Australian wife.

"I thought it'd be a good idea just doing nothing," Myrtle said. "There'll be horses for the kiddies to ride, and if we're still liking it at the end of the week Dick says we can stay on for as long as we want to. Dick and Mavis won't be using the house now until they go down there after Christmas."

Wallanulla homestead was old, rambling, and comfortable, made of weatherboard and filled with Victorian furniture, much of it in red cedar. For the Lamberts, Wallanulla had everything they'd expected of the Australian bush. Here was the heady mountain air, the dazzling light of full noon, the great gums that stood with not as much as a leaf moving in moonlight bright enough to read a newspaper by. The nearest township, Bidgebyne, was ten miles off and consisted of a pub, a combined general store and post office, a butcher's shop, a garage and blacksmith's, and less than a dozen houses with corrugated iron roofs shimmering in the heat.

For the first time in her life Barbara was put up on a horse, a quiet old mare on which she followed the others, wearing a wide straw hat with a brim that flopped up and down as she bumped along.

One day while driving to a picnic on the Snowy River they came across a flock of sheep on the road. They stopped the cars, got out, and stood in the dust driven up by the pounding of thousands of feet, marveling at the dogs as they barked and wheeled about the edges of the flock. The drovers looked down at them from their horses and spoke to them, lean men under sweat-stained felt hats. When Barbara saw a red kelpie jump on the back of a sheep and run clear across the flock to the other side without once touching the ground she shouted and clapped her hands, calling out to Nelly to look, look, look! Percy turned away from her, a sudden lump in his throat, savagely angry that such a joy in living had so little time to run.

Percy and Les did the shopping. Most mornings the two men would take Myrtle's old Holden and drive into the township, park in the shade of a blue gum in front of the general store, pick up the bread and milk, the vegetables and meat, perhaps fill up with gas, and then go to the pub and have three or four pints, talking to the hotelkeeper and a few of the locals or the occasional traveler wetting his whistle on the way through.

One morning there was a state Forestry Department utility truck parked outside the pub, and when they went in Les knew the driver. "Heard you were back," the driver said to Les. "This is better than the Big Smoke, eh?" The driver's name was Tom Eastwood and Les introduced him to Percy.

Eastwood looked Percy up and down. He reminded Percy of one of the drovers they'd seen with the flock of sheep. "We got quite a few of you English around here," Eastwood drawled. "Over Cooma way on the Snowy scheme. You migratin'?"

Percy shook his head.

"This is a great country," said Eastwood. "What'll y'have?" Les said they'd have a couple of pints. When he'd pulled the beer the publican said to Eastwood, "They doing any more sprayin' over there these days, Tom?"

The publican was drinking beer out of a lady's-waist, a small narrow glass, because it was early in the day and he had a lot of drinking to do before it was over. Percy was fascinated by the enormous fold of fat under the man's chin — brewer's goiter, Les called it — and by the way he downed the beer, as if pouring it down a drain, apparently with no need to swallow at all.

"Yeah, a bit, Pat," said Eastwood.

"What are they up to now?"

"Ah, you know these scientific jokers. Always tryin' somethin' new. They're going to give the Shelsey block another dose of that stuff we sprayed about six months ago."

"What's the sprayin' for?" asked Percy.

"Search me," said Eastwood. "It's from the air, y'know," he

[35]

explained, leaning one elbow on the bar, hooking his foot over the rail. "One stuff they put on was a growth suppressant. I think that's what they called it. They're always tryin' somethin' new. The department's got an experimental forest area out near Brownin's Junction." This was for Percy's benefit. "They spray all kinds of these here chemicals. I wouldn't know what they were up to. I only drive the utility. And help loadin' the plane. They're going to do some more soon. If you'd like to see the plane sprayin', I'll drop in an' let you know when they'll be doin' it."

"The children might like to see it," said Percy, thinking of Barbara.

"Yeah, well, I'll let you know," said Eastwood.

He was as good as his word. Two days later he called at the homestead, late in the afternoon. Myrtle had made a batch of scones, and they were sitting on the wide verandah, looking down the valley, eating some of the scones with slabs of butter that melted and dripped from them, some with strawberry jam and the clotted cream Les and Percy picked up in the township in the morning. They drank tea from a big brown pot, the biggest Nelly had ever seen. There were still some scones left when Eastwood arrived, and Myrtle got another cup for him.

"That plane," Eastwood said to Percy. "You know, doin' the sprayin' like I was telling you about. Well, she'll be over this way tomorrer afternoon. I saw the pilot an' he's goin' to have a look in at you when he's finished. About four o'clock, he reckons."

"You mean he's going to come *here,* to the house?" asked Barbara, her bright eyes popping in astonishment.

"Why not?" Eastwood turned to her. "I told him all about you an' he said he'd like to come and see a nice little English girl."

"Will he land?" Barbara's mouth didn't close and her eyes seemed to grow in size.

"Y'never know y' luck, he might." Eastwood grinned at her and, taking out tobacco and papers, began to roll a cigarette.

"Would he have room to give us a ride?" asked Caroline.

"Not in a cropduster, he wouldn't. She's only got one seat. You kids been makin' any peashooters?"

"What's peashooters?" Barbara asked.

"What, you don't know what peashooters are!" Eastwood's

mock horror was dramatic. "Don't you have peashooters in England?"

"*I* know what peashooters are," said Caroline, then, quickly springing to Barbara's defense, added, "and I suppose they have them in England, too. But we can't have them here because we haven't got any peas."

" 'Course you got peas," said Eastwood.

"I know," cried Betty. "The peppercorn trees! Will you make us a peashooter, Mr. Eastwood, please?"

" 'Course I will. Wait till I light up and I'll make one for each of you."

The children followed Eastwood to the clump of bamboo that stood near the remains of a rose garden. With his cigarette dangling from his mouth he took out his pocket knife, picked out a suitable length of bamboo, and cut it. Then with the children on either side of him he sat on the edge of the verandah and, choosing the longest sections between the nodes, cut three lengths. One end of each he sliced off diagonally, the other he cut straight. "That's the end you put in your mouth. Now, let's get some of those peppercorns."

The trees stood on the north side of the house, one of them almost touching it. They walked in under them and began stripping the hard green seeds from them. "Now," Eastwood said, grinning at them, "you just watch this." He threw away his cigarette, popped several peppercorns into his mouth, raised the blowpipe, and in quick succession peppercorns began bouncing off the fly wire over one of the windows. "That's my room, where I sleep!" cried Barbara. "Oh, do let me try."

Caroline and Betty could do it. Barbara's first efforts barely got out of the end of the bamboo pipe. Then they sat on the verandah's edge, swinging their legs, popping off a stream of peppercorns. Barbara sat beside Eastwood, and he showed her how to work her tongue against the end of the peashooter. Finally she had it, and the girls shouted and laughed and fired at Nell and Myrtle as they cleared away the tea things. Then Eastwood got some gum leaves and showed them how to hold one of the leaves between their thumbs and by blowing and cupping their hands make a tune. "You should hear the Abos playin' a gum leaf," he said, and when Barbara managed a faint squeak out of her leaf Eastwood said they'd make a dinkum Aussie out of her yet.

The next day the children could barely eat their midday meal for excitement. A little after four o'clock the plane arrived, dropping down from behind the big stand of gums east of the homestead so quickly that none of them heard it until it was there, rushing over the house. The children dropped the dolls they'd been playing with, jumped off the verandah, and ran out.

"Oh, he's going away!" cried Barbara.

"No, he's not! He's turning!" shouted Caroline.

"He's turning, he's turning! Mummy, come and look, Mummy!" Barbara shouted, and the machine banked and flattened out and came down so close to the ground that dead leaves and pieces of bark swirled up into the air. It climbed away and made a circuit and then banked again. After a moment the engine note died and the aircraft began dropping.

"He's going to land!" shouted the girls, jumping up and down.

"He's pointing straight at us!" cried Barbara, her eyes wide in fright and excitement.

The plane came in steeply, wings waggling a little, floating as the pilot held it off with a trickle of power and then dropped it down sweetly. Barbara ran to Nelly and grabbed her dress as the machine came bumping up to them, the pilot sitting high in the cropduster's cabin. Finally the propeller jerked to a halt and the pilot lifted the canopy.

"Y' just in time for tea," said Les, moving forward.

That was on a Wednesday.

The next day it rained, and though Les and Percy went into the township, neither the children nor the women went outside the house.

On Friday Barbara was sick. Nelly took her temperature and found she had a slight fever. She was irritable and couldn't be comforted. By midafternoon she was obviously no better. Had it been Caroline or Betty, so slight an indisposition would have passed virtually unnoticed, but because it was Barbara and because of what they thought it might portend, as the day passed and evening began to settle, a shadow fell over the house. Caroline and Betty played on the verandah, but they did it quietly and put their dolls to bed and nursed them, because the dolls too had fevers and weren't well.

The next morning Barbara was worse after a night during which Nelly and Marilyn got little sleep.

"Would you like me to go and get the doctor?" Les said at breakfast. "I can run into the post office and find out where he lives. There'll be one somewhere about."

Nelly looked at Percy. Already they had discussed it. She had told Percy what she wanted to do.

"I think, Les," Percy said after a moment's silence, "that Nell wants to go back."

Myrtle took it up quickly. "And that's a very good idea," she said in her slow way. "My word it is. We can pack up this morning and get away this afternoon if you like. Or if you'd rather go straight away, Nell, Les'll drive you an' Percy and Barby, an' we'll tidy up here and come on up to Sydney tomorrow."

"I wouldn't like to just leave you like that, Myrtle," said Nelly anxiously.

"Oh, fiddlesticks! I think that's what we'll do. Eh, Les?"

"It's a good idea, all right. We can drive straight through."

"Tomorrow's Sunday, isn't it?" said Nelly, looking apprehensively at Percy. "What about the tickets?"

"What tickets?" said Myrtle. "You don't need any tickets."

Percy cleared his throat and looked from Myrtle to Les and back to Myrtle. "What Nell means," Percy said, "is that she wants to go back."

"I do, Myrt," Nelly said earnestly.

"Well, that's all right, Nell. I'd feel the same way, up here an' all that."

"I don't know why it is, Myrt," Nelly went on, "but it come over me last night. I told Perce. I want to be 'ome with 'er."

"Home?" said Les, getting it before Myrtle.

"That's right, Les," said Percy. "And I can understand 'ow she feels."

"Oh," said Myrtle. She was at the stove, getting more bacon and fried bread and tomatoes for Les. She turned around, an egg slice in her hand. "You mean right home, do you, Nell? Back to England?"

Nell tried to speak but the word stuck in her throat.

"That's right, Myrt," said Percy. "That's what she means."

There was a long silence, then Les said, "Well, if we're goin', we'd better get started. How long will it take you to pack, Nelly?"

"I'm sorry, Myrt, I really am," Nelly managed to say. Percy sat with his knife and fork in the air, looking at Nell, thinking she'd be better to let it come and have a good cry.

Myrtle, secure in her own children's health, saw the tension and anguish in Nelly. She put the egg slice down and went around the table to her. "I know how you must feel, Nell," she said gently. "I'd be the same. My word, I would." For a moment the two women looked at one another, then Myrtle brightened and said, "Now finish up your breakfast and you two go and pack — I'll cut some sandwiches for you to eat on the way. There's nothing fresh in the house at home, Les." She turned to her husband, "I'll give you some of the sausages and eggs for tonight, and the apple pie. There's plenty of tinned stuff at home, but you better hop into the butcher's at Bidge' now, while Percy and Nell are packing, and get a roast for tomorrow."

They made good time on the road, and going into Sydney that evening Les said to Percy that he had remembered he knew a chap at Qantas. When he got in, he telephoned the man and found him at home, mowing his lawn. An hour later he had got them four first-class seats on a flight leaving for London the next morning.

"You leave Sydney at seven in the morning on Flight . . ." Les looked at a piece of paper torn from the telephone scratch pad. "On Flight 003 for San Francisco. You get to San Francisco at five past seven on the same day because you lose a day, see? Then you change to TWA and fly straight on to New York, where you arrive at ten past six the next morning. You change to British Airways, BA Flight 590, and that gets you into London at nine-fifty at night."

"She's goin' to be a stinker," Les said the next morning, driving the Lamberts to Kingsford-Smith Airport, "real 'ot day. You'll be well out of it once you get in the air."

Les was doing his best to ease the tension in the car. Looking at him as he drove, Nelly saw that Les was wondering whether they were doing the right thing. Les had said nothing directly, though he sensed that if Percy had had his way he would have opted for staying in Australia. But to Les it was none of his business, though he did say to Percy that there were plenty of good doctors and hospitals for kids in Sydney. All Percy said was that he supposed so. He didn't quite look at Les when he said it but glanced at Nelly, out of earshot at the time, stroking Barby's cheek and telling her she'd soon be home and she'd be better then. She was in Marilyn's arms, propped against her breasts. Les had seen them to the departure lounge but hadn't waited until the aircraft took off. Deeply troubled, feeling very much that the visit hadn't turned out at all the way he'd thought it would, Les drove sadly out of Mascot to await Myrtle's return from Wallanulla with the children.

In the aircraft Percy, Nell, and Marilyn took turns nursing Barbara. It soon became more and more difficult to comfort her. Her limbs ached. She felt hot, looked flushed, and before they landed at Los Angeles she had begun to develop a cough.

"It's the smog," said Nelly. Percy said nothing. There was no smog, not that he could see. In the transit lounge at Los Angeles Nelly said, "Marilyn, see if there's a chemist's shop where you can buy a thermometer." Marilyn couldn't, but at the airline counter she was overheard by a fellow passenger, an Australian who said he was a doctor and who asked if he could be of any help. Marilyn brought him back to Nelly and Percy.

The doctor introduced himself. "Pyke. Roger Pyke." A slightly built man of about thirty, he seemed embarrassed. "I'm not so much a clinical doctor," he said quietly, "as one who does research."

"I'd be very pleased," said Percy. Normally, as it was Barbara, he'd have looked to Nelly for approval, but now he did not, and Nelly acknowledged that the decision was Percy's by standing and saying, "Put Barby on the chair 'ere, Marilyn, so the doctor can see her properly."

Walking back from the inquiry counter, Marilyn had told Pyke that Barbara had leukemia. Pyke sat and smiled at Barbara. He took her hand in his and with two fingers felt for her pulse. He asked her where she ached and she said all over, and he asked if the light hurt her eyes. Was that why she hid her head? She said yes, it was.

The call to board the airplane interrupted his examination. On the way to the exit gate Percy let the women go ahead and dropped back with Pyke. " 'Ow do you think she is?" he asked.

"I don't think it's anything to do with the leukemia," Pyke said. His eyes were on Marilyn and Nelly walking ahead. "Do you know whether she's been in contact with anybody recently who's had flu?"

"Not as far as I know." Percy shook his head.

Pyke glanced sideways at Percy. "I think you ought to get her to a doctor. She might have to go to hospital. You can't nurse a child properly in a hotel room."

"We'll be in London soon," said Percy.

"Yes," said Pyke, but he said it slowly, as if hesitating whether to say it or not. "I'll be stopping off in New York to see my brother, who's at an astronomers' conference."

Because Pyke was a doctor and because the child was so obviously ill and the airplane lightly loaded, after Pyke had twice visited first class to look at Barbara, the steward said he could sit there with the Lamberts. Percy thanked him and said he'd pay for Pyke's drinks, but the steward smiled and said that there was no need for that.

Past the halfway mark across America, somewhere near Chicago, Barbara complained of a headache and then, as Marilyn was handing her to Nelly, she said her neck felt stiff.

Percy called Pyke to the bar. "Why's she afraid of the light?" he asked.

"It's a condition called photophobia," Pyke said.

"Is it bad?"

"It's a symptom," said Pyke. "I'd say perhaps the result of a mild encephalitis."

Percy stared into his glass; he didn't like the sound of encephalitis because it was something he didn't understand, couldn't come to grips with.

They were on time at Kennedy. Marilyn carried Barbara, who was more restless now that she was off the airplane. She began to cry, and Pyke said, "Perhaps I'd better have another look at her."

Marilyn put Barbara on an upholstered bench. Pyke bent over her and began to undo the buttons on her dress, saying, "Nothing tight . . . her breathing, you see."

When Barbara next coughed it was stronger, harsher, a curiously dry cough that Nelly hadn't heard before. Finally Pyke straightened up and looked at Percy. "The doctor who saw her, here in New York," he said, "do you have his telephone number?"

Percy nodded.

"It's early." Pyke glanced at his watch. "Only a quarter past six. It's too early for him to be up, I suppose, but I'd like to speak to him."

The airline steward reached the number and Percy introduced Pyke to Dr. Spellman. He waited in agony while the doctors spoke understanding nothing of the jargon. Finally Pyke put the phone down. "It's as I thought," he said as he turned to Percy, "Sorry, but she can't go on. Not yet, at any rate. She must go to hospital."

"Jesus!" Percy murmured softly. Then, more loudly, "What 'ospital? You know where it is?" he asked.

"Saint Luke's. He's given me the address, but he's sending an ambulance."

"We'd better move quickly, then," said Percy, "an' get our luggage taken off."

When the ambulance had gone with Barbara, Nell, and Marilyn, Percy and Pyke found a taxi. The bitterly cold rain was carried on a fierce wind that snatched at the taxi's open door. "What about your brother?" Percy said. "Isn't he supposed to be meeting you here?"

"He's coming from Arizona, so he won't get to New York until tomorrow." Pyke had to shout above the noise of a jet taking off. "Would you like me to come to the hospital with you?"

"We'd appreciate that very much," Percy shouted back.

The Royal Free in Hampstead, London, or Saint Luke's on Morningside Drive in New York — to Nell one was nothing like the other, yet there wasn't all that much difference between them, either. She felt dazed and full of a great need to cling to Percy and Marilyn once she had lost the fight to get Barby home.

Lethargy and malaise overcame Barby. Quickly the cough be-

[43]

came still harsher, racking her smallness. She began to vomit.

It was Pyke who said he'd go out and see about hotel rooms.

Through the remainder of that day and through the night Barbara grew steadily worse. Soon the cough began to hurt her. Her temperature rose and then fell; from burning heat, drenched in sweat, she'd slip within minutes into an icy coldness and, shivering, teeth chattering, would cry out for blankets.

When Percy, Nell, Marilyn, and Pyke went to the hospital the next morning, Barbara was in an oxygen tent. Percy spoke to Spellman in the wide corridor. "If it's the flu," said Percy, "— you still think it's the flu?"

Spellman nodded, his glasses glinting.

"Well then, can you cure the flu?" Percy asked.

"Mr. Lambert, I'm not going to say we can't cure Barbara, but she has a fulminating viremia."

"Is that the flu then?"

"Why, yes, but it's a bad attack, let's put it that way."

Spellman sounded a little harassed. "You must understand, Mr. Lambert, it's an overwhelming infection and it's combined with respiratory failure. I'm sorry, but I can't say more, not at this stage."

"I'm the one that ought to be sorry," said Percy, suddenly chastened, realizing how aggressively he had tried to pin Spellman down. "It's just that, well, you know how it is . . . worried about her, and the wife, an' all."

The oxygen tent was of clear plastic.

"What's the noise, that bubbling?" Percy asked Pyke.

"The humidifier," Pyke answered.

Percy nodded. "Look 'ere," he said. "Call me Percy, will you? Or Perce. I been in Australia. I know what you're like out there, straight away on first names."

Pyke impressed Percy; he told Nell he was one of the nicest people he'd ever met. "Clever chap, too, y' can always tell."

And Pyke was useful to them, and to Spellman. He became the one who stood between Percy and Nell and the mechanics of Barbara's illness.

On the second morning Percy said to Pyke, "What about your brother, shouldn't you be seeing him?"

[44]

"He's happy," said Pyke with his quiet smile. "He's very busy with his conference. Don't worry, I'll see him before I have to go on to England."

"When do you 'ave to go back?" asked Percy.

"I'm due to start work there next week."

"What kind of work, in a hospital?"

"Not really. Medical, but in a laboratory. Under Sir Julian Reece."

"Oh, I've seen 'im on the telly. 'E's a scientist, isn't 'e?"

"Yes, a research biologist, one of the best."

On the afternoon of Barbara's second day in Saint Luke's, first Pyke, then Marilyn, then Nell, and last of all Percy realized that Barby no longer knew who they were. She tossed about on the bed, seemingly unable to find any position that gave her rest. At noon Pyke noticed that her lips and nails were turning slightly blue. Uncharacteristically, Percy saw this almost as soon as Pyke did — uncharacteristically, because it wasn't in Percy's nature to recognize the bad signs unless he saw also that they might signal defeat. He took Pyke down the corridor and asked him what the blueness meant.

Pyke hesitated and Percy said, "Don't 'old back, I can take it, better I know."

"Well, it means," Pyke said, thrusting his hands into his jacket pockets, "that she's lacking oxygen."

"An' that's bad, o' course."

"It's respiratory failure," Pyke said, "not responding to treatment."

By that evening Barbara's breathing had lost its even rhythm. She was now grunting, each breath a separate, exhausting effort, draining her of strength.

"Poor little bitch," Percy said, staring at her, her nostrils flaring open, her throat muscles straining, her chest wall sucked in between each rib, and her tummy heaving with the effort.

None of them stayed in the room for long at a time. Neither Nelly nor Percy could stand it, and the mechanics of the attention given to Barbara intruded. Every fifteen minutes a nurse would chart temperature, pulse, respiration, and blood pressure and observe the flow of intravenous fluid, the drip now necessary since Barbara could spare no effort for drinking. The oxygen flow was monitored, the humidifiers checked. And doctors, some they'd not seen before, came to look at her. At five that evening Percy and Nell watched as Spellman unzipped the tent side, snapped his stethoscope into his ears, and began listening to Barby's chest.

It was after this examination that Percy followed Spellman outside. "What about drugs?" he said. "I mean, you know these wonder drugs an' all. Another opinion, eh?"

"You've seen other doctors in the unit there, looking at Barbara today, Mr. Lambert?"

"Yes."

"Those men are your other opinions. Each of them is an expert in his own field. As to drugs, we are doing all we can, but the wonder drugs, as you call them, only work wonders with particular diseases. The general public seems to figure we can cure all kinds of respiratory infections — and so we can, we cure a lot of them — but Barbara has one of the influenzas, and it isn't a simple bacterial infection that can be treated by conventional means. For a viral infection of this kind there is no such medication, Mr. Lambert."

Later that evening Pyke added to what Spellman had said. Percy asked him why they "couldn't kill a virus like it was any other germ."

"It's not all that easy to explain," said Pyke. "A virus lives inside the cells of the body, and therefore to destroy the virus you'd have to kill the cell as well. You can't do that without killing the patient, so the only course is to treat the symptoms. We try to help the patient fight the fever, the dehydration, the need for oxygen. This is where real nursing counts, the sort Barbara is getting now, nursing with skill and care. But no amount of good nursing really attacks the basic problem — that Barbara has a virulent, pathogenic organism invading her body against which there's evidently no protection. The body has defense mechanisms," Pyke went on quickly, "and Barbara's body is doing its best now to repel the attack by making antibodies against the virus, but it takes time."

"Funny," Percy said to Pyke that evening — Percy had bought a bottle of Black Label — "funny isn't it, 'ow life turns out? I mean, 'ere we was worryin' ourselves to death over that leukemia an' what 'appens — she goes an' catches the fuckin' flu. I never knew it could be so bloody awful. Listen, Roger, I'm not a bettin' man, an' I'm not asking you to stake your reputation as a doctor, if you see what I mean, but when do you reckon she'll go?"

For a moment Pyke was surprised; then he realized how much of the realist there was under Percy's bounding, aggressive optimism. "I'll tell you why I'm asking," Percy went on, reaching out for the whiskey. "I'd kind of like to, well, to get Nell ready a bit like, see?" Percy was suddenly embarrassed. This he'd not yet learned about himself — that death embarrassed him. He decided it was probably because he'd never had a great deal of time to think about it, and it was something, he also concluded, that evidently did need thinking about. He also found himself realizing that he wasn't being quite honest with Roger Pyke. Certainly he was anxious to do what he could to prepare Nell for Barby's death, but as much, or more, he felt the need to prepare himself.

Pyke's estimate was wrong, but only by about an hour. Pyke said it would be about midmorning the next day. As it was, Barbara lasted almost until noon.

Percy got it first; as Spellman wearily stood back from the tent, catching Percy's eye, he put his arm around Nell. Then she too understood.

Nell screamed and plunged for the tent. Spellman and a nurse moved between her and the bed; then Spellman nodded, and another nurse began to take down the tent. Percy held Nelly until Spellman stepped back and then he led her to the bedside.

# 3 〜〜〜〜〜〜〜〜〜〜〜〜〜〜〜〜〜〜〜〜

Elizabeth was on the ground when the small brown men surprised her. She tried to struggle up and knew she was shrieking. Before she could strike out, her arms were grasped and held. Desperately she fought to get to her feet, but the small men's strength was too much for her. Slowly she was forced down until her head was hanging, her hair falling about her face. Their warm, oily smell was strong in her nostrils. For a moment she lost consciousness; then she realized the men were no longer holding her but stood in a ring about her, incredibly fierce-looking; a more primitive people she could not have imagined.

As she moved they began to chatter excitedly. Then one of them started to give directions, pointing to her and around him. The man wore through his nose a curved boar's tusk planed down to a thin slip. He spoke sharply, took a step toward her, and touched her gingerly on the shoulder, as if trying to tell her that she should stand. The others watched her intently, and as she looked about at them she saw in their expressions a hint of fear.

The tallest of them was about four feet nine inches; their hair was woolly and short and some wore beads. Their eyes were large, round, and sad-looking. Except for a curiously shaped half gourd that they wore over their genitals they were naked. Each

[48]

was armed with bow and arrows, and the one with the boar's tusk through his nose wore a helmet of plaited coconut fiber. Others had strips of fur around their foreheads and some wore necklets of seeds, bones, and small gourds and had birds' claws hanging from their ears. Their most elaborate decoration was on their satchels. Most of them wore two: a large one slung across the shoulders and another, smaller one hung around their necks. These bags were beautifully made, consisting of fine fibers of different colors woven into complex patterns.

When Elizabeth got to her feet, the man with the boar's tusk began to push forward. The men chattered more quietly now, looking about with their big, sad eyes. She sensed an urgency in them, as if they were afraid of lingering. As she began to move she remembered Steve. She stopped, but Boar's Tusk pushed her forward. She stumbled on blindly, sick with fear for herself and for the loss of Steve. Her legs shook and she nearly fell.

She found herself on a path so narrow that the party had to string out in single file. Boar's Tusk went behind her, pushing her, sometimes helping her when she stumbled. Her anguish had reached the breaking point, her strength was beginning to run from her, when from ahead came the chatter of voices and then, unmistakably, the sound of Steve's voice.

"Steve!" she shouted, "Steve!" She felt strength return and pushed past the little dark men, jostling them aside to get to him. Steve was lying on the path on a kind of litter twisted out of lengths of vine slung between two long poles. She dropped down beside him. He looked much grayer now. "Gee, honey, am I pleased to see you." He grinned weakly up to her. "I've been trying to tell these guys about you." Her pleasure at the sight of him was such that she could not speak. "I guess they've solved a lot of our problems." He spoke slowly, obviously in much pain. "They must have a village hereabouts." Then he added, "They're kind of cute-looking, aren't they? Pygmies —" He tried to add something, but as he did the man with the tusk spoke up loudly and the litter was lifted. Steve cried out as the movement wrenched his leg. She tried to keep beside the litter, her hand on his arm, doing what she could to steady him as he swayed along the trail. They walked for well over an hour before they came to the village, approaching it by a knife-edged ridge. The first sign of it was a palisade of poles barring the path and extending down into the jungle on both sides. The opening in the fence was so narrow that they nearly rolled Steve out of the litter getting him through.

Some twenty houses were dotted about the steep ground, houses raised up on long poles, so wildly thatched with palm that they looked to Elizabeth like hairy insects that had only just stopped staggering about on their many legs. Because of the steepness of the ground, some of the houses were ten or twelve feet from the earth at one end, the other being no more than three or four feet high. Smoke was filtering through some of the thatches. Their arrival caused intense excitement among the women, who were about four feet tall, and their tiny children, all with enormous, grave eyes.

They stopped before one of the houses and Elizabeth was appalled at the thought of getting Steve into it. The ladder was not only steep but narrow, two poles lashed together with vines, the ties forming the rungs. A narrow porch stood at each end of the house, covered by wide eaves from which the fan-palm thatching hung raggedly.

She was still wondering how they were going to get the litter up when she saw that the far end of the house was so close to the jungle that it all but melted into it. Like the others, the house was only about four feet from the ground. At this end the men were surging about, chattering, setting up two new poles, tying and lashing them together at a much less steep angle than the ladder, at the foot of which they had set Steve down. The speed with which it was done surprised her. Then, with much more shouting, pushing, and pulling, they got Steve up and slid him, still on the litter, inside.

Elizabeth was surprised to see what a good house it was within. The walls were made of laths split from some long-grained wood. Big sheets of bark were lashed to the outside of this inner wall. The floor was made in the same way but covered with mats woven from fan palm or pandanus. In the middle of the house was a raised box filled with earth, and in it were dead embers. Above was a rack with dry firewood. Against the wall opposite the door stood a low platform. This was covered with mats —

obviously for sleeping — and there they placed Steve. Then they left the house. The man with the boar's tusk in his nose was the last to go.

Elizabeth sat on the edge of the platform and put her hand on Steve's arm. His eyes opened and he gazed up at her.

"Gee, honey, was I pleased to see you back there."

"You couldn't have been happier than I was. How do you feel? You must be in pain."

"I guess," he said slowly, "that stretcher wasn't exactly an air cushion." Then he added, "Do you know what happened to the whiskey?"

She shook her head. "I've no idea. Nor the aspirin. I'll look." A spasm of pain hit him and his body stiffened. Then he said, "Maybe those guys brought it along. They could empty Macy's with those dilly bags they've got."

"I'll try and see if I can find it."

Outside, the wet heat of the jungle fell on her. Boar's Tusk was waiting for her, and as she got to the foot of the ladder he pointed to his leg, then up to the house, plainly referring to Steve. Then he pointed at an old man who was shuffling toward them, followed by several younger men. They were carrying sticks, pandanus leaf baskets, and wooden bowls. Obviously they were going to do something to Steve's leg. As she turned to go back to Steve, to warn him, she saw the neck of a bottle of Johnny Walker sticking from a basket carried by one of the women. She put her hand on the basket and the woman gave it to her.

As she came back into the house and Steve saw the bottle he said, "Good girl. I guess you could do with a shot of that, too."

"I think," she said, as she sat beside him, "that they want to do something for your leg."

"The hell they do!"

"I know how you must feel," she said gently, "but I think if they want to then we ought to let them."

"But that's one hell of a bad break, honey."

"Which is all the more reason for not just leaving it untreated. After all, they must know about such things as compound fractures — and about medical treatment. Do let them have a look at it."

"Can you give me a drink?"

"Wait until I see if there's a cup here." She rummaged around in the basket and drew out one of the plastic mugs.

"Then pour me the father of all shots, will you?" he said.

From what Elizabeth could see, the pygmies had brought everything she'd taken from the wreck of the aircraft. She poured whiskey into the cup then helped Steve sit partly on one elbow while he drank it.

Elizabeth hadn't misunderstood Boar's Tusk. The old man was a doctor; "witch doctor" jumped into her mind. He looked incredibly old; the flesh on his buttocks and thighs and arms hung so slackly that it hardly seemed part of him. Slowly his rheumy old eyes wandered all over Steve. Then he began touching him, feeling his chest and neck and the muscles of his arms. Elizabeth sat at the head of the platform, watching, desperately afraid for Steve. From the old man's earlobes hung bundles of small white bones that clicked together as he moved. This and his movements were the only sounds in the house.

Finally he seemed satisfied. He straightened up painfully and muttered something so quietly that Elizabeth barely heard it; a much younger man came forward with a cup made from a half coconut kernel, black with age. In it was a dark, greenish liquid. The man looked from Elizabeth to Steve and back again to her. Then he gave her the cup.

"You're to drink this, Steve," she said.

For a moment she thought he was going to protest; too ill for that, he let her put the cup to his lips.

Once the old man began he worked quickly. When it came to the actual setting of the bone Elizabeth turned away, looking past the others to the door and the late afternoon heat outside. Several times Steve cried out. Once, he screamed. It took almost an hour, but when it was done Steve's leg had been splinted and the wound packed with shredded leaves, with other, larger leaves then tied over them to keep them in place. Elizabeth's skin glistened with sweat, which trickled down her neck and between her breasts.

Steve did not open his eyes after the men had gone. She spoke to him but he neither answered nor moved, and she guessed the drink he'd been given was a soporific.

Dusk came suddenly. Steve lay unmoving. Once, overcome by sudden panic, Elizabeth felt for his pulse to reassure herself. She found it thready, but strong enough. Forlornly, she looked at his watch, and when she saw it was just after six o'clock she remembered the whiskey. A bowl of water had been left in the house and she got the whiskey, poured two fingers into one of the cups, decided to make it three, added as much water, and going back to the platform sat beside him, gazing down at him as she sipped.

Ten minutes later she was startled by another presence in the house. She swung about and saw two women in the doorway holding wooden bowls heaped with food. Bending swiftly, they set them down, and without as much as glancing at her went out again.

In one bowl were pieces of boiled yam, in another cassava, in another what looked like sweet potatoes, and in the fourth a kind of stew, vegetable pieces she could not identify mixed with meat that she took to be pork.

For a long while Elizabeth stared at the food. Then she ate a little, but soon a weariness began to steal on her. How much of it was due to the strength of the whiskey, how much to the ordeal she had gone through since the crash, she could not decide. But, with the whiskey and the food and the knowledge that her responsibility for Steve was no longer entirely her own, with the quiet softness of the shelter of the house about her, she felt the first stirrings of relief seeping into her. Leaden-limbed, she looked about for a place to sleep. There was room on the platform with Steve, but the sight of him lying there in the last glimmerings of the day — his leg so grotesquely splinted and strapped, his gray face with its new stubble, his arms thrown out beside him in the helplessness of his drugged sleep, and, the crowning incongruity, the tattered remains of his shirt and jacket over the brief underpants — filled her with such compassion for him that she could not bring herself to disturb him. With virtually no conscious thought of what she was doing she moved to the side of the platform, lay down on the floor, and fell asleep.

The next morning Steve's condition began to deteriorate steadily. He was conscious but moribund, aware of her presence, of her solicitude, her eagerness to do what she could to help him, but a steadily growing weakness plucked at his wish to reciprocate. "Honey," he said in the middle of that next afternoon, "I thank you from the bottom of my heart for all you're doing for me, but I'm just not worth it, not worth it."

"Let me be the judge of that," she said as quietly. "Values don't mean anything when you've nothing to measure them by. For me, you are all I have. It's as simple as that."

By late afternoon she was sure Steve had a fever. She longed for a thermometer. He asked her for whiskey, and thinking aspirin might help before the whiskey, she gave him two of the tablets. Twice that day the old surgeon came and looked at Steve, disconcerting her by his sudden arrival and total disregard of her presence. Twice, also, the young women brought her food and early in the morning led her to a place outside the limits of the village where she could relieve herself, then to a stream where she could bathe.

That second night Elizabeth slept fitfully. She dreamed much and woke sweating and frightened, only to fall off into sleep again and repeat the pattern of her agony. When she finally woke it was full daylight and men were bending over her. She cried out, fighting her way to her feet amid the tangle of their bodies.

"Take it easy, honey," croaked Steve. "You just woke up at the wrong time."

"What's happened?" she gasped.

"They took me to the john," he said weakly. "You were asleep by the bed here. You woke just as they were putting me back. Relax."

On the third day Steve felt slightly better.

When Elizabeth awoke Steve was smiling down at her. At once she saw that life was returning to him. "Would you like some coffee?" she asked, sitting up. "Or, I forgot, I've got some tea bags, too."

They decided to make it coffee. Carefully she stirred the ashes of the fire, put on more wood from the rack above the fireplace, and blew it into flame. He lay watching her as she moved about. She had now tied her hair back with a piece of sennet. He liked the way she did things; she was practical and moved easily with economical movements. They had almost finished their coffee

[54]

when a man came to the door and looked in shyly. He was holding one of the passenger's overnight bags, which he put down just inside the doorway before he turned and disappeared down the ladder.

Steve said, "Want to bet, honey? I say the contents belong to a woman." Her hand was on the zipper.

"And I say they belong to a man. How much will you bet?"

"Oh, let's make it worthwhile. Say a grand. I only bet on certainties."

"What's a grand?"

"Thousand bucks."

Steve lost. She drew out a pair of men's pajamas, then a shirt, socks, a well-stocked toilet kit, and an electric razor. They were wet and already had begun to smell of mold. "Go ask that guy with the tusks if he has 110 or 220 volts here."

"I wonder where they found this bag," Elizabeth said. "Would they have taken it from the cabin?"

"It's hand luggage," he said.

"Where was the baggage compartment in that plane, Steve?"

"In the rear."

"In the part we were in?"

"Uh-huh. Why?"

"I was wondering if I could get them to take me back. I might find more of the luggage."

"I guess they might have done that already, honey."

Steve's guess was right. Late that morning, and then again in the afternoon, the men brought a sorry collection of passengers' baggage and personal belongings. There were three suitcases — all of them burst open but now tied together with vines — a couple of overnight bags, sodden and torn, and finally, at the end of the afternoon, a package virtually unharmed. As soon as Elizabeth saw it she seized it and took it to the platform. "Steve," she said excitedly, "look what I've got."

"Take it easy, babe. It's probably something we really need, like, say, a carton of golf balls."

"But it isn't. I *know* what it is. It's *my* parcel and I know what's in it —" A flicker of interest lit Steve's face. "— It's a radio I bought in Manila!" Frantically she fumbled with the package while he watched her. "There!" she cried, lifting it out. Her eyes were shining with pleasure. "Wait until I switch it on."

"It's had a hell of a jolt." He was afraid of her disappointment should the set be damaged. "You had them put the batteries in?" he added.

"Yes. Yes, I did," she said quickly. Just as suddenly the memory of what had happened in the shop hit her. She gave a groan. "Oh, God, no, Steve, no, he didn't put the batteries in." Her shoulders slumped and she stared dejectedly at the useless radio.

"You're quite sure?"

"I'm sure." She shook her head. "He didn't put them in. He was a fool of a fellow. I was in a hurry, and as he was about to put in the batteries a woman came into the shop and started yapping away at him. I stood it for about ten minutes and then said I couldn't possibly wait, would he please pack the whole thing up and I'd take it as it was."

"So you didn't get the batteries?"

"Yes, I got them, but I put them in my suitcase. Oh," she added quietly, "I could wring that bloody man's neck."

"It'd be fine to have a radio."

"I want to hear whether they're looking for us. It'd be on the news, the Australian and New Guinea news, wouldn't it?"

"Sure it would. But you don't doubt that they're looking for us, do you?"

"I'd feel a lot happier if I heard them say so."

They fell silent in the damp heat of the house, he lying very still and gray, trying hard not to let her know how ill he felt.

Suddenly she said, "Sorry, Steve."

"What have you got to be sorry for?" He opened his eyes and smiled at her.

"For grumbling. Talking about being unhappy when I'm uninjured and you're hurt. And you're not complaining. You're a sweet man and I'm wicked to grumble."

"Hell, that's not grumbling. I'd like to hear that they're looking for us just as much as you would."

"Yes, but you're not grumbling about it. You accept it."

"Got to. Gee, I've been in worse scrapes than this and got out of 'em before."

"Where?"

"In the war. Don't you go worrying your pretty head, they'll find us. Bet you before the week's out — well, it might take a little longer than that — but you'll see, it won't be long before they'll find us and have a chopper in here and lift us out."

Quickly she smiled at him. "Want to lose another grand?"

"Like I said, I only bet on certainties."

That night Steve was in a lot of pain and slept fitfully. There was a bright moon, and its light slanted in through the open door. If he moved his head and looked down, he could see her on the mats on what had now become her sleeping place on the floor beside his platform. She was wearing one of the dresses she'd got from the broken suitcases the pygmies had found. She was lying on her side, turned toward him, the thin stuff of the dress tight across her hips and thighs. Her long hair was spread out around her head. She was breathing evenly and deeply, though sometimes she gave a little shudder and whimpered, reminding him of a black Labrador he had had when Fay, his wife, was alive, a dog who used to lie asleep before the fire, twitching his paws and whimpering, eyelids fluttering, while Fay said, "Look, Steve, Sam's dreaming, chasing something."

He watched her a lot that night, wondering about her, about who she was, what her husband was like, if she had children.

He'd said they'd be found within a short time, but he didn't believe it. He remembered how it had often been in the jungle during the war, when crashed aircraft had been searched for at treetop level and had been missed. He knew how quickly the rain forest rearranged itself, healing even a large scar in a matter of weeks, even days. There was also the paramount importance of their position at the time of the crash. He wondered what kind of a position-fix Search and Rescue — he guessed that would be at Port Moresby — might have been able to get on them. They must have been way off course to fly into the mountain. In such a violent electrical storm there had probably been instrument failure, too.

The more Steve recalled what he'd learned of the jungle during the war and the more he searched his memory for facts about the size of New Guinea, the more he believed that they would be very lucky people indeed if they were found. The fact that none of the pygmies knew even a few words of Pidgin English, the lingua franca of New Guinea, was proof of the remoteness of the country into which they had fallen.

How much would it matter if they were not found? Once he was well again could they not walk out of the jungle? Other people had done it, passed on by natives from village to village until they reached the coast or some outpost. But this prospect became clouded because he knew enough about New Guinea to know that connections were not always friendly between remote tribes. Very often these villages were small nations at war with those surrounding them. He remembered that every man of the party that had brought them in had been armed. He dredged his mind for more facts about New Guinea, recalling the hundreds of different languages spoken, the immense variety of its flora, a flora so vast that he knew there were botanists who thought that here may have been the cradle of life on this planet.

The moonlight finally touched her body. He watched her, listening to her breathing, seeing the faint movement of her body under the thin cotton dress. Say they weren't found, and say they couldn't walk out because his leg wouldn't let him undertake such a journey? What then?

He decided that didn't bear thinking about.

Or say — and when the thought struck he winced physically as if it had been a dart of pain — or say that he didn't survive, that the wound in his leg became infected and she was left here undiscovered and alone, without hope of finding her own way out?

When Elizabeth woke it was full daylight. Steve, on his back, was staring into the smoke-darkened timbers and thatch of the roof. For the first few moments he didn't realize she was awake and looking at him. Then he heard her move and he turned to look at her, but she didn't quite meet his gaze because she didn't want him to see in her face the recognition of how much worse he looked this morning.

She pulled the front of her dress together, sat on the edge of the platform, and smiled at him. "How did you sleep?" she asked.

"Best night I've had for a long time," he said. "I feel just fine." He sounded much weaker this morning. "It's the country air." He smiled at her. "Honey, do me some good, will you? Give me a shot of that whiskey with the coffee before those guys get here to take me to the john."

She went to the fire and stirred it. As he watched her kneeling there, putting on dry sticks and stirring the embers, he was moved by the sight of her breasts through the opening of her dress. "They'll never believe it when we get back," she said. "Whiskey and coffee for breakfast in darkest New Guinea."

For a long moment their eyes met. Then hers dropped and she turned away and bent again to the fire, afraid he would see her fear.

The following morning Elizabeth said, "You always say you feel fine. But please tell me, just how do you feel? Is the pain any better, or worse?"

"I always feel fine in the mornings, first off when I see you."

"Flatterer. But this morning you sound a bit croaky. I hope you're not catching cold."

"The coffee and the whiskey will fix that. We've still got whiskey left?"

"Plenty. We're not through the first bottle yet. The coffee I don't make very strong. But please tell me how your leg feels." She was sitting on the edge of his platform, looking down at him.

"It throbs some," he said quietly. "But I guess that's all."

This was the sixth morning after their rescue. Steve looked much grayer now, and the skin on his face seemed to be stretched more tightly over the bones. When he was lying on his back she could see that his arms were thinner, as if the flesh was wasting away.

As the sounds of the village beginning its day and the scent of wood smoke from newly stirred fires drifted into the house, Elizabeth set water to heat. Steve watched her as she moved about the hut. The scratches on her legs and arms were beginning to heal; she'd found a comb, and pale lights moved in her hair. He noticed this morning how long and well shaped her legs were.

Suddenly she turned from the fire. "You embarrass me," she said.

"How come?"

"Because you watch me so intently."

"I like watching you. It does me good. I keep telling myself how lucky I am. Instead of you it might have been some whiskery old guy crouching there fixing my coffee. I told you that before."

"You might yet come to wish it was a man . . ."

"Hell, no, not that. Maybe today, maybe tomorrow, that chopper will come for us and they'll whisk us off, me to a hospital somewhere and you back to your husband, and maybe I won't see you again."

She gave a short, rueful laugh.

"That's not funny," he said.

"It wasn't meant to be funny."

"Not that kind of a laugh, huh?"

"No. It was about the chopper, as you call it, the helicopter."

"What about it?"

She got up, her eyes still on the fire and the pot of water heating on it. "Just that I don't think it will come today." She looked around at him. "Or tomorrow. You see, I don't think we're going to be found as easily as you say we will."

"You're not getting depressed, are you? We haven't been here long, you know." She noticed a slightly critical edge to his voice.

"I knowing we haven't," she said, suddenly smiling at him. "you're the dearest man to keep encouraging me. I should be encouraging you. You're the sick one."

"Hell, I'm *fine*. Our being found is like — well, it's a matter of opinion. We've got to hope — even a beggar has to have hope."

"I remember something about hope," she said. "I know: 'Hope is the second soul of the unhappy.'"

"Is that a quote?"

"Goethe."

"That's like discovering that a woman you love has been unfaithful to you. If you love her enough to want to stay with her you *hope* she won't do it again. But that's all the guarantee you've got, isn't it — the *hope* that she won't. The chances are," he paused and added ruefully, "that she will, having done it once. And what's more, she'll know that as sure as you do. I guess old Goethe was about right."

"Yet you say one should never give up hope."

"Ah, but hope is where you find it. Besides, our position is different."

"You mean there are different kinds of hope?"

"Maybe there are. The guy with the woman who's been unfaithful has one kind of hope. I nearly said luck. Mind, he's an optimist, as I figure him — or a sucker for punishment, or just a plain fool. But we have another kind of hope. We're hoping for the tangibility of rescue. In fact" — he smiled at her — "we're *expecting* it."

"If we're lucky."

He changed the subject. "You like Goethe?" he asked.

"My husband does."

She gave him the coffee, well laced with whiskey. She sat on the edge of the platform and they drank it. "I'm going to give you a warm wash this morning," she said.

"You hope to." He grinned at her, but she saw how hard he was trying to hide the weakness he felt.

"It'll make you feel better. When they've brought you back from the loo," she said gently.

"So now this is going to be as bad as being in the hospital. At any rate, you have washed me. You did yesterday."

"Only your face and hands."

"Let's talk about Goethe. And your husband. He likes Goethe, huh?"

"Some of his poetry, yes. I don't think he admires him as a man."

"That's a relief. Say, what does your husband do? What's his name?"

"He's a scientist, a biologist, and his name is Julian."

"Where does he work?"

She nearly said he was head of the Institute; instead she said, "In a laboratory attached to one of the big London research institutes."

"And you're a scientist, too?"

"Sort of. But I'm not full-time. I only do occasional consulting work now."

"That 'sort of' is all my eye and Fanny Adams," he said, watching her. "I've remembered now. Geoscan doesn't hire anybody to

[61]

make reports for them unless they're really good. I heard something about you in Manila. I remember it now. You have any children?"

"No. Do you?"

"Uh-huh. Two."

It was long past midday before she had the heart to wash Steve. When the little men brought him back he lay, pale and exhausted, staring into the roof timbers. She gave him two aspirins and said he must try to sleep. In the middle of the afternoon Boar's Tusk came into the house. He darted her a shy look, then stood with his big sad eyes on Steve, who turned his head and smiled up at him. Elizabeth watched Boar's Tusk's face. He barely acknowledged Steve's recognition as his eyes, so mobile in the all but expressionless face, moved slowly up and down Steve's length. Elizabeth noticed that Boar's Tusk was wearing the dried claws of a bird in each of his earlobes but not his helmet. In the sunlight striking in through the door the blackness of his hair was dusted with gray. Finally he made a curious clicking sound with his lips and turned and went out. As Elizabeth resumed her seat on the platform Steve said, "That guy looked about as cheerful as an undertaker at his mother's funeral."

"Don't be silly. They always look sad."

"Next he'll be back with his tape measure." A few moments later there was the sound of someone on the ladder. "What did I tell you?" Steve shifted a little, looking anxiously at the doorway. Three times the doorway darkened as there came into the house the old surgeon, followed by Boar's Tusk and one of the younger men Elizabeth remembered as the surgeon's assistant when they set Steve's leg. The three men stood looking down at Steve, whose eyes switched from one to the other in turn. Now, for the first time, Elizabeth saw plain fear in Steve's eyes. She sat at the foot of the platform and put her hand on his good leg so that he looked down at her. "What do they want, honey?" he asked quietly.

"I think they've just come to see how well you're getting on."

"The hell they have."

The old surgeon then spoke to the younger man, who left the

house while the surgeon resumed his doleful gaze at Steve. Suddenly it was over. As if on a signal both Boar's Tusk and the old man went off, the old man's feet shuffling dryly on the mats.

"These guys are up to something," Steve said, watching them as they went out. "I don't trust that old bastard."

"Well, you must," she said earnestly. "He set your leg."

"Sure he did. And I figure he's just written it off as a bad job. What a bedside manner! That guy must be the high society doctor for miles around. I bet he's got a practice that never allows him a moment's rest. You notice how he just *oozes* confidence. If I hadn't had this leg broken for me I'd bust it myself, just to be under his care. How you can bear to be so fit and healthy with a medical adviser like that on your doorstep beats me."

As Steve said this they heard someone on the ladder again. Steve groaned. "Here's Galen back," he muttered, turning his head to the doorway. "Christ, no," he said as the younger man came in again, "it's Hippocrates."

The man came with a small, steep-sided wooden bowl. He looked at Elizabeth and, lifting the bowl to his mouth, made as if to drink. Then he lowered the bowl and pointed to Steve.

Elizabeth got up and looked in the bowl. The man's eyes never left her. "There's not much of it," she said, looking at Steve. She held him under the shoulders while he drank. "What did it taste like?" she said as she took away the bowl.

"Hemlock. You'll be an accessory."

"I think I know now," she said later that afternoon, "who you are. I've been doing some remembering, too. You're the VIP this aircraft was sent for, aren't you? They said something about you when they offered me the seat. I was about to book on a normal flight."

"Why in God's name did you change?"

"Because this way I'd see more places . . ."

"Primitive mountain pygmy villages, for example."

"Correct. Now go on, tell me more about yourself. You're an engineer. Didn't I hear them say that?"

"I guess you could call me an engineer. But not a very good one. I'm good at *employing* engineers. Instead of a slide rule, I carry around a list of guys who are good with a slide rule. Or good at chemical analysis. Or just damn good at sitting around and thinking something out. I'm a kind of a private thinking machine who thinks he sometimes knows a lot more about another man's business than he knows himself."

"You're a consultant, then?"

"I guess you could call me that. Sometimes when a big company has a problem and wants an outside view of it they call me in, and because I maybe go about the problem in an unorthodox way I often manage to solve it for them. Sometimes a company will call me in before it has a problem, wanting to know whether it's likely to get one or not. Sometimes a government will ask me to look at some scheme or other. I get to have quite a few corporations asking me to have a look at some of the things they're doing."

"You sound like a very clever man."

"No, honey, there you're wrong." Steve shook his head. "I'm not clever. But I *am* lucky. Fay used to solve some of my problems."

"Fay?"

"My wife. She was cleverer than I. When she died I all but folded. I wasn't really ambitious, you see. I only thought I was. What I mistook for ambition was really a desire to do well in her eyes, not something I wanted to do for myself. When she went I suddenly realized I'd been stacking dollar on dollar, going from one job to the next, because I wanted to make good for her sake. When she died I lost the reason for working. It took me three, four years to get it back. The funny part of it was that after we'd reached a certain point she kept urging me to quit. While she was there I didn't want to. When she went I had nothing to go on working for."

"You must have loved her."

"I was crazy about her. She was small and she was dark and beautiful. She was a musician, and when I was away from her I used to call her up and tell her to play the piano, and she'd put the phone on the piano and she'd play. Not much, just enough to keep me going until I got back to her. Why I kept having to go away from her I'll never know, except there was that desire to keep on always being successful in her eyes. She didn't want that. Once we had enough, she didn't want any more. She just wanted me. When she died I gave most of my money away. Money after a certain point doesn't do anything for you that's good, and having it only complicates life. I used to have five Japanese gardeners. Now I have one."

"Whom did you give your money to?"

"Oh, we built some fine animal houses in zoos here and there and set up a few trusts to study and take care of wild animals and birds, and a friend of my daughter's had an autistic child which brought home the nature of that problem to me, so we helped set up a permanent study program."

"So you didn't give it to your children?"

"Oh, I took good care of them as I went along. Rose is worth a packet, and Dave gave his to the Benedictines when he joined them. I've never seen the sense in rich old bastards hanging on to it just so they die the richest corpse in the graveyard. People like that get their values wrong. I don't mean just about money but about damn near everything. They're like the German army officer who went to see *William Tell* and came back and reported to his commanding officer that it was all about civilians shooting fruit. It isn't hard to make money, the hard part is in using it; some people are good at carpentry or have green thumbs, others have the knack of making money. In a way, you remind me of Fay. She was sensible and practical and so are you, and you ask the same kind of questions."

"What did she die of?"

"She didn't die of anything. Not in that sense. She was healthy. She went out one night to mail a letter she'd written to me and a maniac jumped her and cut her to pieces."

It was the hottest day they'd known since the crash and that afternoon the village lay silent, as if drugged by heat. Steve dozed or stared at the dark roof timbers or turned his head and looked out of the doorway across the clearing to the mountain ranges that enclosed the village. Flies and other insects flew in and settled on the floor mats and rose buzzing when Elizabeth moved. Early that afternoon the women who brought the food came with more mats for her, and she spread them beside the platform to make a softer bed. "I feel like a heel," Steve said, "hogging all this platform. That's not comfortable for you on the floor, Liz. Or maybe these guys can make you a bed like this."

"You just lie quietly and leave this to me," she said. "I want to stay right where I am. I like being near you."

That day the women also brought her bundles of dry ferns and showed her how to spread them between the mats to soften the bed and how to make pillows.

At the hottest part of the afternoon, when Steve was sweating a lot, she took one of the torn dresses and from time to time fanned him with it. He seemed much weaker that evening and she didn't want him to talk. Nor would he eat when the food came. She ate a little, then when it was cooler went and sat outside the door. She noticed that not many people came near their house, and when they did they darted only the shyest of glances up at her as they passed, large sad eyes in the dusk. Then the breeze died and the smoke from the cooking fires climbed straight and the night insects began to sing.

That night Steve cried out in his sleep and awakened her. She lay listening to him calling over and over again. It took her a while to realize that he was calling for his wife.

Finally his voice died away and she sat up, long into the night, thinking of Julian. What would he be doing now? Would she ever see him again? She ached to see his tall, gangling figure; her sudden longing for him was strong enough to make her cry out. She'd had a sister widowed and had seen the frantic hurt. Her head fell and her hands clutched at her face and she felt her nails beginning to tear her skin; she got up and lost her balance and stumbled in the dark and grabbed for the split bark of the wall and stood there and sobbed and knew a sense of loss greater than she could have imagined possible. Twelve hours . . . Was that the time difference between here and London? And which way did it go, was it yesterday in England or tomorrow? Julian was surely due to give one of his television talks . . .

# 4 〰〰〰〰〰〰〰〰〰〰〰〰〰〰〰

After Julian's telecast, Draper, the producer, said, "Went very well, Julian. Come and have a drink." Draper was a large man, smoking a cigar, with a fat face and hard eyes. A man who didn't smile much.

The drink was in an anteroom off Draper's office. Julian's producer and four other senior people followed them, with two young men bringing up the rear, plainly feeling more important for getting the nod to join the big brass for a drink.

"We wondered," said Draper, "about some of those clips. Those children with kwashiorkor. I made the decision. Put 'em in, I said. Let 'em see how bloody horrible it really is to die of a deficiency disease."

"It's a difficult subject," Julian said. "There's so much to say. And so much of it has all been said before. Yet it's hard to make people see the seriousness of the situation. Without boring them."

"It's a fact of television life that people are easily bored," said Draper. "Especially if you're trying to educate them."

"There's that, no doubt," said Julian. "But there is also in all of us the conviction that it won't happen to me, personally. Or that if it is going to happen, it won't happen in my lifetime. Otherwise practical, down-to-earth people just don't seem to be able to grasp what is happening now. Every time your pulse throbs there are two new mouths to feed. You put it to people but they don't see it; if they did they wouldn't go on having children, because what we'd call a normal decent person wouldn't deliberately have a child in the certain knowledge that it would grow into a person who'd die of starvation or a deficiency disease."

"Yet normal decent people do go on having kids." Draper let the smoke trickle from the corner of his mouth.

"It depends who the people are. What we'd call the normal decent Indian peasant on the poverty line does it to provide himself with labor. The white-collar worker, one of your chaps here, for instance, on a reasonable salary, does it out of conceit."

"Conceit?"

"Why else? So that they pass on their own so-precious genes. Don't misunderstand me; there is of course a biological force at work also. But a good bit of the urge to procreate, especially among women, has been inculcated. From childhood they've been brought up with the notion that one day they'll be mothers."

"Perhaps they're masochists." Draper chuckled. "Awful thought. Husband madly rodgering wife to produce children who he knows will come to sticky end."

"Just imagine, Draper," Julian said, "every month there are more than five and a half million extra people. That's about the population of Rome and Paris put together. It's more than Peking, double that of Toronto. Every month! Quite apart from being unable now to provide enough food to cope with a population increase of that magnitude, we've no hope of being able to provide every month the services a great city needs: the water supply, the sewage systems, the hospitals, the electric power, the schools, the roads, the houses, public buildings, and so on. And the trained people necessary: doctors, nurses, teachers, engineers, plumbers, electricians, and the like. We can't even do it *now*. At this moment, here in England and in all the so-called developed countries, we need more schools, more hospitals — more everything. Poverty even in a country as rich as America is appalling. Imagine what it will be like in thirty years, when our present world population will have doubled. Have you ever been in Africa?"

Draper nodded. "But only in a few of the big cities."

"If there is to be any future for man, we've got to think globally. The future of mankind is indivisible. What happens in Africa will and must affect what happens here in England, or America, or Australia. Anywhere. And somehow we've got to make people see this. In Britain there is one doctor to every 870 people; in the Upper Volta there is one doctor to every 80,000! Go and see it! It's unbelievable. Dysentery, diarrhea, TB, polio, schistosomiasis, pneumonia, and all kinds of tropical diseases. One dentist to every half-million people, Draper. Children in Africa, India, with enormous bellies because they've nothing to eat. Or they're infested with worms. Thin sticks for limbs, twisted by polio. We may not be our brother's keeper — though I'm not so sure about that — but unless man stops breeding and takes stock of his resources there's just no hope for his survival."

Julian stared at his glass, swilling around the whiskey that remained in it, setting the ice to chink.

"No news, no fresh news," said Draper, "about your wife?"

"No fresh news, no." Julian looked up at him.

"I take it," Draper said, looking sideways at Julian, "that it was a private aircraft. That right?"

"A company aircraft. It belonged to a firm called Geoscan Incorporated. Their head office is in Chicago. My wife does an occasional consulting job. Oil people need first-rate paleontologists, and Geoscan had some interesting cores in Sydney. They made her a good offer to look at them. It was my fault. I urged her to go. I said she'd enjoy the trip," he added bitterly.

Draper shifted uncomfortably, embarrassed by Julian's remorse. Draper had long since made it a policy never to admit mistakes. "Have the other half," Draper said, and gave the merest nod to one of the young men.

"Why New Guinea?" he asked.

"Well, Geoscan has an operations base at Port Moresby. They're doing all they can, of course. They've sent their chief pilot to New Guinea and canceled all their survey work in the Pacific area to make as many aircraft available as possible. And the Australian authorities are conducting an official search." Julian stared into his glass. Draper noticed how very tired Julian looked, more than he had on the monitor on which Draper had watched the program.

"Nothing we can do, I suppose?" Draper asked.

Julian looked up. "Afraid not. Wait and hope, that's all there is to do."

The door opened and a young man came up to Draper; he frowned, then bent his head to listen. "I thought the order was explicit," Draper said, looking at the young man from under his heavy brows. "No telephone calls to be accepted for Sir Julian Reece. Not on any account."

"We explained that, sir, and the caller said not to worry Sir Julian, but would he please ring him when he got home tonight. It's not about the program. It's a Professor Saunderson."

"Saunderson?" Julian looked around sharply at the young man. "Did you say Professor Saunderson?"

"Yes, sir."

"Is he on the line now?"

"I think so, sir. He said he'd wait to be sure you got the message."

"I'd like to speak to him," Julian said to Draper. Then, by way of explanation, "He's my number one at the Institute."

"Have it put through to my office," Draper said. Then, to Julian, "Bring your drink."

"Sorry to worry you, Julian," Saunderson said over the telephone. "I enjoyed your broadcast very much. But I'm ringing to tell you that Pyke has died."

"Thank you, Clem. Who has died?"

"Roger Pyke, that young research chap from Australia. On a travel grant, one of ours. Arrived on Wednesday but was ill. Remember I told you on the phone about how I got him into digs with Chris Leach pro tem?"

Julian remembered. Pyke was from the Walter and Eliza Hall Institute in Melbourne.

"I asked Chris if he'd have him for a few days," Saunderson went on, "because Chris is always helpful and because they're both working on much the same kind of thing."

"Chris is on leave though, isn't he?"

"He is now. He went yesterday, with a chap from Guy's, I think. Climbing or something like that in Italy. I didn't want to

[70]

worry you about Pyke but thought you ought to know straight-away . . . No news of Elizabeth, I suppose?"

"No. No, not yet. You say Pyke was ill when he arrived here, Clem?"

"Well, yes. All rather worrying, actually. The day after Pyke arrived I went around to see him and diagnosed influenza. Leach offered to postpone his leave, but I said no need to do that. I'd see to him myself. But he got worse, and a couple of days later I called in Colin Ringway. Colin agreed it was the flu, but thought it a kind he'd not seen before. Clever chap, Colin, bags of experience, as you know. Colin wanted him in hospital so we rang around and got him into UCH. Well, he died tonight. Do you mind phoning Ringway, Julian? I think he'd like to speak to you."

"I'll do it as soon as I get home. I'm leaving here now."

Alone in the taxi, Julian sat thinking about what Saunderson had told him of the young Australian's death. Then thoughts of Elizabeth intruded. Had they been killed outright? Had the aircraft fallen into the sea? Or might she be alive, perhaps in a rubber dinghy? If she had been killed, had she known much about it? He had often tried to imagine the scene in the cabin of an aircraft falling out of control. If their seat belts were on, the passengers would be held in their seats. Or pressed against the sides of them by the centrifugal and G forces. There would come the moment when they knew . . . It was at that point — if you had any imagination — you stopped thinking of the scene in the cabin . . .

He shook himself and deliberately went back to thinking of what Clem had said on the phone. Clem had sounded somber, worried, even perhaps a little out of his depth, which was unusual for Clem. Julian had a moment's mental picture of Clem, sandy-haired, bristling moustache . . . Then Julian remembered that Clem was supposed to be on leave, building a garden at his new house. Wonderful chap, Clem, the sort who'd spend his leave working on Institute business — especially any difficult staff matter — and not worrying anyone unless he had to.

"Influenza's one of those bloody boon words," Ringway said to Julian on the telephone, "both for the medical profession and the poor bloody patient. I diagnosed Pyke as having influenza, but what the hell is influenza? These days, almost every time we get an outbreak of what we call the flu it seems to be in a different form. Extraordinarily complex and variable symptoms, as you know. In Pyke's case the respiratory type seemed to be indicated, an infection progressing from the larynx and trachea to the bronchi. And it went like hell too. But, you know . . ." Ringway paused, thinking, "It wasn't, Julian, what you could call a normal, straightforward, respiratory kind of flu. It . . . Well, it puzzled me. I've never seen one quite like it. A rapid viremia, that's what killed him; no sign of pneumonia, no real time for any of the pneumonias to develop. Tell me, Julian," Colin went on, "this chap Leach, right? The chap in whose flat Pyke was staying. He's one of your bright young men, too, isn't he?"

Yes. He's on leave now."

"I know, walking in Italy, so Clem tells me. You haven't heard anything about Leach, have you?"

"Nothing. Why? Should I have?"

"I was wondering whether he might have caught it from Pyke, being in the same flat."

"You think it's as infectious as that?"

"Well," said Ringway cautiously, "influenza is, of course, an acutely infectious disease. This Aussie died bloody quickly, Julian. Bloody quickly. Nice chap, too. Any idea where he could have picked it up?"

"None at all."

After Julian had spoken to Ringway, he called Saunderson back. "What about Pyke's next of kin, Clem?" Julian asked. "Do we know much about him?"

"Well, there's the information on his application form, of course. He seems to have only a brother, a physicist who was connected with that radio telescope at Parkes in Australia — so Pyke told me — but is now in America on some radio astronomy thing there. Pyke told me he stopped off in America, in New York, and saw his brother on the way over here. Pyke had about a week in New York, so he told me."

"Ringway asked me if I knew where Pyke could have picked up this flu."

"Yes, he's interested in that. Oh, I imagine New York. By the incubation time."

[72]

"You're supposed to be on leave," Julian said then. "I'm sorry you've been worried by this, Clem."

"Well, you know how I like to settle these chaps in, especially if they come from overseas. By the way, I've cabled Pyke's chief at Melbourne. I didn't want to worry you with that. I've asked them to try to get approval from his brother to have him buried the day after tomorrow."

"Damn," said Julian. "I'll be at Mill Hill, the Common Cold Unit."

"Don't worry," said Saunderson. "I'll represent the Institute."

"I can't see how I can make the funeral, Clem."

"Forget it. I was going anyway. He was an awfully nice young chap. I suppose the petty cash will stand a wreath?"

"From the Institute, yes, certainly. And order one from me, would you? Let me know how much and I'll send you a check."

"Wait and give it to me when I come back from leave."

"Well, make sure it *is* leave, Clem. Forget the Institute for a while. How's the new garden coming along?"

"Oh, great guns. Though I'm sure the builders could have built another house out of the rubble they've buried, damn their eyes! You'll ring if there's any news of Elizabeth, won't you?"

"Of course I will."

After he'd hung up, Saunderson sat by the telephone thinking of Elizabeth's disappearance. He wondered how he would have taken it had it been his own wife, Peggy. Julian was taking it remarkably well, remarkably. That telly appearance tonight . . . In Julian's circumstances Saunderson decided he couldn't have done it. Julian had looked strained, but as Peg had said, not as strained as he might have looked. The devil of it was the not knowing whether she was alive or not. Peggy called from the bedroom that she'd have to get him a new black tie for that young man's funeral. When he went into the bedroom Peggy was wiping her eyes. "I must be overtired," she said, blinking at him. "First Elizabeth Reece and now this young man Pyke. Don't you go flying off to Australia, will you, Clemmy."

Julian finished speaking to Clem, hung up, and poured himself a whiskey. The house was utterly silent; not a car passed outside along the little-used street in St. John's Wood. Standing with the whiskey, loneliness and loss hit him again. How could he mourn for Elizabeth without her? The one person with whom he could share such a grief was no longer there.

Mrs. Bennett, his housekeeper, had drawn the curtains over the big window in his study that looked out to the garden at the back of the house. The room was warm and safe, its book-lined walls soaking up the light from his wide desk and magazine-spread table. Yet the room seemed so horribly empty. Julian dropped into his leather armchair. He felt the deathly silence. Restless, he got up again and took a pipe from the rack, filling it from the tobacco jar Elizabeth had given him three years ago, on his forty-third birthday. She had designed this room, and there was nothing that he could see or feel that was not her. Before the contract had been signed she had said, "Julian, the big room at the back, looking over the garden, we'll make your study. I'll have a big window put in it. So you can look at the silver birches. And I'm going to make a fish pond and have the lawn relaid . . ."

He couldn't go to bed. Not yet. Nor even stay in the house. It was cold outside. And the night was clear and sharp.

He went out and stood holding his whiskey. The stars were frosty sharp. He stood at the pool's edge. The water-lily pads were gone now until spring. The water was as smooth as black glass, peppered with star points. Then a fish came swelling to the surface and wobbled the star points and split them and sent them reeling.

Elizabeth was here, too, planting water hawthorn and dropping in water soldiers, telling them that come spring they must come up again and stand to attention like good soldiers, the summer through. "You can stand at ease, or whatever it's called, when winter comes . . ."

She was at the stone table, too, and it was a hot summer's night again; there was the laughter and chatter of guests, her lawn was greenly smooth and the birches silver. And Clem and Peggy Saunderson were among the guests and Elizabeth had said, "Peggy, when you get your new house and have your pond I'll give you some of our newts. They have the most marvelously colored bellies . . ."

Now she was at the swinging seat, too, and he was there beside her, letting the evening flow over him, looking at her roses and begonias blazing in the dusk, and she was getting up, setting the seat swaying and saying, "Pour me my other one. Mrs. Bennett will be going in a minute and I want to see her. I won't be long," and he was watching her tall figure and fair hair as she crossed the lawn, asking him as she went into the house if he had seen how well Nelly Moser was doing now she'd been moved to the other wall ...

And her pride in him. The surprise party she had given him for winning the prize. He had felt such a fool that night because he had cried. Clem had kept him, delayed him at the Institute with an excuse so patently clumsy that he'd wondered what had come over Clem. Then the coming home and the street full of cars and the sound of taxis; the house bulged with guests and waiters from the caterers. Old academician Veronoff had got a little drunk and had begun to talk politics, which he wasn't supposed to, and an embassy car had come for him ...

Could one know she was still alive? Could one tell these things, as some wives and mothers said they did when they refused to believe their men were dead at war ...

It began to get cold in the garden, and though he did not want to go in he started to shiver and returned slowly to the house, closing the door softly behind him — and even in that action she was there with him because it was a door she had so often closed, and opened ... come through, when it stood open against the stop, with a tray for summer lunch at the stone table, calling to him through the open study window that he was to stop working and if he wanted another drink he should have it because they'd be eating in twenty minutes ...

Hope. He must hold fast to hope ...

Though there could be danger there; hope could grow until it became more horrible than black consuming certainty ...

Suppose she was injured ... alone ...

That was worse; far easier to face the kinder thought of death.

Speculation, and suspense. These were twin devils, and with them lay power enough to build a dream that could take possession of his mind.

But how to stop the thinking, the hoping?

[75]

Speculation, that damnable child of uncertainty . . . The pilot, Ferris said when he'd telephoned from Chicago, the pilot may have made a forced landing. "Gone in on some beach . . ." There'd been something almost touching in the confidence of Ferris: "This is Claude C. Ferris, president of Geoscan Incorporated . . ."

To Julian, Clem Saunderson's death a week later ranked as a shock second only to Elizabeth's disappearance. Peggy Saunderson telephoned Julian at the Institute. "But Clemmy's *dead*, Julian, and I *don't* believe it. Colin Ringway says so, and I've seen him, Julian, I've *seen* Clemmy. But I don't *believe* it. Just not."

"Listen, cock," said Ringway when Julian rang him after speaking to Peggy. "I've a thing, a feeling about this bloody flu of Pyke's. I've sent material to the Common Cold boys at Salisbury, but I hope I'm wrong. My God, I hope I am. No news about Elizabeth yet?"

Julian said there was not. And then there was silence until Ringway said, "I *am* sorry, Julian. Clem Saunderson was a fine chap and I know what he was to you."

"He was one of the best men we've got. That the Institute has ever had. I must say this has floored me, Colin."

"So bloody quick, you see. And the devil of it was that he'd started to improve. I spoke to you last on Thursday, didn't I? About that Aussie, Pyke. Clem fell ill on Saturday and Peggy got me round on Monday. We got Clem into hospital on Tuesday, lunchtime. By Thursday he looked to be over the worst of it. I, naturally, concluded it was just another uncomplicated case — though seeing Pyke go the way he did I must say I did have a, well, a feeling about it, you know. But never mind that. On Thursday I was beginning to wonder whether I'd overestimated Clem's danger. And he got quite a bit brighter, too, even talking a bit about his new garden. Then, like a wolf on the bloody fold, Julian, on Friday he suddenly copped it. Properly, a massive viremia. Sputum pink and frothy, and lots of it."

"No pneumonia?"

"No. But I called in Harry Peacock. There was also a sign of some peripheral circulatory failure. Harry was going to do an emergency bronchoscopy to clear the airways, or a tracheotomy. But Clem died. And listen, Julian — he was cyanotic. His face was practically midnight blue. I'll tell you something else, it scared Harry Peacock, too. 'Harry,' I said when I phoned him, 'I want you to have a look at Clem Saunderson's bellows.' Peacock kept asking me when the symptoms had first developed. Didn't seem quite to believe me. Or the X rays. But it's flu, Julian. Flu all right, but I'll be bloody interested to see what the MRC chaps make of it. One other thing," he went on, "that chap Leach who's gone on a walkabout in Italy, you haven't heard anything about him, have you?"

"Nothing."

"Well," said Ringway gloomily, "bad news travels fast. I suppose we'll hear soon enough if Leach has caught it, too."

Julian hung up and sat thinking about Ringway's comments. The man wasn't an alarmist; it might well be they had something as infectious as the Hong Kong influenza on their hands. If they did, the virus would certainly be interesting; but the public health side of the effects of it didn't concern him: he was a research scientist.

Julian's telephone buzzed and Miss Marler, his secretary, was saying, "It's Dr. Ringway again. Do you want to speak to him?"

Miss Marler was fat and fifty, a superb secretary with but three passions in life: a cat called Edith, a mother who was blind, and Julian. Put to it, she would have hesitated to say in which order to place them. She bullied all three unmercifully.

"Listen, Julian," Ringway said when Miss Marler put him through, "were you thinking of going to see Peggy Saunderson?"

"This evening," said Julian.

"I thought as much," Ringway said.

"Why?"

"Well, it's none of my business really. In one way, that is. In another way I suppose it *is* my business. But, listen, Julian, if I were you I wouldn't."

"But for heaven's sake why not, Colin? Peggy and Clem are among my oldest friends. Quite apart from Clem's position here."

"I know that," Ringway said quickly.

"She'll expect me. Besides, I want to go. I must go. She's in a hell of a state, so tell me why I shouldn't."

"Michael Canning, used to be a student of yours, friend of mine, epidemiologist, remember?"

"Of course. He's been to my house."

"He's just phoned me. Seems he knows Chris Leach. Early this morning Leach telephoned him from Italy and said he'd tried to ring me last night to find out how Pyke was but I wasn't in. Leach asked Canning if he'd give me a ring and find out if Pyke was getting over the flu okay. Canning said he'd do that. Then he told Leach about Clem Saunderson's death. Before they rang off, Leach asked Canning to call his cleaning woman and tell her he'd be back earlier than expected. So Canning rang the woman, but her daughter answered and said that her mother was in hospital, in an oxygen tent — dying, so she said, of the flu." Ringway paused.

"You think there's a connection?"

"I don't know, but Canning found out that this cleaner was in the Brompton Hospital. So I rang there — and it sounds exactly the same as Pyke's flu, Julian. I'll stake my reputation on it. Some slight differences, but that's all. The old girl's for it."

"So that's Pyke, Clem, and now this woman. What you're saying, Colin, is keep away from Peggy as she might be incubating it?"

After a moment Colin said, "Look, Julian, I could be wrong. I hope I am. But well, yes, that's what I'm saying."

"What about yourself?"

"So far touch wood. Of course, in a general practice you seem to pick up a certain immunity. But it's a startler, isn't it? One hundred percent mortality. So far."

"If the cleaning woman goes."

"Oh, I'm afraid she will — and not by any staphylococcal pneumonia or anything like that either, Julian — the way old people and kids usually die after flu. I've told you, Clem and Pyke died of an extremely violent viremia. Nothing bacterial had time to get going. When I rang the Brompton they gave the old girl only an hour or so."

[78]

That evening Ringway rang Julian in St. John's Wood. "Canning's just phoned me again," Ringway said. "He's spoken to Leach and told him about his cleaning woman being ill, and then guess what? Leach said he was probably getting it, too, that he had a temperature and was feeling like hell, had been since midday."

There was a long pause, then Julian said, "I wonder if there've been any other cases reported?"

"Well, there must be others, of course, unless" — Ringway gave a short, grim chuckle — "that poor bastard Pyke invented the bloody thing. I asked Canning if he'd heard of any flu about — it's right up his alley, public health, epidemics, that kind of thing — but he said nothing unusually virulent. What worries me is that I've never seen anything quite like it before. It's flu right enough, but if it's not a new one I'll eat my bloody hat." For a moment he paused, then said, "Look, Julian, I'm not a lab chap like you. I'm a GP and I've been in practice a long time. A lot of the medicine *I* consider good medicine is the sort you practice by the seat of your pants, a matter of good common sense helped by experience and by reading all the new literature you can. Listen, my father went through the 1918–19 flu. In those days, as you know, they didn't know that flu was caused by a virus, but I remember him telling me that the type of bacteria found in the lungs varied from country to country, even from district to district. Now that'd seem to indicate that if a particularly nasty virus spreads itself around the world and finds nearly everyone susceptible to it, it must be able to make all kinds of alterations to itself while adapting to different pathogenic, disease-producing bacteria. It must have been the virus that did the initial damage, that made the lesions which let the bacteria in, so to speak, but it was the bacteria which did the actual *killing*. Right. But this, Julian, is something different — unless I'm very much mistaken. And I'll tell you something else: my old man told me that in 1918 they were dying with black faces. Do you know, Julian, I didn't believe him; I thought he was exaggerating. But listen, I saw it myself, with my own eyes, in the '58 epidemic. They were blue, some of them, before you could get to them, just like Clem. In Fulham it took a fortnight to get them buried."

When Julian got to his office the next morning Miss Marler said, "A Dr. Canning just phoned." She sniffed. "Said he used to be a student of yours. He wants to know what time it would be convenient for you to ring him. Did you sleep last night?" Julian had long since grown used to Miss Marler's habit of tacking personal questions to the end of totally unrelated statements.

"Fairly well, thank you."

"You look as if you hadn't slept a wink. I'll get that doctor on."

In a moment Canning came through on the phone. "I say, sir," he said, "Colin — Dr. Ringway — told you I spoke to Chris Leach, didn't he?"

"He did."

"And he told you Chris was ill?"

"Yes."

"Well, there's more bad news, I'm afraid. Ringway's got it now. Says the symptoms are those of influenza —"

"But that needn't necessarily mean he's got what killed Professor Saunderson, Michael. Or Roger Pyke. Flu can make you feel bloody without being lethal."

"I suggested that to him . . ."

"I'd better get straight around and see him."

"That's why I thought I'd ring you," Canning said quickly. "You'll be wasting your time, sir. If I may say so. He says he won't see anyone. He's sent his nurse home, told his char not to come, and he's canceled all his calls, rung his patients, and told them to get someone else."

"Have you seen him?" Julian asked.

"No. I spoke to him on the phone, rang him to discuss Chris Leach's illness. I know Chris well; we studied together and I've sometimes crewed with him in his father's boat."

"But this is absurd," said Julian. "Ringway will have to go into hospital — if he's really ill he can't nurse himself. I'll go and see him."

"Well, perhaps you'd better ring him first. By the way, sir, I thought you might like to know, this morning I rang a friend of mine in the WHO office here in London. He says there's been nothing abnormal in the overseas reports in the way of influenza."

"Did you tell Ringway that?"

"Yes, sir."

"What did he say?"

Canning paused a moment, then said, "He muttered something about hollow laughter. He seems rather frightened of this flu."

"I know. What did Chris Leach actually say to you, Michael?"

"Well," said Canning guardedly, "Ringway just might have something, you know — I mean, about the acutely infectious nature of it — because when I spoke to Chris last night he said he wasn't well. Ringway seemed to be expecting it, said it only confirmed his suspicions. Chris was in the flat for two days with this Australian chap, Pyke, who died, you see. Ringway pointed out to me that, as far as he knew, everyone who'd come into contact with it had got it. Epidemiologically speaking," Michael went on, "if that is so, it's something new. I mean it's a popular fallacy that in a big flu epidemic everyone, or nearly everyone, gets it. That doesn't happen because the disease burns itself out. The point is that the lines of infection tend to peter out as immunity levels rise and the proportion of susceptible people reaches a lower level. But I must say, if Colin Ringway's right about the mortality rate to date, then he's got every reason to be as scared as he is. Mind, we don't know the number of recovered cases, do we? Only the fatal ones."

"I still find it difficult to believe that influenza can be quite as infectious as that, Michael. Or as fatal."

"Well, yes. Unless, of course, it's like no flu we've ever seen before. Always a chance, I suppose." Then he added, "I think Colin has something like that in his mind."

"Listen," Ringway said when Julian got him on the telephone, "you haven't seen this bloody thing, Julian. I have. And I'm positive I've got it. I've shut up shop here, put the chain on the door."

"You've got to go into hospital, Colin."

"And bring this with me! Not bloody likely."

"I'll arrange the strictest quarantine . . ."

"Wasting your time, cock."

"But you're not being treated . . ."

"Physician, cure thyself."

"That's not very helpful, Colin . . ."

"I'm being bloody *un*helpful, cock. Look, Julian" — Ringway's voice fell — "I appreciate your solicitude, I do honestly, but right from the first I've had a bloody uncomfortable feeling about this flu. If it is flu."

"What else do you think it might be?"

"Well, Christ Almighty, Julian. Look, hardly a year passes that we don't hear of an outbreak of something caused by a newly discovered virus, or by a known virus that's suddenly become important. The devil of viruses, as you bloody well know, is their capacity to vary in virulence depending upon the strain they come from. Look at that Lassa virus they found in 1969, which knocked off those people in that mission in West Africa and then did the same to those laboratory workers in America who were studying it. We've just had another case of it, right here in England. Christ, let a virulent strain of something like that loose . . ." His voice trailed off. Finally he said, "Flu or not, whatever this is, it's a killer. It has several curious characteristics about it. Flu usually depresses the spirit, as you know, but this does more than that. One of the characteristics of rabies is a sense of impending doom. In the premonitory stage. Now rabies," Ringway paused, as if summoning up his energy, "that's another bloody awful virus, and look how it can change, or at any rate exist in a mutated form. It was only in '67 that a quite new rhabdovirus — the Marburg virus — killed seven chaps in that laboratory handling African monkeys, in Germany."

"But you're not suggesting —" Julian began.

"I'm not suggesting anything at all, Julian. I'm only a bloody GP that happens to have caught something from his patient. What I've caught is for the clever lab boys to discover. I think it's a myxovirus. Maybe, who knows, it's another influenza A mutant, or something related to that respiratory syncytial virus which has knocked so many kids . . . Who knows? It could be any bloody thing at all, as far as I'm concerned. Where was I? Oh, yes, as I was saying, a characteristic of rabies in the premonitory stage is the feeling of impending doom. Ghastly feeling. Now I don't say this flu is as bad as that, but it's something like it. And remember, I *have* seen a case of rabies. Unfortunately. And I saw this fear in

[82]

Pyke and in Clem Saunderson. At the end. Now this is what I'm going to do. I've got one of those little tape recorders here and I've got a stack of cassettes, mostly with music on, but I can record over the music and wipe it out. I'm going to record all my symptoms. And I want you to have those tapes. By the way, I've sent quite a bit of material to Salisbury, and I've taken the liberty of asking them to shoot their examination results through to you. All right?"

"Of course. But God Almighty, Colin, the idea of you, alone, ill, in that house —"

"Stow it, cock. I can look after myself. And if I can't, then that's just too bloody bad."

At four that afternoon, the Institute's administrative office rang through to Julian and told him that Dr. Leach's mother had just telephoned. The Foreign Office had just told her that Christopher was dangerously ill in a Bolzano hospital.

At five o'clock Ringway rang Julian again. "Guess what. Harry Peacock's got it now," Ringway said. "Interesting incubation period. He saw Clem — his only definite contact so far as we know — three days ago. That might be a bit longer than usual — flu is generally supposed to be from twenty-four to forty-eight hours. Now I saw Pyke a week ago. By the way, I rang UCH — where we got Pyke in — and they've got it there. Four cases. But like mine, a longer incubation period. Evidently with this virus individual incubation periods and resistance vary quite a bit.'"

"Where is Peacock?"

"Oh, home. We're treating one another by telephone. Peacock and I have been talking about the possibility of this thing being caused by a virus that isn't really a true flu virus at all, though it may be related to one of our known flu viruses. Take monkey herpes, for instance. People die of that because it's about as lethal as rabies, no cure; but it's harmless to monkeys, as harmless to them as herpes is to us. Now these two herpes viruses must have evolved from the same stock. Who's to say this new virus is not as different from the flu viruses we already know about as the herpes group of viruses are different from one another? There's

[83]

chicken pox, too, that's another herpes, and herpes Zoster, shingles. I put that up to poor bloody Peacock. He said he saw no reason why there should still not be a virus around that existed in a common ancestor of man, monkey, and pig. Mammalian host, you see. And he also reminded me of some theory that the major changes in influenza virus are caused by a double infection of a single cell with a human flu virus and a nonhuman one, say a swine or bird type. Natural selection in the raw, eh? Julian, I'll have to hang up, old man."

"Before you do," Julian said quickly, "are you absolutely adamant that you won't let me come around there —"

"Absolutely. Wasting your time."

"Who's looking after Peacock?"

"His wife. Trained nurse, old Guy's girl. Now listen, Julian, I told you about recording my symptoms. Well, I'm doing Harry's too — blood pressure, temperature, everything we can do for ourselves. I've also got some more material, blood, feces, sputum, urine. Will you send around for it? Tell whoever comes to ring the front doorbell three times and I'll slide it through the letter slot."

That evening Julian got home at seven o'clock. Mrs. Bennett, who had kept house for Elizabeth for nine years, was on the telephone as Julian put his key in the lock. In the hall he heard her say, "Oh, here he is now . . . It's America, sir . . ."

"Claude Ferris, Sir Julian, president of Geoscan . . ."

Julian dropped into the chair by the hall phone, his heart thudding suddenly as Ferris said, "Now first off, to get you off the hook, Sir Julian, I'm not calling with any positive news. Not positive. But that doesn't mean it's bad news. Now the position as of two hours ago is this . . ."

For the third time now Ferris told of the size of the search for the missing aircraft. Told it as if he was selling something. Of the thousands of square miles flown over by helicopter and fixed-wing aircraft. Of the alerts circulated to all shipping and civil aircraft operating in the area. All of which Julian had heard before, an agony of fruitlessness repeated.

"The more we figure it," Ferris said, "the surer we are that our airplane came down over land. We now have a fairly complete meteorological picture of the situation on the afternoon the aircraft disappeared. It was a violent storm. And it covered a lot of territory. An Australian government patrol officer has reported one of the severest electrical storms he's experienced in thirty years in New Guinea. That was in the Mount Albert Edward district. Now as you know, Sir Julian, we've got our chief pilot down there at Moresby and he's got full cooperation with all the authorities. It's a mammoth search we're mounting. And I want you to know that. They call me every day with a position report. The problem is, of course, the denseness of that jungle down there. But the experts give a reasonable to high survival chance. We've never yet lost an airplane, and that one was in the hands of one of our finest pilots. And I want you to know that, Sir Julian. Our chief pilot figures that, given any chance at all, Zuckerman — that's the pilot's name — could have ditched that plane into the treetops, like putting an airplane down into the sea. We are very, very hopeful, Sir Julian . . ."

The words flowed over Julian, heard, understood, appreciated, but meaningless. The agony of being able to do nothing, the despair of helplessness . . . Could he go out there?

"Well now," Ferris said quickly, "if you would like to do that, Sir Julian, why we would, of course, put any part of our organization at your service. And we'd be prepared to pay for your flight out. But is there anything you could do there that isn't already being done? I assure you we are doing just everything that can be done to find that airplane and bring Lady Reece and the other passengers and crew out of there. Why, there's the Royal Australian Air Force, there are planes from a U.S. Navy carrier, there are now four of our own airplanes down there, and another due sometime tomorrow. There are also . . ."

"I realize all this, Mr. Ferris. And I'd probably only be in the way."

"Well, no, Sir Julian, you wouldn't necessarily be that, but, frankly, I don't see what you could do. Why not wait until we find them, then fly down and bring Lady Reece back to England?"

And that was how it was left.

Sleep was Julian's problem. Like many men with a vast medical knowledge, he had an aversion to taking drugs unless absolutely necessary. That night he found sleep impossible. Ferris meant it as a kindness, but this continued repetition of the details of the search only seemed to Julian to emphasize the futility of it. And of all things at a time like this, there was this influenza that had so frightened Ringway. Ringway, Julian knew, was too experienced a physician, too much the steady doctor, to let himself fall victim to unreasoning panic. As with Elizabeth's disappearance, it wasn't something to dwell on if you had a vigorous imagination. At one o'clock that morning he found a bottle of sleeping pills in Elizabeth's dressing room and took two of them.

At seven o'clock the ringing of his bedside telephone woke him.

"Ringway, Julian. Sorry, cock, to phone you this early. And I don't want to sound melodramatic . . . First of all, any news of Elizabeth?"

"No."

"They'll find them. No melodrama, Julian . . ." Ringway paused. Julian could hear his breathing, as if it was already requiring an effort. "I won't waste my energy now telling you my symptoms, they're all on the tapes. But this I do want to say. I want you to do something for me."

"But of course, Colin. Anything. Let me get an ambulance and come around now and get you into hospital . . ."

"Nothing doing. Not that. What I want you to do is to take this bloody flu seriously."

Julian was shocked that Colin might have thought otherwise; he began to say, "My God, of course I'm taking it seriously —" but Colin cut him off. "Sorry, I didn't mean you weren't. All I'm trying to say is that right from the start I've . . . bloody unscientific this, reading of entrails . . . but I've had a . . . feeling about this flu. All right, I'm not ashamed to say it: a premonition, if you like. You're an eminent chap — they'll listen to someone like you. Will you do it?"

"But of course."

"Then, look, Julian, go to someone high up. Someone in the government who can act. Get it across to him that this thing is a killer. Has anything come through from Salisbury yet?"

[86]

"No."

"This is something new, Julian. I'm sure of it. I've been thinking about a mutation of an existing virus. Listen, go to someone in the government." Julian wondered whether Ringway was beginning to ramble. "Got to be *contained*, Julian. It's got to be stopped before spreading. Peacock thinks so too. Quarantine, all that kind of thing. If you could find out where it came from . . . I'm not wrong about this. And I'm damned frightened. Not for myself. Had a fair innings. Funny, I'll tell you something — when your time comes you start thinking of all the things you might have done and didn't. Do you know what I always wanted? A thirty-five-foot sloop, or a little ketch, with a raised deck and shallow draft that'd go up creeks and be at home in estuaries, a Maurice Griffiths."

The fruitlessness of hope. Of saying, "But Colin, you'll get your boat. When this is over you'll be able to take things a bit easier . . ." The futility of saying anything like this to Colin, of all people, of *comforting* him — though there were doctors you could say it to because hope springs as vividly in a medico's breast as it does in an undertaker's. But *was* Ringway as ill with as virulent a disease as he believed? It was monstrous and absurd that he wouldn't go to a hospital.

Colin was saying, "You can't cure me. Any more than Harry Peacock or I, or anyone else, could have cured Clemmy Saunderson. Or that nice young Aussie, Fyke. You've always argued that there was no technical reason why there shouldn't be a disease for which there was no natural immunity, and if this is one, and there's no specific for it, then by trying to treat my symptoms you can only get the bloody thing yourself. Now be a good chap and do as I ask. And send a man around for the material. I've got two cassettes filled now. Tell him to ring three times and I'll drop the stuff through the letter box."

"So we've had yet another good night's sleep by the look of it." Miss Marler sniffed and frowned at Julian when he arrived at his office at nine the next morning. "You should sleep on a hop pillow. You're to ring a Dr. Burgess. Don't go yet and I'll get him for you. You're never very sensible on the telephone when you speak from up there." "Up there" was how Miss Marler referred to

[87]

Julian's laboratory, which she tolerated only because it was where Julian did his work. No one had ever seen her in it, but Julian maintained that not so much as a cover slip or a petri dish was lost or broken that she didn't know about it.

Burgess had a practice in Acton. In his high-pitched, slightly fussy voice he asked Julian if he would be guest of honor and make a short speech at the annual dinner of a small medical society of which he, Neil Burgess, was honorary secretary. "But what with Elizabeth missing, Julian, I did say to the committee that it might be asking a bit much of you. No news yet, I suppose?"

Julian said there was not.

"I saw," Burgess went on, "that Professor Clement Saunderson died suddenly. Very sad. What did he die of?"

"Influenza," said Julian.

There was a pause, then Burgess said slowly, "Actually, I've got Moira down with the flu. Rather a nasty type, too. I've had to put her in hospital, but I must say she's not making the progress I hoped she would. I rang Sir Harry Peacock to have a look at her, but they say he's away ill. I'll ask Brinkman to see her, I think. Chest, you know. And Moira's always had a weakness there. Well now, Julian," Burgess went on, "I won't take up any more of your time. Think over our proposition, and if you'd rather not do it we'll understand completely. We've not settled the venue yet but we're trying to get the Apothecaries. And please, Julian, do believe me when I say how much our thoughts are with you over this dreadful business of poor Elizabeth."

Julian put back the telephone and picked up his pipe. Should he have told Burgess? Told him what? That his wife, Moira, probably had *the* flu? That the reason he couldn't get Harry Peacock to look at Moira was that Peacock had it, too? Plenty of people got the flu and got over it. Unless, of course, Moira Burgess had what Ringway had . . . Ringway's flu . . . Ringway's virus . . . ? Even so . . .

Julian didn't doubt that Ringway had good reasons to be pessimistic, yet he couldn't quite bring himself to believe it was as bad as Ringway believed. What really nagged him was the fact that it *was* Ringway; he could think of plenty of other doctors whose opinion wouldn't nag him in the same way ...

His eye fell on *The Times Atlas* Miss Marler had borrowed so he could look at the map of New Guinea. What mountain had Ferris mentioned? He opened it at the marker placing New Guinea. Mountains and more mountains; the Owen Stanley Range and Mount Victoria and here it was, Mount Albert Edward, 13,300 feet. What chance would an airplane have coming down in that kind of country? Suppose she was alive, lying injured, alone ... ? He sat staring at the beautifully printed page, not seeing it anymore, bleak and cold in his heart ...

Miss Marler opened the door and saw him bent over the atlas. She hesitated a moment, then said, "They're asking for you up there."

At eleven o'clock Miss Marler called Julian in the laboratory. "It's that Dr. Burgess on the phone again. I told him you were busy, but he seems upset. Shall I put him on?"

At first Burgess found it difficult to speak. Finally he managed. "After I spoke to you, Julian, they called from the hospital. She ... she died at ten past ten. I got Trenchard — he was in the hospital. We did everything. But not a chance. She just — just went ... Did I tell you, Moira had a weakness in the chest? Even so ... *terribly* quick, Julian. They said ... severe bronchospasm. Really, there, well, there just wasn't time . . ." Burgess paused. "You said, didn't you, Julian, that Clement Saunderson died of influenza?"

"Yes, Neil."

"Well, Moira's was influenza right enough, but Trenchard was puzzled. You don't happen to know anything about it, do you? You see, there's another case, one of mine — black woman, Jamaican, I think. On the buses. Julian, I'm broken. Moira was the light of my life. Literally. So dreadfully *sudden*. At the end."

"Neil," Julian said carefully, "I might know something about this flu . . ."

Coming from Burgess, the vigor of the reaction surprised him. "What the devil do you mean by *might*, Julian? Surely, either you do or you don't."

"Sorry, Neil, I expressed myself badly. I know nothing clinically. I know no treatment for it."

"But it *is* influenza, isn't it?"

"Almost certainly, though I've not yet any report on the virus."

"Is it a new one?"

"It could be, yes," Julian said guardedly.

"Well then, something's got to be done. Who knows about it? I'm going to get in touch with our MOH straightaway. You must tell me all you know, Julian."

Julian hesitated only a moment; at that instant he made up his mind. "Neil," he said, "could I ask you something? Would you mind not informing your Medical Officer of Health?"

"Well, he'll know anyhow. I'm not sure, but I think he sees all the certificates."

"I mean, not go out of the way to direct his attention to it? Not just at the present?"

"But for God's sake why, man?"

"Because . . ." Julian didn't quite know how to put it to Burgess. But he had promised Ringway he would do something, see some government bigwig, though who this would be he didn't know.

"Why, Julian?" Burgess was insistent, his voice rising.

"Because I want to start somewhere higher up the scale, Neil."

"I see." Though Burgess sounded as if he didn't. "God, Julian, we did everything . . ."

"Of course you did. Now don't torment yourself, dear chap."

"You knew about it." There was more than a hint of accusation in the statement.

"Something. Not much. But this has made up my mind."

"Perhaps, who knows, if I could have got hold of Harry Peacock." Remorse was mixed with the anguish in his voice. "But when I rang his rooms yesterday I didn't know he was dead, poor fellow."

Now it was Julian's turn to register shock. "Peacock's dead?"

"So they told me when I rang again yesterday to see if he could have a look at Moira. The day before, his receptionist only said he was away ill. I must go, Julian. But . . . Oh, God . . ." Burgess broke down and hung up before Julian could speak.

Julian stood in the little soundproof telephone box in the laboratory and felt for his pipe. Now he *must* act. Peacock dead. Did Ringway know? And what had Burgess said about a patient, a Jamaican, on the buses? Conductress, he supposed. The thought was a decidedly chilling one. If it was an influenza it would spread by droplet infection, and a bus conductress was in contact with hundreds of people on one shift alone.

He went back to his office and asked Miss Marler to check on the report of the material Dr. Ringway had sent to Salisbury. He wanted it as soon as possible.

He sat pulling at his dead pipe, then struck a match and put it to his pipe, but the match went out. He didn't light another. Who to see in the government?

Who?

Suddenly he thought of someone he knew who was high enough up, a minister. But he had nothing to do with health. Besides, he was an unsympathetic character — and a bit of a fool to boot.

Why not deal with the people he knew? Why not the Medical Research Council? Why not any of the boards he was on? But what Ringway wanted, and what he'd promised him, was someone actually in the government. He reached for the telephone and asked Miss Marler to find the minister he knew.

It took her twenty minutes. "Parliament's not sitting," she said. "They're all on holiday. But I've got his secretary. Will he do?"

The minister's secretary was a very superior young man who patiently explained to Julian that the minister was giving a luncheon at his London house that day and immediately afterward was driving to Manchester. Could the minister possibly, asked Julian, give him just ten minutes between his luncheon and leaving London? The superior young man was almost certain the minister couldn't, but because he was no fool and knew who Julian was he decided to risk putting the proposition to the minister. He asked Julian to wait. It was a long wait because one of the minister's principles was never to be too easily available to people who could not directly further his own or his party's advancement. Intellectuals were seldom useful in either respect. But, as the minister's secretary hinted, it *was* Julian Reece and no doubt Reece could always go elsewhere . . .

"While you were on that line," Miss Marler said, putting her head in at the door, "I had a call from Salisbury. They said the report will be through soon, but that the material contained what was almost certainly a new mutant. They'll know more to-morrow."

"Will you please get me Dr. Ringway on the phone?" said Julian. "And, Miss Marler, I shall be out for some time this after-noon."

# 5 ～～～～～～～～～～～～～～～～～～～～～

The minister liked to think of himself as firm, forceful. He knew his own department. It was a damned pity virtually all the cabinet were out of London, because if Reece wanted to see someone, ten to one it would be for something scientific, probably medical, the minister supposed, and he had nothing to do with anything scientific, or at least as little as was possible. Clever chap, Reece, he mused. Not that he got on well with intellectual types, but you had to hand it to people as clever as Reece; those television things he did were damned interesting, even if they did seem a bit exaggerated.

Parts of a recent telecast came back to him as he waited . . .

Julian's sparsely built figure, longish fair hair, his thick-rimmed glasses, and his quiet, well-modulated voice, yet a voice with power in it, authority, the kind of sound the minister understood . . .

*"Eight thousand years ago there were but five million people on this earth; today there are over three thousand seven hundred million . . ."*

And the shots of those hollow-eyed, emaciated, sticklike people staring out of the TV into the warm luxury of the dimly lit room.

*". . . two point four extra people are now born every second . . . Every month there are six million extra people on this planet; in one month more than the present population of all but a few of*

[93]

*the world's biggest cities . . . in seventy years' time there will be
one thousand people to every square mile of the earth's arable
urban land.*

*". . . instead of seeking ways to conserve our resources we have
sought only to exploit them. Expansion and development have
been equated with progress. We have invented the wrong kind of
heroes. In our blindness we have lavished praise on the pioneers,
those brave people who populated new worlds so that we could
proliferate in them, cut down their forests, pollute and silt up
their clean, swift-running streams, pull the very earth to pieces in
insane rushes to plunder it of its wealth . . ."*

Reece had quoted Conrad; the minister remembered that because there were one or two of Conrad's books he'd quite enjoyed. *" 'To tear treasure out of the bowels of the land,' "* Reece
had quoted, *" 'was their desire, with no more moral purpose at
the back of it than there is in burglars breaking into a safe.' "*

Then there had been that picture of that woman nude. A poster,
wasn't it? Reece saying, *"In some parts of the world the amount
of DDT in the milk of lactating mothers is as much as six times
the amount allowed in milk sold commercially. The California
protesters are quite right: milk in such containers as the human
breast may well be unfit for human consumption. Rightly, a
woman with .30 parts per million of DDT in her milk who at-
tempts to breast-feed her child should be prosecuted, as would
the milkman down the road if he was selling DDT-adulterated
milk . . ."*

*". . . even the PCBs, that group of industrial toxic chemicals
used in products as diverse as food packaging, electric trans-
formers and copying papers have turned up in human milk, yet
when fed to animals the PCBs cause cancer, reproductive dis-
orders, skin eruptions, hair loss, metabolic disturbances, and other
illnesses . . . according to the Manufacturing Chemists' Associa-
tion six and a half thousand chemical products come on the market every year, yet not half of them are tested for their ability to
cause cancer even though a cautious estimate is that between
sixty and ninety percent of human cancer is brought on by factors
in our environment . . ."*

After the interview, in the taxi going back to the Institute, Julian wondered whether he'd done the right thing in going to that man. They'd met before, but that was all there had been to it: the odd meeting at functions Julian hadn't been able to avoid attending. The minister had greeted him warmly, not all of it just the politician making sure his fences were in order; his concern for Elizabeth and his sympathy for Julian were plainly genuine.

Julian had got quickly to the point — the story of Pyke and Clem and all he knew of it — and when he had finished the minister had sat back in his chair and pointed out that surely there weren't many cases as yet?

"It's not the number, Minister, it's the apparently extremely virulent nature of the disease. If what I fear were to happen — I make no prophecies — if what I fear *were* to happen, then our public health services would be overwhelmed. The effects could be catastrophic. No public service could cope with it." He'd explained that the cases were characterized by a singular virulence, "a virtually unbelievable one hundred percent mortality rate, from what we've seen so far."

The minister had wanted to know if Julian had any theories why this should be so, and Julian had said, "It's impossible to do little more at this stage than speculate, but it would seem almost certain that we're dealing with a virus we've not seen before."

This statement had puzzled the minister. "I thought you said it was influenza," he said. "Do you mean a new kind of bug altogether?"

Julian had paused, choosing his words carefully. "No." He paused again. "Rather," he'd said finally, "a new type of an existing bug. Not that a virus is a bug. A virus isn't an organism."

"Really? Must be something — animal, mineral, vegetable — no?"

"It's not an organism because it has no metabolism. It's entirely dependent for its replication on conditions supplied by its host cell. You could call it — this is putting it as simply as possible — a lump of nucleic acid surrounded by a protein coat." Julian had gone on to say something about the nucleic acid molecule, either DNA or RNA, being only able to replicate within living cells. The minister had interrupted him. "So, summing it up, Sir Julian, I

[95]

take it you're worried that we're going to have another nasty bout of Hong Kong flu on our hands."

Julian had experienced that sinking of the spirit that accompanies the failure to communicate. "I'm afraid," he had said slowly, shifting his long frame, feeling for his pipe in his pocket yet not really wanting to smoke, "that I've not made myself sufficiently clear. I mean something much worse than that," he added. "Much worse."

"Well, how much worse?"

Julian thought for a moment. "Look," he said, leaning forward, "I'm not an epidemiologist, I'm in another branch of medicine, but in the recorded history of man there have been three great pandemics." He paused. "One of them was influenza."

"In, let me guess, 1918?"

"Right," said Julian quickly.

"And the other two?"

"The Black Death, and the Plague of Justinian sometime about A.D. 540. The flu in 1918 — the Spanish flu, so called — is said to have attacked more than half the world's population. God alone knows how many people died, certainly many millions. But why I've come to you, Minister, is because I want the government to know as soon as possible that if I'm right — and, mind, I only say *if* — then what we might have now is a virus much more virulent than the one that caused the Spanish flu."

At that point there had been a long silence. The two men stared at one another. Then the minister said, "Yes, but that was 1918, Sir Julian; now we have antibiotics, all kinds of drugs, vaccines, eh? I mean, do we really have to fear plagues on that scale anymore?"

"Antibiotics can only work if they've something to work on. I don't know yet and therefore can't say, but if it is as I suspect and the influenza A strain has undergone another change, then it might well be one capable of killing before antibiotics have had a chance to work. Antibiotics," he explained, "don't actually work on the virus itself. They work on the results of the effects of the virus. If you get the flu and then get pneumonia as a result, the antibiotic will kill the organism that causes the pneumonia, but if the virus was virulent enough you'd die from the effects of it alone, before pneumonia or any other respiratory tract infection set in."

"Why do you say A strain?"

"There are three types of influenza virus — though this is simplifying the thing — A, B, and C. C we can discount because the A and B types are the ones that cause the trouble. Pandemics, more or less severe, due to the A type, tend to break out about every thirty years. That's why it's called influenza; it's cyclical, and the old observers thought it was brought about by the influence of the stars. It's an Italian word," Julian added, "that came to England at the time of the epidemic in 1782. The problem with influenza, what makes it such a potentially devastating disease, is that every time it appears with sufficient potency to cause an epidemic or a pandemic it does so because it has, so to speak, changed its spots. The influenza virus has a remarkable ability to form mutants, and just as the world population has got used to one particular form of it and built up a pool of immunity, it forms a mutant, does a flip, a quick change, and in the new form spreads quickly in a world where people have no resistance at all to its new form." Julian had stopped, staring at the minister, hoping desperately that he was getting his message across.

"Go on," the minister said.

For a moment Julian had played with the idea of not saying it, then he added, "But really it's even more complicated and bloody than that, because the Hong Kong outbreak you referred to a moment ago — what virologists call A2 Hong Kong '68 — was a different virus, unique, or virtually so, with practically no cross-relationship with previous A2 viruses. As you know, Mao flu killed many thousands of people throughout the world and cost untold sums, about two hundred million pounds in England alone."

"Look, Sir Julian" — the minister had sat even farther back in his chair — "you've said that if, repeat *if*, the kind of pandemic you're thinking of occurred the health services would be overwhelmed. Now I see that as a distinct possibility, too — *if* this were to happen. But as of now there aren't many cases, and in the meantime surely the proper authorities are keeping their eye on

[97]

the thing? Whose responsibility is it to watch for this kind of trouble?"

"Worldwide it's the World Health Organization. Each member country reports to a common center. For influenza, it's the World Influenza Center here in London. But first the virus has to be identified. The Influenza Center examines hundreds of influenza strains every year. The virus — it's called seed virus — is flown here and grown in eggs." The slightest smile touched Julian's face. "A lot of eggs, about four thousand a week —"

"Four *thousand!*"

"That's average during an outbreak. The eggs are candled — they're live fertilized eggs — then the embryo is killed by chilling, the virus taken out, in its turn killed — with formaldehyde — then it's concentrated to form a vaccine."

"Look, I was going to ask you about a vaccine. Two years ago I was vaccinated, so was my wife, but we still got the flu."

"That's because vaccination usually only works against a known virus. If we get a new one — and they are mostly new ones — the vaccine you've had won't work."

"But say this thing really got going. Couldn't they then make a vaccine that would kill it?"

"This is the obvious course to take, but the catch is that it takes almost six months to make a new vaccine, and by that time the strain would have got itself around the world. In fact, with air travel it can get from one side of the world to the other in a few hours. And then there's the physical difficulty of producing so many doses: that's another reason I want someone such as yourself to know of my fears, because at our present capacity in England today we could only make about three million doses. The Americans can do better, but during the whole of the Mao flu they were only able to produce about twenty million doses. And that, of course, only after it had spread throughout the world."

"So what you're saying is that if this is as bad as you think it might be, we've got no chance?"

"More or less, yes."

"And you've no idea where this new strain has come from?"

"No idea at all. This young Australian biologist, Pyke, could have caught it from someone in Melbourne, or he could even have invented it."

"Invented it?"

"Well, a new strain has to start somewhere. If, say, he picked up a flu strain from a human contact and then, for instance, went riding, he could pick up another strain from the horse. That could result in a new strain, which if it was virulent enough could give you a pandemic."

"Wait and hope, eh?" said the minister.

"Oh, no, I'd like to see us do more than only that."

"What? Give me something positive, Sir Julian. Facts."

"That is not so easy, Minister. There are over one thousand different strains of influenza group A viruses stored in the freezing chambers of the World Influenza Center here in London, frozen at minus seventy degrees Fahrenheit. You just can't go poking about there and expect to come up with the answers. What I would do is to get together a high-level committee directly responsible to, say, the prime minister. A committee with top priority for whatever action the committee thought fit."

"My God, you *are* pessimistic!"

"Respiratory tract viral diseases spread so damnably quickly because so many virons are distributed in the air when infected people sneeze or cough. And don't forget that even if you were to get the whole community vaccinated you'd be bloody lucky to get even sixty percent protection. Flu vaccines aren't like the Broad Street water pump, you know."

"What the hell's the Broad Street water pump?"

"That's the pump that first taught us about cholera. In 1885 John Snow, a London doctor, drew a map of the cholera-affected areas of London and found they lay around the Broad Street pump. It was one of the great landmarks in epidemiology. Snow," Julian added, "was an anesthetist at Saint George's Hospital, though curiously there's no memorial to him there."

"Well, what happened to the pump?"

"They took the handle off it and cholera virtually ceased to exist here. Cholera is a waterborne disease. I wish we could say the same with this influenza."

"What?" The minister had sounded scandalized.

"In the sense that we could *contain* a pocket of infection, seal it off before it spread through the community. The Russians did that with cholera in 1970. They closed whole cities —"

"Ah yes, I remember that. But the cholera got out, didn't it?" The minister jumped on this. "It got out," he said again. "Come now, Sir Julian, you're not seriously suggesting that because of an outbreak of flu we ought to shut off whole cities. Can you imagine the effect upon business, upon — everything? As for arguing that the Russian expedient of closing whole cities is useful, just look at the facts — the cholera got out."

"This is not the classical strain of cholera," said Julian. "This is El Tor, which broke out of the Celebes as recently as 1961. No, the Russians did well to do what they did. The frightening thing about that outbreak was that it occurred in cities with good sanitation."

They had sat staring at one another. Finally the minister had said, "I'll tell you what I'll do, Sir Julian. I'll get my parliamentary private secretary to prepare a minute of this conversation and I'll see what action we can think about taking on it. Fair enough?" It was not really a question because as he added it the minister had got to his feet and said, "I do so hope, Sir Julian, that you'll soon get good news of Lady Reece. I understand the Australian authorities are doing all they can, but if there's anything our chaps out there can do please don't fail to let me know."

It was a dismissal but, Julian had to admit, superbly done, because at that moment the door had opened and a discreet voice said gently, "Minister, I hate to interrupt, but ..."

"Yes, yes," the minister said fussily, as if he had really been interrupted, "I'm coming just now." As Julian had gone out into the street it crossed his mind that the minister must have pressed a bell as he got to his feet. Clever bastard, Julian thought; it would never have occurred to him to have something like that — and God knew he'd had to deal with some clods, especially politicians, in his time — but then, he realized, he wasn't a cunning bugger. Mentally, he gave himself a bad mark. Then he had grinned to himself because he suddenly had a picture of Miss Marler bursting in when the bell rang.

At the Institute Miss Marler looked up from her typewriter. "That friend of yours who's a politician, Mr. Braithwaite, he's been on the phone," she said, "only just rung off. He wants you to telephone him when you come in, but I said you were very busy."

"Get him, will you please, Miss Marler?"

"Julian," Peter Braithwaite said, "I just rang to ask if there was any fresh news of Elizabeth, but that nice secretary of yours says there isn't. We're so frightfully sorry, old chap. Is there anything we can do?"

"Nothing, Peter. Nothing at all, but thank you so much for asking. How's Helen?"

"Oh, very well, thank you, Julian. Actually, we were wondering: what about dinner with us one evening soon, say this week? House isn't sitting at the moment."

"I know you're not sitting at the moment. I'll take a rain check on that very kind invitation, Peter, but I'm absolutely up to the ears in work at the moment."

"Just get your secretary to give Helen a ring, will you? She keeps tabs on our social life. Right, then, we'll look forward to seeing you as soon as it suits you. Bye, Julian."

Julian had the telephone halfway to the cradle when it hit him. "I say, Peter," he said much too loudly, "are you still there?"

"Yes." Braithwaite seemed rather surprised.

"Look, I have a problem, and it's just struck me that you might be the very chap to help me. As an MP you might be able to advise me. It's something I'd rather not discuss on the phone. Can you have a drink with me this evening?"

It took Braithwaite a minute to discover that he was free at half past five. "Then can you come to my club?" asked Julian.

"Sure, I'll meet you there."

Braithwaite was Julian's age, but whereas Julian was tall and lean Braithwaite was stumpy, round-faced, and balding. On the way to the club Julian decided to tell Braithwaite the whole story.

When he finished Braithwaite gave a low whistle. "Harry Peacock, eh? I must have missed that in *The Times*. I knew Peacock slightly; he looked after my father. Lung cancer. I say, this is a steep one."

"It could be. Very."

"And can't anything be done to contain it?"

"That was what I was trying to do this afternoon." And Julian told Braithwaite of his visit to the minister.

"Christ Almighty, man," Braithwaite exclaimed, "what in the hell did you pick on *him* for?"

"Because I knew him slightly. And all the health or environment or Home Office chaps are out of London."

"Pity you went to him," Braithwaite said, frowning.

"But surely, Peter, he didn't think I'd just waste my time and his going to see him about nothing."

"That wouldn't occur to him, Julian. You're an intellectual and a conservationist — though I hate that bloody word, we really ought to try to find something better — and he's a businessman and a politician. You certainly picked a wrong 'un that time. What about the medical councils and committees? You're a member of some of the most important of them, if I remember correctly."

Julian shook his head. "I don't want to do it that way. I could leak it to the newspapers too. One telephone call to Fleet Street and the country would be in a panic. What I want is someone high up in the government."

"The trouble now," Braithwaite said slowly, "is that everyone's away on holidays. If only the House was in session . . . The Opposition are all away, too." He sipped his sherry, then said, "I might, just might, be able to get you a junior minister." He sounded rather doubtful.

"I don't give a damn who it is. Just so long as he's not got solid bone between the ears and is prepared to use his influence."

Braithwaite sat in silence for very nearly a minute, then said, "Where are the telephones?"

He was away about ten minutes. "Not much help, I'm afraid," he said as he dropped down into his chair again. "But there's a chance I'll be able to get this junior minister later. The maid says he's in London for the day and should be at his flat about eight o'clock, but he's returning to the country tonight. Julian, I won't have another drink if you don't mind. I'll get off and try running your fox to earth. I take it you'll be available at any time."

"At home tonight. And tomorrow at the Institute."

When Julian got home Mrs. Bennett told him two things: one, he was having lamb cutlets for dinner with potatoes and green peas and she'd opened a half-bottle of white Burgundy to go with it, and, two, she had been answering the telephone all day to reporters who wanted to interview him about Lady Reece. "It's worse than when you won that old prize," she added indignantly. "They're like flies around a honey pot. Some of them actually come to the door, but I tell them all the same thing, 'Can't you let the poor man in peace for a minute,' I say. And there's a message for you on the telephone pad in your study. He rang about ten minutes ago and would you ring him back. He sounded like a very nice man, a Dr. Canning."

Canning answered immediately. "More bad news, I'm afraid, sir. It's about Chris Leach. His mother phoned me about an hour ago. He died in Bolzano. Foreign Office rang her," Canning went on. "Poor thing's in a terrible state. I must say it's a shock. I've known Chris for years."

"How sure is she about it being flu?"

"All she knows is what the FO told her, of course. She's flying out tomorrow. But it's what Colin Ringway was expecting. I've not rung him. I thought I'd better not, seeing as he's got the bloody thing too."

"We still don't know of any other cases, do we?"

"Not as far as I know. I rang Freddy Cook, a friend at WHO, and told him about Leach dying, but he's not heard of anything. Nothing's been reported officially."

"So that means that Roger Pyke is still the first case we know of."

"I'd say so. Of course, that doesn't mean much, does it? Not by itself. Pyke must have been incubating it when he arrived here. God knows where he picked it up. I told Cook about Pyke coming from Australia, but Cook says no reports of it have come in from Australia. He says if there were anything big on he'd have seen it in their general reports, which are being regularly circulated."

"Look, Michael, you're an epidemiologist, I'm not. Tell me something about this World Influenza Center here in London."

"There's not much to tell, really. WHO has a system that ties up about eighty-five laboratories in fifty-five countries. The

[*103*]

Chinese don't play, which is a pity, because in my opinion — and I'm not alone in this — some rather strange things have happened to the influenza virus in China. All these centers send material to London. You see, I believe, and I think most virologists would agree with me, that at least one of the really deadly A-strain viruses is still with us, living in pigs. We gave it to the pigs, and for some reason the poor bloody pigs are still harboring it, though it's no longer surviving in man. I am, by the way, speaking of a specific strain of A flu: the one that caused the 1918 pandemic."

"I've been speaking about this today — to a politician."

"As I think you know, Colin Ringway believes we've something even worse than 1918. There's no reason why our present swine flu virus couldn't be a descendant of the 1918 job. Some people believe a virus can go underground, that it can exist without actually causing influenza until, snap, crackle, pop, for some reason we don't understand, it breaks out and kills a lot of people. But Colin's thinking way past that, sir. He's thinking of a mutation, no doubt, of some existing strain, or if not that, then a new one altogether that is highly lethal."

Julian had just put down the receiver when Ringway phoned.

"Julian, there's another tape in the machine. I can't get the bloody thing out. Jammed." Ringway's breathing was now very difficult. "It's for you. And it's got poor bloody Peacock's voice on it too . . . describing his symptoms . . ."

Ringway's voice died away, faintly. Julian pressed the receiver hard against his ear in the effort to hear.

"You . . . you're doing something?" Ringway said faintly.

"Yes, Colin."

"Can you hear me? Damned difficult . . ."

"I can hear you, old chap."

"You'll do something?" The voice sounded pathetically alone. "And, and listen to this, Julian." There was the faintest trace of irony in the voice, "I've solved the, the bloody riddle. Death's the cure for life. Awfully sorry about Elizabeth . . . she was a bloody fine woman. Bloody fine . . . Brains, too . . .

"Helpless . . . We're all helpless, Julian. Have you ever thought how really bloody helpless we all are? We think we can stand alone when our parents have finished bringing us up, but we

[104]

can't. We can't feed ourselves without the butcher or the baker, can't cover our bodies without tailors, can't cure ourselves when we get ill . . . Self-sufficient? Masters of our fates? God, we're not even pawns. It's all luck . . . And who knows whether it's good or bad luck?

"I'm rambling. Can't be helped . . . It's not death that's frightening, it's the dying. All societies, Julian, all religions — they all try to offer some compensation for death. You know: life after death, reincarnation, heaven. And hell, too. Patients . . ." Julian heard the breathing in the pause. "Patients usually come to, come to understand they're going to die. I've often noticed even weak characters get some kind of strength then . . . I'm rambling . . . Julian?" There was a pathetic note in the voice.

"I'm here, Colin."

"Yes. Don't go. Don't go yet, Julian. Not yet. There are lots worse ways to die. I know now just how it'll be with me. It's on the tapes, but the bloody machine's jammed, did I tell you that?"

Again there came the silence except for the harsh sound of Ringway's breathing, and listening to it Julian began to wonder how much longer it would be before he wouldn't have the strength to talk, let alone dial a phone number. Listening, Julian began to envisage something of the pathology . . .

The inhaled virus, almost certainly a new mutant, breathed in, sticking to the respiratory epithelial cells, using the metabolic processes of these cells to go on reproducing. The infected cells losing the battle as their metabolism failed in the process . . . The damaged epithelium in the windpipe and bronchi sloughing away . . . Bacteria infecting these injured areas, fluid and debris plugging the bronchioles . . . But there didn't have to be any bacterial infection, the virus alone could do it. *Would* do it. That lesson was learned in the 1957–58 flu epidemic . . .

"Julian, be Crito for me. Will you? We ought to offer a cock to Aesculapius. Remember old Socrates saying to Crito, 'See to it . . .' That's what he said, Julian. I've worked that out now. None of this nonsense about physician cure thyself. Had a, a feeling about this flu, right from the start . . . Told you, didn't I? From the bloody beginning . . ."

Julian heard a thump, as if the handset had been dropped, and then a noise as if, he thought, a hand was groping about.

"Colin," he called. He called again and again, but got no answer. Then he dialed the operator and finally was told that the number wasn't answering because the party must have left the instrument off the cradle.

Julian got to his feet and stood in his study, uncertain what to do. He must go to Ringway, that was certain, but he had told Braithwaite he'd be available that evening. Had Braithwaite been able to get the junior minister yet?

Braithwaite answered at the phone's first ring. "I've been sitting here trying to reach you, Julian, but you've been engaged. Now listen, I'm awfully bloody sorry, but I've drawn another blank, I'm afraid. That damned maid forgot to give the minister my message. He's left London now, gone to his place in the country. And he's dining out. But I know where, and if I can't get him at home I'll catch him during dinner. I'm most awfully bloody sorry, Julian —"

"Peter, there's another complication now. Colin Ringway has just phoned me. He's obviously very ill. He's quite alone in his house so I must go there straightaway."

"How long," asked Braithwaite, "do you think you'll be out?"

"I'll take a taxi, that's quicker than parking my own car."

"Could you be back home by eight-thirty?"

"I'll try. If he's not already dead, I'll get Ringway into hospital. Tell the minister to call me at half past eight," said Julian. "I should be back by then."

"How free can I be with the information you've given me?"

"In confidence, tell him anything you like."

As soon as Julian put down the phone it rang.

"It's Michael Canning, sir. Sorry to trouble you again, but I've just remembered something Chris's mother said —"

"Michael," he said quickly, "how important is it, can it wait until later?"

"God, yes."

"Then listen. I've just spoken to Colin Ringway. He's either dead or dying. I'm going to his house now, but I have to be back here by half past eight. If he's alive, I'll get an ambulance, but I'll

[*106*]

need time to arrange a bed in an isolation ward. Could you help me?"

"Leave Colin to me," said Canning. "I'll whip around there now. I can arrange a quarantine box —"

"Get there as soon as you can. *But don't go inside*. Wait for me in the street. Got that?"

In the kitchen Mrs. Bennett protested that Julian had had nothing to eat. He told her to go home but she said, "Oh, I'll wait for you, sir, certainly I shall. It's not that, it's the food spoiling. I've done the potatoes."

"Well, if you could wait," he said, pulling on his overcoat, "I would appreciate it if you could prepare enough food for two. I may be bringing Dr. Canning back with me."

Julian's car shot into Herbert Crescent and then into Hans Place. Canning was already there, a big man in a short camel's-hair coat, his massive shoulders hunched up against the bitter cold. Julian told the driver to wait and got out of the car as Canning came up, bare-headed, dark-haired, an Irish face, with eyes very deep-set in the harsh street lighting.

"There's no light showing," he said. "But his bedroom's at the back. Best way in might be down there." Canning pointed to the basement area, the black iron railings gleaming dully in the light of a passing car. "We'll have to break in, and the front door's a bloody heavy one. There's glass in the area door."

"We can't break in without the police, Michael."

"Let me go down and put my shoulder to that area door," Michael replied. "Or bust the glass. To hell with it. You can explain to the police afterward. Matter of life and death."

Julian shook his head. "Where's the nearest phone?"

"There, I'd say." Michael pointed to the house next door, where windows were lighted on every floor. "I've always wanted to dial 999."

Together they ran up the steps and Michael pressed the doorbell. Julian had a card ready in his hand.

"Mummy's in the bath, Daddy's playing the cello, the maid's having a baby. And I'm in charge," said the thirteen-year-old girl who opened the door.

"Oh," she said, looking up from Julian's card, "what fun! At last someone really famous! There's a phone in the hall," she went on briskly. "Come in. I'm going to tell Daddy. We know Dr. Ringway. He comes to dinner with us sometimes. And he plays the flute with Daddy on cello."

Michael made the call, and the girl's father came down in shirtsleeves and stood with them in the doorway and said that now that he came to think of it he hadn't seen Dr. Ringway about for a day or so. The girl said, "Daddy, you'll catch your death of cold out here without a coat, for heaven's sake." They all heard the *hoo-haa* rising pitch and fall of the police car siren. "I thought the fuzz only got there as quick as that," she said, "on the telly. Wheee . . ."

"Please, Miranda," said her father. "I rather think we can do without your comments at a time like this."

Miranda rushed to the edge of the areaway and hung on the railings, looking over and down. In the dim lights and the darting flashlight beam she could see Michael's bulk with Julian beside him, and in front of them the dark shapes of the two policemen. One was squatting, examining the lock on the house door. Then he straightened up and turned to Julian. "We could force it, sir," he said slowly, "if it's really urgent . . ."

"It's extremely urgent," Julian said.

The policeman nodded and turned to his companion. "Right, Jack," he said. "We'll knock in the right-hand panel of glass."

Miranda heard the sound of breaking glass. Then the policeman's voice again. "Mind your hand, Jack, on that glass." As they moved about below her, a flashlight shone suddenly up into Miranda's face, blinding her, but she heard the lock snap back and the door creak open.

Then Julian's voice came up, sharp and decisive. "Officer, if you will both stay here, please, while Dr. Canning and I go in."

"Well now, listen, sir," began the policeman's voice, but Julian said, with a hint of apology in his voice, "I'm very sorry, Officer, but I am afraid I shall have to insist. As I've told you, I have every reason to believe Dr. Ringway is suffering from an acutely infectious disease. I'll take full responsibility, but I insist you men are not exposed to possible contagion."

The policeman sighed. "If you say so, sir," he said. The voice was resigned, tolerant, the voice of a man who'd seen and heard it all before, who was long past being surprised by anything the public might do or say, especially if they happened to be bigwigs.

"Gosh!" exclaimed Miranda, swinging about on the railings, looking at her father. "What's Dr. Ringway got? Will we all have to be fumigated? Perhaps I won't be able to go back to school. I'll have to stay in quarantine, pale and poorly, waiting to get my strength back, being fed on spoonfuls of beef jelly."

One of the policemen came up from the areaway, crossed to the squad car, and spoke into a microphone. He clipped it back, and with notebook and pencil at the ready went up to Ringway's neighbor.

"Perhaps you could give us a few details about the occupant, sir," he said, gesturing toward Ringway's house. "Purely routine — full name, that kind of thing."

"Daddy's a solicitor," said Miranda, then swung back to lean as far out as she dared over the railings and peered below.

Julian stopped at the foot of the stairs leading up from Ringway's entrance hall. "Wait here, Michael. No point in both of us exposing ourselves." He stopped speaking suddenly; from somewhere in the darkness came a curious screeching sound, suddenly eerie in the stillness. "What's that noise?"

"It's a howler," Michael said, groping for the light switch. "The Post Office puts one on the phone to let you know that it's off the hook. Just a moment, sir, Colin Ringway's as much my friend as yours." He found the switch. In the light, Michael's eyes were blue, the brows over them thick and dark. The Irish openness of his face made him look younger than his thirty-two years. "If anybody's to be exposed to it, far better me than you."

"I fail to see why."

"Oh, for Christ's sake, sir." Michael liked many people, respected a few, and regarded Julian Reece with little less than awe. After his graduation and medical degree, he had sat for his Diploma of Public Health; it had been while studying for this that he had attended some of Julian's lectures. "I'm going up," he added, and he put his hand on the newel post.

Julian's voice snapped, "I think I may be said to be senior to you, Canning —"

"I'm not disputing that, sir. It just so happens that if one of us is expendable, it's me. Senior to me you may be, professionally and otherwise, but as doctors we're equal in the eyes of the law. You can't order me not to go up."

For a long minute they looked at one another. Then Michael said, "If he's dead, I'll call you up. If he's alive, leave here and take the police with you. Go to your meeting and I'll see to Ringway." Then he added earnestly, "Isn't it because of what you believe to be the acutely infectious nature of this that you're seeing the minister? Tell me honestly. Say you go up there, Ringway is alive and breathing, and you examine him. Would you be prepared to go to see this minister chap, or anybody else for that matter, knowing what you may be carrying? I know you and your conscience. No, you wait here, and I'll come to the top of the stairs and call down to you." With that Michael turned and went up the stairs two at a time, looking very big, fading into the darkness until only his coat could be seen. Julian heard him knock into something and curse as he felt about for a light switch.

Julian stood waiting, looking up the stairs. He took out his pipe and sucked on it, but didn't light it. Michael was not gone long. He came to the top of the stairs and stood bulking massively in silhouette in his short coat looking down at Julian, who could not see the expression on his face, only the drooping lines of the big body.

"Did you touch anything?" Julian called up.

"Only light switches. No need to touch anything else."

"You've still got your gloves on?"

"Yes."

"Then come on down."

"What about the arrangements?" Michael said as he stepped heavily off the last tread.

"We'll do them at my place. I'll ring the local MOH in the morning."

"No certificate, you see," said Michael. "Nobody treating him. Inquest. PM. You spoke to him, what, two hours ago?"

Julian nodded. "He could speak a couple of hours ago, you see," Julian said softly.

"What I mean is that —"

"I've got what you mean. You didn't see any positive evidence?"

"Oh, lots of bottles. Pills, drugs. Glasses, too." He shrugged. "Medication . . ." Michael's jaw began to work. "Poor devil . . . Alone. Awful mess. His face . . . Oh, God, why Ringway? He was one of the nicest, best men I've ever known."

"He was a very brave man," Julian said softly. "Let's find the police and have the house shut up." When they got to the areaway Julian's eye fell on two large plastic garbage cans. "Drop your gloves in there, Michael," he said, pointing. "Then let's get some methylated spirits."

Miranda watched the men file up the areaway steps, but she was as quiet as a mouse and watched as fearfully.

The junior minister called Julian at a few minutes past half past eight. "Peter Braithwaite tells me that you wanted to see me rather urgently, Sir Julian." The junior minister's voice was confident, assured. "Unfortunately, I'm rather busy just now," he went on. "Braithwaite said something about meeting tomorrow, but I'm afraid I'll be tied up all day. And the day after. Which brings us almost to the end of the week. But I have to come up to London again next week, and I'll be much less busy then. We could have a chat, say, next Wednesday, if that suited you?"

Julian paused before answering. He was very tired and deeply shaken by Ringway's death, but he knew that, above all, he must keep his temper. "I'm afraid next Wednesday wouldn't do at all, Minister." He looked at Michael, who sat staring at the whiskey and water in a hand that smelled strongly of methylated spirits.

"I just might be able to fit you in on Monday." The junior minister sounded doubtful. "It's a health matter, isn't it?" he went on. "Braithwaite said something to do with influenza. Don't you think it might be better to wait until the minister of health returns. I think he's in Brussels . . ."

"Minister," said Julian as calmly as he could, taking a deep breath, "I am English enough to have a deep-rooted dislike of the dramatic. But I am going to be dramatic, if not melodramatic. I must see you as soon as possible, within the next few hours, in fact."

"Well now, Sir Julian," the minister gave a little half laugh, half cough, "I'm afraid that would hardly be possible. You see —"

"Please let me finish. Unfortunately, what I have to say can't very well be said on the telephone, but I hope to convince you that we may have a health situation developing that will demand the swiftest action being taken at the highest possible level. One fear that always dogs a scientist is that he could be wrong. Well, I may be. I hope to God I *am*, but, Minister, if I'm not, then any calamity that has occurred in your lifetime will seem like a Sunday school picnic compared to this."

There was a long pause. Suddenly Julian felt exhausted. He let himself down into the chair at his desk and saw that his hands were clenched so tightly that the knuckles showed white.

Finally the minister spoke, "You are, I take it, at your home now, Sir Julian?"

"I am."

"Just where in London?"

"St. John's Wood."

"Would you give me your exact address, please? I should be at your house in about two and a half hours, traffic and weather permitting."

When Julian hung up he went to the drinks tray and poured himself a stiff whiskey. Michael watched him. "Wherever I look," Michael said softly, "I keep seeing poor Ringway's face. Did he ever have guts! You know, courage like that makes you feel suddenly worthless, makes you wonder whether you could do it yourself."

Julian sat in his big leather armchair, and silence flowed between them. Finally he said, "Michael, I'd like you to do two things. One, stay here tonight while I talk to the minister; I can give you a bed, if you like. And two, would you undertake to check on Pyke for me? It'll mean your working for me for a few days. I'll clear it with Professor Day; he owes me a favor anyway."

"Certainly I'll do it."

"As an epidemiologist it's up your alley. I want to try and find out just where Pyke got this bloody thing. He came to England by air. Professor Saunderson's secretary ought to be able to give you the name of the airline from the personnel file. I can't tell you much, I'm afraid," he went on wearily. "It's a pretty tall order, but do the best you can, will you? And keep away from personal contacts, direct contacts; use what poor Ringway called the aseptic electric telephone. You're no use to me in the mortuary."

"Any suggestions where I ought to start?"

"I'd say with Marge Wood, Clem Saunderson's secretary."

"Listen, when the official bods get onto this, won't they do a check on Pyke?"

"I hope after we've finished with this chap tonight they'll be doing a damn sight more than just that. But that's in the future. And I want something *now* that we can control ourselves. I want as much information as I can get. Ammunition, if I have to put up a fight." A faint grin flickered on his face as he remembered the man he'd seen that afternoon. He mimicked him now: "I want *facts*, Michael, as that bloody senior minister said. Facts!"

"The trouble with this sort of thing," Michael said gloomily, "is that trails go cold so bloody quickly. Before you know where you are you've got a dozen of them, all going ahead in different directions — and which one is the real scent?"

"There's just a possibility," Julian said slowly, "that Pyke might have invented this disease. A new one has to start somewhere."

"God, think of that, eh?" There was awe and wonder in Michael's voice. "To be in on the birth of a new disease . . . Sort of midwife to it. I don't mean merely to be the first to describe a new disease — though that would be fine, like having a plant or an animal named after you — but actually to be able to pinpoint the body in which it first showed itself. That would really be something."

# 6 ～～～～～～～～～～～～～～～～～～～～

At just after eight the next morning Julian got to the Institute. His meeting with the junior minister the night before had gone far better than he had dared hope. Miss Marler arrived to find him looking in the telephone directory. "Humph," she said, glaring at him. "Whose number are you looking for? Give me time to get my hat off and I'll get it for you."

"Sir Henry Benwell," he said. "If possible I want to catch him before he leaves home."

Miss Marler managed that.

"I must say, Julian," Benwell said in his hearty, forthright voice, "Harry Peacock's death gave me a hell of a shock. What's going on? Do you know? I rang Clara — Harry's wife — as soon as I heard, and some friend of hers answered the phone. Clara's ill. Did you know that? Well, she is, and what's more, she won't let me come to see her. They've shut up the house!" Benwell sounded most indignant. "She's there, on her own, except for this woman friend. I said I'd go around straight away and have a look at her, but she said she wouldn't let me in. Preposterous. So unlike Clara, too. Most sensible woman. Only the undertaker's men being let in. Never heard anything like it in my life. And if what this woman told me is correct, Harry wouldn't have anyone in to see him either. Or go into hospital. She said something about someone treating him over the telephone. The *telephone!* Never in all my life heard anything so damned stupid. What's up, do you think?"

Julian told him. Benwell listened without interruption and then said, "I've met that junior minister chap. Bit stuck up, but I happen to know they think something of him. Well, this is a bit of a teaser, isn't it? What's he going to do about it?"

"Telephone the PM this morning. He's in the South of France."

"You don't think you're going off half-cocked by any chance, do you?" Benwell sounded anxious. "Pretty slim evidence, eh? I mean, not many cases —"

"But, as far as we know, almost one hundred percent mortality. So far."

"Well, yes. Even so . . ." Benwell sounded even more thoughtful.

"What would you have done?"

"Now that you ask me," Benwell said after a moment, "I'm damned if I know. You're quite sure of your facts? I mean" — he added quickly — "there can't be any doubt about it, eh? No," he went on, answering his own question, "if Peacock was as scared as that, I suppose there can't be. You too. Ringway I didn't know."

"He was a damned fine physician."

"No doubt. All right then, Julian." Benwell suddenly sounded as if he'd made up his mind. "What do you want me to do?"

"I told this chap last night that ideally, I'd like to see a high-powered committee directly responsible to the PM or the minister of health set up as soon as possible. I'd like you to be part of it."

"Well, I suppose I could do that, yes. Try Claude Fisher — and Dame Dorothy Sellers, too, she'd give them hell. I'd like to think this over and then call you back."

"Certainly. When would you ring?"

"Give me until about ten-thirty. And, Julian, I hope for your sake that you're right," he added, "and not going off at half cock — they'll have your skin for it if you are."

"And if I'm not?"

"Ah." Benwell chuckled ruefully. "Then they'll say you didn't act soon enough."

At twelve o'clock Michael got to the Institute. Julian had spent most of the morning telephoning, sounding out the people he would like to see on the committee he envisaged. None of them had heard of any particularly virulent flu going about, but all had agreed to be ready to act should they be needed. Politically, he could only hope he had played his cards well. He hoped particularly that he hadn't missed anyone whose advice he should have asked and who, slighted, might be able to plant the seed of doubt somewhere, a doubt still a bit too close to Julian's own thinking to be comfortable. That morning he wished desperately for the help Clem Saunderson would have given him. In the quiet, unobtrusive way in which Clem had worked there was a feel for and a knowledge of medical politics that Julian knew he did not himself possess. And Julian's method of going about things had been queried more than once, notably by Dame Dorothy Sellers. "You're being too polite, Julian," she said in her clipped, couldn't-care-less way. "If I'd got onto something like this and seen that fool of a minister, I wouldn't have wasted time trying to see another. I'd have rung up the GMC and told them what I was going to do. Then I'd have blown it to the papers."

"Well, don't blow it now, for God's sake. Not yet."

"If you say so. But you know the only way you'll get them to do something? By letting them see it spread," she went on, answering her own question. "Very well, if you need me you know where to ring me. But don't be surprised if you only get waffle — until it's too late. And remember one other thing, Julian, you are not a politician. You're a laboratory man. And I never knew anyone who was good at both. Good luck," she said and hung up her telephone.

"It's beginner's luck, I shouldn't wonder," Michael said. "But I've gone a long way further on finding out about Pyke than I'd have hoped to in such a short time. But before I get to that — after I left your house last night I suddenly remembered the London Transport daily flu report figures. I wondered if you had checked on them."

"I've never heard of them," said Julian. "But remember, I'm not in public health."

"No. Well, for some years now the daily absentee rate due to influenza among conductors and drivers on the London Transport has been sent weekly to the Department of Health and Social Security.

"It gives a continuous check on the incidence of influenza in the community, you see. Influenza costs this country thirty million pounds a year in medical services and sickness benefits as well as millions of days off work, so they keep an eye on it. By keeping tabs on the LT people, the Department of Health can pick up an epidemic that might be developing. It's a bloody sensitive index, too. Conductors, because they're in actual touch with more people than drivers, probably develop a bit more immunity than drivers — though the figures don't always bear this out. But if there's anything like an epidemic of respiratory infection starting in London, these figures ought to show it."

"And they're sent in weekly?"

"Unless an epidemic has actually developed; then they go in every day."

"How can we get them?"

"I can do it now on the telephone. Can I have an outside line?"

"Ben," Michael said when he'd been put through to the right extension. "I don't need actual figures, but could you tell me whether there's been any rise lately in the London Transport index of respiratory infection?"

Michael sat back, waiting, and glanced at Julian. He remembered that he'd forgotten to ask Julian if there was any fresh news of Lady Reece. He hesitated, then asked. Julian took his pipe out, shook his head slowly, and said, "Nothing, I'm afraid."

"They'll find them," Michael said. He was about to add something else when the phone crackled. Michael bent his head, listening. Then he said, "No, don't bother with actual numbers, I know you've got 12,340 drivers and 7,980 male conductors." He grinned. "All I want . . ." He was silent, listening, then he said, "So on a four-day-absence-from-work basis the graph is steady, that right? Nothing unusual. Normal for the time of year. Thanks, Ben." He was about to hang up when he added, "If the graph shows an upward movement, would you let me know? Well, we just might be expecting something. But yours is about the most sensitive yardstick. How old are your figures? Two days. If we think we need it, could you supply on a daily basis?" Julian then heard Michael say, "Sir Julian Reece." Then Michael gave a short laugh and hung up. As he put the phone back on its cradle he said to Julian, "Nothing unusual."

Julian put a match to his pipe; he was thinking of Neil Burgess and his patient, that Jamaican woman who Neil thought was "on the buses." "Tell me," Julian said, speaking through the pipe smoke, "what you found out about Roger Pyke."

"Ah, yes." Michael sat forward in his chair. "Now first off, did Professor Saunderson happen to mention to you anything about friends of Pyke by the name of Lambert?"

Julian shook his head. "Who are they?"

"It seems Pyke traveled from Australia with them. This is what I've been able to discover so far. Professor Saunderson's secretary had a cable from Pyke in his file giving his arrival date, by British Airways. Well, I rang BA, but they couldn't give me much information other than to confirm that a Dr. Pyke actually traveled on that flight on the seventh. This wasn't a great deal of help, but then the girl I was speaking to suggested I ring a chap in their office at Heathrow. I finally got onto him, but he couldn't, or wouldn't, tell me much. Maybe he didn't know much, or perhaps airlines are cautious about giving away information about their passengers. Anyhow, I gave him a line about an official health follow-up on passengers. He was a bit suspicious and asked why I hadn't got onto the airport health department. I told him a lie. I said I had. He finally told me that he couldn't help and doubted if anyone in their office could now, except perhaps the fellow who was his opposite number, who had been on duty when Pyke's flight arrived. Well, after a bit of argy-bargy he gave me this chap's telephone number at home. So I rang him. Now," Michael paused, "at first I spoke to his wife, and she told me her husband was ill. In bed. Guess what with?"

"Flu?"

"Yes."

Julian grunted but said nothing.

"Well," Michael went on, "I gave her some guff about a medical follow-up and she went away and her husband came to the phone. I must say he didn't sound too bright, but he was a helpful sort of chap. At first he couldn't remember anything about the flight. Then, after he'd thought for a bit, he remembered it perfectly. His wife heard him say the seventh, you see, and she called out to him that that was the day after they'd come back from a holiday on the Costa Brava. His first day back at work, you see. What fixed it in his mind was that there was a party on the flight consisting of a man and a woman, husband and wife — he couldn't remember their name — and a young woman. And — grim bit this, which is why he remembered it — they claimed a parcel contained the ashes of their daughter who'd died, he thought, in New York. Well, this parcel had been left behind in New York, by mistake, along with a suitcase belonging to another passenger, a man, who seemed to be traveling with them, though the party of three with the ashes was first class and the chap with the lost suitcase had been tourist. Well, when I heard about the lost suitcase I pricked up my ears, because Professor Saunderson's secretary had mentioned something about Pyke's baggage having gone astray."

"I didn't know any of this," said Julian.

"Well, that's what happened. Now this British Airways chap couldn't tell me any more than this, and as I say he didn't sound at all well so I didn't want to press him too hard, and besides it seemed a dead end, so I thanked him and hung up. Then, thinking over what he'd said about this chap with the lost suitcase — who might just have been Pyke — and the lost ashes, I rang BA back and mentioned the ashes. This they knew all about, because when the ashes had turned up with the suitcase on a later flight, and when they'd cleared them through Customs, they delivered them to the Lamberts. Luck again — it was a London address, in Chelsea. Chap by the name of P. A. Lambert.

"So I looked him up in the phone book and rang. A girl answered. At first she wouldn't say much. Then she thawed and told me she was the au pair girl from next door. Strong accent, sounded like Dutch. She said she'd only come to Lambert's house to feed the canary. The Lamberts — the whole family, father, mother, child — were dead. As was the little girl's nanny, who'd also been to Australia with the Lamberts."

"Did she say what they died of?"

Michael snorted and grinned wryly. "It's getting like a cracked gramophone record. The flu."

"The child — she of the ashes — too?"

"Yes."

"You're sure of this?"

"That's what the au pair told me. And I was able to check it. But I'll come to that."

"Before you go on, am I to understand," Julian said carefully, "that Pyke is no longer the first case we know of? I'm particularly interested in that," he added.

"That's right!" Michael said enthusiastically. "The first case that we now know of is this child. Her name was Barbara. Of course, there may be others before her, who knows? She evidently caught it in Australia."

"Not in New York?"

Michael shook his head.

"Have they got this flu in New York?"

"Cook — that's the WHO chap here in London — says not as far as he knows. I rang him again earlier this morning. He's checking with their departments, surveillance centers, that kind of thing. But one thing is certain, if we're interested in where this flu came from," Michael went on, "then Pyke is no longer of primary interest. But this child, Barbara Lambert, is. She's definitely one step nearer its origin than Roger Pyke. Obviously her parents and the nanny caught it from her, because she predeceased them."

"Did this au pair girl know where these Lamberts died?"

Michael shook his head. "Only some hospital, here in London. But, wait, I haven't finished yet. It was sheer beginner's luck, but the girl at Lambert's number told me that the nanny's mother lived in Folkestone. Name of Petworth. It seems the two girls were friendly. She'd even spent a weekend with them, at Folkestone. Well, I got the old girl's number and telephoned her. She's a kindly old trout, terribly upset at the sudden death of Marilyn, her only child. I'm wondering if I oughtn't to go down to Folkestone and see her —"

"You can't — the mother must surely have been in contact —"

"That's just it, sir. The mother told me she was staying with" relatives when the Lamberts arrived back from Australia, and by the time the police made contact Marilyn was already dead. All she saw was the coffin when she went up to London to get her buried."

"If you're sure of that . . . When did the Lamberts die?"

"Actually, Marilyn was the first. Five days after they arrived back from America. On the twelfth, so her mother told me. Pyke died on the eleventh. The au pair said Lambert and his wife died about three days later, she thought, and Mrs. Petworth confirmed that. Evidently, when she went up to bury Marilyn the Lamberts were already in hospital and she couldn't see them."

"Very well, then," Julian said after a moment. "Go and see the old girl."

"She says she's got letters from Marilyn. They may just be useful. Cook said he'd have a special check run on recent Australian and U.S. respiratory infection figures, just in case he'd missed something . . . Of course, some countries try to hush up epidemics and don't report them as they're supposed to for fear of damaging their precious tourist trade. And not only underdeveloped countries, either — remember Switzerland and that typhoid epidemic?"

Michael's telephone impression of Mrs. Petworth had been right A nice old trout in a gray wool coat coming up Cheriton Road to her gate pulling after her a little shopping cart on two wobbly wheels that squeaked. "Oh, I'm late for you, Doctor." She wheezed a little, stopped, smiling at him, and patted her chest. "Bronchitis, you know. Every winter now since Mr. Petworth fell overboard and got drowned. He was on the boats, the ferries to France. Now come in out of the cold. Do you like crumpets? I do. I'll put the kettle on, pop the crumpets under the grill, and then we can talk." As she pushed open the door a budgerigar started chattering at the end of the corridor that ran down one side of her little semidetached house. "I'm coming, my little Eddy-bird," she cried. Then she wheezed and said, "Now you go and wait in there, Doctor, while I see to the tea." Off she went down the corridor, wheezing, calling to her Eddy-bird, pulling the little wobbly wheeled squeaking cart after her.

The crumpets and tea lay between them on a shaky card table

before the gas fire in the parlor. "Marilyn, Doctor," Mrs. Petworth wheezed, "was such a *good* girl, the best daughter a mother could have and no mistake. What I shall do without her I just don't know. She was so thoughtful . . . 'Ere, Doctor, another crumpet? Oh," Mrs. Petworth exclaimed, her red-rimmed eyes shining with pride in her daughter, "she was *ever* so good, Doctor. When she was in London she rang me regular, once a week. And all the time she was away on that trip all that way out there in Australia — that killed her, you know, she caught something out there, she did, *and* Mr. and Mrs. Lambert and dear little Barby, too. Awful place it must be, simply awful. What was I saying? Oh, yes, every week while she was away out there she wrote to me, sometimes twice a week, and postcards and photographs, too, she sent. She was such a thoughtful girl, Doctor."

It hadn't been all that easy to get the letters and photographs from the old girl; strict was the understanding that they'd be sent back within a day or two, by registered post, after they'd been photostated. "Just *fancy*, Sir Julian Reece being interested in where Marilyn went for medical research reasons. Makes you think, doesn't it. I *so* much enjoy him on the telly. Though I must say in all honesty, though you needn't tell him this, he's certainly a Jonah, isn't he? I don't know what Mr. Petworth would have made of him, I'm sure I don't. Mr. Petworth was always so *cheerful*. No," she added, shaking her head dubiously, "I just don't know what Mr. P. would have made of Sir Julian Reece at all."

"So this child had leukemia," Julian said thoughtfully, and felt for his tobacco jar.

"But she died of influenza," said Michael. "Marilyn's letters make that quite clear. No doubt about the diagnosis. Not only did she die in a big, well-equipped hospital, but Lambert spared no expense in calling in every specialist he could lay hands on."

"I know Saint Luke's Hospital," said Julian. "By the way, no sooner had you gone this morning than a preliminary report came in on the material Ringway and Peacock sent to Salisbury. It contains what is almost certainly a new variant A-strain influenza. The virus shows marked changes in the outer envelope when compared with the Hong Kong, English, New Zealand, A/Vic-

toria 75, or any previous A strains. And Colindale confirms that.
I've now got Berman and his chaps here in the Institute on it, too.
As you know, they've got the disease at UCH, four cases now
since Pyke died there. You're quite certain this child got ill while
she was in Australia?"

"Got the flu there, yes. The letters are quite positive about that.
I must say this girl Marilyn was a bloody marvelous correspon-
dent. She's also positive about the diagnosis of leukemia in New
York. A chap by the name of Spellman made it."

"And Pyke traveled all the way from Australia with the Lamberts?"

"Even including a week's stopover in New York. Pyke also saw
his brother in New York, and introduced Marilyn to him."

"Then Pyke's brother might have it?"

"I don't know where to get in touch with him. He's a radio
astronomer, evidently, in America on some exchange scheme.
Coming up in the train," Michael went on, "after rereading Marilyn's letters, I thought our next move might be to check with
Saint Luke's Hospital in New York. We know Barbara had flu
when she got there. It might be instructive," he added grimly, "to
know what happened there after she died."

Julian reached for the telephone and spoke to Miss Marler.
"What's the doctor's name again?" he asked Michael.

"Lucius Spellman. New York's five hours behind GMT."

Julian sat back in his chair and lit his pipe. "You've given
Marilyn's letters to Miss Marler for photocopying?"

"Yes. And she's also getting some of the photographs copied;
they might just be useful, for identification."

"Where did the Lamberts spend their time in Australia?"

"At first in Sydney. Then at a place in the Australian Alps with
a strange-sounding aborigine name, Wallanulla. She says it's near
the New South Wales–Victorian border."

They were silent, Julian pulling at his pipe. "You know what
I'm thinking?" Julian said suddenly.

Michael nodded and replied, "Maybe I've already thought of it.
I wouldn't need much time. If I was going to stop off in America,
I'd need a visa."

"I can fix that."

"Just the ticket, really," said Michael.

"Shots?"

"I've got them all. Had them for that conference in Cairo last month. My passport's valid."

The telephone rang. Miss Marler said, "The call to Saint Luke's is through now. I've got a Dr. Lichtheim on the line. Dr. Spellman's dead, he says, and he wants to know is there anyone else you'd like to speak to?"

When Michael left the Institute he went into a telephone booth.

Jane's voice spoke, full with relief. "Mike! For heaven's sake, where have you been? I've phoned and phoned. At the lab, the flat, *everywhere*. Are you all right?"

"Janey, I'll be with you in twenty minutes."

"Whatever's happened?"

"I'll be there —"

"Take a taxi. Have you eaten?"

"No."

"We'll go to that little place near Montpelier Street."

"I'd rather eat at your place."

"Omelettes then? Or —"

He cut her off. "Omelettes."

"I've got parsley. But get a taxi, be here *soon*."

She helped him shrug himself out of his coat. He turned, smiling at her, and as she lifted her face to be kissed he said, "You get lovelier and lovelier every time I see you."

"I've got a recipe for it. Being in love."

"Your mother?" he said.

"As well, as they say in hospitals, as can be expected. It's poor Daddy, too. I'm so sorry for him. Why is it so slow?"

"Your mother's not a young woman, and cancers are funny things — they tend to go slower as you get older."

"Come and have a drink," she said, and led the way into the long L-shaped living room where the kitchen was at the short end. It was small, but the furniture and the pictures were good because Jane was a partner in a little antique business near Regent's Park. "Tell me," she said as she went to the refrigerator, "have you heard anything more about Elizabeth Reece?"

"Nothing good," he said.

"The poor man. I wonder how he's been taking it. Have you seen him?"

She turned with the ice tray in her hand and he said, "Yes, that's why you couldn't get me on the phone. But I left a message at the shop with Claude," he added.

"Oh, *damn* Claude," she exclaimed. "He's having one of his regular tiffs with Leonard, and when he's like that he forgets everything. Leonard's got this big part in the new ballet and he's a bag of nerves. That's the trouble with queers, they're so unpredictable. Though I mustn't be too hard on Claude; he *is* a dear, and I'm sure I couldn't have a better partner in the business, aside from all the money he's put into it. What was the message?"

"I'm going to Australia," he said.

The ice tray made a little crashing, skidding sound on the counter beside the sink. "Damn," she said under her breath, then bent to the cupboard for the whiskey. As she straightened he studied her profile, her long hair and brown eyes; an intelligent, alert face. He watched her come from behind the kitchen counter with the drinks. She was dressed in what she called her winter shopwear, plain skirt and sweater. Her taste in clothes was as sure as it was in her business; she was smart enough to make not only men but women notice her, and Claude Zorwell, her partner, knew that some of their best customers were men who came to the shop and bought because it was Jane who looked after them. She also knew a good bit about porcelain, enough to write about it in expert reviews and to be asked for advice by knowledgeable people.

"Another conference?" she asked as she gave him his drink.

"I suppose you could call it that."

"How long will you be away?" They were both conscious of the slight strain in her voice.

"I don't know," he said, after a second's hesitation.

"Oh, please, Mike" — now there was a distinct edge to her voice — "there's no point in being mysterious. You must have some idea."

"That's just it, I haven't." He sat, silent, for a long moment.

Jane swallowed, and he felt her stiffen on the couch beside him. "You've applied for a job out there —"

He cut her short. "No. Well, it is a job, of course, but not in the way you mean. I'll be going for Julian Reece." He went on quickly, getting it over with, "and before you say anything more you'd better listen and I'll tell you what's happened."

She listened, staring at him wide-eyed.

"There's only just one more bit to add to that and it's a question: Will you come with me?"

"I can't," she said instantly.

"Yes." He paused, letting his breath run out. "That wasn't very fair of me to ask."

"I just couldn't leave Daddy now, Michael."

"I realize that. It was bloody stupid of me to ask. But suppose," he said after a moment, "that I was to be out there for some time, would you come then?"

"You mean when Mummy . . . ?"

He nodded.

"Of course, Michael," she said. She spoke with a catch in her throat. "But it's all so sudden, isn't it?"

"I'd want to get married," he said. "Listen, Janey," he went on, "I do understand just how you feel. You know that, don't you?"

"Oh, yes, but of course I'd come," she said.

"What would you do with the shop?"

"Oh, Claude would buy me out. And give me a good price for it, too. He's rolling in the stuff, and he'd make a good offer as a sort of wedding present. He's like that."

Michael laughed. "You mercenary little bitch," he said.

"Well, I am a businesswoman, aren't I? Or supposed to be."

She let her head fall against his shoulder, and for long minutes they let the silence of the room enfold them. She said finally, "Oh, God, Mike, if *only* I could come with you." She sat up quickly, staring at him. "You *do* believe how much I love you? I don't just mean the sexual side of it — I'm not so stupid as not to know that sex for kicks can be so bloody unrewarding, so damnably horrible after it's over, after it's spoilt something. You do know I know that and really that I love you, Mike, don't you? For *everything* we have. Mikey, you do know how I feel about being faithful to you, don't you? I hope I don't sound horribly old-fashioned, but loving you as I do, I couldn't go to bed with anyone else. I'd, I'd

feel . . . all creepy. Right now, imagining it, it makes me feel —
you know that goosey feeling when people say it's someone walking over your grave? It's just exactly like that. You do understand,
Mike, don't you? And trust me?"

"Of course I do, Janey. Here, come here." And he pulled her
down so she lay against him, and he felt her weight and warmth,
the strength of her. And the trust.

# 7 ∿∿∿∿∿∿∿∿∿∿∿∿∿∿∿∿∿∿∿∿∿∿∿∿∿∿∿∿

Sleep did not come easily to Steve. After an hour or two he would wake with the pain in his leg and move gingerly on his platform, seeking to ease muscles cramped by the position in which he was forced to lie. Often Elizabeth would hear the platform creak; waking, she would get up and help him turn, or put her hands under his grotesquely splinted leg and move it for him. Then she would take the pillow she'd made for him and tease out the fern fronds in it. When he was comfortable she would sit on the edge of his platform, and sometimes they would talk softly until the day began to creep out of the sky and into the village.

On those mornings they would talk mostly about themselves. Something in the hush of the dawn prompted confidences. He told her about dogs he'd had; how, he said, Fay could teach a dog to do just about everything, though she wouldn't teach it tricks. He told her how he'd been wounded in Italy, in Tuscany on the Futa Pass, on a cold winter's morning near a little town called Sasso Marconi, and how in Burma he'd been shot down in a Dakota on a supply drop mission between Yandoon and Prome on the Irrawaddy. "I was lucky," he said. "I'm always lucky, honey — see how I've got you."

"Were you hurt?"

"Not much. Two of us managed to bail out. Whether the other fellow knew his parachute was on fire or not I don't know. I guess it had an incendiary bullet in it. Mine opened perfectly, but his just kind of tore up in long shreds. He left a trail of smoke after him, right into the ground."

For Elizabeth the being lost didn't hurt so much as the sense of loss she suffered in her separation from Julian. Over her every waking moment hung her grief. Night after night she would waken, suddenly terrified by the strangeness of the incredible house she was living in, and she'd sit, not sure whether she was awake or dreaming, engulfed by the fear of what might happen and by a grief even stronger for the loss of Julian. She would become aware of her wakefulness and sit there, rigid, battling for control so that she would not make a noise and wake Steve; she would bite her tongue and clench her hands until the nails cut into her palm to stop herself from crying out for her love and need of Julian. Then slowly the dreadful longing would become clouded by the practical need to live, if not for herself then for the desperately sick Steve. She would stand and watch him and listen to his breathing and then ease her way as silently as she could across the mats to the door. She would let herself down onto the porch and sit there, trying to come to terms with a life she had never even imagined and, what was worse, a life she doubted she could long survive.

One night Steve groaned a lot and clutched at his abdomen, and she wondered whether he'd been hurt internally and was only now beginning to show it. Mornings brought some relief as the village came to life and she could go about her chores, wash Steve, and try not to be too depressed. Often this took an effort that all but exhausted her.

As the days passed they talked less and less about rescue. It was no further from her mind, but she was becoming, of necessity, more and more involved with the mechanics of their immediate survival.

One morning she said that she supposed the worst part of disappearing, for the anxious relatives and friends, was the uncertainty of whether they were dead or not. "I mean," she said, "everyone in that plane is dead, except you and me, and yet all the outside world knows is that we've disappeared."

"Do you," Steve asked, "and your husband have a lot of friends?"

"We're not what you'd call social people."

"Strange how some folks are," Steve said. "Drive clear across town for the olive out of a martini."

"Julian suspects people who go out a lot. I think it's got something to do with being all things to all men. Probably it's no more complicated than talking to people who have nothing to say. Do you have a lot of friends?"

"Before Fay died we had some good friends and, yes, a good number of acquaintances. People were very kind to me when Fay died, but after that they just didn't seem to mean the same to me anymore. I'd have thought it would have been the other way around."

He watched her as she began to poke about in the fire, stirring the coals, adding sticks, blowing it all up into bright flame.

"I smell all smoky," she said when she'd put the water on to heat. "It's a funny feeling. I bathe every day in the stream with the women, but one seems somehow to absorb the smoky palm-thatch and pandanus smell of the house."

"You're doing fine, honey."

She smiled down at him. "You're really very good at morale building. But you know you talk too much."

"How come?"

"You should rest more. Talking is tiring. And I'm selfish. I let you talk because it does me good."

"Like say I was a visit to the hairdresser's?"

"A visit to the hairdresser's," she said slowly. Suddenly it seemed unfair, grossly unjust. She sat bolt upright as the thought gave rise to a vivid picture of the inside of her hairdresser's in Kensington. At that moment she could even smell it . . . Images came tumbling into her mind, fretting at her courage. She was in the Brompton Road, with the doubledecker buses roaring away from the stop; she was under the dryer, writing letters, hearing out of one ear the chatter and the gossip . . . The day Julian had telephoned her there, Stephen, mincing up: "My dear, your famous husband is on the phone. *So polite...*"

"Baby." Steve's hand came out and rested on her arm. It took her a second or two to recall herself. She looked down at him, blinking. "I guess," he said quietly, "the beauty parlor was one below the belt."

She let her breath out and was back in the house again. "No," she said quietly. "It just made me think of things. That's all," she added simply. "Things now better forgotten."

"They'll come again," he said.

"It happens to you?"

"Sure it does."

"Only you're too kind to let me see."

"Happens mostly nights," he said matter-of-factly. "When you're not awake to see. You know what I decided the other night? I said to myself that when" — he almost said if — "we get out of here I'm never ever going to bawl anyone out again, not ever!"

"Do you bawl people out?"

"Uh-huh. Sometimes. Putting up with fools is not my strongest point. Life is a matter of survival."

"And sacrifice," she said, surprising herself by the suddenness of her remark.

"Sacrifice," Steve said, "is part of survival in that survival for one usually means sacrifice for another. As I remember it, Aristotle in the *Poetics* speaks about grace being temporary, but what is ever with us is the imagination of disaster. Once we had heroes, godlike, good people. Now, in fiction I mean, the hero, if you can call him that, is usually a victim, sacrificial if you like, but a victim. Yet somehow determined to survive. Which gets harder and harder to do. You only need some guy in the Kremlin or the Pentagon to call a meeting and the tanks are rolling into Prague or the B-52s are wiping out whole communities in Vietnam. You know something, in a way it's the *lack* of imagination of disaster. *Power has no imagination.* Just think of those guys in the Kremlin or the Pentagon and try to get anything but despair out of it.

"Maybe survival, personal survival, takes precedence over everything else. But that also means a moral choice. I guess that some concentration camp survivors don't like to remember what they had to do to survive. It's no trick to die when to stay alive is a miracle. Perhaps that's why martyrs are such successful, happy people: they get what they want *and* they don't survive. Life really is one hell of a thing."

" 'Just the awful choice.' "

"Did someone say that?"

"Browning."

"It about sums it up."

"Steve," she said earnestly, "suppose, just suppose we aren't found."

"Okay," he said after a moment. "I'm supposing." Then he added, smiling at her, "Just for your sake. Academically."

"I don't think I could survive," she said finally, looking up at him.

"Sure you could."

She shook her head. "I don't think so."

"You're not on your own, girl. Nor am I. We've got one another. And the pygmies, too. Oh, sure, they're strange to us, and it's hard to imagine becoming part of them. But we've got them, nevertheless. Hey, look at me. What's the matter with you, having a bad day or something?"

She shook her head. He saw she was near tears. "I tell you, I know."

"But I know you'd do it, if you *had* to. It's as simple as that."

She looked at him. "Why?"

"Because" — he gave a little shrug of his shoulders — "you'd have no choice. Sometimes life's even tougher than Browning figured it. Sometimes there is no choice, awful or otherwise."

For Elizabeth that day was memorable for its misery. Above all, she felt her inadequacy. Some of her depression she realized — triggered by Steve's mention of her hairdresser — could perhaps be put down to her period being due. But much of it, and growing the greater as the day dragged by, was brought about by Steve's condition. In the morning he lay very quiet and by evening was too exhausted to be tempted by even a morsel of food. She offered him whiskey, and he refused that too. With the dark he fell asleep so deeply that he appeared to be almost in a coma. If his wound had become septic she supposed it would smell; she bent over the leaf-wrapped bundle that was his leg but smelled nothing except the sharp moldy odor of the recently dead leaves, green when the surgeon had finished dressing the wound but now brown, reminding her of a battered cigar. She took his pulse and found it weak and thready.

That night she lay before sleep wondering not for the first time what she would do if she heard an airplane. The obvious thing would be to light a fire. But she had already learned that open fires in the village were taboo because of the obvious danger of setting one of the tinder-dry houses alight. Nevertheless, she decided that night that she would never let the woodpile under the house go down; that if she heard an aircraft she would light a fire, even — if she could get Steve out in time — set fire to their house if it meant a fire would be seen. Rescued, they could easily compensate the pygmies for the damage she had done. But suppose she lit a fire and it was missed. And the fire got out of hand? The houses were so crisply dry that they would flare into fierce heat within minutes, impossible for the pygmies to put out. She was sickened by the realization that they would see it as an act of criminal recklessness done by people to whom they had only shown great kindness.

While a prisoner of the Japanese, Steve had seen a compound fracture that had become infected and so knew how slim his chances of survival would be if septicemia set in. Whenever his leg throbbed he wondered just how good the dressing of leaves on it might be. Could be, he told himself hopefully, that these pygmies had discovered a leaf with good antiseptic properties. He tried to keep his fears from Elizabeth, but there were times when the pain weakened him and his defenses fell. One night when the pain was bad and she was sitting very still beside him on the platform as he lay sweating, he said, "I sure hope those leaves are good medicine, honey."

For a long moment she was quiet, then she said, "Purge me with hyssop and I shall be clean."

"That the Bible?"

"It's a psalm. The fifty-first, I think." She was silent for another long moment, then she said, "Yes, now I remember. Sir Alexander Fleming had read that one of the penicilliums had been originally recognized by a Swede — a chemist by the name of Westling — on a specimen of dead hyssop. I remember Julian saying that that psalm contained the first known reference to penicillin. I think that's why I remember it. Because of all the thousands of different fungi that Fleming might have stumbled on, his spore was the same one that Westling had found on the piece of rotting hyssop."

"Don't you cook with hyssop?"

"It's a potherb, yes. It's related to sweet basil and lavender and balm and rosemary."

The next morning Boar's Tusk came, looked at Steve through his round, sad eyes, and went away again. "He's gone for Galen and Hippocrates. Want to bet?" Steve stared anxiously after Boar's Tusk, watching him swing onto the long ladder and away out of sight. "I sense trouble. They figure I'm beginning to recover, and that won't do at all. Want to bet they're fixing to make certain this time?"

"You really are the most ungrateful wretch —" she began.

"It's not *your* leg —"

"They probably want to change the dressing."

"Heave on the hyssop. Well, I wish they'd leave it alone. It's coming along fine as it is."

"And who is that thanks to?"

He grinned at her. There were voices outside and his grin died. "Oh, ho, here come the Mayo brothers," Steve said, and he lay watching the door apprehensively. Boar's Tusk led in the old surgeon and the man Steve called Galen. Several more men followed, carrying leaves and a large wooden bowl.

Elizabeth moved to the head of the platform, where she would be out of the way yet near Steve. "Now you be good," she said softly, leaning down and putting her hand on his shoulder.

She was right about what they were going to do. Without disturbing the splints, the old surgeon began to take the leaves off Steve's wound. He undid the hibiscus bark binding and layer by layer lifted the leaves and dropped them on the floor. At last only the finely shredded leaves that he'd packed over the wound were left, and after poking about their edges with a knobby, shaking finger he lifted them as if they'd been a single plaster. As he did, Steve, who was staring into the roof timbers, flinched. Elizabeth felt it, too, and began to sweat. She closed her eyes, afraid of what she might see. Then she looked. The wound gaped at her, larger than she remembered it, but it was clean. "Steve," she whispered. "Oh, Steve, dear, it's going to be all right." The sweat was trickling from Steve's face into his hair. She pulled up the hem of her skirt and wiped his forehead. "Believe me, Steve, it's going to be all right."

"If you say so, honey," he breathed up at her.

"There's no suppuration at all." She wanted to say more but relief choked her.

"I guess," he said after a moment, "you were as scared as I was."

The old man looked at the wound for a long time, though he didn't touch it. Finally he seemed satisfied and the man with the bowl came forward. In the bowl were more of the same finely chopped leaves. These the old man spread over the wound as he had when he'd first dressed it. Over that layer he placed larger leaves, and finally the binding of hibiscus bark to hold it all in place. When he had finished he did not so much as glance at Steve's face but turned and shuffled out through the door. The others followed him except for Boar's Tusk, who stood staring down at Steve. Then he smiled, very faintly, and kept the smile while he looked up at Elizabeth. For a moment his big, sad eyes met hers, but as she began to move toward him, wanting to show in some way the gratitude they felt, he turned, went quickly to the door, and climbed down.

"Steve," she said softly, and she sat again in her usual place where they could look at one another properly.

"It looks," he said as quietly, "as if you're going to have me around for a while yet."

She started to speak again, but he put out his hand for hers, and as their fingers touched she let herself down onto him and buried her face on his shoulder, seeking his flesh with her lips.

That night as she lay awake listening to Steve's breathing, it seemed lighter in a way she couldn't quite describe, the sleep of a man who breathed more easily. "It looks," he had said, "as if you're going to have me around for a while yet," and in that truth — for she knew it was almost certain that Steve would recover — in that truth lay the only comfort that stood between her sanity and its destruction. Yet, in the way of all such extremes of the human predicament, in that very comfort was also the numbing realization that since Steve would be around for a while yet, as he put it, then she would not be with Julian. She lay in the pandanus and fern and smoky-sweet smell of the house and craved for Julian with an anguish that made her turn and bite into the fern-filled pillow so she would not cry out and wake Steve.

# 8 ∿∿∿∿∿∿∿∿∿∿∿∿∿∿∿∿∿∿∿∿∿∿∿

Michael's booking was British Airways to New York, TWA to Los Angeles, and Qantas for the long hop across the Pacific to Sydney. Now Michael sat beside Julian in the latter's ten-year-old Aston Martin; there was rain on the road to Heathrow, windshield wipers going back and forth in the downpour.

"Now you've got how many copies of my précis of Ringway's tape recordings?" asked Julian.

"Miss Marler gave me six. And Angelino's telephone number in Los Angeles. Archy Nolan's number in Sydney I haven't got, but he's practicing there and I can look him up in the book."

"Give Nolan my regards. He's specializing, isn't he?"

"GU. I think."

"Angelino just might be useful. He's a curious, amusing chap. Don't be put off by his manner. As I told you, he makes medical instruments and scientific equipment. He's in a big way of business. We use his micromanipulators. He came to London a couple of years ago and visited the Institute. He knows a lot of medical bigwigs in Los Angeles and might well be very helpful. Now listen, Michael, we know this is a long shot, and as I've already said probably a forlorn hope, but I want everything, absolutely everything you can get on the Lambert child. And don't waste time before getting up to that place the Lamberts went to, what's it called —"

"Wallanulla."

"Get there as soon as you can. I want water samples, dust out of the house; you've got that little battery-run vacuum cleaner for samples of bed mites. Any food scraps they might have left, anything at all you think might be useful — and even things that might not be!"

"Now what about Spellman's prescriptions from Saint Luke's Hospital? The chap you spoke to will have them ready?"

"He'll have them ready and he's already sent samples of the drug. But there *is* some slight confusion, because from what Dr. Lichtheim said on the phone, Spellman's secretary was too ill to be coherent before she died, but she believed that Spellman supplemented Barbara's treatment from other sources. We just don't know. Did Miss Marler give you Lichtheim's home number in case he isn't at the hospital?"

"Yes," said Michael.

Julian added, "And ring me every day. Don't forget, as soon as you have a number for me to phone, let me have it. What did you arrange about Fiji?"

"There'll be about an hour's stopover there, but I'll be able to see the airport health officer. I've sent him a cable to say what flight I'm on. God, what a bloody long shot it all is."

They were waiting for Michael at the late arrivals desk. A ground stewardess at his elbow said, "Please, sir, the flight's being held for you." There was only the chance to wave to Julian, then he was walking to the airplane, tired after making all those last-minute arrangements — but not, he suddenly decided, too tired to take pleasure in the pretty, plump bottom and the legs of the stewardess as she went ahead of him.

He slept on the airplane. At Kennedy there was a sleety rain blowing against the big windows. Michael got to a telephone, dialed the number, and stood waiting to speak to Dr. Lichtheim, watching the passengers as they wandered about, hung around with bags, or sat waiting for their flights to be called. Airline passengers in the mass, he decided, didn't look like a particularly happy bunch.

[138]

"Say," said Dr. Lichtheim, "you English don't let any grass grow under your feet. Now I figure I've got some of the information and drug samples Sir Julian wants, but I haven't got them all; at least there's some doubt. I only have access to Dr. Spellman's treatment records for Barbara here in Saint Luke's, I've no access to his private office files."

"Not even in an emergency?"

"Well, his files have been sealed by his accountant and the state tax people. He wasn't dodging taxes, but his books are under seal until —"

"I understand," put in Michael, "we call it probate. Tell me," he went on, "how much have you been able to discover about the child's treatment?"

"Well, as no doubt you know, she had acute lymphoblastic leukemia, typically a disease of children, and normally you can get a fairly complete hematological remission with an initial treatment of vincristine and prednisone. I guess about a ninety-five percent remission rate. Now whether or not Dr. Spellman used a concurrent administration of L-asparaginase I can't say, but I do know he was interested in evaluating it. I have here a paper of Dr. Spellman's on an intensive chemotherapy clinical course lasting twelve weeks —"

"Have you sent that to Sir Julian?" Michael asked.

"Yes, I have. Along with the drug samples. And I've got Zebito — that's the upstate pharmaceutical company I told Sir Julian about — to send him full evaluation reports of any of their preparations that were used on this child. Whatever the initial cause, this influenza is really something — or" — he paused significantly — "or maybe I should call it the Ringway virus?"

"So you've already got Sir Julian's telex?"

"We certainly have. Just who is this Dr. Ringway?"

"He was a very fine physician."

"Was, huh?"

"I'm afraid so, yes."

"This sure is one hell of a thing."

"Do you know yet whether it is still confined to your hospital?"

"I'm afraid you'd have to contact the city health office for that information. We have emergency planning on several diverse

[139]

possibilities and eventualities here in the hospital, Dr. Canning, and one of them is in operation right now in our pediatric section. It's about as complete an isolation as is humanly possible. But now, since Reece's call, we've been doing some thinking here. Do you happen to know much about the movements of this Lambert child? Since Sir Julian called us we've checked it out, and we're positive she was the first case here at Saint Luke's."

"All we really know about her is a list of places she visited in Australia. I'm on my way out there now to see if I can discover anything more."

"That's a mighty tall order!"

"We realize that, but there is, you see, just that million-to-one chance that she invented the disease. If that could be proved, who knows? It may lead to something of therapeutic use. So far, in the few cases that have been treated in England, our therapy has been useless . . ."

When he had finished talking to Dr. Lichtheim, Michael had a drink, and waited for the call to board the aircraft, becoming just another passenger, waiting, bored, worried . . .

At Los Angeles impressively big jets were landing side by side. Michael dialed Arturo Angelino's telephone number. He spoke to Mrs. Angelino, who invited him over immediately.

Angelino was short and dark with a ring of hair around a bald head, a big mouth, and a gravelly voice, and wearing a bright yellow terrycloth robe. He opened the door to Michael, smiling broadly. "Come right in, Dr. Candling. Say, this is just *great*." His enthusiasm was genuine and infectious.

"Canning," Michael said gently.

"Sure, my wife told me. How's tricks with Sir Jules? He still right up there with it? I'm just getting in the pool. Hey, Momma, here's Dr. Calling . . . I guess she's busy elsewhere. Now you got time to relax in the pool. Momma . . ." Mrs. Angelino came in smiling and took Michael's hand. "There's a suit for Dr. Candling from England?"

"Sure . . ."

The house was of wood and stone, with floors of black polished basalt. All the lighting was hidden, and the room into which

Michael was ushered rose like a great tent of wood, open on one side through glass to a pool that flowed out to a terrace where a fire fountain blazed, the heavy column of water interlaced with flame from the gas jets around the water nozzle. Far below the pool the city was a shimmering strip of flashing lights.

"You like my fountain?" Angelino didn't wait to be told. "You know what? First night I lit it I was lyin' there in the pool on that air seat sippin' a highball and looking at it and I hear sirens, and Momma calls out, there must be a fire in the street. Next thing I know I got the whole of the Los Angeles fire department right here in the pool with me. Some guy saw my fountain from the boulevard, figured Hollywood Hills was on fire, and gave the alarm. What do you know about that? Finally the fire department got so many calls they rang up one night and asked if I could shield it. I got my architect in and that's what the curved rock shield is for. You go change, Doctor. There . . ." He pointed to a plain wooden panel in the stone wall at the right side of the pool. "Hey, Momma, have Pedro fix the highballs, will you? I guess Scotch for you, eh, Doctor Candling?"

As Michael approached the door it slid open and shut as silently behind him. The room was air-conditioned, with starkly molded olive green chairs and a black polished basalt floor. Through another door he could see a bathroom. On a table that matched the chairs were two pairs of new swimming trunks in heavy plastic envelopes initialed AA. Before changing, Canning peeped into the bathroom. The floor was covered wall to wall with white goatskins. If this was only the pool shower room, Michael wondered what Angelino's own bathroom could possibly be like.

As he came out Angelino shouted, "You bringin' the highballs, Momma? Doctor Candling, now come right in. Used properly, water and alcohol are two of the greatest boons man has."

Angelino was half lying, half sitting in an air-filled plastic couch. Two others floated at the far end of the pool. "Grab yourself one of those, Doctor. The highballs will be here in a moment. Now tell me all about Sir Reecey. Say, isn't he a great guy? He was so goddamned kind to me in London, Dr. Cannaling, so goddamned kind to me. Showed me all around his laboratory and then had me to his club for lunch. A great London club. A great guy. Great. I got all his books. An' you know what? I gave a set to all my closest medical friends here in LA for Christmas. I got them all signed by him before I had them shipped over here. Hey, Momma, where's those goddamned highballs?" But as he added this Mrs. Angelino appeared, followed by Pedro in a white jacket, carrying a tray of bottles and glasses. Hidden in a wall space near the changing room door, behind another plain wooden panel, was an icemaker. From this Pedro chilled the drinks.

Mrs. Angelino wore sequin-studded pants and a scarlet silk blouse. Her hair was dyed ash blond.

While Angelino sipped his drink, paddling himself slowly about the pool on his raft and admiring his fire fountain, Michael told him why he was on his way to Australia. When he'd finished Angelino said, "Look down there at the city, Doctor Canling. See that sorta yellow glow? That's the smog. Why we aren't all dead of it I don't know. We ought to be. Maybe it's because we're waitin' for this Ringers disease of yours. Say, what exactly is it now?"

"I've got copies of Ringway's notes on it."

"Show 'em to me. Momma, get my pool reading outfit, will you?"

Michael got out of the pool and gave the photostats to Mrs. Angelino, who slipped each of the three pages of Julian's précis into transparent, waterproof, plastic envelope with an adhesive flap. Angelino paddled over, took them, and began reading. Michael relaxed, feeling the water and the drink beginning to soothe him after the strain of the flight. As he floated about he watched Angelino's face, the quick-moving eyes; it was, Michael decided, the face of a man far more intelligent than he liked to appear. Suddenly Angelino stopped reading and looked at Michael. "Say," he said, "isn't this just the most unheard-of thing you ever heard of?" He paddled to the pool's edge and flipped the plastic-sealed sheets up onto a wide green swinging seat. "You mind," he asked, "speaking to one of our medical big shots?"

"I'd be only too pleased to."

"Momma," said Angelino, "get the telephone and dial Hiram Drake, will ya?"

[142]

Michael didn't see where the telephone came from. Mrs. Angelino dialed a number, waited a few moments, and then handed the receiver down to Angelino. "This is a waterproof outfit, special," he said in his gravelly voice, grinning at Michael, then, "No, I don't mean you, Hi. About the only thing you ain't is waterproof. Listen, can you come right over? Now, I mean. Would I be callin' you now if it wasn't important? Hell, no, an' if she was we got a doctor right here, a great doctor. From England. That's why I'm calling you. He's a big, important guy working for the great Sir Reece. And listen, Hi, you may not know it, but we got trouble. Big trouble. It's bad news, so come right over."

It seemed to Michael that he didn't wait for an answer. He held the telephone up and waved it about until Mrs. Angelino put down her Autobridge board and took it.

Hiram Drake was Angelino's opposite in almost every particular. He was tall, spoke quietly, and was elegantly dressed and aloof. Angelino said, "Meet Dr. Candling and read those," and pointed up from the pool to the plastic-covered sheets. "They're written by Sir Jules," he added before pushing off again and turning around to admire his flaming fountain.

Michael watched Drake as he read: the narrow face with the long nose, the easy way he sat in the deep green chair, legs crossed, his cream silk cuffs showing just the regulation length below the dark blue jacket sleeves. When he finished Angelino said, "Tell him, Dr. Candling."

Drake listened, sipping a sherry. Finally he said, "When do you leave, Dr. Canning?"

"In about two and a half hours' time."

"Momma," said Angelino, "tell Pedro to be ready to drive Dr. Canley to the airport."

"I think I'll call Nordstrom first," said Drake.

Again the telephone was produced, this time at the table where Mrs. Angelino sat. Michael didn't hear much of what Drake said. He spoke for only a few minutes. When he put down the telephone he said, "Nordstrom says it might fit. They've had about three reports, he thinks, one from Palo Alto and one from somewhere in the San Fernando Valley. But one of these cases has now been diagnosed as lymphocytic choriomeningitis."

"That must be since the earthquake," said Angelino. "Those damn little mice, peein' all over the place. They carry it. Nordstrom" — Angelino said aside to Michael — "is from the city health department. Just imagine, lettin' those little mice go pissin' about diseasin' everybody. Though, y'know, I *like* mice. I like the little bastards. We're all polluted to hell here, Dr. Canling. I'll recite you a poem that great English journalist you got here — what's his name? Alistair something . . . I know, Cooke — a poem he quoted the other day:

'I shot an arrow in the air. / It stuck.' Say, isn't that great?"

"So far," said Drake, "they've heard nothing from Washington. Nordstrom is going to call someone there right away. I'd like to have this copied," Drake added, holding up Julian's précis. "Would that be possible?"

At Honolulu a 707 had overshot the runway. Nobody had been seriously hurt, but some passengers were being taken to the hospital for observation. Canning got the telephone number of the airport doctor, but after trying three times and getting only a busy signal he went to the bar and had a drink.

As Michael came down the airplane steps at Nadi airport in Fiji he was reminded of Marilyn Petworth's letter to her mother — the shock of the wet heat that hit him, after the air-conditioned comfort of the plane, was really something to write home about.

The Mocambo bar was cooler. The airport doctor was waiting for him. "Though you're in transit, I've arranged to winkle you through Immigration and Customs so we can talk up at my house."

The doctor was a slight, earnest man in white trousers and an open-necked shirt who had an Australian accent. As he drew under the carport his wife came out to greet them. "You look a bit stunned by the heat," she said to Michael. "Take Dr. Canning onto the verandah, Frank, and I'll get him a drink. Or would you rather have tea?"

"A drink, if I may," said Michael.

"So would I, if my biological clock were being assaulted as yours was on that bloody plane," said the doctor.

[*144*]

With only an hour's layover, Michael told his story quickly. Then he gave the doctor one of his copies of Ringway's condensed notes. The doctor read them through, frowning. Finally he said, "My word. You might be right about this thing coming from Australia."

"You've heard of it there?" Michael was instantly alert, his travel tiredness banished.

"No. Nothing like that. But," the doctor went on more slowly, "we might have had it here."

"Really?"

"I only say *might*." The doctor glanced at his watch. "If I could get through to the director of medical services in Suva I might be able to check. Tell me, could Ringway's be mistaken for encephalitis lethargica? I ask because last week two women tourists were taken from a hotel at Deuba — that's well up the coast from here — to Suva with a query encephalitis. I didn't hear the end of it though."

"The early symptoms of encephalitis have sometimes been mistaken for influenza. But encephalitis can look like, oh, syphilis, meningitis, botulism, and other things, too, in its early stages. Do you happen to know where these two women were from?"

"No. But as they were tourists I'll try and see if I can find out. I've fixed it with Qantas to phone here when your plane's ready to leave."

When the doctor went into the house to telephone, his wife came out and sat with Michael. "By the numbers I saw in the airport lounge down there," Michael said, "you seem to get a lot of tourists here."

"Too many," she said. She was in a short-sleeved cotton dress and sandals; if anything, Michael noticed, her Australian accent was even flatter than her husband's. "They're said to be good for the economy. Tourism earns more than sugar does now in Fiji. But I personally think it's a shortsighted policy. Frank does too. He's not really the airport health officer; he's only doing it temporarily while the real chap's away on leave."

"Why is it shortsighted?"

"Oh," she laughed shortly, "it's only our idea really. But we're both very interested in the native peoples of the Pacific. My husband studied ethnology and for some time did research among the aborigines in Arnhem Land — that's right in the north of Australia. We think, you see, that tourism tends to fix cultures; because they're laid on specially for the tourist they become ossified. In this sense the tourist in an underdeveloped country becomes, well, almost a kind of polluter."

"But surely the same thing happens in a developed country?"

"Not in the same way. In a developed country, say England or America, tourists don't make nearly as much impact as they do in a little place like this. Small island cultures could be so easily submerged by what is virtually something artificial that is manufactured for the tourist's benefit. Such as you've got happening here."

Michael remembered seeing a plastic boomerang in a house in Earl's Court in London and said so.

"That kind of thing, yes," she said, "but it's much worse than that really. Here we've even got a phony native village, built by the government, with phony 'chiefs' dressed up in what amounts to fancy dress, for the tourists to be taken to, to goggle at. It's degrading both for the islanders and for the tourists. Like all prostitution. Fiji has now, so friends overseas tell us, the reputation of being the fastest-growing tourist trap in the world. There's a film that's been shown —"

"I've seen that," Michael said, "on English television. Not, I fear, a pretty picture."

"Well, we've not got television here so we've not seen it, but what's happening here is not the fault of the people, it's the fault of the government that exploits them for the money tourism brings in. And inevitably tourism makes for discontent and breeds social tensions among relatively unsophisticated people. And brings greed and envy in its train. The locals see them as people with unlimited wealth, able to buy, duty-free, anything they want.

"The Greek Orthodox church," she went on, "has a prayer now, I'm told, exhorting God to have mercy on those Greeks 'scourged by the worldly touristic wave.' What the government is too shortsighted to see is the bitterness tourism can lead to in small, poor countries, especially if they're proud of their traditional cultures.

[*146*]

Tourists are escapists, largely free of the checks and balances on their normal behavior. Frank says they're something like soldiers; not as bad as soldiers, but almost as inconsiderate. But try telling *that* to government officials who can see nothing but the money tourism brings."

The doctor came back onto the verandah, carrying a scratch pad. "They've been able to tell me that there were three cases, not two as I thought. Tourists, from Neutral Bay."

"Neutral Bay?" Michael sat forward quickly. "That was where this English child stayed in Sydney. Have you got the addresses of these people?"

The doctor looked at his note pad. "Kurraba Road," he said. "I don't appear to have the numbers, but I've got the names."

"Wait until I write these down," Michael said. Then, "And you're sure it wasn't encephalitis?"

"Absolutely. It was influenza. Or, I suppose," the doctor added, "I should now say the Ringway virus."

"It needn't be Ringway," said Michael. "It could be just a normal kind of flu. As you know, there are God knows how many different symptoms —"

"I doubt it." The doctor shook his head. "I also spoke to one of the doctors at the Colonial War Memorial Hospital, the biggest hospital in Suva." He paused. "No, it's Ringway, right enough; a normal flu would hardly kill all three of them. What impressed my colleague particularly was the heliotrope cyanosis; he'd never seen it before."

"When did they die?" Michael asked.

The doctor glanced down at his pad again. "Two of them on the twelfth, one on the thirteenth. Bloody worrying this, you know," he went on, frowning. "My colleague at the CWM — that's the hospital — also told me they've got about another half-dozen cases there now, and someone has just died at Labasa — that's a place on the other big island in this group — of what the doctor there described in his report as the worst case of influenza he'd ever seen."

The telephone rang. The doctor glanced at his watch. "Drink up," he said, "that'll be them wanting you at the plane."

In the airport lounge Michael joined the tail end of the line of

[147]

passengers being checked onto the flight. He shook hands with the doctor. "Good luck," he said.

"And the same to you." The doctor didn't smile. He had a narrow face that frowned easily. "I think we might be going to need it. I've a friend here, an old man who remembers what he calls the Spanish flu. That went through the Pacific like a dose of salts. In Suva they were burying people in huge communal graves. A good fifty thousand South Sea Islanders died then. But there are destructive factors outside those caused purely by the disease itself, you know," the doctor went on. "I've made something of a study of the measles epidemic here in Fiji in 1875. Exact figures are hard to come by, but as many as forty thousand Fijians died in that outbreak. About twenty percent of the population. Now the Fijians didn't have any particular racial susceptibility to the measles. No one, of course, was immune, but the excessive death rate occurred because their morale went to pieces. Islanders are riddled with superstition, and they saw the measles as a visitation. Socially, their village communities were soon completely disorganized by the appalling psychological effects of the disease. Maybe there were some secondary bacterial infections present, too."

The doctor stood there, shaking his head, not looking at Michael. "It's not exactly a cheerful prospect," he said, "thinking of what might happen if we got a big flu through here, among this lot."

Qantas put Michael into the Wentworth Hotel in Phillip Street. First he placed a call to Julian. Then he called for a drink, washed up, and was looking at the tourist map of Sydney on his dressing table and finding Neutral Bay when the call came through. Julian's voice was as clear as if it had been a local call, but he sounded very tired.

"Have you rung Archy Nolan?" Julian asked.

"Not yet. I've just arrived."

"Well, Lichtheim's samples and photostats have arrived and I've spoken to the Zebito company, which is being very helpful. We're sending someone over to see them. We've also notified the federal health authorities in Washington and they're going to

[148]

send someone, too. We want to see the full series of checks and animal tests Zebito did. Mind, I'm not for one moment saying it has anything to do with Ringway's, but it just *might*. You saw Angelino?"

"I did. Amusing, as you said, but nobody's fool. He rang a medical friend who phoned someone in the public health department. They think they may have a query Ringway's somewhere near Los Angeles. In Honolulu I couldn't get hold of anyone, but I spent some time with the airport doctor at Fiji. From what he could discover I'd say they almost certainly have it there. The Lamberts only had an hour there, normal stopover time, as I did, but the three cases were tourists. They could well have caught it from Barbara if they traveled on the same plane. But there's also another possibility: they might have got it in Sydney because, significantly, they came from Neutral Bay, which is where the Lamberts stayed while they were in Sydney. And Barbara was ill when she left there."

"Do you know when these tourists died?"

"That's the real crunch. On the twelfth and thirteenth. In other words, within a day or so of the Lamberts' and Marilyn's death. Pyke died on the eleventh."

"So Barbara is still first."

"As far as we know, yes. Perhaps you'd better let Cook know about these Fiji cases. This airport doctor is going to notify his own authorities and I left with him a copy of Colin's notes, but he's something of a medical historian and he's a bloody worried chap. Tell me, sir, do you know whether WHO has notified the Australians yet?"

"Cook rang me about that. They're now preparing a provisional warning for general circulation that, of course, the Australians will get too. But listen, Michael, no matter what WHO or Canberra or anyone else decides, I want you to go ahead on our own investigation. If you need the help of the authorities out there let me know, and I'll get a request made from this end at the highest governmental level. We're doing well on setting up the committee I want here. Fortunately, for once, the government seems to be pulling its finger out. And don't forget I want you at Wallanulla as soon as possible. When can you go?"

"As soon as I can hire a car. Have you heard of any more cases since I left England?"

"It's spreading more quickly than I'd have thought. It's already showing up in that London Transport index. I'm urging containment, quarantine. If we can pinpoint outbreaks and seal them off, we just may be able to contain it. Cook has two top people from WHO arriving here tomorrow. He's done a follow-up on Chris Leach's death in Italy: they've already got it badly at Bolzano and Udine — Milan, too — and someplace over the border into Austria. And a query in Klagenfurt. It's out of London now; and quite a number in the Midlands, in the West Riding, and right up into Scotland. There's also a query in the Scillies. Anyway, look for anything at all unusual you might be able to discover in the child's environment while she was out there. I've been speaking to Lichtheim again; he's first rate, and he now seems certain that Spellman was using L-asparaginase. Well now, Lichtheim's traced the supplier and we're in touch with them; I want some of the actual strain of guinea pig they're using and not just the guinea-pig serum. One difficulty I didn't count on was Spellman being dead because we are a bit in the dark about the actual brand drugs he used, let alone the batch numbers."

"Marilyn, the nanny, tossed all that stuff away."

"That's bad luck. The corticosteroids — and we know Barbara was almost certainly given prednisone — are extraordinarily complex substances. How do we know how they or any other drugs are going to react in man in specific and particular circumstances? A drug is such a hit-or-miss affair. Tests in animals aren't really the answer, and drug companies can't afford to go on testing, so they take a chance and put it on the market."

"And you get a thalidomide."

"Exactly. Even if a drug does prove itself reasonably safe you can't say how it's going to react, what the effect will be in man or some other animal, when some new insecticide or food additive comes along. Fortunately Barbara wasn't irradiated, but who knows what natural radiation received out there in the Australian Alps mightn't have caused a mutation of one of the A-strain or other swine influenza viruses. And don't forget, if you have to speak to a probable suspect use the telephone. Clement the Sixth sat between two huge fires during the plague. Rather interesting that, the plague bacillus is extremely sensitive to heat."

"Clement was weak on faith. And besides, he wasn't in Sydney. It's ninety in the shade here, and they tell me that if the weather holds it might warm up in a day or two."

From the photostats of Marilyn Petworth's letters Michael found Robinson's address in Neutral Bay and asked the hotel operator to call the number. He sat waiting until she came back on the line and asked if he reached the number. "I'll try it again," she said. A minute later she was back. "It's been disconnected." She sounded like a very friendly girl. "Perhaps they haven't paid the bill," she laughed. Then he asked her to call Archy Nolan's number in Rose Bay. It was engaged. "You're not having much luck," the girl said cheerfully. "I'll try it again in a few minutes."

Michael sat on the edge of the bed, looking through the window. The sky was a pale, hot blue . . .

Angelino's pool, he thought, with no Angelino in it . . . The flaming fountain unlit, corroding, the gas leaking away . . . Julian's laboratory, those rather shabby rooms in that big shabby institute that was known and respected throughout the world because of what Julian and men like him had done there. Julian's lab empty, the benches, the instruments, the apparatus under dust and webs spun by patient, unmolested spiders. The Uffizi, the National Gallery, the Prado, the Tate, the Metropolitan, the Pitti Palace, miles of pictures, portraits that would stare out at one another . . . until decay sent them crashing to the floor. Books would molder, machinery redden with rust. Ships would rot until some storm sent them to the bottom or a spring tide beached them. And without man vegetation would creep into every place it could find nourishment.

Yet was it so impossible that there in a little girl's body could happen the accident that could bring all this about?

In a sense, he thought, the real wonder was, once you started to think about it, that it hadn't happened before. For three billion years bacteria had been the dominant life on this planet. Burnet and White had pointed out the "utter expendability of the individual," an expendability that made it impossible to define a bacterial species — or this was how Michael understood it. Any change in its environment and a more or less different bacterium would grow and flourish in the place of its forebears until some environmental change caused it to change again and flourish in the place of its old form, mutations that, in man, would need millions of years to accomplish. And these were changes that were constantly taking place; in any culture vessel thousands of mutant organisms with anomalous DNA were being tested. Most were unfit to survive but an enormous number did, and such was their "genetic flexibility" that it was probably now all but certain that from bacteria there had emerged sex and viruses — perhaps nature's two most successful inventions.

It was quite possible that the virus mutant that was Ringway's had started in Barbara. The Black Plague had taken, some authorities said, half of the population. In whose or what kind of a body had the particle that began it become effective? Where in the chain of rat, flea, and man did the final change take place? And why? In whose body did the *spirochaeta pallida* first cause syphilis? It wasn't in that of the ancient hero Syphilus — that would be too easy; the hero had only picked up what was going about. If *pertenuis*, which causes yaws, be the father of *pallida*, might not a little girl have known the first mother yaw? Who was first to have typhoid or cholera, diphtheria or pneumonia, dysentery — or invent the Ringway virus?

"Not Mike Canning!" Nolan's voice on the phone was high with surprise. "Mike, you old bastard. How *marvelous* to hear you." The accent was no stronger than Michael remembered it from the London days at Saint Thomas's. "Where are you? Why aren't you out here? How long are you staying? Christ, I've got to see a patient, old chap I did a prostatectomy on this morning, but Molly can go in straight away and get you."

"I can get a taxi —"

"Rubbish! Hey, Molly . . . Hang on, Mike." He heard Archy calling his wife. Heard him say, "At the Wentworth." Then he was back. "Mike, pack up, pay your bill, and Molly will be there in about an hour and a half."

Molly was forthright, rangy, cool-looking, with a wide mouth and dark red hair. Impressive, thought Michael; a woman who would stand out in any crowd with her good looks, poise, and presence.

In the Honda, which Molly drove expertly on the way out to Rose Bay, Michael told her why he had come to Australia. In the worst of the traffic Molly said little, but as they climbed William Street to Kings Cross and got onto Bayswater Road, she relaxed and said, "You know, this won't altogether surprise Archy. Tell me, was he a pessimist in England? Because ever since I've known him he's been saying there's a catch somewhere. He says we're bullying nature, that it's only a fluke we've so far escaped a calamity that'd make the thalidomide tragedy seem no more than a slight touch of dandruff. We're rather hot on this correlation between drugs and abnormalities here. As no doubt you know, it was one of our doctors, William McBride, who first discovered the toxicity of thalidomide. Archy thinks there's not nearly enough basic research done into the effects of new drugs. He's also pretty scathing — well, that's an understatement — on the subject of drug companies. Mind, he's not the only doctor who feels like that."

Archy's house was built on a slope landscaped with rockeries; a big house with wide, low rooms, some good pictures, squat, comfortable furniture, and outside a big terrace from which you could see the harbor, where the Nolans ate and drank during the summer. Michael liked the feeling it gave him, open and friendly.

Michael was on the terrace, beginning to unwind after the flight, when Archy came home, sweeping up the drive in an American-style station wagon. Archy came out onto the terrace. Apart from an aura of success, he hadn't changed much. "Mike, it's *so* good to see you. We've got to have champers tonight, Chook. Got some on ice?"

"No."

"Stick it on, then."

"Birdy's coming. I rang him."

"Chook?" said Michael, looking from one to the other. "I thought it was Molly."

"Only a Pommy," said Archy, "wouldn't know what a chook was. Tell him, Chooks." But before Molly could speak Archy went on, "A chook, Mike, is a fowl, a hen —"

"It's nothing of the sort," said Molly. "It's a tender young chicken."

"It's a tough old boiler, Mike, and don't you believe her. Before she came up in the world and managed to trap me, her name was Fowler. Hence — Chook."

At that they heard a car coming up the drive. Molly said, "This'll be Birdy."

Richard Birdwood, Archy's partner, bustled onto the terrace, shook hands with Michael, flopped into one of the foam-cushioned easy chairs scattered about, and fixed his gaze on Michael, summing him up through small dark eyes set in deep wrinkles, a smallish, plump man of forty-six, balding, dark-skinned, a man who looked as if he spent a lot of time in the open air. "What's the bad news?" he asked, and when Molly put a whiskey and water into his hand he still didn't take his eyes off Michael.

"Worse than that," said Molly.

"Mike," said Archy, "start at the beginning. I haven't heard it properly myself yet," he added to Birdy.

When Michael had finished his story he gave them a copy of Ringway's description. Archy read it over Birdy's shoulder. "Right," Birdy said when he'd read it. He pushed the sheets into Archy's hand and stood up. "I'm going to phone Bill Wilcox. I might catch him still at the office. At the health department," he added for Michael's benefit, and he stumped off the terrace into the house.

"Where's Wallanulla?" asked Michael.

"Search me," said Archy. "Do you know, Chooky?"

"I've never heard of it. I'll look it up on a road map."

"Now just so I get this straight, Mike," said Archy, "Julian Reece thinks this disease started here in Australia, with this English kid —"

"I don't think he'd be as positive about it as that — not yet. But in the absence of any case before hers, then yes. So far, we know of none before her. That's why he wants me to go to Wallanulla as soon as I can, before the trail goes cold. Can you arrange for sterile bottles and sacks?"

"Sure, I'll get onto this chap Willcox in the health department."

"And where can I hire a good car?"

"Hire one? Oh, damn that, take mine. I can use Molly's." Archy sat silent, thinking, rubbing the side of his face.

"Birdy came back, picked up his drink, and looked at Michael. "You've got Billy Willcox worried," he said.

"He's heard of it?"

"Something like it. At All Saints," he said to Archy, and then back to Michael, "That's a hospital over Mosman way, in Ella-matta Avenue. He's ringing them now. He said something about a new A strain in South India."

"We know about that," said Michael. "This is nothing to do with that."

Molly brought out a road map. She opened it on the table and they bent over it, looking for Wallanulla. Willcox called back. After a few minutes Birdy called, "Molly, bring me those notes of Mike's, will you?"

At length Birdy hung up. "It's Ringway all right," he said grimly. "Symptoms agree with Ringway's description. And a bas-tard of a thing it is, too." He stopped, staring at Michael with new respect. "They've tried about everything at Mosman: all the wide-spectrum antibiotics, even the prostaglandins, the bloody lot. No go."

"Did you mention Wallanulla?" asked Michael.

"He's never heard of the place."

"I can't find it on this map either," said Molly.

"I told Willcox," said Birdy, "of WHO's interest and he's going to phone someone at Canberra. But they've got a dozen cases at Mosman."

"Did he say how many had died?"

"Ten."

"Now, this is most important," said Michael. "Does he know when they died — specifically? What we're really interested in is the date of the first death."

Birdy gave a wry grin. "All of them," he said, "after your Lam-bert kid. The first death was on the eleventh —"

"That," said Michael, "was the day Pyke died in London."

Birdy grunted. "It's even more significant than you think," he said. "It was a male, aged forty-two, and his name was Leslie John Robinson. The kid's uncle's name *was* Robinson, wasn't it?"

"Yes."

Birdy reached for his drink, and there was silence on the terrace until Birdy grunted again, looked at Archy, and said, "You going with him?"

"Going with who where?" said Archy.

Molly answered, "With Mike to Wallanulla. Yes," she added, "he is."

"Hey, wait a minute," said Archy, sitting up quickly. "What about my cases?"

"Pethwick and I between us," said Birdy, "can handle them."

"Archy," said Molly, "go and ring Jim Pethwick now."

"The second person to die," said Birdy, looking at Michael, "was Robinson's wife. Then their two kids. I didn't think you'd be interested in the names of the others, but they're all from around the same area, two of them in Robinson's street, one of them an old codger who died in two days flat."

"What do I tell Pethwick?" Archy looked at Michael. "He's a nosy sort of a cove."

"What you mean is," said Birdy with a wry grin, "*do* you tell him or don't you." He sipped his drink, looking at Michael over the rim of his glass.

"You'd better tell him," said Michael. "But ask him not to broadcast it. Unless I'm much mistaken there'll be some kind of an official warning or statement soon. But we don't want to panic people."

"I've phoned Kate," Molly said, and everyone looked at her as if her statement had something to do with what Michael had just said. "She's coming over," she added.

"Then you'd best tell Mike about her," said Archy.

"When," asked Birdy of nobody in particular, "does the expedition to Wallanulla take off?"

"Tomorrow morning," said Molly.

"My God," Archy said to her, "you *are* an organizer, aren't you. First Kate, then off we go tomorrow morning."

"At seven. Well, Mike's got to get there as soon as possible, hasn't he? And as for Kate, why shouldn't she know what's going on? Kate," Molly added to Michael, "is my sister." She paused there and for a moment looked away, out over the harbor where dusk was giving way to a scatter and flash of lights in the soft purpling of the warm night. "There's not a great deal, really, to tell about her" — Molly glanced at Birdy for an instant and then went on — "but by way of explanation, she's three years younger than I am, which makes her thirty. Eighteen months ago, Tom, her husband, went to pick up their two kids after a birthday party. It was a wet evening. They were coming from Woollahara, and as they turned into New South Head Road one of those big articulated lorries got out of control. His brakes failed —"

"They locked," put in Archy.

"Yes," she said. "He skidded into them and drove them against a lamp standard. They had to be cut out of the wreckage. The little girl was alive when they got her into the ambulance, but dead at the hospital. Tom and the little boy were killed instantly. I'm only telling you because Kate is only now really beginning to get over it. Birdy's been wonderful to her, because for about, oh, nine or ten months afterward she virtually disintegrated."

Birdy grunted. "She had all her eggs in one basket," he said. "Frazer was the only, and I mean the only, man in her life. All very romantic, no doubt, but it doesn't make for an easy adjustment if you're cooking the dinner one minute, the next learning that your man's been blotted out, along with the kids. Not if you're built the way Kate is."

"But she's all right now," Molly said.

"She's about over it," agreed Birdy. "Though there are cases where the human spirit takes such a knock that it never really completely recovers. But Kate's all right now, as Molly says."

"Thank God," said Molly.

"I'm going to have a drink," said Birdy.

Kate Frazer had Molly's dark reddish hair and the same wide-apart blue eyes; she was slightly fuller in the figure than Molly — and better, thought Michael. Well dressed, no jewelry except a wedding ring and a gold watch. Michael decided that had he not been told about her he might have missed the odd sign of tension: the occasional sideways dart of her eyes, the sudden crossing and uncrossing of her legs, the quick clutching at her wedding ring as if to assure herself it was still there. There was also, he felt, a tendency on the part of Molly and Archy and particularly Birdy not to ignore her — she was too alive for that to happen — but to keep a shield, so to speak, ready, which they could drop between her and remembrances of times past.

Molly and Kate served the dinner. Tomato soup — "Out of a tin," said Molly, "because I didn't know I'd be having a dinner party tonight." After the soup, roast beef, Yorkshire pudding, baked potatoes, green peas, and horseradish sauce. Archy stood at the head of the table and carved the beef. The wine was an excellent Hunter River red. "Oh hell, Chooky," said Archy, "weren't we going to have champagne?"

"With roast beef?" Molly said.

"Shut up, Archy," said Birdy. "If," he went on, "this Ringway's disease is as bad as Mike seems to think it is, ideally no human being in the world at the present moment should come within spitting distance of another. Right?" He looked at Michael.

"Right," said Michael.

Birdy grunted. "Fat chance," he said. "I saw cholera in India, among the refugees. One road I remember well, the verges of it were littered with curious sticklike things that stank. It took me a while to realize they were bodies. Where do you put the dying? How do you isolate cities? Troops aren't all that good. Besides, how do you stop an army from catching something spread by droplet infection? And who's going to bury the dead? It won't work." He shook his head. "You couldn't just isolate Sydney from the rest of Australia by tomorrow morning. Or New York from America. Or anywhere else from any other country. And you can't stop people from congregating. If you shut down the slaughter-houses and the milk-bottling plants and the bakeries and can-neries and wholesale markets, how are you going to feed a city?"

"Surely you can have a quarantine," said Kate.

Birdy looked at her and shrugged. "When I was about four-teen, before your time, there was an outbreak of what was then called infantile paralysis. We call it polio now. They put a ban on interstate travel. I remember it well; we had cousins at Geelong, in Victoria, and couldn't visit them. But it didn't do any bloody good. God knows how many kids got it."

Archy said, "Remember what McFarlane Burnet said about that almost unimaginable catastrophe of a "virgin soil" epidemic involving all the populous regions of the world."

"Yes," replied Birdy, "but Burnet was talking of the dangers of accidental or deliberate meddling with the genetics of viruses. He was afraid of the possibility of some new ultravirulent virus escaping from a laboratory and taking hold in a population with no natural resistance to it. A new cancer virus has been made in the laboratory by accident, a major and permanent genetic change did occur, no doubt of it, whereas before it had been infective only to mouse cells — afterward it didn't infect them at all, *but became highly infective to human cells!*"

"I don't want you two sleeping in any pubs when you go to Wallanulla tomorrow," said Molly. "You're going to take the small tent and the camping gear."

"We can sleep in the station wagon," said Archy.

"The tent's at your place, Birdy," Molly said.

"I'll bring it around," he said.

"No," Molly said, "Kate and I'll do that, after we've stacked the dishwasher."

"Well, the tent's in the garage," Birdy said. "Look here," he went on, shifting uncomfortably in his chair, "if this Ringway virus is going to be a mass killer, shouldn't we be taking a few precautions?" He puckered up his eyes and looked around at them.

"Such as?" asked Archy.

"Well," Birdy said slowly, "I know hoarding is antisocial and all that. But we're quacks, aren't we, and this is a medical emergency. I think we ought to stack up on food. Tinned stuff, nothing perishable. No bloody good having the deep freeze stacked if the electricity goes off. No fancy stuff: plain meat, fish, vegetables, things like that. Vitamin tablets, I suppose, too."

Archy looked at Molly. He couldn't quite bring himself to this idea. "Mightn't that be rushing things a bit?" he asked. "Being a bit previous?"

"I couldn't agree more," Molly said.

"With me?" asked Birdy. "Or Archy?"

"With you."

"Emergency, y'see," Birdy said. "Otherwise out of the question." He seemed relieved by Molly's support.

"Where would you go for it?" said Archy doubtfully. "You'd have to offer some explanation. I mean we're not a grocer's shop."

"Oh, Levett," said Molly.

"I'd forgotten about old Levett," Archy said. Then to Michael he added, "Levett is a patient of mine."

"He's a big wholesale grocer," added Molly.

"But won't he think it a bit peculiar?" said Archy.

"Tell him you're buying it for a friend who's planning a yacht voyage around the world," said Kate.

"I't be some yacht if she gets the quantities I've got in mind," said Birdy.

"Why can't I tell him the truth, Michael?" Molly asked.

He gave a little shrug. "I don't suppose there's really any valid reason why you shouldn't. If it goes on as it has been, there'll have to be a worldwide announcement soon. Reece, of course, wants a proper quarantine."

"Bloody remarkable that," said Birdy, shaking his head. "We have to come to the edge of fucking doomsday before man's got the sense to try to pull together for the common good." He shook his head again.

"As I think Birdy's right, tomorrow I'm going to get those groceries — and," Molly added, "at wholesale prices too. Kate," she went on before anyone else could speak, "why don't you stay here tonight with us?"

"I've not brought Crackers." Kate paused, as if making up her mind, then added a trifle acidly, "You told me not to."

"Go and get him," Molly said quickly.

Kate said nothing but stared stolidly at Molly, who looked slightly disconcerted. Then Molly said, "Get Crackers and then you'll be here early in the morning to lend a hand. While Archy and Mike pack the big car, we can go and frighten the hell out of old Mr. Levett."

"But you'll need the big car for the groceries," said Archy.

Molly shook her head. "I'm going to hire one of those drive-yourself vans."

"Christ," said Archy.

"Well, if we're going to do it," said Molly, "there's no point in doing it by halves."

"Couldn't agree more," said Birdy. "Will you lay in a stock for

[160]

me, too? Remember, I don't eat anything out of the engine room, no kidneys, liver, lights, balls, brains —"

"They don't tin offal," said Kate. As she spoke she got to her feet. "Well, I'll go now," she said.

"Go?" Molly looked at her sharply.

"For Crackers," said Kate.

Molly said, "Wait a minute, Kate. Michael, wouldn't you like to go with Kate? It'll be company for her. And a run in the car after the heat of the day might cool you off before bed."

"I'd love to," said Michael. As he followed Kate out through the big room and down the stairs, Archy said quietly, "You really are a bloody little organizer, aren't you, Chooky?"

"You mind your own business."

"He's a nice bloke," said Birdy, helping himself to his second brandy. "Married?" he added, cocking an eye at Archy.

"Not as far as I know," said Archy.

"He's not," said Molly.

"How do you know?" asked Archy.

"I asked him."

Archy got up and was about to take a cigarette from the table when he stiffened and, bending forward, looked Molly straight in the eye. "And I'll tell you something else," he said, drawing each word out. "You *told* her not to bring Crackers. So that if she stayed here she'd have to go back for him. What do you say to that, Birdy?"

"I say there's nothing the matter with our lovely Kate now that a course of concentrated copulation won't put right."

"This is a nest of vipers," said Molly, getting up and going inside to refill the ice bucket.

"Right!" Archy called after her, "Trouser snakes."

Kate's car was an open VW and the top was down.

"Who's Crackers?" asked Michael as he got in beside her.

"A dog."

"What sort?"

"Half kelpie. Half border collie. Sheepdog. He belonged to my son. I suppose they told you I once had a husband and children?"

"Yes, they did."

"Then we don't have to talk about them, do we?"

"No, we don't."

She shifted into top gear and they went the rest of the block in silence. Then she said, "Sorry if I sounded sharp then —"

"You didn't —"

"Oh, yes, I did. I've had three drinks, a lot of wine, and two of Archy's mammoth brandies. I'm also very angry with my sister."

Kate looked sideways at him for an instant, then back to the road. "She's what Archy calls an organizer."

"I don't understand," he said.

"Do you know what Molly told me on the phone? She said they'd had foisted on them a very proper, stuffy, old-fashioned, retired Army surgeon, a relic from the Khyber Pass, and would I please come over and help along with what was going to be a very dull and sticky evening. Crackers was to be but definitely left at home." Kate began to laugh, showing her even teeth in the light of a street lamp. "I'm *furious* with her. I could *murder* her. And I will, too. You, of course, played right into her hands —"

"How?"

"That business about a run in the car before bed. After the heat of the day. 'Oh, I'd love to go,' you said, nearly falling over yourself getting out of that chair."

"Well, it has been a hot day. At any rate, it has been for me, after England. It's practically snowing there."

"This isn't hot. Wait until next month. And the month after."

"I won't be here then."

"Oh?" She glanced at him out of the corner of her eye. Then added, "Oh, no. I suppose not."

As she put her key in the lock Crackers started yelping and whining with pleasure. Kate opened the door and the dog hurled himself at her. "He isn't used to being left alone," Kate said, doing her best to hold Crackers with one hand while she felt for the light switch with the other. Suddenly a change in the dog's voice warned Michael, but Kate beat Crackers to it. "Down, Crackers!" she said firmly. "Down!"

When the light snapped on, Michael found himself faced with a particularly handsome dog who hadn't, as yet, been properly introduced. A dog who, just as obviously, placed great store on a proper introduction. The hair along his back rose, and a menacing rumble came from somewhere behind the incredibly white teeth.

Kate dropped down beside Crackers. "This is Mike," she said quietly, laying her face alongside that of the dog. "Now, be a good Crackers and say hello nicely to him." For a long moment Crackers continued to show his teeth. Then suddenly he relaxed and came forward, brushing past her. Michael held out the back of his hand and Crackers sniffed it cautiously. Finally he seemed satisfied, turned away from Michael, and went back to Kate.

"I'd rather have Crackers as a great and lasting friend than otherwise," Michael said as he too relaxed.

"When David was in his pram in the park or on the beach nobody could get within fifteen feet of him. He's very possessive. Tell me, Dr. Canning, are you a possessive type, too?" Before Michael could answer she went on, "I think I must be slightly drunk. Speaking so freely to total strangers. So unlike Crackers."

"I suppose I am," he said.

"What, drunk? Like me. Or possessive? That's also me."

"Possessive."

"Birdy thinks it's a bad thing. He might be right, too. He very often is, is old Birdy. His name's Richard, you know — Richard Birdwood. At school they called him Dickey Bird. Not surprisingly. What will you have to drink?"

"I thought we only came for Crackers."

"Because the Boer War surgeon — or was it the Khyber Pass? — couldn't bear dogs in the house. I hope Molly's lawn dies. May her clematis get the wilt and her roof leak. Did you know that during the Boer War the native women when being chased by rude British soldiery used to rub a handful of sand into their private parts?"

"I think you must be a little bit drunk." He was laughing at her and with her, for once enjoying himself.

"Because I happen to know something of England's glorious imperial past does it mean I must be drunk?" Kate said. "I thought you, as an Englishman would be pleased to see how deeply I'd delved into the deathless saga of British military history." She was standing under the light in the little entrance hall,

[163]

light that fed the rich red darkness of her hair. He noticed how smoothly dusky tan her skin was, and again how wide and blue her eyes. Her lips had the full curves of her body and she wore no lipstick. "What," she went on suddenly, "are you going to have to drink? You realize, of course, that you'll have to drive back to my wretched, organizing sister's house. Come out onto the balcony where we can be cooler and can see forever. I, of course," she added as she turned and went into the living room, "should by no means have another drink, but I am going to. Crackers" — Kate stopped, turned, and looked at the dog as he came past Michael — "you have never seen me drunk, have you? Why tonight?"

"There are times," Michael said, "when we seem to have less resistance to alcohol."

"Crackers," Kate said, not taking her eyes off the dog, "is *enormously* resistant. Perhaps it's because he drinks beer."

"Tell me," Michael said, following her onto the balcony, "about Birdy. He interests me."

"Birdy's marvelous. Bit of a dark horse, though. More important than he makes out. Was in Vietnam, during the war."

"You mean serving as a doctor?"

"As a doctor, yes. But on some official inquiry, I think. Don't know, really; Birdy doesn't say much about things like that. Went up there twice, no, three times I think. Birdy," she added, suddenly serious, "saved my life — and if you want your life saved for you that's a very good thing. It was only after he'd done it that I realized I did."

They sat on the balcony with their drinks, looking out over the harbor into the dark purple night. Kate sat well back in the chair, gazing out to where a brightly lit ship was passing. "That," she said more quietly, "is the Manly ferry . . ." She sipped her drink. "I am going to have the father of all hangovers in the morning but I don't care. I just don't care because for now I am happy. So I will drink my drink very slowly . . . Then, 'I, an old turtle, will wing me to some withered bough.'"

"*The Winter's Tale*," he said.

"Don't be funny. It's summertime. And you like runs in the car after the heat of the day. Remember? We'll have our drinks very, very slowly, and it'll serve that wretched sister of mine right.

[164]

She'll be furious if we're not back within half an hour. So let's make her really mad, shall we?" The conspiratorial flash in her eyes was charming.

When they got back to Archy's place, Michael asked if he might call London. "Use the phone in the old surgery," Molly said. "I'll take you down there. If you have to do much phoning, you can use it as an office."

He rang Jane's shop number, making it person to person. It came through quickly, catching Janey five minutes after she returned from lunch.

"Darling! Oh, Mike, what a wonderful surprise! How are you?"

"I'm fine."

"But you didn't just ring to tell me that." Always Jane got right down to the point; nobody Michael had ever known got to the point as quickly as Jane.

"I want you to do something for me —"

"Mike, if you're asking me to come out there —"

"I'm not," he said. "Now listen. I don't want to be too specific over the phone, but you know why I'm out here." He paused, wondering for an instant how to put it. "It looks," he went on, "as if it's going to be worse than we thought."

"But there's been nothing here in the papers about it, Mike. I've been looking."

"Maybe the government has slapped a D notice on the papers, I don't know, but it's spreading, believe me. Now what I want you to do, darling, is this: shut up the shop and your flat and go and live at your father's house; you can help him and the nurse with your mother."

"But, Mike, darling, I just can't shut up the *shop!*" she protested. "What about Claude?"

"Haven't you got some holidays due?"

"I suppose I could manage to go home for a bit." Jane sounded doubtful. "But for how long?"

"God alone knows. There's food too."

"What?"

"Look, Janey, you've got to get in plenty of canned food." Michael remembered what Birdy had said. "No frozen stuff, that would go if power was cut. Plenty of good straight nourishing food: meat, dried beans, vegetables, porridge, tinned milk, that kind of thing."

"Mike," Jane said carefully, and doubt was strong in her voice, "are you sure it's as bad as all this? Aren't you perhaps —"

"I might be," he said quickly. "But then again, I might not. Besides, I'm not the only one who's scared of it. Jane, my love, will you do what I ask?"

There was an anguished pause. Then she said, "I suppose I'll have to if you say so. Where are you?"

"With the Nolans, the people I told you about."

"Give me your phone number."

He gave it to her with Archy's address. Another time beep sounded and she said, "Oh, Lord, darling, if only you were here. I love you so much. Oh, do, do *please* come back soon. Won't you?"

"Just as soon as I can."

"Promise?"

"With all my heart."

It was Janey who broke the connection.

Of all the unsatisfactory things, Michael decided, nothing could be quite so bloody as a long distance telephone call. When he went up, Archy offered him a nightcap, but Molly said, "For heaven's sake, you've both had enough to drink and talked enough for one night. And you've got a big day tomorrow. Now you two go to bed," and she kissed Michael on the cheek. Molly, he concluded, was an extremely perceptive, kind human being.

Later in his room Michael sat under the table lamp and wrote to Jane, urging her to do as he asked. Then he told her of Archy and Molly and Kate and Crackers and Birdy. "You'd get on well with them," he wrote, "because they have your honest forthrightness. It's not an English characteristic."

At breakfast the next morning, eaten in an alcove off the kitchen, Archy was in high spirits. Molly, still in her robe, looked fresh and handsome, though not, Michael decided as he watched her pour his coffee, quite as good-looking as Kate. The heat was already beginning to wash through the house.

"Kate," Molly said, "has a hangover. What did you two have to drink around at her place?"

"Ker-rist," said Archy. "Don't tell her, Mike. See those bags under her eyes? Insomnia, old cock, lying awake all night wondering why you two were so long."

"Don't be such a bloody fool, Archy," Molly said.

"Here, Mike" — Archy winked at him — "have some toast to keep you going until the Chook brings the bum nuts."

"My God, you're getting more and more vulgar, Archy. How you ever hope to build a respectable practice I'm damned if I know."

The telephone rang. Molly took it and then handed it to Archy. "Hospital," she said.

"Nolan speaking." Archy gave a series of instructions, slowly, clearly, and concisely. And politely. Michael was impressed; this workaday Archy Nolan was obviously a man to be reckoned with. He was doubly glad he was coming to Wallanulla with him. He had forgotten the enormous amount of concentration Archy Nolan was capable of.

Archy put down the phone and winked at Michael. "Chook," he said, "can't be helped, but there'll be a short delay. I've got to go to the hospital. As well as pick up the sterile bottles and packets for Mike's samples. Now what you want, Mike, is, I take it, a sort of health inspector's specimen sample kit, right?"

"Yes. Sterile bags, jars, and bottles — things like that."

Kate came down as Archy shot out of the back door, banging the fly-wire screen door behind him with Crackers leaping about, barking, seeing Archy off. The dog came back with much grinning and tail-wagging. "Beast," Kate said, fixing her eyes on him. "Oh, how healthy he looks. I feel simply bloody. Have we time for a swim? Would you like that, Mike?"

"Love it." Then he looked at Molly, who shook her head. "Time, as usual, is the enemy," said Molly. "Have your coffee, Kate, then take Mike to Birdy's. If Archy's delayed we might have time for a swim later."

The lower part of Birdy's house was faced with three large doors. Michael pulled the VW up in front of them and they got out. "That's the garage," Kate said, pointing to one of them. "I'll go and get the key. His Mrs. Badlaugh should be here by this time. The tent and the other gear is through that door there." She led him into a large storeroom dominated by a fiberglass speedboat on a trailer. "It does over sixty and I once won a race in it," Kate said, pointing to the name in huge letters along its side. "See, it's called *Kiss Me*."

"Is Birdy in love with you?"

"Birdy's not in love with anyone. But that doesn't stop him being a wonderful person. It could, I suppose, but it doesn't."

They brought the tent back to Archy's in the VW. Molly had a checklist for the gear that went with the tent: sleeping bags, stove, waterbag, ax, cooking pots, cutlery, first aid box (including snake antivenom); she ticked the items off while loading them into the station wagon. As Michael and Kate got out of the car she said, "Archy's just phoned. He's been delayed at the hospital with an emergency, but he says he'll be back for lunch. So I vote that when the car's packed we all go for a swim. We'll have lunch and then you can get straight off to Wallanulla, Mike."

Rose Bay Beach was practically deserted. They all ran down the sand and Crackers beat them into the water. Kate played her game with Crackers, diving under him and swimming around below him while he yelped and barked and ducked his head in a frantic effort to get down to her. Then they swam farther out and trod water, luxuriating in the limpid coolness. Suddenly Michael felt crazily, indescribably happy. He was looking at Kate, but he thought of Janey and saw a likeness, a curious almost sardonic downward twist of the mouth when they both smiled. Why hadn't he and Janey married yet? Thinking of all that *could* be, of love, harmony, and no administered (accidental or contrived) hurt and cruelty. Was it possible? How much had they, or anyone, to alter themselves to have such happiness? One would be the trusted, one the truster; it would be the trusted who would break the link, the truster who would know the numbing unexpectedness of the shock of sudden disillusionment.

Kate began to swim for the beach, calling to Crackers, but he was last out of the water. "I hate to see him out there on his own," Kate said, panting from the swim, and she called loudly to Crackers to hurry up.

"One morning," Molly said, "Kate was here —"

"A little way farther down," put in Kate, pointing along the beach.

"— for her morning swim. With Crackers. A man was throwing a stick into the water for his dog. One moment the dog was swimming, head up, making for the stick, the next he was gone. Just like that."

"All we saw was the dog's head and then a swirl in the water," said Kate, bending to grab Crackers by the collar.

"Heart failure," said Michael. "Dogs get coronaries, too, you know."

"Shark," said Molly.

Crackers shook himself furiously and led them up to the car. They put towels on the seats and Michael drove. The afterglow of that sensation of sudden, unexpected happiness was still with him, disturbing . . .

Archy was home earlier than he'd expected. While they were having drinks Molly said, "I'm going to give you boys a big lunch. Try to keep out of cafes and pubs. And motels. All public places. I've put in enough canned food, beer, and whiskey for a week."

"We won't be that long," said Michael.

"I've put in Ryvita, too, so you won't have to buy bread, and there's wine and lots of water. Make sure you get plenty to eat, Mike. Archy's such a fool."

Archy was only half listening; he had a road map spread out before him and the photostats of Marilyn Petworth's letters. "We'll have to get to Bombala first, Mike. Wallanulla isn't shown on this map." He picked up one of Marilyn's letters and read it for a few minutes. "The trouble is that they did such a hell of a lot of driving around after they got there. All these picnics. One day they went to Jindabyne, to the Reservoir; another to Nimmitabel. Then they went to Bemboka. Bega, Bibbenluke, and they got as far as Eden and Twofold Bay. Marvelous country altogether. The Snowy and the Monaro Ranges —"

"Here," said Molly, "if you don't get on with it you'll never get away. Now finish your beer and come and eat."

During the meal Michael noticed that Kate seemed quieter. He often glanced at her but never quite caught her eye. Archy was full of praise for the beauty of the country they were going to see. "Australia's highest mountain, Kosciusko, is down there, right near Jindabyne. I don't know how high it is exactly, but —"

"It's 7,314," put in Kate, getting up to help Molly clear away the first course.

Archy looked up at Kate. "Wonders will never cease," he said.

"And I won the essay prize."

Michael didn't quite know how it happened that he didn't say good-bye to Kate. He and Archy went ahead to the car, followed by the women and Crackers. There had been a general saying of good-byes, Archy kissed both women and Molly raised her cheek to Michael. Then Crackers had to have a pat. Archy started the car and said, "Come on, Mike, for Christ's sake. We've got a long way to go." Michael couldn't see Kate and looked around, thinking she'd be at Archy's window, but there was no sign of her. Turning back he caught Molly's eye. She gave the slightest shrug, stood back from the car, and called good-bye. Crackers barked and the car began to move. Archy lost no time. Twenty-five minutes later he said, "Now we're on the Prince's Highway."

"How far will this take us?"

"To Melbourne — if we wanted to go that far."

Driving south out of Sydney, Michael soon began to pick up place names Marilyn had mentioned in her letters. Tom Ugly's Point was one of the first, and Michael was surprised at the number of beaches they passed. They got to Sutherland and then bore southwest. It was hot. Archy guessed it to be ninety-five degrees: "Maybe knocking ninety-eight, ninety-nine. Keeps up like this and she'll hit the century in a day or so. Then it might begin to get really hot."

As they drove they decided that while it would slightly delay them in getting to Wallanulla, it would be better to check off each town the Lamberts and Robinsons had stopped at as they came to them now, rather than doing it on the way back. "It really needn't delay us at all," said Archy, "because we can drive at night."

Woollongong was the first town they stopped at. "I made a phone call and picked up a few names this morning. I've got two doctors here," Archy said, turning the pages of his notebook.

They found the post office and Archy made the calls. He came out of the booth, shaking his head. "Neither of them have had cases of anything like influenza. Let's have a beer before we push on."

They also stopped at Kiama. One phone call there. Still negative.

It was dark when they got to Nowra, where Archy made another call. "Negative," he said as he got back into the car. "What say we go on as far as Jervis Bay and then call it a day?" But as it happened they went farther than the big Australian navy base. "All this part here," Archy explained, "is federal capital territory. Same as Canberra." It was pleasantly cool driving at night. Not far from Ulladulla they found a place where they ran the car well off the main road and rolled it to rest under a big blue gum. Archy rigged his electric camping light, which was fed by the car's heavy duty battery, and they got out the camp chairs and ate Molly's sandwiches. "Will we boil the billy?" asked Archy. "Or have beer?" They decided on beer. They were tired and slept heavily on their air mattresses, under their sleeping bags. They woke soon after daylight, and while the billy was boiling they stood breathing in the eucalyptus-scented air. "I've smelt it vaguely ever since I arrived in Australia," Michael said, "but this is really strong now."

"It's the first touch of the sun on the dewy leaves that does it," said Archy. "It's about the most beautiful smell I know, a summer's morning in the Australian bush. You know, Mike," he went on more slowly, "sometimes when I'm in the bush, I think I love Australia as much as I love Molly. And that's about as hard, I reckon, as I can love. It's funny, but you can compare a country to a person. The mixture of good bits and bad bits, easy bits and difficult bits, nice and nasty bits. On the whole, I reckon the good bits about Australia, and Molly, outweigh the bad. I was thinking last night that you could perhaps do worse than stay out here, you know. My word, you could," Archy added earnestly.

"The thought had occurred to me."

"Really?" Archy's face lit with pleasure.

"Bad time, though, to go thinking of the future. You tend to end up asking what future."

"Which brings us," said Archy, "to the job in hand. Let's get cracking. With luck we'll find Wallanulla by tonight."

"You think so?"

"If all goes well we ought to. We'll get to Bega, go inland to Nimmitabel, and then south again to Bombala. That's the way Les Robinson went."

On the way to Bega they stopped at Batemans Bay, Bodalla, and Narooma and went off the Prince's Highway to Bermagui — this was the way Robinson had gone. At all these places they telephoned. If the doctors were out Archy spoke to their wives. "Reports still negative," Archy said. "Though there's some chicken pox about."

"Chicken pox is a strange virus," Michael said some little while later. "What fascinates me is the way it doubles its chances of survival."

"I know," said Archy. "You get it as a kid and that gives you immunity — from chicken pox — but when you're about fifty or sixty it comes up fresh as shingles." He was driving fast and they both had their eyes well on the road. Archy had made this drive before, but to Michael it was a day of revelation. Often they were in sight of the Pacific Ocean, blue and endless under a sizzling sun. At Bega they got their first positive.

"No, not a patient of mine," said the doctor, "and I don't think there's one in Bega. But down at Pambula, that's just south of here, I hear there are two or three cases of a very nasty kind of flu. As a matter of fact, I think a couple have died of it. That wouldn't be the same as they've got in New York, would it? Is it going around somewhere, do you know? Why I'm asking is that it's funny you should ring about this; my eldest boy is a radio ham and a couple of days ago he was talking to one of his friends in New York who told him that a bad flu was going around over there. Have they got the flu up at Sydney?"

Archy said they had. The doctor then said he was a keen fisherman and had a good boat if Archy would like to go out after some of the big stuff. Archy said he wouldn't have the time this trip, thanked him, and rang off.

They were soon in big mountain country, climbing through forests of tall trees, running along rich valleys. Michael heard

[172]

birds he'd never heard before, sat marveling as range after range of blue and purple mountains were revealed. They stopped at two pubs for beer, boiled the billy, and made lunch in the shade of a cider gum. The road ahead of the car shimmered in the heat. "If you want to see the Australian marsupials," said Archy, "you have to go out at night with a torch. All the gliders and possums, some big, some about the size of mice, are nocturnal. The little ones look like paper darts swooping between the trees."

Soon they were into ghost- and snow-gum country, and in the middle of the afternoon they got their first news of Wallanulla. They saw a horseman and pulled up. He was a man of about fifty with a long wrinkled face under a wide-brimmed hat. Horse and rider stank of horse and sweat and leather. Archy asked the question.

"Now let me think," the horseman said slowly. "Wallanulla . . ." He lifted his hat by the brim between thumb and forefinger and scratched his head with his little finger. His mare dropped her head and began cropping the grass. "Y'know, I've heard of it, my word I have," he drawled. "She's somewhere over Bombala way. I ought to know it. I was born at Bombala. I don't reckon she's much of a place," he went on. "Isn't it a station? Yeah, I think it was a station."

"Railway station?" asked Michael.

"No." He did a slight double take as he looked at Michael. "They had horses an' cattle in there once. Look, you're not far from Bibbenluke now," he went on. "Stop an' ask in there. I reckon she might be somewhere between Bibbenluke an' Bombala. Ask at the pub. Or the post office. You mightn't have to go as far as Bombala."

They asked at Bibbenluke, but nobody had heard of Wallanulla. On the way out of the town they stopped and drank a bottle of beer. Archy said he reckoned that the temperature was now over the century. Their shirts were soaking wet.

In Bombala they went to the post office. A middle-aged official said, "Wallanulla isn't really a place at all. It used to be the name of a station. But the homestead is still standing."

Archy said, "Where's the copy of that photo that Marilyn Petworth sent her mother, Mike?"

Archy showed the print to the man behind the counter, who peered at it for a moment, then said, "Wait a minute," and he disappeared through a door at the back of the room. When he came back he said, "I thought it was, but to make sure I asked the wife. That's Wallanulla homestead all right. It's a bit hard to find from here. The nearest place to it is Bidgebyne, which is hardly a place at all really, it's very small. Did you know there's been some sickness over that way?" He looked with some apprehension from Archy to Michael and back again.

"We'd heard something of it, yes," admitted Archy.

The man was silent for a long moment, then he said, "All right, I'll tell you how to get there. Now you take the Delegate road . . ."

An hour later Archy was driving the big car very carefully along a rutted bush road. "I don't even know if we're still in New South Wales," he said. "We might be in Victoria."

Michael had seen the Snowy River and said he thought it would have been much bigger. "No Australian rivers are very wide," said Archy, "except up north, in the wet season. Christ, if the car broke down in here, we'd have some walk to get out. I wonder why Robinson brought them here."

"To show them the great Australian bush," said Michael.

"He showed them that, all right."

Suddenly they came to a two-chain road, not sealed but regularly tended. "This'll be the way into Bidge'," said Archy. The Australian habit of knocking off syllables intrigued Michael.

"The roaring metropolis of Bidgebyne," said Archy about half an hour later. The road widened, shaded by a few gums. On one side was a pub, a single-story wooden building; a hundred yards farther on was a general store, also of wood. Opposite that was a blacksmith's shop and next to it a garage with two hand pumps outside it. A short street ran behind the pub on one side and behind the blacksmith's shop on the other. About eight or nine houses lined the streets. They, too, were of wood, with galvanized iron roofs. Some of them looked as if they had been lived in recently, but none of them as if they were being lived in now. Archy drew up at the pub. They got out and stood in the heat, looking up and down the main street. The hotel was shut. A faint breeze rustled the big round leaves of the gum on the corner.

"It's deserted," said Michael, puzzled.

"Bloody ghost town," said Archy, sounding even more surprised. "That's what it is, mate, a bloody ghost town."

They walked up to the general store. It was shuttered and bolted. The garage, too, was shut, the double doors tied together with a loop of fencing wire. The hard earth in front of the doors was black with oil. Old forty-four-gallon drums were scattered under a stringy-bark tree. The blacksmith's doors hung open. They went in. Spider webs stretched across the forge. In the dark heat at the back of the shop stood an old-fashioned machine with a big handwheel on it. Michael stood staring at it. "They used to have to make one of those before they finished their apprenticeship as blacksmiths," said Archy.

"What's it for?"

"Bending metal, I think." Archy went and stood in the shade just inside the door, looking out at the deserted town. "Rum, isn't it?" he said.

Then they heard the motorbike. They went outside and stood in the shade of the stringy-bark. The bike came slowly down the road. An old man was on it. He wore a greasy felt hat with a fly net rolled up over the brim, a collarless flannel shirt held together at the neck with a brass stud, moleskin trousers patched at the knees, and old military boots. Fine yellow-gray dust covered him, sitting high on the hairs on his sweating forearms. The bike was an ancient BSA, the cylinders sticking darkly out of an oil-and-dust-encrusted mass. It had no front mudguard. Slung over the luggage rack behind was a pair of hessian sugar sacks.

The old man didn't see Archy or Michael, so intrigued was he by the station wagon outside the pub. He stopped the bike, got off slowly, snapped it up onto its stand, and stood looking at the car. Then he felt for a knife, drew a plug of tobacco from the pocket in his shirt, and holding the plug between the thumb and forefinger of his left hand expertly planed a few slices into his palm. In one action he snapped the knife in his right hand shut and with the other transferred the tobacco to his mouth. Then he stood quite still, staring at the car, slowly working the tobacco into a quid.

[175]

He heard Archy and Michael as they left the shade and began to cross the road toward him.

"Arr . . ." he said slowly, turning around, "I was wonderin' where you was."

"Just having a look around," said Archy.

"Wouldn't take you too bloody long to have a look at all there was around here," the old man said.

Archy said, "My name's Nolan."

"So's mine," said the old man.

"Well I'll be damned. This is Dr. Canning."

"Where you from?" The old man squinted at Archy. He had small eyes surrounded by crow's-feet, sharp, dark eyes that reminded Michael of Birdy's.

"Sydney."

"You too?" He looked at Michael.

"He's from England," said Archy.

"Arr . . ."

"Do you live here?" asked Archy.

"Not on your bloody life. See all them houses? Every one of 'em either dead or ratted out. Not that I blame 'em for goin'."

"We're looking for a place called Wallanulla," said Archy. "Do you know it?"

Nolan nodded. "What the hell you want to go there for? She's out this way." He jerked his thumb over his shoulder, shifted his quid, and then spat. The spittle made a little crater in the soft dust. A faint stink of gas drifted from the bike.

"Could you tell us how to get there?" Archy asked.

"I reckon I could." Nolan shifted and spat again. He was plainly not going to ask again why they wanted to go there, but just as plainly Archy saw that they would not get much help from him unless they told him. "Mike," he said, "have you any objections to telling Mr. Nolan what we're here for?"

"None at all," Michael said quickly.

Nolan stood listening, chewing steadily, occasionally nodding his head, from time to time glancing at Michael, sometimes spitting. If they had expected him to show any surprise, or to make any comment when Archy was done, they would have been disappointed. Archy fell silent, and Nolan drew the back of his right

[176]

hand across his mouth and said, "Well, you follow me on the bike, then. But first I got to go to the store an' feed the bitch. She's on heat. When she's over it I'm takin' her out to my place. That's why I ain't got me own dog with me now."

"Tell us," said Archy, nodding around at the deserted township. "How long has this place been like this?"

" 'Bout . . ." Nolan stared at his motorbike, thinking. "Reckon the last of 'em — old Ma Walker — went just over a week ago. She wasn't too sick, though. She went because there was no one else left here in Bidge'. Her son come an' took her into Delegate. Wait 'til I feed the bitch."

They followed old Nolan to the store and then behind it to a shed. "This used to be the kero store," he said. The door was open. A red kelpie, hearing them, came rattling out into the sunlight, chain clanking as she shook herself, tail wagging, whining for joy. While she climbed on him Nolan unsnapped her chain. She bounded about him as they went back to the bike. There he took one of the gunny bags and pulled from it the remains of a cooked leg of lamb on which there was a lot of meat. He put this on the saddle of the bike while he felt about inside the sack, grinning at the bitch, who stood staring up at him with her soft eyes, a trickle of saliva hanging from her mouth. He then pulled out a plastic sack of rough meat trimmings and went back to the shed, the bitch trotting at his heels. He snapped the chain back on her and put the food down. Then he checked her water bowl, patted her, told her he'd be back tomorrow, and said to Archy and Michael, "In a few days she'll be over it an' I'll take her out to my place for good. She used to belong to Jim Pierce, who kep' the store. He an' his missus is dead now, y'see."

"How long ago did they die?" asked Michael.

Nolan spat and then thought for a moment. "Well, Jim died the day Mona got out. It was a Saturday. I reckon she was a couple of weeks ago."

"You're quite sure it was two weeks ago?"

"Yeah, I'm orlright. Because I remember I had a hell of a job gettin' Mona back. She's a bloody remarkable runner."

"Well, now," said Archy, "all the other people who used to live here — you really mean most of them are dead?"

"Too right, I do. Dead or cleared out."

"Would you happen to know when the first of them died?" asked Michael. He noticed that his heart rate suddenly increased; this was the little township Lambert and Robinson had shopped in, drunk beer in. If Julian was right, in all probability Bidgebyne would have been the first place to fall victim to Ringway . . .

Nolan chewed a little and then said, "Well, the first of 'em to croak was Tom Eastwood. He went 'bout . . ." Nolan paused and stared at the ground. "Now I can work this out, I reckon, because I saw Easty in his van 'bout a week before he got crook. You got a calendar on you?" He looked from one to the other.

"Here," said Michael, taking out his diary and handing it to Nolan. The old man opened it, held it well away from him, and began flipping through the pages. Suddenly he grinned, "I heard of Convent Garden," he said. Then, "Now, 'ere you are, first of the month was a Tuesday. That's right because Dave Seymour's dog got bit by a snake an' died the day after, an' Easty tol' me about it. Now I remember that when I heard Easty had croaked I worked out the last time I seen him, an' that was 'bout ten or eleven days before. Eleven, she was. Yeah, Tom died on the eleventh."

"You're absolutely sure?" Michael was trying to hide the excitement he felt. "And sure this man Eastwood was the first of them to die?" Michael looked very hard at old Nolan.

"Course I am." Nolan began to bridle.

"Same day as Pyke died," Michael said.

"Who?" asked old Nolan.

"A man in England," said Michael.

"Arr. Well, I'm sure it was the eleventh orlright. 'Nother reason I remember is because every now an' again I used to do a bit o' work for the Forestry Department that Easty worked for. Well, just before the start o' the month I sees Easty here in Bidge' an' he calls from the ute that they want me to give a hand down the airstrip. That's where they do their forest spraying from. Well, I tol' Easty to tell 'em they could work their job up sideways as far as I was concerned." He paused there. "I had a disagreement," Nolan went on, then spat. "Not with Easty but with one of them Forestry Department scientific codgers after the rats died in my creek, y' see. Yeah, Easty croaked on the eleventh, orlright. An' then his missus dies an' the kids. An' his missus's sister, too, I reckon."

"As long as you're absolutely sure of that date," said Michael.

"Y' still want to go to Wallanulla?" Nolan asked, screwing up his eyes at Archy, ignoring Michael.

But it was Michael who answered. "More than ever," he said.

"Well, you better foller me on the bike," said old Nolan. "I got nothin' much to do at the moment."

Michael thanked Nolan, who patted the bitch again, said something quietly to her, and went back to his motorbike.

The old bike roared into life and Nolan got slowly onto it. "She'll be orlright for the first five or six miles," he shouted to Archy at the wheel of the car. "After that we come to the Wallanulla turnoff an' she'll be a big rough. Orlright on the bike," he added to himself and let in the clutch.

"Bit of luck, finding him," said Archy as the car began to roll.

"Incredible luck," said Michael. "My God, wait until Reece hears about Eastwood dying the same day as Pyke *and* being the first case to die here. He must have caught it directly from Barbara. I wonder if he's the chap who made them the peashooters?"

"Is he mentioned in Marilyn's letters? I've forgotten."

"Not by name, but she speaks of one or two local people and the pilot of the cropduster. And what do you make of what this old chap says about the rats dying in his creek?"

"They'd be water rats, I suppose. I noticed that, too. I don't know much about water rats. They live in the banks of streams, I think. And they may be protected by law."

Big gums lined the road up to Wallanulla homestead. It was closed by a gate that old Nolan rode up to and bumped open with the front wheel of his motorbike. As Archy drove up after the bike Michael felt excitement rising.

They stopped and got out at the spot where Marilyn had taken her photograph. The house was long and low with a corrugated iron roof, a verandah around two sides of it, and the three peppercorns shading part of it. It stood about three feet from the ground on rough-hewn posts capped with sheet iron to stop termites working their way through into the floor timbers. Behind and to the left of it was a barn and a machinery shed; behind them the land ran away into hills that folded into mountain ranges. It was all very tranquil and beautiful, and Michael saw instantly why Les Robinson had wanted to bring his English relatives there.

Nolan snapped his bike onto its stand and came up to them, his head on one side, chewing steadily.

"Why doesn't anyone live here?" asked Archy. "It looks a good house. Isn't the property worked?"

"She's worked," Nolan said. "But when the place was sold up a few years back this 'omestead here was cut off with only a bit of land, about a hundred or so acres, I reckon. That bit, and the house here, was sold to this codger from Sydney who likes ridin' horses and only comes up here for his holidays."

As they walked up to it Michael could feel excitement growing. If they were right, it was just possible that this was the birthplace of Ringway's virus. They were at the back of the house, one end of it dominated by three large corrugated iron water tanks. "Where does the water in those tanks come from?" Michael asked.

"The roof," old Nolan said. "She's rainwater."

It was dead easy to get into the house. The third window they tried lifted. Nolan slipped the large blade of his IXL pocketknife under the bottom of it and worked it up until he could get his fingers under. The sashweights rattled as he threw up the window.

It was dark in the house because the blinds were drawn. It had a hot, shut-up smell. The furniture was well worn, Victorian, some of it good, all of it heavy. On the tongue-and-groove board walls hung colored prints of lakes in mountains that might have been anywhere, or nowhere. There was Landseer's *Stag at Bay* in a black frame.

Michael went to the car and brought back the boxes that held the specimen bottles and envelopes. First he took a sample of the floor dust in each of the rooms, sweeping it up into little heaps, then brushing it into the envelopes and sealing them, one for each room. The room Barbara and Marilyn had slept in was easily identified because it was the only bedroom with a peppercorn tree outside its window, and this tree Marilyn had mentioned in one of her letters. The beds had old-fashioned black iron frames, and there was a dressing-table, a small table under the window, a wardrobe, a chest of drawers, and a couple of chairs. "That's a nice piece of furniture," Archy said, pointing to the chest of drawers. It was of red cedar, made in the early days before Australia's great red cedar stands had been ruthlessly exploited.

Michael spent a long time in this room, taking dust and lint from inside drawers, from the top of the wardrobe, from the wire mattresses. He found two long fair hairs on the fly-wire screen over the window; in the chest of drawers Archy found a pair of laddered tights. "I suppose they'll be Marilyn's," said Archy. "Do you want them?"

"We'll take everything," said Michael. "And I'll get an air sample in this room too. Didn't we see a bucket in the kitchen?"

"I'll get it," said Archy.

Michael took a stoppered bottle of sterile water from the specimen box Archy had provided, stood in the middle of the room, held the bottle upside down over the bucket, pulled out the cork and let the water run into the bucket. When the water had run out the air that replaced it was his sample.

He took water samples from the kitchen and bathroom, first taking the temperature of the water and then sterilizing each tap with a twist of cotton wool soaked in methylated spirits and set fire to. They searched for food scraps but found nothing.

When they'd drawn the blinds again and shut the house, Nolan said, "Where are you two chaps goin' to stay tonight?"

Archy said they'd sleep in the car.

"Why don't you come along to my place?" Nolan suggested. "She's only a humpy, but I got some good stew in the pot. She's about nine miles from here, that's all."

Nolan's humpy consisted of one room on the edge of a creek that ran into the Snowy. Made of battered pieces of corrugated iron, odd lengths of weatherboarding, and unsawn timber, it was shaded by gums. On a bench outside was stretched the skin of a copperhead snake, drying. At the back of the humpy was a vegetable garden with beans climbing up on chicken wire and well-staked tomatoes. Sweet peas in full flower clung to wires near the door, and all was neat and well kept. Down by the water's edge was a setline for fish.

As they parked the car, a Queensland Heeler came bounding

out to meet them, barking wildly. Nolan called him Bluey and told him to shut up. The dog whined with pleasure while Nolan set his motorbike under a shelter made of two pieces of corrugated iron. Then the dog went trotting to the car, the ridge of its back rising. "Don't take no notice of 'im," Nolan shouted. "He don't see many visitors an' he's not used to 'em."

Archy brought out half a dozen bottles of beer and some cans of food. Nolan looked at it. "Y' can leave the beer, but take the tins back."

"That's not fair," said Archy. "We'll eat you out of house and home."

Nolan shook his head. "Not tonight you won't. If you camp here for a few days you can kick in with some tucker, but tonight she's on me."

Inside, the hut, clean and fresh, smelled pleasantly of wood smoke. There was a bunk bed, an old wood-burning stove set back in an iron hearth and chimney; a table in the middle of the room, covered with a plastic cloth, was set on sapling legs buried in the hard-packed earth floor. On the wall was a calendar with the passing days struck off. Near the stove hung a frying pan and saucepans, and an iron pot stood on the stove. Nolan lifted its lid, peered in, and said, "I reckon she's about done." Then he clanked open the fire door, picked up a piece of firewood from the box at one side of the stove, poked around in the fire with it, and finally shot it in. In a few minutes the fire was burning brightly and the sweet scent of burning gum drifted into the room. At the table there were three chairs with molded plywood seats. Above the table hung a Tilley pressure lamp. Near the door hung two hurricane lamps. There were gum boots, too, and a pair of axes with wooden guardboards over their edges. The bed was covered by sugar sacks that had been opened up and sewn together, then washed and bleached until they were almost white; above the bed was a little transistor radio on its own shelf.

Nolan opened two bottles of the beer, brought out glasses, and began pouring. Bluey lay in the doorway, watching. It was late in the afternoon and the shadows were beginning to lengthen. It was very hot and still. This was something Michael was not yet used to: the uncanny silence of the Australian bush.

"Well, here's to yer," said Nolan, raising his glass. "Reckon this won't touch the sides." When he put down the glass it was very nearly empty, as was Archy's. "Now," said Nolan, after he'd re-filled the glasses and sat back with his legs straight out before him, "you reckon this 'ere complaint that's killed 'em at Bidge' might 'a started at Wallanulla, eh?" He had thrown his hat on the bed, and the top of his forehead was startingly white against the darkness and stubble of the rest of his face.

"If the dates you've given us are right —" began Michael.

"See that calendar." Nolan pointed to it. "I cross every day orf as she goes. I'm good on dates."

"Then as the disease was not reported anywhere else earlier, there's not much choice left, is there? Tell me about the rats dying."

"In the creek. Yeah . . ." Nolan took another pull at his beer, wiped the back of his hand across his mouth, and went on. "First time was 'bout six months back. I was workin' for the Forestry, givin' Tom Eastwood a hand on the truck. I got up one mornin' an' as usual went down to see to me setlines and I saw a dead water rat go floatin' past. Then I see another one. An' another. I counted six in all. So when I went to work I took one of 'em with me on the bike and showed it to one of them Forestry scientific codgers. I told him as I reckoned it was the bloody chemicals they was sprayin' from the air, see. He got shirty and told me to mind my own business. I says that it *was* my business. That they had no right to go killin' animals that didn't belong to them. He said there was no reason to think the chemicals were bad just because a few water rats had kicked the bucket. In fact, the joker said outright that the sprays wouldn't hurt animals. But what killed 'em, I asked him. 'Tell me that,' I says . . . 'Scientific bullshit,' I says to him. That's why, when I'd finished out me month, I told Tom Eastwood I wouldn't go back to work for the buggers. I don't have to work for no man, leastways not for any of these scientific no-hopers.

"Here, now just a mo'," Nolan went on, as if suddenly remem-bering something. "I got a cutting from a paper that'll interest you chaps, my word it will." He got up and went to a packing case nailed to the wall above the head of his bed. In it were a few dog-eared paperbacks, an alarm clock, and several rolled oat cans. He took down a tin, fished around inside it, and brought out a newspaper clipping.

"Now here," he said, his eye glinting at Michael as he sat again, "you just listen to this. 'People,'" he began to read, "'living in a forest area of Arizona are suing the United States Government for more than four million dollars, claiming that spraying of defoliants on the forest has caused them medical and other disabilities. One of the complainants has said that women in the district have miscarried and given birth to deformed children because of the sprays. Six kinds of defoliant were sprayed on the Tonto National Forest to destroy brush and improve the flow of water for an irrigation scheme. Ranchers allege that animals drinking from the streams in the forest have given birth to deformed offspring, some species have died out altogether, the earth has become less fertile, and the inhabitants have suffered unexplained illnesses. The complainants also state that medical tests show that some people have enough herbicide residue in their bodies to shorten their expectancy of life. Damages are also being claimed against the company that did the spraying for the government and against the makers of the chemicals.' Now" — Nolan looked up and tossed the cutting onto the table — "what about that, eh? An'," he went on quickly, "somethin' else — I read in a paper the other day that recent studies in America 'aven't been able to find any less DDT in forest soils ten to fifteen years after the last time they used the stuff. You'd think that in fifteen years the bloody stuff'd begin to go away, wouldn't you?" Nolan fixed Michael with his eye. "But 'ere in Australia they're still allowed to use DDT, an' I 'eard one of 'em scientific no-hopers up at the depot say he didn't think DDT did any harm to anything!"

"What were they spraying here for?" asked Michael.

"Christ knows. An' I don't reckon they know either, 'alf the time."

"You don't know the names of the chemicals?"

"Nope. But they're up there, at the depot. At the strip."

"I'd like to see someone at the depot," said Michael. "Where is it?"

"Up at Browning's Junction. But there's nobody there now.

[184]

They only open it when they're goin' to spray, an' they've stopped it now."

"Would the chemicals still be there?"

"Well, they might be," Nolan said slowly. "Unless they come an' took them away. If you like, we could run up there in the mornin' an' take a gander."

Michael opened his mouth to say he would like that, very much, but no word came. Archy saw Michael's mouth open, saw the startled look on his face. Then Michael said, "Archy, look — for Christ's sake! —"

Archy jumped to his feet, staring in the direction that Michael was pointing to, under Nolan's bed.

Suddenly Nolan, too, leaped up. "Holy Moses!" he shouted, "shut the wire!" and he bounded for the door. Bluey yelped and shot outside as Nolan hurled himself at the wire door and banged it shut. "That give me a start," he said, coming back to the table and sitting down again with obvious relief. "What with us not bein' used to visitors I clean forgot about Mona." He picked up his glass and began to drink again. When Archy saw what Michael was pointing at he shot around to the other side of the table.

"She's 'ungry," said old Nolan. "That's orl. She'd give you a nasty nip, though. Fancy me forgettin' to close the wire. She'd have got out sure as God made little apples."

"It's an iguana!" said Archy.

A huge lizard was now emerging from under the bed. Michael had never seen anything like it. It looked incredibly dry and dusty, its skin seemingly so loose on it that there would be room for another iguana inside. It fixed the two men with a glittering eye, and as it moved it rasped on the hard earth of the floor. "She won't hurt you," said Nolan. "She's 'ungry, that's orl."

"I've never seen such a thing," said Michael. "It's enormous."

"I 'ad a bigger one than 'er once," said Nolan proudly. "Ever see 'em run? Blimey, they can go. An' y' know what, if an iguana bites you, every year on the anniversary of the bite the wound opens again. Practically impossible to cure, an iguana bite is."

"I think they scavenge," said Archy. "So they've probably got pretty dirty mouths."

"Now come on and sit down," said Nolan. "You'll make 'er nervous, standin' up like that. Orlright, you old halligator," Nolan went on, smiling at the iguana, looking at her over the top of the table. "I'll give you some tucker afore bedtime."

"I think I'll sit on your side of the table," Archy said to Michael.

"An' I'll tell you somethin' else about them, too," said Nolan. "There's nothin' in the world better for a touch of rheumatism than a good rub with iguana oil." He looked over the table at Mona again, his face cracking into a smile. "But it's orlright, old girl, we ain't got rheumatism."

Nolan's stew was excellent. By nine o'clock the last light was out, and they went to sleep listening to the call of the mopoke. Nolan cooked them fish for breakfast, redfin from the creek, and by half past eight they were at the Forestry Department depot.

"Y' goin' to break in 'ere, too, then?" Nolan said as he got out of the car.

It was very obviously a government building, standing at one end of a grass landing strip and made of green weatherboard; it was surrounded by a cyclone fence, six feet high, also painted green. There were two sets of double gates to the enclosure, one opening on to the strip, the other onto the dirt road. Both were chained with heavy brass padlocks. As they went through the calf-high grass Nolan said, "Watch out where you put your feet. I dunno why, but there's always a lot of snakes around here."

He led them behind the enclosure, walking along the fence, peering at it closely. Finally he stopped. "Here she is." He drew from the hip pocket of his moleskins a pair of pliers. "One of them bloody scientific no-hopers lost the key one day an' we had to cut a hole in the fence here." The opening had been rolled back into place and tied with wire. With his pliers Nolan untwisted the ties. He held the fencing back while Archy followed Michael into the enclosure.

They found the window in the end wall open; the glass was broken and it appeared to have been forced. Nolan stood looking at it, chewing, his head cocked on one side. "There's a lot o' flies around that 'ole," he said. "I don't like that."

Archy got through, disappeared; in a moment his head appeared. "We're going to need strong stomachs," he said. "There's a dead man in here. Wait and I'll see if I can open the door from inside."

Archy opened the door and they stood looking at the body of a man propped against the wall in the room with the broken window. "He's been dead a good ten days," Archy said. He looked at Nolan. "Do you know him?"

Nolan shook his head slowly, went to the window, and spat through it. "I dunno," he said. "Even his mother wouldn't know him now."

"What are we going to do about him?" Archy said.

"Nothing for the time being," said Nolan. "Here, you get on with whatever you want to do and let's get outa the bloody place."

"Should we notify the police?" said Michael.

"You do what you come to do," the old man said stubbornly. "Then we can decide what to do about him. If anythin'. We go to the johns, they'll start askin' what we were doin' here."

"Well, listen, Mr. Nolan," said Archy, "don't you touch anything — fingerprints, see."

"Ah, the police won't do much. He's probably some swaggy and it'll be what they call natural causes. For want of a better name," he added, and he led them through to the middle room where a number of drums were stacked. "That's the stuff they been spraying," he said, pointing to the drums.

There were four different chemicals. Michael wrote down their names and then said he wanted samples. He went to the car and brought back some plastic sacks. As he was filling and labeling them Nolan said, "Where you sendin' all these samples?"

"England," said Michael. "I'm taking no chances. We want to know exactly what's in them, not just what's printed on the outside of the drums. If this stuff has been sprayed around here, it might be in the Wallanulla homestead water tanks."

"It'd be there all right," said Nolan. "Wallanulla was the end of the southern run when they were sprayin'. I seen it myself."

"Seen what?" said Michael.

"I seen the plane come over the 'omestead with her sprays workin'. We was down there, Easty an' me, one day when the plane was sprayin', with one of those scientist chaps. The plane come right in an' sprayed right over the 'ouse. Course the spray would be in the water at Wallanulla. It'd be on the roof, right? An' the first rain would wash it into the tanks. Why, I reckon the dew at night would be just about enough!"

# 9

Birdy was expostulating with great vehemence. "It's all bloody well to have a perfectly feasible plan, but plans need people to carry them out. You can't assume you're going to have an uninfected half of the population able to minister to the infected half. Yet if you don't make such an assumption you can't plan. The social disorganization that takes place in great pandemics is fantastic. It's quite different from what happens when people are bombed. There is the same interruption to water and power and food supplies. But whereas bombing strengthens a people's resolve — the only people never to learn that are the unbombed Americans — an epidemic saps it. Read any account of the great pandemics and compare it to intelligence reports on great classical bombing raids such as Dresden, London, Hanoi — virtually anywhere — and you'll see that." Molly interrupted the flow to call Michael to the phone. "It's London," she said. "Sir Julian Reece."

"The Wallanulla samples," Michael told Julian. "I've packed them in three strong wooden boxes. Water, air, dust, lint, chemicals — everything I could find there. Qantas has sworn they'll be leaving here on their first flight out. That should be in about an hour from now. There'll be a crew change somewhere along the flight, but our boxes will be the captain's personal responsibility. Now, here's the flight number to ask for at Heathrow . . ."

"Cycogel I've heard of," said Julian. "It's a fairly well known growth suppressant, and I would have said it was harmless enough. The other sprays I don't know."

"What should I do now?" asked Michael.

"Oh, stay there, please. This is only a beginning. You'll be available at Nolan's?"

"Yes. Are there any more cases?"

"It's uncanny the speed at which it's spreading. Yet people can't seem to grasp it. Which I suppose isn't all that surprising. Cook tells me they're beginning to get worldwide confirmation of it now. On the whole, governments seem to be cooperating, but it all takes so much *time*." Michael thought Julian sounded very tired.

"What about quarantine?"

"Well, we're about to begin to close off large centers here. Or try to. It's now in the newspapers. Though the government has slapped a kind of D notice on them, asking them to keep off it as far as possible until the WHO international warning comes out. That shouldn't be long now. Birmingham is already badly hit and it's reached Glasgow. Cook tells me there are signs of panic in Rome and Madrid. So far nothing like that here, thank God. The supply problems look like being insoluble — I mean things like electricity, food, milk, gas. They're planning to close the schools here as soon as the WHO international warning comes out. Cook says Geneva isn't going to wait for all countries to agree to issue a warning. If they don't get full approval they'll go ahead anyway. It's the countries riddled with bureaucracy that cause the trouble . . .

"The Institute? Oh, I didn't consult anyone about that. I've got a tight quarantine here now. You remember that warehouse next door to us that was empty? Well, we've taken that over. We've banged a hole through into it and staff are going to sleep in there. They're in quarantine at Mill Hill, too, and Cook tells me Geneva is now urging all laboratories working on it to do the same.

"Our football fixtures have been canceled. Not soon enough, I'd say, but then, that's part of the inertia. Pitches, stadiums, racecourses, and camping sites are being turned into isolation centers . . . Time, that's the problem. The official mind needs time to function. Civil servants — and most politicians — have got where they have by vacillation; but this is not like a war where they can have time and opportuniy for a splendid load of patriotic spouting about their backs being to the wall. This is a *real* emergency. To these people, writing minutes — as they call them — to one another is more important than *doing* anything. Some of them, usually those who have seen someone die — and are therefore themselves doomed — do appear to recognize the danger."

"My God," said Michael, "it sounds ghastly. Nothing like that here yet —" and he gave Julian a quick rundown on the reported Australian cases.

Michael came back from the telephone and told them what Julian had said.

"Caulfield crabs," grunted Birdy.

"What are Caulfield crabs?" asked Molly. "Talking of crabs, Birdy, are you stopping for lunch?"

"I know," said Kate, "you boil them."

"When the war broke out," said Birdy, "they shoved me into a uniform, told me I was a captain, and before I went overseas they shot me down to Melbourne, to the Caulfield racecourse. That was one of the places you had to report to when you were first called up. In one of the latrines some wag had scrawled, 'No use to kangaroo this seat. Caulfield crabs jump nineteen feet.'"

Molly cried, "You don't deserve lunch."

"Sorry," said Birdy, grinning.

"Filthy little man," said Kate.

"Give him," Archy said, "shellfish."

"James the First," said Birdy, "said he was a bold man who first swallowed an oyster. But Reece is right. For years I've tried to get officials interested. The official mind is a simple one. It might be devious but it's simple, and being simple I've always tried to put problems in the plainest possible form. Years ago they warned us — one of them was Professor J. R. A. McMillian, right here in Sydney — there just wasn't enough water for man to survive unless he became largely vegetarian with the population growing the way it was. I did my best in official quarters to get facts like this across. I told them that to make just one car you need forty-five thousand gallons of water; that to grow enough wheat to make *one*, just one, loaf of bread, you need *two and a half* tons of water — but they still weren't getting the message. A ton of water is needed to enable a fowl to lay *one* egg." Birdy went on. "Most of what we read in the newspapers is crap anyway, yet it takes two hundred and forty thousand gallons of water to make one ton of newsprint."

"It's a change," said Kate.

"What's a change?" he said.

"You're usually sounding off on the more violent side of man's nature."

"Christ," Birdy grunted, "what could be more violent than destroying our water resources? Katie, you like steak. Right! It takes fifty tons, *fifty*, mark you, of water to make one, *one*, pound of meat."

That afternoon Archy went to the hospital. Molly said, "Why don't you two go for a swim? Mike has been on the go ever since he left London."

"Yes, let's," said Kate.

They changed, Michael putting on trunks and a terrycloth shirt while Kate changed into her bikini and pulled a dress over it. Kate drove, and when they got going, "Mike," she said, "if, I say only *if*, but if this disease is really going to spread, what will I do with Crackers?"

"In the plague," he said, "and I quote: 'in the dwellings encumbered with corpses, wild beasts and dogs took up their abode.'"

"You know a lot about the plague, don't you."

"As an epidemiologist I've always been interested in it."

"So I have to put Crackers down, do I?"

"If you want your *i*'s dotted, yes."

Kate was silent, absorbing this. Then she said, "We're going to swim on a little half-moon of beach I used to go to but haven't for quite a while. I'd given it up because I used to take the kids there. And sometimes on hot summer mornings, early, just before dawn, Tom and I . . ." Her voice died. She was driving well, rather fast, Michael thought, but well . . . She went on, "On those hot nights, just before dawn we used to make love and then come

[*192*]

down here to this particular beach and swim. Listen, Mike, isn't Saint Rock, or Rochus, or whatever he's called, the patron saint of people suffering from the plague?"

"And of dogs," said Michael.

"It's not far now," she said. Then, as she swung the car around a corner and let it begin to sweep down a curving road, she added, "Can I ask you a question?"

"But of course."

"You sound terribly English when you say that."

"*Terribly* English?"

"Very English."

She was concentrating on her driving, pulling the car into a narrow parking place under trees where the air was suddenly cool under the shade. Crackers leaped out and went streaking down to the water, sand kicking up behind him. She pulled on the hand-brake. "You're not married, are you?"

"No, but if you want to know if there's someone, yes, there is," he said.

"You don't frighten easily, do you?" She was leaning forward, looking down over the front of the car watching Crackers standing stiff-legged in the shallows, looking up at them, waiting.

"I've had my share of scares," he said. "Why?"

"And plenty of women?"

"Again, I've had my share."

"Loved them?"

"*Liked* them. I've got to like them. No good otherwise."

"I suppose not. And how many have you loved? Really *loved*, I mean."

"Two."

She opened the car door, got out, and in one smooth action pulled her dress over her head and stood full-breasted in her bikini. "Race you into the water," she said. He pulled off his shirt and tossed it into the car.

"Wait!" Kate called. "I've got to put on my cap."

But Michael had started to run.

Crackers bounded about in the shallows, barking. Michael hit the water and dived. She caught him as he broke surface. "You cheated!" she called. "You started before I did."

He tried to dodge but she was on him, ducking him. He came

[*193*]

up spluttering, throwing back his head. "There!" she cried. "That's what we do to cheating Pommies," and she swam away from him powerfully, Crackers paddling after her. Then she rolled onto her back. "Oh," she shouted, "isn't summer wonderful? Isn't water wonderful? Why isn't life all summer and sea? And dogs like Crackers!" Crackers caught up with her and began nuzzling her, licking her face, making her shout with laughter so that Michael didn't hear what else she said.

"Keep an eye out for sharks," she called when he came up with her.

"Thank you very much," he said.

"Actually," she said, "we're probably a little too far out. Let's go in nearer the beach. At this time in summer they come into Sydney harbor to breed, but they prefer steeply shoaled rocky places. But as far as I know, only one person has ever been taken on this beach." She called Crackers, and they swam in slowly until they were only just out of their depth.

By the middle of that afternoon the temperature was over a hundred degrees.

"I am a turtle . . ." Kate said and rolled onto her back and floated. " 'When turtles tread . . .' "

"Not the withered bough again?" he said.

"Nope." She dropped her legs, let herself under, and popped up beside him. "I am treading, see?" Again she dropped her legs, shooting straight down, then came popping to the surface, shaking the water from her face, laughing at Crackers, who swam around and around her barking. "He can't bear to see me disappear under the water like that."

" 'When shepherds pipe on oaten straws' . . . Michael, get me an oaten straw, will you? I've always wanted an oaten straw."

"You shall have several."

" 'And merry larks are ploughman's clocks. When turtles tread . . .' I *am* a turtle! Look at me treading. Oh, I am *so* happy."

"And what about the rooks?"

"Oh *good*, you know it. '. . . and rooks, and daws. And maidens bleach their summer smocks . . .' " She stopped there and laughed at him. "I feel like a crazy idiot!"

"You're very lovely," he said.

She swung about quickly, calling to Crackers, and as he came paddling up to her she started in to the beach.

At the car she said. "When we get to Molly's we'll have tea. I'll make a batch of scones. They can cook while we're showering."

They ate hot buttered scones and drank tea in the kitchen. Kate gave Crackers his second scone and Molly said, "You'll make that dog fat." Kate didn't look at Molly but continued to watch Crackers.

Michael guessed what she was thinking. "In the plague," he said. Then he stopped, realizing he was perhaps about to say the wrong thing.

Kate looked at him. "In the plague? Go on, what were you going to say? Something in defense of dogs, I hope."

"I was going to say that in the plague the dog was the only creature that remained faithful to the end. The literature is full of legends and stories of the devotion of dogs."

"But surely of people, too," said Molly.

"No," he said. "One of the most terrible consequences of the fear of infection was that the sick were forsaken. Even by their nearest and dearest. Trust, faithfulness, love, all evaporated. People died the loneliest of deaths. Children called for their mothers, husbands for their wives, lovers for the beloved, in vain."

"It's the one thing that frightens me about dying," said Kate. "I can't bear the thought of dying alone. I want someone to be there, to tell me it's going to be all right. I'm the opposite to the animal that crawls away into some dark place to die on its own. I want plenty of light around me. What I'd really like would be someone to go with me."

"But mightn't this neglect of loved ones," Molly said, "have been part of a social pattern of the time? I can't imagine leaving Archy. Especially if he was dying."

"It's one of the curiously characteristic aspects of the plague," said Michael. "Centuries after the first pandemic, in the plague of London in 1665, it was the same. When it finally passed and a general cleaning of the houses began, decomposed bodies were found everywhere — on floors, in beds, on stairways, in attics and cellars. They'd virtually all died alone. A great, explosive epidemic is extraordinarily morally degrading. For instance, the men who collected the bodies and pushed the corpse carts around were from a poor and deprived section of society. And they had never had it so good. They had access to the richest houses, and they carried off plate, gold, jewels, everything of value, often piling it on the corpse of its late owner. There was nobody to stop them doing whatever they wanted to do, and because it was good for their business, they tried to spread the plague, too. They smeared pus from the buboes over door frames and on eating and drinking vessels that they hoped people would touch."

"But these people must have caught the plague, too," said Kate.

"Of course. That's the point I'm making about the moral degradation. People knew they would more than probably die of it, but that didn't stop them from committing what we would regard as socially unacceptable or criminal acts. Not only were women and girls, and boys, too, raped as they lay dying, but the violation of corpses was commonplace. Often done in public. Once sanctions are removed from social behavior, it doesn't take people long to break down the barriers that keep them law-abiding. Look at ordinary decent soldiers, for instance, in a captured town."

"I think I'd have committed suicide," said Kate.

"Well, many did," said Michael. "And many went mad with horror, and of course pain — threw themselves from windows or hanged themselves; often they'd rush out to the great communal graves that were dug outside the towns and throw themselves in. Others had to be battered to death when they went berserk. Uninfected people often went mad, too, because of the general horror about them, the streets littered with decomposing bodies.

"But it may have done some good, too, you know," he went on. "It shook the very foundations of the rigid caste system of medieval times, and, perhaps more important, it produced a consciousness of the equality of all men before God that probably hastened the Reformation. Even cardinals and bishops remained unburied and were eaten by starving dogs, a fact that didn't go unnoticed."

"But surely we're more civilized now," said Molly.

"I doubt that —"

"You mean if Ringway's disease spreads we'll see scenes like that?" asked Kate.

"I don't think we've changed all that much," Michael said slowly. "Look what the Germans did to the Jews; that's during our lifetime. Look what the Americans have done in Indochina."

"Would you commit suicide?" Kate asked Michael.

"I don't think so."

"Why not? If you knew there was no hope," Molly said.

"It's not that I disapprove of it — quite apart from whether I'd have the guts to do it. But I think it's a bit different for a doctor. And for a priest. For them it would be the ultimate recognition of failure."

"Would you help another to kill himself?"

"A doctor's not supposed to."

"But they do," said Molly. "I've been a nurse, don't forget."

"In the sense that a doctor will withhold purely palliative treatment in a terminal illness where there's no possible hope of recovery, yes."

They were sitting on the terrace in the shade. In spite of the heat they were all feeling restless and uneasy.

"The radio," Molly suddenly said. "I'll get the portable." She hurried inside. Molly returned with the radio, which was blaring nondescript music. As she set it on the table the music died away and an announcer cut in:

"Here is an important government announcement. Since one o'clock Eastern Standard Time today, when the federal Department of Health in Canberra released the text of a worldwide epidemic warning issued by the World Health Organization in Geneva, Australian state and federal health authorities have been holding urgent discussions on the most effective means to combat the threat. State health departments are now receiving details of an illness described as a form of influenza known as Ringway's disease, which in the last few weeks has spread rapidly through the British Isles, the continent of Europe, the USA, Africa, and Russia and is now confirmed as having appeared in Australia and New Zealand.

"Special warning will be broadcast on all radio and television stations, urging people to avoid public places. In a statement just released, the federal Ministry of Health stresses the need to remain calm and says that it will shortly be announcing the precautions the government intends to take to prevent the spread of the disease. Among immediate measures to be taken, vigorous health checks are to begin at all Australian sea- and airports. Please listen for further announcements."

The announcer stopped.

"Is that the end of it?" asked Kate.

"Short and sweet," said Molly, "like a donkey's trot."

"Mike," Birdy said that evening, "I'm secretary of the local branch of the AMA. Would you come and give our members a talk on what you know about the Ringway virus?"

"I should have thought," said Kate, "that a doctor's trade union would have been the first to comply with the government's request not to congregate."

"This is different," said Birdy, though for the moment he was taken aback by Kate's logic.

"If you think it will help," said Michael.

"Men are so stupid," said Kate, and she stalked off the terrace.

"I must say," Molly said, "there is something in what Katie says."

Birdy looked at Michael and was about to speak when Molly jumped to her feet and said, "We'll miss the news," and she crossed to the terrace table and switched on the radio.

". . . cases have now been reported as far south as Hobart and as far north as Townsville. The minister said that stringent measures must be taken to isolate those suffering from the disease. While there was cause for grave concern, he said, he was confident that there would be no panic. Planning to provide emergency isolation centers is already well advanced.

"As announced earlier, it is hoped that anti-infection masks will soon be made available. These will be distributed by local government authorities. Do not — repeat, do not — call at your local shire or town hall for these masks. They will be delivered to householders as they become available. Until this distribution takes place, people are advised to make their own masks. If possible they should be made of surgical gauze, large enough to cover the lower part of the face, including the nostrils. If gauze is not available, any fairly porous cloth can be used as a temporary substitute. Masks should be worn at all times."

"Oh, balls," said Birdy. "Fat lot of good *that'll* do."

"Have you got any gauze?" asked Molly.

Archy said, "I'll bring some masks home from the hospital."

". . . and," the radio went on, "in neighboring Yugoslavia along the Dalmatian coast. Elsewhere, French and Spanish news sources report a growing number of isolated outbreaks, so far largely confined to well-known tourist centers. It is also reported that cholera has appeared in the Spanish tourist resort of Marbella. In the Sicilian capital of Palermo ten policemen and about thirty people were injured when a mob attacked an outpatient department of a local hospital. It is believed the rioting began after a rumor spread that doctors in the hospitals were leaving their posts and fleeing into the surrounding countryside. Many arrests are reported . . ."

After the broadcast warnings what surprised most people was the speed with which the general public reacted in those first few days. Rumor spread news of cases when none existed. Shopkeepers noticed an immediate drop in turnover as fewer people went out. Some shops and hotels closed, and three days after the warning Archy came home and said he wasn't imagining it, there were definitely less people about on the streets. "And on the beach," said Molly. "Kate and I took Mike to Bondi today. It was practically deserted."

There was no panic in Sydney. Nor, at first, did there seem to be many people who actually knew someone who had caught the disease. But there was a curious air of expectancy. Molly summed it up by saying, "It's not that I don't believe it's possible — I suppose anything is possible — it's just too big and too overwhelming to visualize. It's like trying to imagine a star one hundred million light years away. You believe it's that far away, but you can't imagine it, not really. How many cases have you actually heard of?" she asked Archy.

"A few," he said cautiously.

"Not many people are wearing masks yet," she said.

"One does feel a bit of a fool in one," he said, "but you ought to wear them."

"We did when we went to Bondi today," said Kate. "I felt an utter fool. I almost went into the water with it on."

Birdy rang that night and asked to speak to Michael. "Mike," he said, "about your talk to the AMA. The suggestion is that we call an extraordinary meeting for tomorrow night. We don't know how many doctors we can get together at such short notice, but the committee really thinks it might be useful to hear your first-hand experience with Ringway's. You're still prepared to do it?"

"Yes."

"Tomorrow evening then, at eight."

Grim-faced, mostly silently, the doctors filed out of the meeting. Any who were inclined to regard the warnings as somewhat overdone — and before the meeting there had been some — were now left in no doubt. Michael's clinically dispassionate account of the swiftness with which the disease struck and killed found quick support. One doctor rose and spoke of the first cases at Mosman. Then came another, a woman, who said she knew of nine in the Isolation Block, the Charles Chubbe House at the Royal Alexandra Hospital for Children at Camperdown. Another said he knew of about twenty at the Royal Prince Alfred Hospital. One spoke of at least seventeen deaths at the Mater Misericordiae Hospital in North Sydney. There were over thirty in the Manly District Hospital. Others in the Fairfield District Hospital. More in the Prince Henry and the Prince of Wales, both teaching hospitals of the University of New South Wales. About twenty had died at the Randwick Chest Hospital, another fifteen or so at the South Sydney Women's Hospital, and perhaps a dozen at the Saint George Hospital at Kogarah. The Women's Hospital in Crown Street had admitted "many" ("How many?" someone asked — "About twenty-five, but that in only the last five or six days"). The Canterbury District Memorial Hospital, the Lottie Stewart Hospital, and Our Lady of the Sacred Heart Hospital in Randwick were also names Michael heard mentioned.

Neither Archy nor Michael spoke until they were in the car. "Now," Archy said, "I can *really* believe in it. Coming out of that was like coming out of a requiem mass."

[200]

"So," said Kate, when Archy, Birdy, and Michael got home, "with all those doctors there, how do you know that you three are not harboring this damned thing?"

"We don't," grunted Birdy.

"Men really are such bloody fools," went on Kate angrily. "Especially doctors. The trouble with doctors is that they think themselves Christ Almighty. As a profession you're probably the most narrow-minded of the lot. So you think you can't get it, do you?" Kate's eyes flashed from one to the other of the men.

Molly said quickly, "It won't help your losing your temper, Katie."

"At least I can get it off my chest. We'll probably all get it now."

"But Kate," said Archy, "this wasn't overlooked —"

"You all had your silly little masks on, I suppose."

"I do see your point," Archy went on, "but we're not quite the fools you seem to think us. Every man there this evening was only there after he'd given his word that he had not knowingly, professionally or otherwise, come in contact with a case of Ringway's. And given that word to a committee member over the telephone. True, Birdy, you did some of the phoning, didn't you?"

Birdy said, "Sure, it's true, Katie."

"You say every *man* there," said Kate. "Weren't there any women doctors present?"

The men were silent for a moment, thinking, then Michael said, "I only saw one woman, I think." He looked at Birdy.

"Only one," Birdy agreed. "I might as well tell you, Kate, you'll only worm it out of me if I don't. I don't know how many women the other committee members rang, but I phoned a good half dozen. None of them said they could come."

"Why?" asked Kate. "Because they'd been in contact with it?"

Birdy shook his head. "They said they wouldn't come," he said finally, "because they didn't think we ought to be holding the meeting."

For a long moment Kate continued to stare at Birdy. Then she gave a toss of her head, turned, and walked off the balcony into the house.

# 10 〜〜〜〜〜〜〜〜〜〜〜〜〜〜〜〜〜〜〜〜〜〜〜〜

Later, looking back on their early period in the village, Elizabeth and Steve came to see the day of Elizabeth's despair as marking a nadir, an all-time low of the spirit, while for Steve it marked the beginning of his return to health.

The next day Steve woke late and felt — as he put it — "a bit groggy." But his pulse was stronger and his color better. He also felt hungry. He asked for tea, and Elizabeth used one of the bags from the carton she'd found in the wreck of the galley. After that she tempted him with a papaw, and he ate half.

The next day his improvement continued. She made another pillow by stuffing a folded floor mat with fern fronds and got him sitting up straighter. "I sure would like a shave," he said, rubbing his hand over the graying stubble on his jaw and cheeks. "This itches like all get-out."

"It'll stop itching when it gets longer," she said.

"Never had a beard. I guess," he went on more slowly, "before we get out of this there'll be quite a few things that haven't happened to me before. Say, last night I got to thinking — how much longer do you figure it'll be before old sawbones lets me try walking on his handiwork?"

"I've been wondering that, too," she said, smiling at him.

"I can move it better every day now. And this morning when they took me to the john it didn't hurt half so much."

It was Elizabeth who made the decision to let Steve stand for the first time. Under mounting daily pressure from him the morning came when she said, "Very well. But only to stand, mind. Not to walk."

Carefully she helped him until he was sitting on the edge of the platform, his grotesquely splinted and leaf-wrapped leg straight out before him. He was heavy for her, and far weaker than he thought he'd be, but finally they managed to get him standing. "Baby, this is just *great*," he said, his eyes swimming with pleasure.

"Soon you'll be able to walk as well as ever you did."

"Here, honey, let me try one step now, will you?"

"Tomorrow. Perhaps we'll get you standing again this afternoon."

Next day he took a few steps, leaning on her heavily. "I'm a big guy," he said anxiously.

"I'm big enough for you," she said.

"My good leg's shaking like hell. I feel dizzy, too."

"We'll have to think up some exercises for you." She got him back to the bed; he lay breathing hard from the effort and, for the first time, his defenses were down. His stubborn refusal to let her see his doubt about their being found had, she saw, hidden until that moment some of his humanity. Then had come the pride in his achievement in taking those few steps and it had lowered the barrier. Sitting there by him on the bed, she began to share his pride — and she, too, felt the spiritual weakness it brought. "You're a very clever man," she said softly, and she leaned over and kissed him quickly on the lips. He moved his hand to touch her arm but she got up quickly, not wanting him to see the tears in her eyes. "I think," she said, turning away from him, "that being as good and as clever as you are means you win a drink."

He watched her, smiling, and said, "How much whiskey have we got left?"

"One whole bottle." Then she added, "And a half-empty one."

"Now there," he said, "that's the difference between us, honey."

His eyes were brighter than she'd seen them. "I'd have said a half-full one."

Somehow she got Boar's Tusk to understand what she meant by crutches for Steve. It took a couple of days, but finally he brought them and, she saw, they weren't new. If they had had them, Elizabeth asked, "Why didn't he just bring them up?"

"Maybe they don't figure I'm ready yet."

"You're not, really, I suppose. But I want to get you moving a bit now. You can come and sit on the little porch outside the door and watch what's going on in the village. And there's a lovely view down the valley. There are girls, too; some of the young ones are quite pretty. With their little bare breasts," she said. Then she added, "And soon they won't be the only topless types about here, either."

"Hell, I'm already topless. Maybe you should keep one of those dresses until the government patrol officer finds us. Can you see your interview headlined in the British newspaper? Quote, I knew I had to be decently attired when the Queen's representative found us, end quote, says rescued Englishwoman."

"The Queen," she said, "doesn't have any representatives left."

"Seriously," he said "in the right climate there's nothing quite so good as walking about with no clothes on. And socially it's the greatest leveler there is."

"I'm told it dampens sex."

"Baby, if you're a man who likes women, or a woman who likes men, nothing — almost nothing — can dampen sex."

The first time Elizabeth helped Steve to the ground from the low end of the house caused almost as much excitement in the village as their arrival. The pygmies had become used to seeing Elizabeth about the village, but for Steve's emergence most of them seemed entirely unprepared. Naked except for his underpants, the whiteness of Steve's body after being in the shade of the house exaggerated not only his size but the difference in his color. The women crowded shyly about him, the tallest of them barely reaching to his chest.

Then, as Steve was able to spend more time out of the house, they began to learn more about the pygmies. He pointed out that though they were small they weren't stunted. "If they were of our race they'd be midgets," he said. "See that development of their calves and buttocks, it's solid muscle; and they walk so easily, that swinging gait with the knees slightly bent and the body leaning forward. They're so obviously a mountain people."

The satchels they wore intrigued Steve and Elizabeth. One day Boar's Tusk showed them the contents of his small one: pieces of shell, ornaments made of the claws of birds, several small stone knives, and a dagger made of a long thin bone that Steve thought was probably a cassowary's. In the big bag was his sleeping mat, tobacco, and fire stick. He was proud of these possessions and Elizabeth said this to Steve. "I wish," she added, "we could talk to him."

Steve said, "It's one hell of a language. Those high-pitched sounds in the nose, along with all those throat noises and glottal stops. And have you noticed how they protrude their lips for some sounds?"

"I couldn't be certain," Elizabeth said, "but I think I know the name of this place. It sounds something like Wimberi or Winberiberi. But how strange we must seem to them. At least we know there are other races, people as different-looking from us as Japanese and Negroes are, but I don't think they've ever seen a white person before." She fell silent, suddenly aware of the significance of the remark.

"Sure they've seen white people," he said quickly. "Why, I bet a regular government patrol comes through here at least once a year. Don't let it get you down, we'll be found."

"We've still not heard one searching aircraft."

"We can hope, honey. Even a beggar must have hope. And think how well off we are. Why, we could have gone down in some part where there weren't any people. Do you realize just how wild this country is? Much of it must be absolutely uninhabited. And if we're not found, why, when this leg of mine is better we'll walk out. For all we know the sea might be only a few days' walk away. Some of these people have seashells as ornaments —"

"And have you noticed how old and how worn those seashells are?" she said softly.

Steve had no answer to that because he'd noticed that the few shells he had seen looked as if they'd been worn for generations.

"I'm not bitching, Steve," she said, smiling at him. "Don't worry, I won't go into a decline because I know our chances of ever getting out are a million to one against."

"I told you, even a beggar has to have hope and we're not beggars. We've got a dry house, all we can eat. We've even got a drink. Where's your stiff upper lip? I thought you English had an upper lip so stiff you could open beer bottles with it."

They began to give names to the people they saw every day. Boar's Tusk kept his name because they seldom saw him without it. They thought they could identify his wife and that her name sounded something like Kiri. They began to be invited into houses where they would sit, with the men mostly, smoking and listening to them talk. Usually the men smoked cigarettes, the tobacco in a wrapper made from a thin slip of pandanus leaf. The tobacco was strong, but when Steve tried it he found it quite pleasant. Some of them smoked it in a pipe, a straight length of bamboo into which a plug of tobacco was jammed at one end, the other being held almost upright in the mouth. One of the younger men with a name that began with a sound something like Hicock — Steve dubbed him Wild Bill — played a kind of Jew's harp, made of a thin piece of split bamboo. They soon found that others, too, played this instrument, but Wild Bill appeared to be something of a virtuoso and was listened to when the others were not. Another instrument was made of two pieces of polished bone fitted together in such a way that when one was rotated over the other an extraordinarily discordant squeak came out of it. Wild Bill made a Jew's harp for Steve, and when Steve finally mastered it — the sound it made was very faint — one of the *castrati*, as Steve called those who played the bones, came and played with him, producing the most peculiarly discordant squeaks as accompaniment while staring with such dour, rapt attention into Steve's face that Elizabeth had to hurry up the ladder and get inside their house before she burst out laughing. "From now on," Steve said when he joined her later, "I'm calling that guy Yehudi. If only the boys back home could have heard *that*. What I would give for a tape recorder! You'd better get used to it — Yehudi and

I are going to practice every damned day until we get it right. Then we're going on tour. Say, I've just thought of something," he went on excitedly. "To hell with Jew's harps; there's bamboo, stacks of it. Do you know what, I'm going to make me a whistle. And, by gum, a flute. And a syrinx! And why not even a clarinet? Watch it, Herr Boehm, here I come."

With Steve able to move about on his crutches Elizabeth's days became fuller. When the first stirring of the village began soon after daylight, they would eat their breakfast of fruit on the porch outside. These were the hours of the day they came to like best. Their house was a little apart from the rest of the village, very near the top of the ridge on which the village stood. Steve developed a theory that it might be a guest house, and one day he spent a long time searching the house for any sign that a patrol officer had ever slept there, but he saw nothing. "I thought I might find a used razor blade stuck away somewhere or a bit of pencil or an old ball-point or something." He also went through the ashes in the firebox, looking for the remains of any metal piece that a white man might have thrown away, but he found nothing.

From the porch where they sat and ate breakfast they could see down a great valley. Often at that hour the peaks of the mountains were wreathed in clouds, and they'd watch first the sun and then the new breeze fret at these clouds until only wisps of them hung, clinging to the tops of the trees. On other mornings there were lakes of clouds in the valley that stayed until the sun was high enough to beat down and dry them. It was a very beautiful and awe-inspiring country, but one that left no doubt about its strength. Nothing — except the pygmies — was small. The steepness of the mountainsides, the height and girth of the trees, the denseness of the jungle, the crashing weight of the rain when it fell, even the butterflies, some of them as large as birds: all were on a scale that Elizabeth, as a European, had never before known.

It was while Steve was making his first whistle that he brought up the question of going back to the crashed airplane. "I'd like to find my knife, honey. The damn thing must be there somewhere. It was in a pocket in my briefcase."

"But you've got your knife," Elizabeth said. "It's there, in your hand."

He shook his head. "I mean my big knife. The same make as this little one, a Swiss Victoria, but with lots more blades, a little saw, and tweezers, a file, the lot. I sure would like to get my hands on it."

"Well, there's absolutely no question of your going back to the crash," Elizabeth said firmly. "We don't want two broken legs."

But he brought up the subject again that afternoon. "I've been thinking over what I said this morning. I still think we ought to try and salvage more from that airplane."

Elizabeth looked at him but said nothing.

"Things like that knife of mine," he went on, "would be mighty useful. There might even be tools. There'll be a couple of rubber dinghies, too —"

"At the moment," she said, "I can't imagine anything less useful to us than a rubber dinghy."

"You never know," he said doubtfully. Then, "Suppose we got to the sea."

"So you mean we go to the crash, find ourselves a rubber dinghy, and then set off for the coast, launch our dinghy, and paddle it to Australia?"

"Now you're making fun of me."

"I'm being practical, that's all."

"So am I, and I think it's crazy to leave things to rot there when they might be useful here."

It was at the washing pool in the stream that Elizabeth began to learn her first words of the language. At first the women didn't understand what she was trying to do, but finally it dawned on them. It became a game. Elizabeth would pick up a stone or point to a tree or to the sky and the women would tell her what they called it. She found the pronunciation extraordinarily difficult, and the women would watch eagerly as she tried to push forward her lips or attempt the curious clicking noises somewhere in the back of her throat. She soon learned to count up to ten. She told Steve that they didn't seem interested in counting past ten. "Maybe they can't," he said. "And there really isn't any reason why they need to. Tell me, do you think they have any idea where they are in relation to the rest of the country?"

She shook her head. "In some ways they seem incredibly childish, in others so sophisticated. How well they run their affairs. There's no poverty. And the village is clean; there's no litter."

"In many societies like this one," Steve said, "the disposal of waste is usually governed by taboo. If a man leaves bits of his dinner about, or doesn't bury his feces, an enemy can gather scraps of it and a witch doctor can work a spell with them, which, once the poor guy's told about it, will kill him. Ergo, they bury the waste so they have clean villages and therefore disease isn't spread. Many dietary laws, for instance, are for that purpose: shellfish carry hepatitis, pigs carry trichinosis — therefore the Jews say it's sinful to eat those foods. When the Christian missionaries reached the Pacific they played hell with the sanitation. They told the people it was a sin to believe in witch doctors, that the old island spirits were heathen devils, and that they were to be thrown out and replaced with the Christian devil, who didn't give a damn about rotting food. And the old missionaries had ways of seeing to it that the people went right along with them — regular visits from a frigate or two, shooting up a village or setting it alight to teach the heathens a lesson — and the villages began to stink and disease spread, especially the new diseases the missionaries and the other whites had brought, diseases such as dysentery."

"And another thing — there's no thieving," Elizabeth said. "They leave anything about and it stays there until they come back for it."

"That's because they have no concept of private property. Thieving only began when we invented the notion of property. Here everybody owns everything and you can't steal from yourself. Unless you're a psychotic and become a miser. I figure the children belong to the community, too, like everything else. It's as simple as that."

"Do we, too, belong to the community?"

"Well," he said slowly, "I guess we do. We're a part of it, and

[209]

anything accepted by the community automatically belongs to it. Sure, we belong. If we didn't," he added, "or ever ceased to, I'd say we'd be in some trouble."

With the passing of the days Steve became more and more obsessed by the idea of returning to the crash. Knowing Elizabeth's objection he went cautiously, only mentioning it casually, never dwelling on the subject, but one day he said, "You know, they could carry me on that litter."

"Carry you where?"

"To the airplane."

She was silent, and he saw that she did not immediately reject the idea.

"If they carried me it couldn't hurt my leg," he pointed out.

"Suppose I went?" she said.

"On your own?"

"Well, with the people, of course —"

"But you mean without me?"

She nodded.

"No." Steve shook his head. "I know something about airplanes, and I'd have a better idea where to look and what to look for, things we might be able to make good use of. Besides, they'd take more notice of a man. Listen, Elizabeth" — he didn't often call her that, and he put down the whistle he was working on — "I'm serious about this. My leg would stand a trip on that litter and I really think we ought to try and make it."

"Well," she said finally, "you're the boss. But if we go, we go on two conditions: only if you're carried, and then, if I see it's too much for you, we stop and come back."

To this Steve agreed.

Once he had got Elizabeth's tacit approval, Steve concentrated on urging Elizabeth to speak to Boar's Tusk and find out if a trip could be arranged. So late on a warmer-than-average afternoon Elizabeth came up the steps of their house followed by the sad-eyed little man.

When Boar's Tusk had squatted himself down on the mats and Elizabeth had sat down on the edge of Steve's sleeping platform, Elizabeth began to try to explain. They were surprised how easily they made him understand what they wanted, but they also saw quickly that whereas Boar's Tusk had always been anxious to help them, then he seemed to shrink from the suggestion. His round head fell and his skin glistened in the shaft of light striking in from the doorway. The great tusk curling up from his nose gleamed creamy white. He pursed his lips and thrust out the long upper one. He shifted his feet under his bulging calves and buttocks. His neck wallet swung gently. He was plainly under tension, and in the silence that grew in the house Steve and Elizabeth looked at one another. Steve thought he saw fear in her eyes.

Suddenly Boar's Tusk broke into a torrent of speech. Words came clicking and snapping out, not one of them understood by either Steve or Elizabeth. Yet the meaning was clear enough. Or so they thought. It was not possible to go back to the crash. Finally Boar's Tusk fell silent, staring down at the floor mats.

"Well, I guess that's that," Steve said softly after a few moments.

"But why?" she asked. "For what reason?"

"Search me." He gave a wry grin. "You heard what the gentleman said. Are we absolutely sure he's the head man? That he's above all those other old guys?"

"As far as I know," she answered. "They all seem to defer to him."

She tried all the words she knew that she thought might fit and Steve threw in his few. She leaned forward, bending so she could stare up into his face, which he seemed to want to keep averted.

"Could it have to do with the bodies in the airplane?" asked Steve. "Spirits, spooks — something like that?"

"I get the impression," Elizabeth said, "that the crash might have been on the edge of their territory. I expect they do have territory that's recognized as theirs."

"If so, I guess it means there must be other people about. Maybe they don't get on well with them."

"They never leave the village without their bows and arrows," she said. "And the two entrances to the village, on either end of this ridge, are palisaded: that can only be for defense."

"Maybe," Steve said after a few moments, "we shouldn't press him too hard, honey. He knows now what we want and we don't want to upset him. Maybe, by persisting, we're behaving badly in his eyes. He's a nice guy. Besides, we can't afford to fall out with him. Go get the cigarettes and we'll all have one."

The tension didn't pass. Elizabeth took a glowing stick from the fire and they passed it around. Boar's Tusk smoked the cigarette as if it had been one of their bamboo pipes, holding it between thumb and forefinger straight up from his mouth.

"Funny they don't want to strip that wreck," Steve said. "There are literally miles of copper wire there, aside from all the other stuff you'd think they could use." He paused. "Well, maybe not. I guess when you have everything you need, and they seem to, you don't need anything more. Perhaps he's right. Maybe *we* don't need anything more than what we've got," he added thoughtfully. "But I'd sure like to get my hands on that Swiss knife of mine."

"I wish we knew the word for war," she said.

"You think maybe they're at war?" he asked. "Surely if there was a war on we'd see some sign of it. Even if they were winning there'd be wounded, and we'd see patrols going out, wouldn't we?"

Boar's Tusk smoked the cigarette down quickly. When virtually only the filter was left, he nipped out the glowing tip between thumb and forefinger and then, as if this was his usual habit, slipped the cigarette butt into the pouch hanging on his chest. Then he went back to staring at the mats.

"How do we break this up?" asked Steve.

"We could try smiling at him."

"If a guy won't look at you, honey, how the hell's he to know you're smiling at him?"

"All the same . . ." Putting out her hand, she touched Boar's Tusk on the arm. Immediately he looked at her. Then, as quickly, he went back to staring at the floor.

"Gee, that was one of the nicest smiles I ever saw on a girl," said Steve.

"What are we going to *do?*" she said desperately. "I feel we've done something terrible, insulted him in some way."

"I wish to God," said Steve into the silence, "that I'd never talked you into agreeing to go back to the damn airplane. I'm responsible for this."

"No," she said, shaking her head. "I think you were right. I'd be foolish to let things that might be useful just rot away there."

At that moment Boar's Tusk gave a grunt and in one smooth motion got to his feet. He looked first at Steve, then at Elizabeth, then went out of the house.

"I suppose," Elizabeth said, looking after him, "you should never start anything unless you know you can go through with it. But I feel we're balanced here on such a delicate edge. I wonder what *they* think? Do they believe that someday someone will come for us and take us away? Or do they think we're here forever? Some kind of a penance visited on them for their sins? Do you think they might want to, well, to *do* something to us?"

"Hell, you *are* depressed —"

"Steve, this is something I've not told you yet. One morning I went looking for the woman who brings our food because I wanted to tell her not to bring so much. You were eating hardly anything, and even when I was hungry there was always a lot left. I couldn't find anyone but old people or children, so I went to that big house over on the other side of the village. I've often seen Boar's Tusk there, though I don't know for sure whether it's his house or not. I didn't see anybody, so I went up the ladder and looked in. The house was divided with a partition made of bark. I was about to go when I heard a little rustling noise behind the partition, so I crossed to the doorway and looked in. There was a very old man there, lying down. He was looking at me, yet he didn't seem to see me. I thought perhaps he was blind. I was suddenly embarrassed because I felt I'd invaded someone's privacy and I began to turn to go out, but as I did — it was very dark and gloomy in the house, not bright as this one is — as I turned, I saw some round things hanging from the roof above the old man." She paused for a moment, then said, "It took me a while to realize what they were. I was coming down the ladder when the penny dropped. You can guess?" she added.

"Heads?"

She nodded. Then after a few moments during which her eyes did not leave him she said, "Mind, I couldn't be certain. It was so dark and gloomy in there. What else could they be, Steve?"

"I'd say," he said slowly, "you probably guessed about right."

There was a very long silence between them, then she said, "I'm glad I've told you now. I've been wanting to for some time."

"It's worried you?"

"Oh, not all the time. Somehow, for all their fierce looks, I can't really see them as headhunters. But at other times when I wake about three in the morning I do feel frightened."

"Now listen, you know what we're going to do about that? From tonight on you're going to sleep up here on this platform with me and," he added more quietly, "whenever you wake at night with the blues, promise me you'll wake me, too, and let me share them with you?"

"I wouldn't want to wake you."

He smiled at her. "No need to. If you're up here beside me, I'll know if you're awake."

That afternoon and evening the village was quieter than usual. Steve had pain in his leg and lay on the platform or sat with his leg propped up, cutting thin lengths of bamboo into whistles, blowing into them, learning how to cut the throat notch to get the tone he wanted. Elizabeth did what she called her housework and brought firewood up from the pile under the house. It was another hot day. Her dress stuck to her sweat-wet body, and when the heat had gone from the afternoon, Steve said, "Why don't you go to the stream and lie in the water?"

"I'd like you to be able to come with me."

"Soon. In another week or two."

"All right," she said. "I'll go." Then she bent and kissed him.

It was full daylight when they woke the next morning. There was a faint rustling sound of someone in the house. Elizabeth blinked, her heart starting into her throat, and, in almost the same instant, she rolled from the bed and stood, alert. Steve struggled to sit up behind her, hampered by the weight of his leg.

"What is it?" His voice was a whisper, hoarse from sleep.

"I don't know." She sounded frightened. "It was someone in here, I think."

Then they saw, just inside the door and to one side of it, a basket woven from coconut fronds.

"That's not ours," Steve said. "Here, get me up, Elizabeth. That's just been put there and I want to see what it is."

She shook her head. "I'll do it." And before he could stop her she had crossed to it. For a second she hesitated, then she squatted beside the basket and peered into it.

"What is it?" Steve asked anxiously.

"Things from the crash — a bag, a hat I think, and a . . . a parcel."

She ferreted in the basket and pulled out the parcel. It was of brown paper, soiled, and Scotch-taped at the ends. Suddenly it hit her. "Steve," she said, turning back to him, "I know what this is." Her eyes suddenly shone. "It's my parcel! The one I told you about. It's . . . Oh, I can hardly *believe* it." She came across to him quickly and sat on the edge of the bed, holding the package on her knees, staring at it.

"Well, for God's sake —" he began.

"Steve, it's the batteries for the radio. It's the parcel they were in. It was in my suitcase."

As she said this there was a sound outside the house. They looked up from the parcel and sat listening. Then came a few words, a burst of chatter in which they both heard the voice of Boar's Tusk.

"You'd better go see what they want," he said. "Here, give me that," and he took the package from her.

She got up and he watched her disappear onto the little porch. Then she was coming back, one last glance over her shoulder. Where a moment before there had been excitement and pleasure in her face, there was fear. Steve started moving off the platform, struggling with his leg.

"About thirty of them are out there," she said, "all armed to the teeth. And so fierce. There's a look about them I've not seen before. Steve, I'm . . . I'm not just frightened. I'm terrified."

He said nothing, and she helped him onto his feet. She put the crutches into his hands and he stumped across the floor, bending at the door to look out. He remained there, staring down at the upturned faces. Then he turned and eased himself back through the doorway and into the house again. "Jesus . . ." he said softly. "Oh, Christ, what's wrong? They looked at me as if we'd burned down the orphanage."

# 11 ∿∿∿∿∿∿∿∿∿∿∿∿∿∿∿∿∿∿∿∿∿

Michael sat on his bed reading Janey's letter.

". . . it's quite obvious Mummy can't last much longer now and the doctor has spoken to Daddy. At the most a week, perhaps ten days, he said. Dad seems — don't misunderstand me — he seems relieved. He's already calmer, but of course the actual moment hasn't yet come.

"About shutting up the shop. You can never tell, can you? When I told Claude he didn't panic at all. As a matter of fact, he knows of someone who knows someone who died last week of the flu. So we're treating it as a holiday. When I told Dad, he said why didn't I fly out and join you in Australia. Wonders will never cease! But, darling, seriously, I might be able to, and when your work out there is over, could you take a holiday, too, and we might be able to go to the Barrier Reef? I've always wanted to go there ever since I saw a super film of it on television while I was still at school. I suppose saying super dates me . . ."

The last part of the letter he read and reread. "Being at home is very comfortable, as you know — it really is a very lovely house — but it's not nearly the same as being in my little flat, because no matter how many million miles away you *actually* are, you are *really* there in the flat with me. I see you all over it: at the fridge, fiddling with the coffeemaker in the morning, putting up those bookshelves, and I never but *never* have a bath without seeing you sitting there, after Claude's big party, with the water all run out, singing that dreadful song about awful Mrs. Long. And the night the furnace chimney caught fire or whatever it did in the basement, and we woke up to find Lenny had used his master key and had let in those enormous firemen, all tweedy and helmeted with big torches and axes in their belts, and they were all over the bed, feeling the wall above us to see if it was hot, and poor Lenny saying how sorry he was because we couldn't have heard him ring the bell (remember those twee chimes they had there when I first took the flat?), and then realizing how much worse he was making it by calling me *Miss* Davies, being as always *so* polite, over and over. But *weren't* they nice firemen? One of them gave me such a lovely friendly wink. But then, all the people we meet when we're together are nice, aren't they . . . ?"

"Listen," Birdy said, "if this Ringway virus really gets going, if it does actually wipe out man, he has still succeeded in making himself immortal. Or just about."

"Well, all that means is that man will live on as part of the fossil record in the same way a dinosaur does," Molly said.

"Nothing" — Birdy shook his head emphatically — "as feeble as that. No, man will live on, and I mean *live* on, as dangerous if not more so than he ever was in an insane but nonetheless positive way, to perpetuate the miserable record of his achievements as surely as if he had solved the secret of immortality."

"Oh, for heaven's sake!" exclaimed Kate. "Birdy, you do tend to talk in riddles. Sometimes I think you do it to be deliberately provoking. And obscure."

"There's nothing obscure about radioactive wastes, girlie. Listen" — Birdy swung around in his chair and stared hard at her — "do you realize that the radioactive waste we're making now, those ashes from nuclear power stations, will not only still be around in a time to come so far away that the mind boggles, but that until that time comes they'll remain unimaginably dangerous?"

"They can be kept safely," Kate said. "I've read about it."

"For a million years?" asked Birdy. "Because that's the time scale we're talking about. Listen, Katie, if you are anything but terrified about the prospect, then you've been brainwashed, and there's a lot of big business with big profits involved, and the last thing they want to see is a well-informed body of public opinion. Do you realize that one, mark you, I said *one*, average-size nuclear power plant, producing about one thousand or so megawatts a year, produces the same amount of radioactive waste that would result from a nuclear explosion equal to the detonation of twenty-three million tons of TNT. And listen, Katie, if you don't think that's provoking enough, let me tell you that man doesn't yet know how long it will take before he can stop isolating radioactive waste from the environment. In all probability it could be as much as one hundred thousand years."

"They're beginning to get worried about this in England," said Michael.

"And no bloody wonder!" exclaimed Birdy. "The British don't only process their own waste, they do it for other countries as well."

"It's an extraordinarily expensive process," said Michael. "The tanks they store the stuff in are only about twenty by twenty feet, yet they cost a couple of million pounds each to build. I think Birdy's right."

"But a hundred thousand years," protested Molly.

"Look, Molly," Birdy said, "we don't know. It's probably longer. What of our political structures? How can we be sure we're going to have viable governments in fifty thousand years? Man mightn't even be around then — quite apart from Ringway's, he is working himself into extinction at such a rate at present that he quite likely won't be. And then what'll happen when this stuff leaks out? The whole planet will be a radioactive slag heap in no time."

"Why can't they make these tanks strong enough to keep it until it's safe?" Kate said. "They seem to cost enough."

"They're not just tanks, period," Birdy said.

"They've got to be kept cool," put in Michael.

"Look, Katie," Birdy said, "once the waste has got to the stage where it can be put into storage — and that's a saga in itself — it has to be kept cool by huge refrigeration plants, and air has to be kept bubbling through it to keep it stirred. Now the first seven hundred years are the most dangerous, because after then the original activity will have fallen to only about a ten millionth of what it was, but then comes the problem of the plutonium. Roughly speaking, the half-life of plutonium is more than twenty-four thousand years, and neptunium, another of the actinides, has a half-life of over two million years. Some nut said there was only one safe way of disposing of it and that was stuffing it into rockets and shooting it off into the sun."

"Sounds like a very good idea," said Kate.

"Does it? A rocket costing about a hundred million dollars off to the sun on the hour every hour. And only one, *one*, mind, failure and a rocket flops back to earth or has to explode anywhere inside the earth's envelope and that puts finis to life on this planet. Come off it." He was silent, then he said, "I haven't worked it out yet, but I'm beginning to think religion is mixed up in all this."

"Religion!" said Kate. "*You*, Birdy — ?"

"Because I'm an agnostic doesn't mean I don't think about religion. But for the first time in the history of man he's come up against eternity right in his own backyard. He doesn't have to look into the sky to see eternity anymore. And talking about religion, if this Ringway virus does get going it's going to be the poor bloody dedicated, the do-gooders, who, as usual, will be the first to suffer. The doctors, nurses, priests, and nuns." Then suddenly quite unconnectedly he added, "Personally I'm all for clearing out."

There was silence after Birdy said this. Archy was the first to speak. "Clearing out?" He said it as if he didn't understand.

"Yes," said Birdy, with a touch of defiance. "Didn't Plato reckon a wise man was justified in escaping from danger? Someone did. But I didn't mean it in that way. You see, society just can't cope with a calamity of this size."

"It isn't a calamity yet," Kate pointed out.

"It bloody well soon will be," Birdy said grimly, "unless they come up with some pill for it. I was thinking of a Noah's ark," he went on, looking around at them. "Collect some kids, teenagers, perhaps a few older ones, too, both sexes, and find some island, some empty place."

"Where?" said Archy.

"Damned if I know. Somewhere up north, I suppose. Masses of islands up there."

"Then come back when this has burned itself out?" said Michael, thinking.

"I thought," said Molly, "doctors weren't supposed to run away from disease."

There was a long silence, then Birdy said quietly, "This one might be different, Molly."

"Sort of going to Fiesole," said Kate. "Is that it?"

"Where?" asked Archy.

"Wasn't Fiesole the place outside Florence where the people in Boccaccio's *Decameron* went to escape the plague?"

"You'd need a boat," said Archy.

"A good big hulking thing, a good sea boat. Lots of room in her for tools and seeds as well as people," said Birdy.

"How many people?" asked Molly.

"It'd depend, wouldn't it, on the size of the boat," said Birdy. "That boat of Arthur Straw's would do, *White Wings*. A lousy name but a good boat for this. What is she, sixty feet waterline? Eighty over all?"

"About that," said Archy.

"Where would you get the kids?" said Molly.

"Oh, kids like Poppy Bennett's girl and Matt Talent's boy. Only one from each family. Quarantine 'em. In a boat of that size you could take, what, twenty — ten boys, ten girls. You'd pick them over carefully." Then he added, "You'd have a nucleus, you see."

"*Lord of the Flies*, eh?" Kate said.

Archy said, "Remember what Wallanulla township looked like, Michael? With only old Nolan and his motorbike and that kelpie bitch?"

"I was just remembering that," said Michael.

"I can't stand thinking of the animals," said Kate.

"Tell you what," said Birdy, "you find a bitch for Crackers and they can come, too."

"I still don't think you, a doctor, can be serious about running away," said Kate.

"So what should I do?" asked Birdy. "Become a bloody martyr?"

"Doctors are supposed to serve the sick, have you forgotten?"

"I've forgotten nothing. But I have remembered something — that there are none so dead as those who lie on a mortuary slab. Always provided, of course, that there's some kind person charitably enough inclined — and *alive* enough — to stick them on that slab."

When the news first broke officially it wasn't taken much notice of. Some countries even ignored it altogether because it was the beginning of their tourist season or they were about to open a big trade fair or because they were made up of people far too obsessed with politics or racial hatred or extending their borders to bother with a warning that came from an agency automatically regarded as ineffectual because it was part of the United Nations.

Then, as nations scattered here and there across the world began to hear of other nations catching it and dying, as they began to hear of acquaintances and colleagues, and then finally when it came close and took a friend or even came into their family and killed a mother or a child or a father — then, slowly at first, but with mounting desperation, came the realization that something stupendous was going on.

In Australia, Michael was surprised by the amount of coverage it was soon getting on radio and television and in the newspapers. Ministers of health issued statements and city health officers were interviewed. The federal minister of health was interviewed on nationwide television, and a week later a second and much more alarming WHO warning was released. The prime minister himself read the text of it to the nation.

Over and over again people were told not to go out without their masks on, not to congregate, and at the first sign of it they were not to call their doctor but to go at once to their nearest reception and isolation center. It would probably be their nearest sports arena or racecourse. Listening to the world news was just as depressing. Everywhere churches were filling. "Bloody fools," grunted Birdy. "Had a patient once who got a chancre from a communion cup."

Then one night there came a power cut that blacked out a large part of Sydney for about fifteen minutes. It had nothing to do with the influenza, but there was a depressing ominousness about and it got wide publicity. That night Archy was called to the hospital to do an emergency operation, and when he got back Molly was in the big storeroom and workshop under the house. "What are you doing in there, Chooky?" asked Archy.

"Wondering whether we ought to get a stronger lock on this door. There's a van of tinned food in here now, don't forget."

"If it gets as tough as Mike seems to think it will, locks won't stop someone breaking in if he's got children to feed."

"How are things at the hospital?"

"Fair. But you can feel the change in people. The army was there today, checking out sites for field hospital tents on the grounds. They've already moved in a bloody great generating set. And Jackson's hit the bottle."

"Ben Jackson? The registrar?"

Archy nodded. "I suggested he go home. You'd hardly credit it, but there are empty beds in all the wards. People in for operations have decided they're not going to have them. Some of the surgical cases have just walked out. I saw one chap being helped out by his wife. I told him to come back, that he'd die. He said he was probably going to die anyway. She got him into a car — he was in his robe — and they drove off. Now I'm going to have a drink."

"Don't you start hitting the bottle," she called after him.

Over the drink Archy said, "One of the strangest things is how people are changing toward us. This almost blind faith some people have in us — something that has always worried me — it seems to be going now."

"They know you've no cure for them."

"Who knows there's no cure? You can't say that, Molly. True, there's never been a specific for flu, but if a vaccine can be developed in time . . ." He was silent, sipping his drink. Then he said, "It's not anything to do with a cure, it's more than that. Even the real blind-faithers, the ones who know instinctively you can't cure them yet persist in wanting treatment, seem now to be losing faith, sliding away, like a snake sloughing off its skin. I think that's what has got Jackson. He always tended to regard doctors, himself particularly, as kinds of supermen who could

[222]

work miracles. And in a way he was right. After all, it is a kind of miracle you work when you treat someone with an antibiotic and the disease or the infection that otherwise would have killed him just vanishes."

"Kate tells me," Molly said, "that Father Reilly has it. He's shut himself up in the presbytery."

"Where is Kate?"

"Just driving out somewhere with Mike. I think she said they were going to South Head."

"Do you think they're in love? I'd hate to see her hurt again."

"Mike," Molly said, "is in love already — he's got a girl and he wants to marry her."

"He told you?"

"He told Kate."

"Pretty fair warning, I'd say. Keep off the grass unless you want to be run over by the lawn mower. You know, Chooks, you can't organize anything like this."

"I don't want to organize anything. It's the way people fit together that counts. You can't organize that."

"I suppose," he said after a moment, "there'll be a good bit of trial-and-error fitting together happening from now on."

"You want to try another for size?"

"No," he said, and smiled at her. "You fit me just fine."

"Come on," she said, getting up. "Finish that drink and let's go to bed. Tonight, the way I feel, I'm not so interested in the fit. Tonight I'd like it to hurt."

Once begun, the alteration of well-established patterns of life continued quickly, grew apace, and took many by surprise. And not all thought logically. Some, who though they themselves had given up going to the office or factory, were surprised the first morning they found their milk hadn't been delivered, or got angry when they found the self-service pump at the gas station was empty. Most people were well enough aware of the danger of congregating and only talked to each other from opposite sides of the street. Some people nailed up their front gates and kept the blinds drawn. Others pitched tents on beaches or took their families into the mountains, where they staked out a little preserve and watched with caustic in their eyes any other car that came looking for a place to pitch camp.

"Resignation," said Birdy a few evenings later. "That's the great social virtue. But I'm damned if I can resign myself to waiting for Ringway's. It's one thing to endorse the actions of the government, even if you know they can't bloody well do anything, but it's another thing altogether to countenance recklessness."

"Don't forget," said Michael, "that it's a menaced society you're speaking of."

"I'd have thought, Birdy," said Kate, "that you of all people would have been more sympathetic."

"I'm frightened," said Birdy candidly, looking around at her. "And sympathy is only a kind of fear. All right, have it your way — it's the sympathetic, what I called the dedicated, that are dying first. What are principles anyway? Why should a quack or a nurse or a nun or a priest beg for it by trying to relieve a symptom? Note, I said to relieve a *symptom*. Not to try to cure the cause; they know they can't do that."

"Surely some people are recovering?" Molly said, looking around at the men.

"If they are, I've not heard of them," said Birdy. "Have you, Archy?"

Archy shook his head.

"I don't think there's any actual reason," Michael said, "why some members of a particular species *should* have an inbuilt resistance to a disease that others are susceptible to, though up to now we've assumed, I think, that it was so. There's the child who doesn't get measles, though all the other kids in the class get it."

"Far as I'm concerned," said Birdy, "there's not much of a saint or the martyr in me. Ringway's would seem to be as fatal as rabies, and in times like this people either react to the conditions imposed by the pestilence, and are destroyed by it, or accept these conditions as being outside their control and they get out — or try to."

"Run away?" said Kate.

"Call it that if you like. Tell me what I can do to fight it without — or so it seems at present — embracing certain death, and I'll do it. Then I'll fight it because I've got a chance of surviving long enough to make a fight of it in order to help people to live.

"I'm not scared of dying." Birdy looked around at them. "I'm not some old fuddy-duddy who the older he gets the less he wants to hear about death. But we're not only the victims — we're the agents of this plague. Old notions of heroism don't apply. Conrad said something about if men were heroes to their valets they'd be brushing their own clothes. What will wreck our will to fight will be the feeling of helplessness that will engulf us as soon as we realize that we're bloody well nothing but inevitable victims."

"We're that anyway," said Kate. "We're all going to die someday."

"But not necessarily as *victims*. The sort of death you mean is the inevitable consequence of life. Ringway's is not. Look," Birdy went on, "in normal times our duty as human beings is clear. We aid the sick. We bury the dead and we ought to do what we can to protect one another. We also consent to our own deaths, however unwillingly we accept death as a fact of life. In *normal* times." He shook his head. "These times aren't normal."

For a long time Birdy sat looking at his glass. "Today," he said finally, "I had a look at *White Wings*. I spoke to her owner on the phone and he'll sell. She was refitted last season and she's in excellent condition. Tomorrow," he added, "I'm going to start to get the kids together." He looked up at Archy. "She's a ketch, you know, big lump of a boat. Engine, sails, the lot, all in perfect nick, even the bottom resheathed last season. Michael, do you reckon a week is long enough quarantine for the kids?"

"Should be."

"I've bought a dozen Elsans," Birdy went on. "I'm going to stick the kids, two to a room, in my house and in the garage, with a pile of tinned food each, water, a plate, cup, knife and fork and spoon, and a can opener. As they finish, if they're clear, I'll take them to the boat. When I've got as many as I think I can look after properly, I sail."

"Where will you go?" asked Michael.

"Well, there are plenty of islands up in the North," Birdy explained. "Some of them are pretty remote. And with long uninhabited coasts. I'll take seeds; I'm buying them already. But ask me where I'll actually settle and I can't tell you. *White Wings* has been north before, as far as Borneo, and she's got a locker full of charts and a rack full of *Pilot and Sailing Directions*. If I find a good place that someone's beaten me to, then I'll go on until I find another."

"And say if you find a good place, settle in, and someone comes along who wants you out of it. What then?" asked Molly.

"God knows. It'd depend, wouldn't it? I mean you'd have to try to reason them out of it, wouldn't you?"

"And if you couldn't?"

"Well, then, that would be something worth fighting for. I've a horror of violence, but if it was a case of protecting what I'd made up there for the kids I suppose I'd not have much fucking option."

Influenza virus is grown by inoculating a tiny amount of virus into the allantoic, or amniotic, cavity of a fertile hen's egg half-way through incubation. The virus grows in the cells of the membrane. Two days after the incubation, fluid withdrawn from the cavity will contain about a million times the number of viruses that were put into it. Technically, influenza is about the simplest of viruses to study.

But there is a catch in developing vaccines against new strains of human influenza virus because of their reluctance to grow well in hens' eggs. If, for instance, a vaccine against swine virus is needed, the virus must be persuaded to hybridize with another virus strain which does grow readily in eggs. There are also problems of production logistics. It takes six months for a hen to begin laying eggs. Then after incubation for eleven days and inoculation with the virus, it takes another three days for that egg to give half a dose of inactivated vaccine, or some dozen doses of attenuated vaccine. Then testing needs another three months — in the case of attenuated vaccines up to a year.

By the time Michael had been in Sydney for three weeks there were few major biological laboratories in the world that were not studying the Ringway virus. For a vaccine to be of any use, time was all-important; the extraordinary virulence of Ringway's made it imperative that a way be found to cut down on the long process of "taming" this new virus to use it to make a vaccine. As Birdy put it one evening, "The strain on all those poor bloody hens' bums laying all those fertile eggs is fantastic."

Technique was, as always, part of the problem. When Ringway's hit, it took at least one hen's egg to make one dose of killed vaccine in England; in America it was as high as four eggs per shot. *If* a vaccine were to be found — repeat, *if* — it was calculated that in the United States alone two hundred million doses would be needed. Thus work turned to the making of live vaccines, so that viruses still able to replicate could be given in far smaller doses. With an effective live virus one egg could provide enough virus for perhaps one thousand shots. The awful catch, of course, about live viruses is that, while they must be able to replicate significantly enough to provoke an immune response in the patient, they mustn't give him the disease. Attenuation was both the answer and the problem.

But time was the enemy. Unlike most viruses, in which the genes are carried on one continuous piece of nucleic acid, influenza A packs its seven or eight genes separately. Thus it is that much more adaptable in juggling genetic material.

Time . . . How to compress selective, evolutionary forces that, in nature, normally operate over a fifteen-year period?

It was half past three in the morning when Julian rang, the instrument beside Archy's bed jingling into life. Molly got to it first, leaning over Archy, fumbling for the light switch. She listened, then, as Archy stirred, she said, "It's London. For Mike. Hold it and I'll go and get him."

Only when she'd put on the light in Michael's room and had woken him did she realize she was wearing the thinnest of nightgowns and hadn't stopped to put on her bathrobe. "What the hell," she thought as she got in beside Archy again. Archy was holding the telephone, waiting to hear Michael's voice on the upstairs phone before replacing his receiver. Molly, too, heard the crackle of Michael's voice. As Archy hung up, he said, "It's Sir Julian Reece. Put the other light on, Chooky, and we'll wait to see if Mike has any more news."

"I think I'll get us all some iced tea," she said. This time she put on her bathrobe. She was pouring out the tea when Archy heard Michael finish speaking and called to him to come up to their bedroom.

"Archy," Michael said, "would the farmers keep pigs around Wallanulla?"

Archy looked puzzled for a moment, then said, "I suppose a few, yes. Perhaps on some of the smaller farms. I wouldn't have thought it was pig breeding country. Why?"

"Reece says they've come up with something at the WHO World Influenza Center at Mill Hill in England, and they're sending a sample of the material to the International Influenza Center for the Americans at Atlanta, Georgia —"

"What's this about pigs?" asked Molly, getting back into bed.

"Reece is wondering whether we could find any pigs around Wallanulla, and if so could we get some smears from their snouts."

"Sounds a jolly occupation," said Molly.

"A virus to protect man against the A2 influenza variety was found in pigs in Taiwan some time ago," said Michael. "The virus has also been found in birds. What Reece is wondering now is whether any pigs around Wallanulla could have caught Ringway's from the infected people there. If they have, from what we know of the success with the A2 influenza virus, we just *might* be able to develop a vaccine that protects against Ringway's."

"Could that little girl have caught it from a pig?" asked Molly.

"It's the other way around. The influenza appears in pigs *after* an outbreak affecting man. Reece is interested because from about 1928 an American by the name of Shope did a lot of work on influenza A virus in pigs in the USA. He was working on a theory that had been developed by another American researcher in Iowa. Shope came to the conclusion that if the Pfeiffer bacillus — which isn't anything very dangerous in itself — acted in concert with an equally reasonably innocuous swine flu virus, they could combine to make something really deadly — something like Ringway's, only not quite as bad — that killed by causing lung damage severe enough to be fatal. And quickly at that."

"I'm a urologist," said Archy, "and what little I ever knew about the finer points of virology I've forgotten, but isn't our modern swine A virus the descendant of that Spanish A job?"

"I think most virologists would agree it is, adapted to the pig, yes. If it is antigenically similar to the 1918 one, what we don't know is why that particular virus has retained its ability to infect pigs yet can't worry man. On the telephone a few minutes ago Reece was saying that the Americans are sending another team up to Alaska to exhume more of the Eskimos who died in the 1918 pandemic."

"I can't think there'd be much left of them by this time," said Molly.

"Not so," said Michael, "they're almost perfectly preserved, since many were buried in permafrost. Reece isn't optimistic because the Americans did this once before, in 1951; they brought back many frozen lung sections, but they weren't able to infect even one laboratory animal. I told Reece I didn't hold out much hope, but he said that when we get to the stage we're at now we try anything. But it's Barbara Lambert he's really interested in. He says that the computer results and reports coming in still haven't turned up a case before hers. In his opinion, some change occurred in that kid's body by virtue of a combination, "a synergistic act," he called it, when an A-strain virus met up with some factor it hadn't met before. God knows what it was — a chemical, another virus, radiation . . ." Michael fell silent and Molly said, "Drink your tea before it gets hot."

"How does Reece sound?" asked Archy.

"Bloody," said Michael.

"He hasn't got it, has he?" asked Molly.

Michael shook his head. "He'd have told me, I think, if it was in the Institute. He sounds exhausted." Michael sat staring dejectedly at the floor. There was a long silence. Then Molly looked at the bedside clock.

"It'll be daylight soon. It's going to be another scorching day. I don't think I'll be able to go to sleep again now. Why don't we three put on our togs and go down for a dip? The water will be just perfect now."

Molly and Archy were already in the car when the telephone rang just as Mike was leaving the house. Michael shouted "Telephone" and went back in. Molly lay back in the seat in her bikini, already beginning to relish the prospect of the feel of the dawn-cool water on her body. Slowly the minutes passed and finally Archy said, "He's a long time, isn't he?"

"It'll be Reece again, I suppose. Did Mike tell you about the priority system on the overseas calls now? Reece, calls like that, have priority. The lines have been jammed with migrants ringing their families back home."

Several more minutes passed.

Archy didn't answer, instead he said, "He's been a while, Chooky. Do you think he's all right? What I mean is, could it be bad news?"

Finally Molly said, "Well, perhaps you'd better go and see if anything's happened."

Archy was gone a long time. When he came out his face was somber in the half-light.

"It's his girl," he said.

"What about her?" Molly got out of the car.

"She's got it."

"Oh, God!" Molly put her hands to her face, then turned to the car and leaned against it.

Archy stood staring at the ground. Suddenly Molly said, "Should I go and see him?"

"Yes," Archy said, "I think so."

Michael was still sitting by the telephone. He looked up as Molly reached him.

"Archy told me," she said.

"Molly," he said, "I . . . You go and swim without me."

"We don't need a swim that bad, Mike. Unless you'd rather be alone?"

"No," he said, shaking his head. "I'd rather not be, actually. There's so . . . there's so little to say, really . . ."

Clearly, as if it was a recording being played over, he could hear Janey's voice: ". . . the nurse, the new one we *had* to have, darling, the nurse brought it . . . It was very quick with Mummy. Only now we're having difficulties about getting her taken away . . . Mike, oh, Mike, and I was so, oh, God, so near to joining you. I'd booked . . . I so wanted to surprise you. But I've written, darling, telling you I'd be coming."

"You . . . You're quite sure? I mean . . . about Ringway's?"

"Oh, God, Mikey, of course I'm sure. Positive."

"Your father?"

"He's in bed. I tried to get you yesterday but they kept saying all the lines to Australia were engaged. Oh, yes, my darling Mike, I've got it."

"Who else is in the house?"

"No one; the nurse has gone. It's quite awful here. They won't even come for Mummy. And there are all kinds of dreadful things happening in the streets . . ."

"You've got food?" he said after a moment.

"That's rather funny, that. Yes, I did as you said, and there's . . . Well, let's put it this way: there's more than enough."

The unbelievable happening, the utterly unbelievable . . .

Janey ringing, saying good-bye . . .

And being brave, conditioning herself so well for the ordeal. "Darling, darling Mikey, don't you go getting it, will you? Promise . . ."

And then suddenly, explosively, her love cried out for him.

When the memory of the moment hit him Molly stood very close to him and took his head and pressed it against her, and he grasped her and dug his fingers into her flesh, and for a moment she felt, in return, a swift welling of desire for him.

# 12 〜〜〜〜〜〜〜〜〜〜〜〜〜〜〜〜〜

A couple of days after Michael spoke to the doctors in Sydney five people in Cairo died of Ringway's. From Egypt it went to Israel. Tel Aviv sent it southwest and it appeared in the Gulf of Masira at Khaluf, then it hit Muscat and, leaping the Arabian Sea (and the Tropic of Cancer), it broke out in Karachi. Cambay and Baroda were the next victims. Soon Rangoon was hit, and at that point reports erupted throughout Thailand and across the South China Sea to Balikpapan and Makasar in the Celebes. Now the paths it was taking began to get so hopelessly crossed that it was soon impossible to say in what direction it was moving, or from where it had come. To some places it came from two directions at once, arriving by sea from the west at the same moment as an aircraft from the east was unloading it.

While an American student was infecting Russia, two girls who had met her at a hostel in Florence were planting it at the Studenthotellet Skogshögskolan in Stockholm. From there it got to Helsinki, also first to a youth hostel, and on the same day, on the other side of the world, Ringway's virus hit Hawaii, breaking out first at the Hickham Air Force Base at Pearl Harbor. And so the land of the Nene, that beautiful goose (itself so near extinction), of Mauna Loa, the world's most active volcano, soon became as familiar with Ringway's as did people as remote as those on Tristan da Cunha, who learned about it from the two surviving members of the crew of a yacht out of Montevideo, a father and son who, with a failed radio, unable to call for help, had cast overboard the bodies of their four shipmates; driven west by the prevailing winds they had sighted Tristan when they had given up hope of ever seeing land again. By the time the people of Tristan knew what was the matter with these men it was too late; they were ashore. Within days a deep depression of the spirit — that substitute for courage — had settled on the island, followed by panic. And then fighting.

" 'To cure sometimes, to relieve often, to comfort always,' " said Birdy when Molly told him about Mike's girl getting it. "I read that in Lord Platt's autobiography, and it's a bloody fine motto for a quack; so what are you doing to comfort Mike?"

"What can we do?" Molly asked.

Birdy went out on to the terrace and stared at Michael through his screwed-up eyes. "Molly's told me," he grunted. "No use my saying I'm sorry, that's not going to bring her back. Why didn't she come out here with you?"

"Her mother was dying."

"Duty, eh?" Birdy grunted again. "Duty is an affliction, like any other." Birdy spoke more softly than usual. "Mike, I wonder if you realize just how serious I am about clearing out?"

"I think I do."

"You know about White Wings, and the kids, don't you?"

Michael nodded.

Birdy went on staring at Michael for a long moment. "What is happening," he said slowly, "all over the world, now, will happen here, to us, right in this house, if we stay here and wait for it to happen. What did Beethoven write on the last movement of his last quartet? 'The dread decision. Must it be? It must be.' Katie — now there's a girl, Mike, if you want duty — Katie's right in a sense when she talks about my wanting to rat out. I do because I'm scared, not scared of dying, but scared of just sitting here doing nothing while waiting for it come blowing onto this terrace one day, Mike," he leaned forward quickly, "will you do something for me?"

Michael stared back but didn't speak.

"Help me to persuade Archy to go," Birdy said.

Michael was about to answer when Molly and Kate came out onto the terrace carrying trays of drinks, glasses, and the ice bucket. Birdy gave a swift cautionary shake of his head to Michael.

"There's been a chap on the radio today," said Molly, "saying that Ringway's must burn itself out."

"Well, every other plague and pestilence have," said Michael, getting up to help Kate, "in the end. Otherwise we wouldn't be here."

"It's not quite as simple as that, old cock," Birdy said. "Why, at the end of the Cretaceous era, did all the principal groups of reptiles just disappear? Went for good, from the sea, the land, and the air. Almost nothing stayed on to compete with the little mammals that soon had the empty world to themselves. We know of nothing that could have done that. Mind, some of these extinctions must have been the result of others: the meat-eating dinosaurs, for instance, wouldn't have had anything to live on when their herbivorous cousins died out. But there's absolutely no known reason why this extinction of so many different groups of reptiles — living, mark you, in such a variety of environments — should have happened so suddenly, so dramatically. These things usually take place gradually."

"I've read," said Molly, "that there are many reasons why animals become extinct. Even cosmic rays might have done it."

Birdy shook his head. "Not with the animals I'm talking about. All these creatures just disappeared, and we know nothing for sure to account for it."

"You don't have to go back two or three million years to find a sudden disappearing act," said Michael. "As recently as about eleven thousand years ago, slap in the middle of the Stone Age, all kinds of large animals suddenly disappeared in the Americas, where they'd been happily living for millions of years. There's not much doubt now about why they went — Stone Age man knocked them off. They just weren't smart enough to get out of the way of man as a hunter of big game."

"Right," said Birdy. "The brontosauri, let's say, died out because they weren't smart enough. In other words, they died because of limited brainpower, eh? They just couldn't adapt. But listen, I don't think we're so much different ourselves or nearly half as clever as we think we are. I believe we're an animal with fantastic potential that we're trying to realize, but we're like those Stone Age giant ground sloths — we're not quick enough to get out of the way of the hunter."

"Hunter?" said Molly.

"Yes, the hunted has a problem, which is the hunter. Our problems hunt us, worry us — they badger us, and that's a hunting simile if you like. What I'm trying to say is that we just haven't enough brainpower to cope with the problems we face. For one thing we haven't self-control — look at the ignominious defeat of the Americans in Indochina. Kids of twelve looking at the telly and reading the newspapers knew years ago that the American generals were stupid. So much power, but not the intelligence to use it. In a way, what happened in Indochina is symbolic of our whole twentieth-century set of values. It's useless being clever enough to build a bomber that flies so high you can't see it from the ground if you aren't clever enough to understand how that bomber and all it stands for can be beaten by a man who lives on a handful of rice a day and pushes all he needs to make war on the handlebars of a bike. Our minds might be more effective than those of those old extinct animals, but unless we can retrieve and effectively use the knowledge our apparently superior intellects give us, then we, too, face extinction as surely as those old animals did."

"But," said Molly, "man's so much more *intelligent*, Birdy. A human child —"

"Human child!" He jumped around at her. "Hell, Molly, the human child is so stupid it's not even funny. Listen, consider a baby: it has nothing, absolutely nothing! It can't speak, it has no ideas, its incapable of concepts. It has no tools, and it has nothing in the way of experience —"

"How could it, if it's just been born?"

"Ever see a pig born, Molly? But the human baby has nothing. It can't decide whether its mother likes it or not — it can't even decide who its mother *is*. It is a *nothing!* The tragedy is," he added, grinning, "that ninety-nine point nine nine nine percent of what those babies grow into never manage to get minds either. If Reece's idea is true, that the Ringway virus evolved because of a mutation brought about by an enzyme or a fungus, or radiation or a chemical, the idea of a great natural disaster such as Krakatoa, which sent particulate matter right around the world, *also* being able to cause a virus mutation isn't so farfetched. A series of such mutations could very well wipe out most of one specific group of animals. Certainly, we know all those giant mammals went. And, in terms of geological time, went bloody quickly, too."

"So we go back," said Michael, "to the prehominid Eden of the Miocene forests of fifteen million years ago?"

Birdy grinned and muttered something about the supposed killer ape of the Pliocene savannas. "The earth must have looked pretty marvelous then." He paused, then said, "I had another look at *White Wings* today."

Archy came out on the terrace quietly, looking worried. "Old Mrs. Spender just rang," he said. "Chooks, has our phone been out of order?"

Molly looked at Kate before she answered. "No." Then she added, looking up at Archy, "I took it off the hook."

It was a moment before this sank in, then he said, "But why?"

"Because it's been ringing and ringing. Listen, Arch," Molly said, "it's been ringing and ringing, and when I answer it's people like old Mrs. Spender asking what they ought to do. I tell them all the same thing. That they should do what the telly and the radio tell them to do. They're not ill. We've not had one genuine call here yet. They want . . . Oh, hell, Archy, I don't know what they want —"

"They want assurance," put in Kate.

"You answered some of the calls." Molly looked at Kate. "Yes, that's it," she said. "It's as Kate says — they want assurance. I'm sorry, Archy. I've never done it before. But what can I say to them?"

"I see," said Archy thoughtfully.

"There's another thing I've been wondering about, Archy," Molly said after a pause, "what would you do if you got a call to go to a house with it?"

"I'd go." For a second Archy continued to look at Molly, then he turned to Birdy. "Wouldn't you?"

"I won't say," said Birdy carefully, shifting in his chair, "that I've never dodged a house call, because I have. I've never dodged an important call. Or what I thought was one. I've dodged calls that were probably, politically speaking, bad for my practice; hypochondriacs are seldom considerate. But I'm not," he went on uneasily, "at all sure about this one."

"Would you, Archy? Or wouldn't you?" Molly looked at him straight in the eye.

Birdy said, "The point Molly is making, you see" — he sounded most uncomfortable — "is that you couldn't do anything *for* them."

"What can you do for a terminal cancer case?" Kate said.

"That's different."

"Because you can't catch cancer as you could Ringway's?" asked Molly.

"You can relieve pain in terminal cases," said Birdy defensively. "You can encourage 'em, too. Surprising how much comfort you *can* bring, even to a person who knows he's for the high jump. All right. I suppose, if you want a straight answer, I'd funk it. Only because," he added quickly, "I knew I couldn't save the patient."

Archy looked at Michael. "What would you do?" he asked.

Michael paused before answering. He was suddenly conscious of Kate staring at him. Finally he said, "You see, Archy, it's the impossibility of being able to do anything — at this stage of our knowledge anyway."

"So you'd refuse a case of Ringway's, too?" Archy persisted.

"I suppose," Michael said slowly, "I would, yes."

"I take it," Molly said to Archy after a moment, "that there is no doubt in your mind?"

"Right."

"Then," she said, "after seeing this case, would you come home here to give it to us?"

Again the silence intruded until Birdy grunted and said, "That's where she's got you, old cock."

"What *should* I do, then?" asked Archy desperately, turning to Birdy.

[237]

"Damned if I know," answered Birdy. "Except this — that you wouldn't bring it home, knowingly. You might be incubating it now. So might I. We go to hospitals — and hospitals are notoriously unhealthy places. But as yet, touch wood, I've not seen a case of Ringway's. If I had," he added, "I wouldn't be sitting here in your house now. Mockridge," he said after a pause, "hasn't gone home."

"Joe Mockridge?" said Archy.

Birdy nodded.

"He's had a case?" asked Molly.

"A ward full of them," said Birdy. "He's a walking infectious disease."

"That's not the chap with the nice wife, what's her name, Alice?" said Molly.

"The same," said Birdy. "And three kids."

"Oh, God," said Molly.

"You mean," Kate said, aghast, "she'll never see Joe again?"

Birdy had got a drink during the strained, silent minutes that followed; then he said, in a deliberately conversational way, "Alice and Joe Mockridge speak to one another on the telephone."

"Perhaps, Chooky," said Archy, "it'd be kind if you gave Alice Mockridge a ring."

"I was just thinking that. I will."

"'Thou must not strive,'" quoted Birdy, "'officiously to keep alive.' Look, Archy." He leaned toward him. "Ages ago we decided that a human being ought to be allowed to die — once. Right?"

"Yes," said Archy.

"We were talking," Birdy said, looking at Michael, "of patients who'd had coronaries, or were in an obviously terminal illness, being kept alive even though their brains were irreversibly damaged. Archy and I both came to the conclusion that if either of us had a heart attack we'd rather be nursed at home where some mischievous bastard couldn't start our heart when it stopped and so leave us with a good chance of dementia because of temporary arrest of circulation. As I see it, this situation now" — Birdy turned back to Archy — "isn't all that different, only it's the other way around. In the one, the heart failure, we don't wish to risk a badly

[238]

damaged life, and in the case of Ringway's, I say we oughtn't to risk a messy, premature death . . ."

Michael wasn't really listening to Birdy. He had now made up his mind what he would do, what he knew Janey would want him to do. And thoughts of her so easily occupied the place of Birdy's urging. It took so little to trigger the memories. And all of them of moments in places now so impossibly far off, all — except for a holiday skiing in the Engadine, staying in Sils, and another doing what Janey called "gallery bashing" in Italy — all of them of Janey in England and the more acutely painful for that because of his own love of England.

A sunny Sunday morning with her in Trafalgar Square; girls laughing, having their pictures taken. A pecking, surging carpet of plump pigeons, fed by tourists and Londoners, blacks, whites, yellows, old and young, sterile and fecund and pregnant. The short-skirted, tightly clad girls and the drifting about of families as they forgot for the time being the wage they earned and where the money went and how they were to pay the next installment, and how and when and if they were to be promoted. And pictures seen from a train window: houses flashing past, the neatness of back gardens; an old couple sitting side by side in the sun, watching the train go by, and next door, another woman, on her knees, making a crazy path, and the lawn around her so green and in a weeping willow a single white fantail pigeon sitting. And out in a brown plowed field a cock pheasant, golden red. And Janey saying over and over, as she always did, how much better everything seemed "when I see it with you, Mikey darling."

"Listen," Michael then heard Birdy saying, "the easiest thing to miss in life is the moment at which the most important thing in it changes."

The temperature in Sydney hovered about the century and then began climbing. It reached 105 degrees, and on that day Archy came home early, not feeling well. Molly stared at him. "It's not what you're thinking, Chooks. It's that bloody appendix grumbling, that's all."

"Why in the name of all that's holy," Molly exclaimed, exasperated, "don't you get Sam Beck to whip that out? I'm so angry with you, Archy. You're just a bloody fool!" And with that she stormed out of the kitchen. A moment later she came back as he was getting ice water from the refrigerator. "Go and lie down," she said more quietly. "I've put the air conditioner on in the bedroom."

After he had gone up Birdy arrived. On the terrace he said to Molly, "You know why he won't let Beck or anyone else whip it out. Because he's a surgeon, that's why. He's like I'd be — scared. Is he vomiting?"

"No. Bit of nausea."

"I've seen him with it," Birdy said. "Classical appendicitis symptoms. It'll probably quiet down. Someday though," he added more grimly, "the bloody thing might pop. Then he'll be in more trouble than he can poke a stick at, especially the way things are going now."

"Anything fresh?"

Birdy screwed up his eyes. "All kinds of things. Some big, some small. Lots more garbage in the streets, litter. That's come rather suddenly. My telephone's on the blink. Also more dogs about." This seemed to puzzle him. "Don't know why, but so it seems to me. Talking of dogs, I saw Crackers in the garden. Is Kate here?"

"She's at her flat, packing. She's going to come here and stay with us."

"Bloody good idea." Birdy's eyes lightened. "Why don't you put her with Mike in the big double guest room downstairs?"

"And Archy," said Molly, "calls *me* an organizer!"

"I'm serious," said Birdy.

"I see that. Kate wouldn't go to bed with just anybody."

"Who says Mike is just anybody."

"I have strong protective feelings for Kate."

"As if I don't know that, God Almighty! But she doesn't need them," Birdy answered, "not from you. Wait a moment," he added as he saw Molly's lips tighten. "Let me finish. She doesn't need them from you now. He'll have them in plenty for her. Provided you don't keep them apart."

"Who said I do? Look, Birdy, why don't you come right out with it and say what you mean, that you're as sentimental an old fool as I am. You want them to fall in love."

"I didn't say anything about love, but now you mention it, I might as well say it: she's in love with him, and what's more I think she fell in love with him the moment she first clapped eyes on him. Kate's in a quandary."

"Why? I mean why particularly now?"

"Because Kate is one of those people who needs desperately to know that her actions are approved of. God knows, it's true of most of us. The average person doesn't want to feel he's earning the censure of those around him. Kate needs approval. You don't have to be explicit, merely let her know you'd be happy to see her with that chap."

"Maybe, but do you think Mike is the sort who'll jump from one bed into another, just like that?"

"Now you're being moral. Morality's got nothing to do with this."

"Then what has it to do with?"

"People like Mike and Kate aren't good at living alone. Which was why Kate disintegrated as she did when Tom died. Besides, it's a fact that in most cases, once you get used to being married, used to being connected with a person — whether of your own or the other sex doesn't matter — if and when that link is broken part of the anguish is not because you've lost a loved one but because you are alone."

"Oh, Birdy!" Molly sounded shocked.

"I don't see anything wrong in that. The more lonely you are only proves how much you miss the her or the him you've lost. If Kate were here she'd tell us what Dr. Johnson said on this subject, and mighty good sense I'm sure it is, too. But just because Mike's lost a woman he's in love with doesn't mean he can't find solace with another."

"So what you are suggesting," Molly said, "is that because you think Mike Canning is a good catch, Kate ought to bore in and get him on the rebound? Is that it?"

For a long, and to Molly a desperate, moment Birdy stared at her. Then he grinned and screwed up his eyes and said, "Molly, I always knew you were smart."

"You mean just that?" Her voice was high and angry.

"I mean," Birdy said, "just that. And listen, Molly, if you think time is on Katie's side — or anyone else's now — you're a bloody fool. It's eat, drink, and be merry now, with a vengeance. Did Archy tell you about Crown Street?"

"No."

"They've shut it."

"How do you mean, shut it? It's a maternity hospital. One of the biggest in Sydney."

"They've shut it because there's no one in it who's not dying of Ringway's."

"But surely, if people are dying, beds would be available for others who've caught it."

"A hospital needs more than beds. It needs staff, too."

"Well?"

"I said everybody there is dying of Ringway's."

"You mean the staff is dying, too?"

"Everybody."

"Christ, the children, too? And the premies?"

"You mean the respirator and the incubator lot? Fortunately," he went on, "someone had the good sense to pull the plug out on them. Always was bloody stupidity keeping a kid alive in a respirator when you didn't know it wasn't suffering from brain damage due to circulation failure. If I had my way I wouldn't have respirators in maternity hospitals. There are two extra mouths to feed every second and we can't feed even half of the world's population as it is, yet we spend enormous sums of money on highly sophisticated equipment to keep prematurely born, probably brain-damaged children alive. Who," he added with rare venom for Birdy, "shouldn't *ever* have been conceived in the first place! Not unless the parents were either ignoramuses or devils."

"Oh God, those children," said Molly softly.

"*You* weren't stupid enough to have children —"

"It's not just that, Birdy. I was lucky, if you like. We — Archy and I — were lucky. It's usually the man who wants a son, that sort of thing, but Arch saw the danger and we decided we wouldn't add to the problem, but, oh, God, I'd not thought about the children, there in the hospitals." Molly stood blinking at him,

[242]

as if not quite able to comprehend it. "Well, what happens?" It was almost a whisper.

"Some of the women try to help one another when their time comes," Birdy said softly. "Some try to feed their kids. But what's the good of that when you know you won't be there in a week's time. Some have strangled their kids. Old Cecil Morassey — remember him? The retired pediatrician? — he rang me this morning and said he was going over there today."

"But what can one old man do?" Molly exclaimed. "Even if he is a specialist. It'll only mean he'll get it."

"Do you think he doesn't know that?" Birdy paused and then added quietly, "Let's put it this way: he's going to make sure none of the kids starve to death."

It took Molly a moment to get it. Then she put both her hands up to her face. Tears fell through her fingers. Birdy watched her but didn't move. "I had to tell someone," he said, as if in justification. "Sorry, Molly, that it had to be you." Then he added, "But it had better stop right there, with you. Promise?"

For almost a full minute she stood as if transfixed. Then her hands fell and she looked at him. "Yes," she said, gulping out the words, "I promise."

"It'll be painless. Cecil has the gentlest hands I ever saw on a man."

There was a long silence and then Birdy said, "Molly, you let Kate know that if she wants any life with Mike she'd better not go wasting any time."

In catastrophe the rights of the so-called civilized are soon eroded. Even though it be in retreat, an army will stop long enough to loot and to rape, just as the army chasing it is doing. And in catastrophe there will always be some bureaucrat so devoted to his pen-pushing and rubber-stamping that he'll ask for copies in triplicate for the issue of blankets to those shivering to death or for cholera shots to the endangered.

As Ringway's went on spreading, in many places the people found it difficult to imagine that what was happening had not either been sent by God or come about because of the crookedness or the incompetence of the government. The Italians and the

Spanish and the South Americans were inclined to put the largest share of the blame on God and begged the Church to do something about it. Someone in Tel Aviv said the disease had come from Egypt, so for a time the Israelis called it Cairo flu. The Vietnamese put the blame on the Americans, and for some weeks the Indians blamed the Pakistanis while the people of Bangladesh blamed them both. The Hindus said it was caused by the Buddhists because they wouldn't take life and so had let the germ go free, and in Memphis, Tennessee, a Fundamentalist sect held it was the work of the devil and got a hellfire campaign going that was harder and harder to contain as the authorities became less and less effective. Quite quickly law and order disappeared, and such is the power of men and women imbued with the spirit of the literal inerrancy of the Holy Scripture that thousands of people died by shooting and bombing and burning in the name of Jesus Christ the Redeemer.

Then the sense of what was private property began to disappear. If people found or saw what they wanted they took it, or tried to, and they were soon prepared to fight for it. For the first time since the war, when a Japanese submarine shelled Sydney, gunshots were heard in Rose Bay. Some shops that had closed had their windows broken; a jewelry shop in Castlereagh Street in the heart of Sydney had its window broken, but trays of watches and rings were left untouched. Yet a few doors away the same night a man died, speared through the neck with a sliver of glass, in a fight over a cheap suit. Day by day there were less police to be seen, fewer ambulances were heard, and a fire once well established was seldom put out. Food shops were an exception; not only were they not broken into, at least in the early days, but somehow they appeared to be fairly well stocked.

Michael had been in Sydney for a month. With Molly and Archy and Birdy and Kate he was on the terrace, in the deep shade of the vine that covered nearly all of it; what breeze there was rustled the vine leaves and blew the sun-bleached strands of Kate's hair about her face. It was, as all those days were, hot, and the men were in shorts and shirts and the women in thin, brief cotton dresses. Molly and Kate were beginning to set the long table for lunch when Molly looked at her watch and went to the radio, which she'd put on a stone sideboard projecting from one of the low walls of the wide terrace.

"You know," Birdy said suddenly, "it'll soon be Christmas."

"It'll be more than that for you," said Kate, "if you talk while the news is on. I heard the end of a news flash about half an hour ago about some nuclear power station blowing up."

"Blowing up!" exclaimed Birdy. "Come off it, Katie. Where was this?"

"America."

"Ah, well then, you could be right. The Americans go in for boiling water reactors in a big way, and if one of them boils over it could be curtains for a hell of a lot of people."

"You know, Birdy," said Kate, "there's no getting away from it — you're the most anti-American bastard this side of the black stump."

Birdy grinned and winked at Molly, who turned on the radio. The voice came sharp and clear onto the terrace. "Reports are still coming in of a disastrous fire in a nuclear power station at Brown's Ferry in Decatur, Alabama, run by the Tennessee Valley Authority. This is the biggest nuclear power station in the world, and since its last fire in April 1975 it has been considerably enlarged, with new reactors each generating well over one thousand megawatts apiece. The area around the plant has now been declared a disaster area, and because of radiation fallout danger, reports of wide-scale evacuation downwind of the plant are coming in. Press agency reports that are still coming in speak of panic on the roads, which are jammed with cars as people flee the danger area . . ."

"There's a damn good German proverb about the plague," said Birdy. "It applies as much to those poor bastards downwind of that busted reactor as it does to us with Ringway's around every corner. 'The best means against the plague,'" Birdy quoted, "'is a pair of new boots used till they break.'"

"Oh, God," said Kate, "for heaven's sake, Birdy, will you shut up and *listen!*"

"Hundreds of people," the radio went on, "have been trampled to death or killed by police riot squads while trying to enter

[245]

Milan Cathedral, where a miraculous vision of San Rocco is said to have appeared on Tuesday night before hundreds of people praying in the church. As the news spread throughout Wednesday and Thursday, thousands of people thronged the square around the cathedral. When they began fighting among themselves for entry into the building, riot police were called and antiriot vehicles were driven at high speeds into the crowd. There was much shooting, and a United Press reporter who flew over the area in a light aircraft this morning has reported that the square and the streets leading to it are jammed with bodies. He could see injured people trying to crawl away from the place while others struggled toward the doors of the cathedral, already piled high with bodies . . ."

"Oh, God, I don't want to hear any more of this. It's just too dreadful."

"I thought," Birdy said, "you were the one who wanted the news."

"Reuters," the voice from the radio went on, "has just reported that they could find nobody at the Vatican willing to comment on the reports of the miraculous statue at Milan . . ."

"I'll bet they couldn't," grunted Birdy. "Did you know that Pope Paul III excommunicated the comet of 1532 because he thought it brought the plague?"

The voice went on: "In Darwin today a retired crocodile hunter shot his wife, three grown children, and his bedridden mother. All these members of his family were said to be suffering from Ringway's disease. He then went into the house next door and had shot a young housewife and her infant son before he was stabbed to death by an off-duty policeman who, hearing the shots while in his garden, ran to the scene of the crime armed with a pair of garden shears."

"For God's sake, turn it off," said Kate.

After Molly had switched it off they were silent. The heat beat down, the faint breeze stirred the big flat leaves of the vine, and away across the blue of the harbor a boat sailed, ghosting with a big genoa just pulling enough to be useful. Then into the silence Archy said to Birdy, "As you know, Birdy, I was against the idea in principle." He laid stress on the word principle.

"What principle?" asked Molly.

"Birdy and I were talking earlier about leaving."

Archy looked at Michael. "Do you," he asked, "still feel the same way?"

"Well, I certainly see Birdy's point of view," Michael answered slowly.

"Only sensible thing to do," grunted Birdy. He swiveled in his chair to Archy and said, "Tell us about the airplane."

"What airplane? What are you talking about?" cried Molly.

It took Archy a moment to shift his thoughts. "Well," he said finally, glancing up at Molly, suspended in the act of setting the table, "it's a Britten-Norman Islander. It's had some pretty hard use, but its C of A is in order. It's got some paint off, but it's a very good airplane. You see, Chooky, I think that Birdy's right."

"Right about what?"

"About going north."

"I see." Molly came from behind the table and sat down slowly, still with the cutlery in her hand.

"I thought we'd fly," Archy went on. "I didn't want to tell you until I knew if I could get an airplane. I can."

Kate looked at Michael, then at Archy. "And what about us?" she asked.

"Yes," said Molly quickly, "what about Kate? And Mike?"

"There's room for all of us."

"Crackers can come?" Kate said; it wasn't really a question.

"Yes."

The breath ran out of Kate in a long sigh.

"This has knocked me all of a heap," said Molly. "Usually things don't. Are you sure, Archy, it's the right thing to do?"

He nodded. "I've still got reservations, of course. But the answer is, yes."

"Where would we go?"

"North," said Birdy. "Same as me. Nowhere else to go. No good going south, down among the fucking penguins and icebergs."

"Then why not go all together? In Birdy's boat?"

Archy said, "We've talked that over, but we've decided it would be safer to split up."

"Safer?" asked Kate.

"The smaller the individual groups," said Michael, "the smaller the chance of infection. Birdy's got a boat full of kids."

There was silence.

"What sort of an airplane did you say, Archy?" asked Molly.

"A Britten-Norman Islander."

"You've seen it?"

"I flew it today." Archy grinned at her like a schoolboy.

Her face lit with sudden pleasure. "How did it go?" she asked. She liked Archy's flying and always urged him to do more of it. "You flew it all right?"

"What little time I had on it, yes. The chap was scared stiff when he learned I was a doctor. He relaxed a bit when I swore I'd not seen a case of Ringway's. It flies beautifully, Chooks. Mind, I've not had many hours on a twin-engined machine. It makes a difference."

"How far can it fly?"

Archy felt in his pocket and pulled out a piece of paper. "This one's a long-range model with wingtip tanks, fortunately." He studied some penciled figures on the paper. "Something over a thousand miles, I'd reckon."

"That's on one fill of gas?"

Archy nodded. "Naturally it depends on headwinds, that kind of thing. But we'd fly with engine settings for maximum range."

"And how many people can it carry?"

"It'll carry ten. But this particular aircraft has only five seats in it at the moment. There's plenty of baggage space, thirty-six cubic feet. It's got a good short takeoff and landing. With any luck, I ought to be able to land it on a beach or small field."

"I can't see how we can afford to buy it," said Molly.

"We can, Chooks," he said quietly. "That part's all right."

"What about getting gas?" said Kate.

"They say that there's still plenty. But you have to help yourself."

"So now we become castaways on some island or lonely beach, is that it?" said Molly.

"It'll burn itself out, you know, Molly," said Michael. "Every other great plague has in the end."

"I'm not so sure this one will," said Birdy.

[248]

"So wait a minute," said Molly. "If Mike's right and it burns itself out ultimately, we then come back here. Is that it?"

"If we're still alive, yes, of course," said Archy.

"But, Mike," said Kate, "you told me that bubonic plague hasn't burned itself out. There are still places in the world where plague exists."

"Controlled," said Michael. "Or so we would hope. The great world epidemic of plague burned itself out. Ringway's will probably die in the same way."

"It'll only die," said Birdy grimly, "if and when there are no more people for it to infect. In other words, when the pool in which it can live dries up. If you can avoid that pool, when the pool has dried up you can come back. Then those who have ratted will inherit the earth. It'll take time. And the world you'll inherit will be a mess. The insects and the rats — the real rats, the four-legged variety — will be largely in possession by then. They'll be walking around Australia Square, up and down Piccadilly, in and out of Times Square and the Kremlin as if they owned them. And by God, by then they will own them. And what's more, they'll be as fat and as pompous and as arrogant and evil and vindictive and ruthless and aggressive as man ever was. Unless, of course, they get Ringway's, too. That's one side of the coin.

"The other is more attractive, because without man wild animals will begin to thrive again, real forests may start to grow, the seas and some of the lakes and rivers might even begin to recover. Without man, or with only a few million people stretched pretty thinly around the globe, the world might have a chance of becoming beautiful again."

The next morning Archy and Michael drove to see the Islander. What people they saw were wearing masks, but they were people who seemed to move differently, who didn't so much walk as scurry along. Some wore industrial dust masks, others gas masks; one man they saw had a skin diver's mask and air bottles. "Not a bad idea," said Michael, "provided he's sure he's not filled the bottles with infected air. Clumsy out of the water, though." The bottles on the man's back were painted yellow, and they bumped up and down as he hurried along.

At the airport there was nobody in the gatekeeper's hut. It was another very hot day and heat waves shimmered over the field. On the tarmac in front of the hangars stood a few light aircraft. Some were tied down between the hangars. A Cessna stood well out on the tarmac, with an open door swinging occasionally in the hot breeze. "The control tower's abandoned now," said Archy. He pulled the car in beside the biggest hangar and they got out. As they did they heard an aircraft at full throttle. In a moment it came in sight, a Beechcraft Baron, heavily loaded, on takeoff, the pilot holding it down, making good use of runway space. They watched it, and as it lifted off Archy said, "Looks like someone else with the same idea."

In the hangar the Islander stood beside a Victor Air Tourer. "Well, there she is," Archy said, "Looks a bit beat up, but she's in first-rate nick." Michael saw that her paint was dirty and there were oil streaks on her nacelles.

"Now you're sure, Mike," Archy said, "you wouldn't rather I got a bit more practice first? I won't be offended."

"I'm perfectly happy," said Michael.

"Well, let's do the preflight checks. Better do it by the book," he added, getting into the aircraft. "And see the maggy switches are off."

When he got out, book in hand, Michael followed him around, looking at the oleos, the tires, and the brake hoses. He turned the left propeller twice, by hand, checked the level of oil by the filler cap dipstick, drained the gasolator, saw that the pitot head was clear, and looked to see that the aileron was not locked. Then he looked at the tail surfaces; on the right side of the machine he did the same checks.

Then Michael followed Archy into the plane and sat in the right-hand seat. "There's plenty of room in it," said Michael, looking back into the cabin.

"Bags of it. She's really a beautiful plane. Normally she seats ten. I was thinking of taking out that fifth seat on the starboard side, to make more storage space, but we might as well leave it in. Crackers can have it. Now, let's do the cockpit checks." Finally he said, "We'll start her in here, in the hangar."

Archy pumped the right throttle twice to prime that engine,

and went through the starting drill. Then the left. Each engine fired almost immediately, though when he selected the magneto switch in the left engine Archy, as well as Michael, was startled to hear the warning klaxon.

"Christ!" exclaimed Michael. "What's that?"

For a second Archy sat puzzled, looking at the warning light glowing brightly. Then he said, "Hey, wait!" He sounded much relieved. "It's the door! Not shut properly."

In the hangar the Lycoming 0-5400 engines made a lot of noise. Without waiting for them to warm up he let off the brake and steered out, using the rudder pedals. On the tarmac he tested the brakes and let his engines warm. Then slowly he taxied toward the end of the runway. As they climbed the slight rise they saw that at the far side of the field a number of tents were pitched, well away from one another. There were also some caravans, with awnings rigged against them. Some of the camps had barbed-wire fences around them.

Archy turned the Islander, stopped, and did the threshold check. Then, satisfied, he opened the throttles slowly to the take-off position. He took a glance to see that Michael's harness was on and then said, "All right. Except for once when I threw her at the ground I didn't do too badly when the chap took me around, so here goes."

Lightly loaded, the Islander came unstuck quickly. At two hundred feet Archy raised flaps and trimmed out the nose-down heaviness. Then he set engines and manifold pressures to power for climb-out. There was some bumpiness due to hot air rising from the sun-baked earth and houses below. At two thousand feet he leveled off. As always he felt that extraordinary sense of freedom when flying his own aircraft. "She's a bloody beautiful airplane, Mike. Let's have a bit of a look around Sydney before the circuits and bumps," and he began a gentle bank away in the direction of the harbor.

Then they saw just how Sydney had changed. The litter in the streets could be seen clearly. There were tents pitched in the Domain and in other parks. In the harbor even small day sailers were being lived in, with sails stretched as awnings over their booms. Beaches were peppered with tents, as was Centennial

Park. At Botany Bay, the international Kingsford-Smith Airport was closed and deserted. Millions of dollars' worth of big jets stood cooking in the broiling sun. Some of the hangar doors were open, others half shut.

The water of the harbor was greeny blue, that of the Pacific outside it deep blue. A ferry was leaving Circular Quay, and its wake was silver white. Beyond the empty harbor bridge tents and caravans could be seen dotted about the Botanic Gardens and among the trees at Farm Cove. "It's unbelievable," Archy said, pointing to the bridge. "Normally at this time of day it'd be crowded with traffic." The huge sails of the Opera House gleamed in the sun, and near the dockyard lay a frigate, its white ensign hanging unmoving. "Christ," Archy said after about half an hour. "This is getting me down, seeing Sydney like this. Bloody fantastic. And it'll be the same in Melbourne and Perth and Brisbane and Adelaide. All over."

Michael said nothing. He was thinking of some film clips they'd seen on television, shots of London from the air, with tents in Green Park and double-decker buses standing in Piccadilly, deserted by their crews, others in Hyde Park where they'd been crashed through railings and set up as homes; there were shots of washing hanging from the windows of huge office blocks on the Embankment. Of ships lying unworked in the Pool of London. And the shots of the pitched battles before the police and army gave up trying to drive people from Kensington Park, from Salisbury Plain, from Windsor Great Park, from any land, public or private, where a tent could be pitched. They had given up because the police force and the army had ceased to exist as entities, their members becoming, like everyone else, merely people desperate to find an isolated place to live in. One shot from those clips had particularly appalled him. It had been taken from a helicopter that had chopped its way along Oxford Street. Barely a shop window remained unbroken, and both roads and pavements were littered with discarded loot, sodden and muddied.

Archy said, "The more I come to think of it, Mike, the more I think Birdy's right, you know. Australia's such a bloody big place and there's so few people in it. It shouldn't be too hard to find somewhere on our own. Not like in Japan, say; small countries

[252]

with big populations. Australia's really big; she's the driest continent in the world yet she's got more snow than Switzerland, and up in the Kimberleys, that's where Western Australia juts out toward the Timor Sea, in the wet season the rivers up there are fifty miles wide. If we can get the gas," he added, "and lube oil, I reckon we'll be damned unlucky if we don't find somewhere. By the way, I heard yesterday that there's still plenty of gas up north at places like Delta Downs, Groote Eylandt, Melville Island, and farther west, too, inland at the Gibb River, places like that. If we can get the juice, by flying for maximum range we can have a damned good look at God alone knows how many hundreds of miles of uninhabited beaches. We can live in the tents until we can build a house. We must take plenty of good axes and saws and woodworking tools."

Forty minutes later Archy began his circuits and bumps. They saw only two other aircraft in the air, a Beagle twin and a Cessna 172. He then tried several balked landings. All of them went well. Finally he came in at 65 knots, turned, and taxied slowly back to the pumps.

"Who do we pay for the gas?" asked Michael.

"Nobody," said Archy. He let the engines idle until the temperatures dropped and checked his magnetos for a dead cut. Then he moved the mixture controls downward into the idle cutoff position. As the propellers stopped moving, he added, "Crazy, isn't it? But, you see, there's no one to pay."

When they had seen the Islander parked and the hangar locked, Archy drove Michael back to the house, dropped him off, and then went to the hospital. Molly was in the kitchen baking cakes. "Mike," she said, "Kate's got the pip. She's been listening to the news and it's got her down."

"Anything special on the news?" he asked.

"Nothing good. And there's another reactor boiled over. They tried to shut it down but couldn't. Take her for a swim, will you? Did you enjoy the flight?"

"Yes," Michael said slowly. "The actual flight I enjoyed. As Archy says, light airplane flying is one of the great joys of living. But we didn't enjoy what we saw."

"I shouldn't think so." Molly shut the oven door. "Mike, do get

[253]

Kate and Crackers and take them for a swim. When Kate gets the pip so does that dog. He looks as if he's lost every bone he's ever buried." Molly went out of the kitchen into the hall and called up along the wide staircase, "Katie, Mike's back and he wants to take you for a swim. Put your togs on."

"It's nearly dark," came Kate's voice back in reply.

Molly looked at Michael. "See what I mean?"

"You heard me," Molly called. "Mike's almost ready to go."

"Oh, very well."

Michael drove in the dusk. He was in shorts with his trunks on underneath; Kate was in her dark green bikini, a color complementing the pale duskiness of her skin, the brief top accentuating the fullness of her fine breasts.

Crackers ran down the beach and stood waiting while they followed. There were not many people on the half-moon of sand, but each little group kept strictly to itself, either on the beach or in the water. Some of the swimmers wore their masks in the water, which Kate said looked silly, just plain bloody silly.

Out of their depth Kate stopped swimming and said, "This was a good idea. I feel better already. Who thought of it, you or Molly?"

"Molly."

"Molly has some good ideas sometimes." Kate spoke as she trod the water, looking away out of the little bay across the wide blue of the harbor. "Can you," she began, turning toward him, "talk about Jane yet? I'll tell you why I ask," she went on quickly, "because if you can't I'll understand. I mean," she went on much more quickly, embarrassed but determined, "after Tom died I couldn't speak about it for ages and ages, so if you can't I'll understand," she finished softly. "I'll bet she was lovely."

"She was," he said, turning to her.

Kate let herself sink, and he saw the redness of her hair floating out and under it the dusky paleness of her body shimmering and weaving in the darkening water. Then she came up, tossed the water from her face, and called to Crackers, who was swimming strongly with his muzzle held high out of the water. "They say," she said as Crackers turned and came paddling back, "that dogs get taken because sharks can smell them a long way off." Then, as if it was part of the same sentence, she went on, "Come on, let's go home," and she struck off strongly for the beach with the dog close behind her. When they got back, Michael showered and changed and went out onto the terrace.

Molly's voice surprised him. "You've not got a drink, Mike." She was at the drinks cart.

"I'll wait for Kate."

"She's lying down," Molly said. She was about to add more, but instead swung around as Archy came quickly out onto the terrace and they nearly bumped into one another. She splashed some of the drink out of her glass, said *"Damn!"* and marched back into the house.

Archy looked after her, puzzled. "Now what's got into her?" he asked.

"Perhaps," Mike said, "I'd better leave here, Archy."

"*Leave* here? Now?" Archy's voice rose in surprise, "what the hell do you want to do that for?"

Michael stood looking out into the gathered heat of the night. There was no wind moving and the lights twinkled and flashed and away somewhere an aircraft droned. Michael remembered Janey with a vividness he'd not thought possible. Jane would have sounded much as Kate had out there in the water. Why hadn't he married Janey? There was no answer to that; all they knew was that one day they would marry and that had seemed enough . . .

"Look, Mike." Archy's voice startled him out of his reverie. "For God's sake, what's got into everyone? I come home and find you talking about leaving here, Molly in a temper, and Kate in a sulk, on her bed. What's up?"

"I'll tell you what's up." Molly spoke from the house door. She turned to Archy. "Kate wants to marry Mike."

"Oh, Christ!" said Archy. "As if there wasn't enough trouble already!"

A softly burbling exhaust noise could now be heard from the drive below the house. Archy said, "It's Birdy, in the Bentley." Birdy's magnificent old car came surging into sight and slid to the gentlest of stops; the engine continued to purr for a moment and then died. Birdy looked up at them and grinned. "I thought," he said, "I'd give her an airing." His screwed-up little eyes glinted maliciously. "That's the charm of Ringway's. Now no one knows for sure just how many more times we'll be able to do things, or even whether we'll *ever* do them again." He paused, staring up at them. "What's up with you two? You look like the girl did when she discovered she'd taken a month's supply of slimming tablets instead of the pill."

Birdy got out of the car and came up. He grunted, bent to the cart, and poured himself a stiff drink. "There's a big fire in town," he said. "How did the flying go?" He joined them, drink in hand.

"That went all right. Yes, we saw the smoke at Circular Quay."

"Well, what didn't go all right? What's up?" He looked from one to the other.

"It's Kate," said Archy.

"It's my fault, Birdy," Mike said softly. "I think perhaps I'd better leave here."

"Like hell!" Birdy said savagely. "Kate's in love with you, isn't she?"

Molly said, "Yes, she is."

"But Kate" — Birdy gestured with his glass toward the house — "has been in love ever since she first clapped eyes on him. Now listen, Mike," he began, but then Molly said, "Hush, she's coming."

Kate came through the big doorway, looking in the light of the terrace lamps so startlingly beautiful that Michael felt his breath draw in.

"She's been crying," said Molly.

"It suits her," grunted Birdy. He moved toward her, not taking his eyes off her. "What is it, Katie? Out with it."

"We're all leaving soon, right?" Kate said. "Today Archy and Mike flew the plane and you've got the boat and the kids, haven't you?" she said.

Birdy nodded.

"Well . . ." She stopped and looked at Michael, and her eyes began to fill with tears.

"Go on," Birdy said.

Kate moved toward Michael. "It's true, as Birdy says. Let me explain a bit, please. You see, I just couldn't ever see myself looking at another man, *really* looking at another man. And then," she went on, "you turned up. Just like that . . ." She looked around from one to the other, and the silence was heavy on the terrace until a dog barked and Crackers got up, went to the edge of the terrace, put his front paws on the balustrade, and growled into the night.

"All right," Birdy said suddenly — he still hadn't taken his eyes off Kate. "So what the hell do you want to do now?"

"I want to marry Mike."

"A shotgun wedding, eh? What can the poor bugger say now, surrounded by the lot of *us*. Who says he wants to marry you —"

"Mike, dear," said Kate. "At least I've got it out now! And now that I've made a fool of myself and done that it'll be easier, seeing you every day."

Kate went and sat slowly on one of the big wide settees. She sat looking at the terrace pavement as if she still hadn't said all she wanted to, and they waited, staring at her. She glanced at Birdy, then looked away into the night. "For some time now," she went on more quickly, "I've known what that bit from Ecclesi-astes means. 'Two are better than one,' it says, 'because they have a good reward for their labor. For if they fall, the one will lift up his fellow.' Then, and this is the bit I was meaning, 'but woe to him that is alone when he falleth; for he hath not another to help him up . . . if two lie together, then they have heat: but how can one be warm alone?' "

She was silent for a long moment and none of them spoke. "You can say I want Mike because I'm tired of being alone, of not being with someone to help me up when I falleth. But it's not quite as simple as that. If I go with a man I want more than just heat. I mightn't be a particularly virtuous person, but I'm not just looking for a bed."

Molly went and sat beside her protectively.

"You haven't made a fool of yourself, Kate," Mike said quickly, earnestly, crossing to her.

"I've thrown myself at you." She began to cry.

"Well, what the fuckin' else do women ever do," growled Birdy, and he went on his short legs to the cart and there came the sound of the whiskey and the ice going into his long crystal glass. "I think," he said finally, "it's the best bit of news for a long time. I told you, didn't I, Molly, that you ought to have put 'em together in the double guest room."

"But don't you *see*," cried Kate, looking up at Birdy, her face streaming with tears, "I want to get *married*."

"Bloody nonsense," grunted Birdy. "Anyway, how do you know he" — he gestured with his glass toward Mike, — "wants to marry you. Have you asked him?" Birdy grinned.

"If you don't mind, I'll do the asking," Mike said.

"Huh! And about time," grunted Birdy, but they could see how pleased he was.

"Dear Kate," Mike said, his heart in his eyes, "will you marry me?"

"She'll think it over and let you know," growled Birdy with mock derision.

"Yes," said Kate, and she stood up and Mike took her in his arms and held her close until Archy cleared his throat and said, "I think I'd better get the champagne."

They drank the champagne in silence. Molly went and looked out over the harbor and Michael sat next to Kate and Crackers jumped up on Kate and she sat stroking his head. Her other hand rested on Michael's. "When," Kate said, "do we get married? When do we leave? There isn't much time, is there?"

There was silence, and then Molly turned and looked at Archy. "Well," she said, "Kate's asked a question, Archy. When do we leave?"

# 13 ⌇⌇⌇⌇⌇⌇⌇⌇⌇⌇⌇⌇⌇⌇⌇⌇⌇⌇⌇⌇⌇⌇⌇

The crowd of pygmies stood at the foot of the ladder in silence, their faces hostile, and stared up fiercely. Elizabeth's voice was tight with fear. "We *must* have offended them. I've never seen them look like this before!" Steve, balancing on his crutches, moved to comfort her.

"Do they want us to go away, Steve? Perhaps they're sick of us. Want to get rid of us, want to take us out into the jungle and leave us —"

"Now come on! I don't think it's that at all. But I must say, I wish to God I knew what it was all about."

"Why do they *look* like that? Sad, yes, they always look sad, even lugubrious, but now they're so *grim*-looking. Why did you say the other day they weren't headhunters?"

"Because I thought maybe you were thinking they were."

For a second she was silent, recalling what she'd seen in the big house. "You notice how quiet the village sounds this morning? I can't even hear the children playing."

"Maybe if we had Boar's Tusk up here we could mumble and make signs at him and sort it all out?" he said.

"I doubt it," she protested. "Look how far we got with him the other day."

"But, honey . . ." he broke off. "Christ, we must have managed to get *something* across."

"But what? This?" She gestured hopelessly toward the door. "We don't even know what they're planning to do with us." Then she added, "Say we just refuse to budge?"

He shrugged. "I guess they'll find some other way of getting rid of us. If that's what they want. In any case, I don't see we've any option but to go with them."

"Could we try telling them we'll go some other time, say tomorrow?"

"What good would that do?"

"And how to say 'tomorrow'?" she said.

"Listen, maybe their looking that way has nothing to do with us. Perhaps there's some other factor we know nothing about."

"Such as?"

"Hell, I don't know. Unless maybe the airplane crash is out of their territory and they don't like going there —"

"But they went before —"

"Sure they did. But it might be different now."

"But it was such a little thing," she said helplessly. "Merely asking to go back to the crash."

"We don't know, honey, how big or how little a thing it was. What worries me now is that we might have lost their trust. I figured the way they had us worked out, they trusted us."

For a long moment he stared at the bright rectangle of the doorway. Elizabeth was about to speak again when he turned to her.

"Let's vote," he said, "whether we go or not." He paused. "I vote we go. How do you?"

"With you," she said, after a second's hesitation. "Can you imagine me staying here now? Seeing them cart you off? Anyway, I don't see that we've any alternative but to go with them. We're in their hands." She was about to move toward the door when she said, "I've only got on this dress I sleep in. There's a heavier one there. I think I'd better change it."

Suddenly there came an increased chatter of conversation from the pygmies at the foot of the ladder. "I think we'd better go on down," Steve said. "I can manage the short ladder by myself."

To Elizabeth and Steve one path through the jungle looked the same as any other. The one sign they may have had that they were going to the crash was that they went out through the same entrance to the village as the one through which they had been brought. "Not that this means much," Elizabeth said after she'd pointed this out to Steve. "There are only two ways into the village, and the path from the other leads no farther than to the stream." Again, it took some maneuvering to get Steve's litter through the narrow, stake-guarded entrance. He wanted to get off and walk, but Boar's Tusk pushed him back, with much head-shaking. There was barely enough room on the trail for Elizabeth to walk beside the litter, her hand resting on Steve's shoulder. The pygmies spoke seldom, loping along with bodies bent forward, bows either slung over their left shoulder or hanging from their hands. Still, the tenseness remained in them, and often Elizabeth glanced down at Steve. When their eyes met he smiled at her. "Don't worry, honey," he said. "I don't think these guys are doin' us wrong."

"I've been thinking," she said. "If they are going to leave us, perhaps we could find the plane? We could live in that," she said hopefully.

"Sure we could. Now don't you go on worrying." He didn't add — if they could find the airplane, what would they use for food? They were as dependent upon these people as a three-month-old baby was upon its mother. The idea galled him and frightened him, and he shifted on the litter. "Are you all right?" she asked, bending to him. "Sure, I'm okay, honey. Watch where you put your feet." She smiled and looked ahead again. He stared up at her. She'd changed into the heaviest dress she had, a blue one of slub linen; he could see the movement of her breasts as she walked.

"Steve," she said a few minutes later, "whenever I've seen the men coming from the jungle back to the village — or when they've been going out — I've noticed that among their arrows are some blunt-headed ones, arrows with flat heads instead of points."

"They're for hunting birds," he said.

"I know that. But I've been looking at their arrows now.

There's not one of them carrying anything but pointed arrows. And you notice how practically every one of them has a strip of fur around his spear?"

"Why that's just decoration," he said, doing his best to allay her fears. "It's cuscus fur."

They walked on in silence, Steve swinging from side to side on his litter, holding onto the sides of it to reduce his rolling as much as he could. He was desperately uncomfortable and in a fair amount of pain, but he didn't want Elizabeth to see that.

They had walked for something over three quarters of an hour and were making their way along one of the steepest parts of the trail when there came a call from somewhere ahead and they stopped. Some of the men began to chatter uneasily. They put Steve down and stood peering forward. Elizabeth dropped down beside Steve. "Don't be frightened," he said softly, and he put his hand on her thigh. "Do they have scouts out ahead?" he asked, straining to look forward from his place on the ground.

"I don't know." She was looking up at the men who'd been carrying Steve and saw that they'd unslung their bows.

"They seem scared of something." Steve struggled up to a sitting position.

"They can't be half as scared as I am," she said quietly.

Suddenly the rest of the men were back, slipping silently along the trail.

"How many do you figure we started with?"

"About thirty," she said.

Steve finished a rough count. "Well, they've sent some on ahead," he said. Then Boar's Tusk was beside the litter. He said something and Steve was suddenly swung into the air again. On they went.

Soon they were moving through what was virtually a dark green tunnel, so thick was the growth above their heads. They could hear water running, and Elizabeth thought she heard a man call out. "It could have been a bird," Steve said. "You get some mighty strange noises in virgin jungle like this."

Twenty minutes later they reached the wrecked airplane. The journey had taken about an hour and a half. Elizabeth's first impression was how overgrown it had become. Already tendrils of creepers were inside or climbing around it. Trees that had showed scars where the plane had sliced into them were already beginning to look whole again.

The men got up to the wreck and put the litter down. Elizabeth helped Steve up and he stood on his crutches. "This is the first time I've seen it," he said, staring. "Jesus wept, what a mess. Let's get in and see what we can find."

"There's one thing, Steve," she said. "The bodies."

Steve was a little ahead of her, moving heavily on his crutches. He didn't answer until he came to the open end of the fuselage. He stood there, the lower part of the shell of the wreck about level with his head. "From what I can see," he said, peering in, "they aren't there now. Jesus Christ," he added, "it's like a mad-woman's breakfast. No, I don't see any bodies; the pygmies must have buried them."

She opened her mouth to speak but then shut it. She had been about to remind him of what she'd seen hanging in the smoky darkness of that house in the village.

"Here," Steve said, "let's get these guys to help me up inside."

Elizabeth followed and they went right forward. Aft of the flight deck bulkhead on the starboard side was a space that held electronic equipment in racks. Opposite it was a crew baggage and service space. Steve leaned in. Then he said, "I can't get down in there. See what you can pull out."

She squeezed past him and got on her knees, pulling away the creepers that were pushing in through the torn skin on the under-side of the fuselage. "There's a metal box here," she said finally.

"Can you get it out? It might be tools. Geoscan often operates their planes from pretty remote fields and sometimes carries an engineer."

"It's jammed," she said. She sat back. "What's this above it?"

"Survey equipment. Magnetometer, gear like that."

"I'll try again."

With Steve's help she finally pulled out an oblong metal box. "That's tools, for sure." He grinned down at her. "Pull those two handles on the top sideways."

The box was crammed with tools.

"Gee, this is just great." Steve's voice was high with elation.

"Now with these tools, see if we can't get the magnetic compass. If it's not bust."

It was a direct reading type with a correction card. And it was undamaged. Elizabeth said she'd get it and worked her way into the pilot's seat. Steve pointed to the screws she should undo. She got the compass and handed it back to him. As she scrambled back she said, "Steve, couldn't we take these two seats?"

The pilot's seat on the left was canted at an angle but seemed undamaged, except for a stain that he thought was blood. The copilot's seat seemed untouched.

"The pilot's seat," he said, pointing to it, "is probably sprung from its fixings."

"I can see the ground under it. The plane's all broken away here," she said.

They were sweating a lot when they finished, but they unshipped the seat and then worked it through to the cabin.

"The other one seems more or less properly in its fixings," he said, moving heavily back. "You'll have to find a wrench that fits the studs."

Propping himself against the bulkhead, he watched her as she wriggled down in front of the seat. The copilot's rudder pedals and the base of the control column had been pushed back, making it hard for her to get herself in a position to bring pressure on the holding-down nuts. Her dress worked itself up around her hips. Once the wrench flew off a nut and she barked her knuckles. She swore, then began to laugh, nearly collapsing in the wrecked and twisted metal. "God," she said finally, "if my friends could see me now."

"One of them can, baby. And you look great."

"I bet I do."

"Did I ever tell you what lovely legs you've got?"

It took them half an hour, but they got this seat, too. The seats looked incongruous in the jungle, heavily padded, dark blue cloth, the webbing harnesses hanging from them as if they were tentacles. Elizabeth put the compass and the tool box with them. The men stood around, sometimes chattering, but, as always, they showed no surprise. The map case was a disappointment. Insects had got at the paper. They found some pages from a *Pacific Air-*

*ways Route Manual,* an Island Group Index chart, and a mileage chart with rhumb-line distances in nautical miles. "We'll take all this stuff, honey," he said, "I might be able to do something with it. We've got pencils now and ball-points. Maybe I can put the pieces together and draw us a map. Let's get some of this cabin lining down; that'll be swell to draw on."

The strips of dress that Elizabeth had tied to the trees were still there and led them to the afterpart of the aircraft. From this they took the galley curtains. They jimmied open a locker door and found a tray of knives, forks, and spoons. As they rummaged in the mess ants began scurrying about, carrying their white eggs. Then they started to examine the wreck of the tail section, which had been ripped open, but they found only two suitcases, both with their lids sprung, the clothing already well rotted.

"I still haven't found my big knife," Steve said dejectedly. "We can use some wire, I guess," he added.

"Wire?"

"I want to get some cable from the plane."

Boar's Tusk was now plainly anxious to go. He kept very close to them, chattering sometimes to himself. When they looked at him he began pointing away. "Okay," said Steve, "we go."

On the way back, Steve said, "Look at these guys carrying me, armchairs, portmanteaus. I feel like some crusty old British explorer on the way to suppress the natives. I guess I'll have to dress for dinner tonight."

"What about me?"

"Those old Britishers didn't have beautiful white girls with them. They lived off the land."

By Steve's calculations they were about twenty minutes from the village when Elizabeth pointed to their left, where a curious, almost bald dome of rock stuck up above a high ridge. "I'd like to go up there," she said.

"Sure, we'll go, just the two of us, when my leg's better."

"How would we get up there?"

"Maybe up that kind of fissure on this end. There's plenty of vegetation there to climb up among."

"What a view you'd get," she said.

"It's an idea. Who knows, we may even see the sea from there.

Now, don't get excited," he went on more quickly. "I'd say the chances of seeing the coast were pretty slim. On the other hand, we don't know where we are, so maybe we might."

Back in the house Steve was in pain. She got him onto the platform, plumped out the fern-stuffed pillow, and sat with him while the men came in carrying their spoils from the crash. Steve was watching them when suddenly his eyes lit up. "Hey, honey, that's my briefcase," he said, sitting up, wincing as the pain came.

"Lie back," she said. "I'll get it for you."

Water had seeped in, and the papers in it were a sodden mess, but in the side pocket, "right where I said it was," was Steve's big Swiss knife. "Gee, am I pleased to see that! All stainless," he said, opening the blades, "not a speck of rust anywhere. Hey, I almost forgot," he exclaimed suddenly. "This is like Christmas morning around the tree. Go get those batteries. And the radio."

She sat, holding the batteries, watching him while he opened the back of the set. One by one he fitted them into the battery pack, then shut the case. "Now," he said, looking up at her, "say a prayer, and keep your fingers crossed way up to your elbows. I'm going to turn it on."

The. blast of radio interference that followed made Steve fumble for the volume switch. Elizabeth gave a great shout of joy and threw her arms about him while he grabbed at the radio to stop it being knocked off his lap.

"It's stopped!" she cried, aghast.

"I turned it off," he said. "You were assaulting me."

"Please," she begged. "Oh, *please* switch it on again."

"You're a wild woman," he said, grinning at her. "Now just sit back there nice and quiet and let me fiddle with it. This is a good set," he added, turning it on again. "It'll get just about all over."

# 14 〰〰〰〰〰〰〰〰〰〰〰〰〰〰〰〰〰

"When do we leave?"

"I haven't decided. Not really." Archy looked at the others. "Is it up to me to decide?"

"Well, you're the pilot," said Molly.

"I'm going," said Birdy, trying to help Archy, "as soon as I can. As soon as I've got my bunch of kids together I'm off. I've enough food and seeds and cloth and tools, even a sewing machine. And got it all aboard, what's more."

"Suppose you get Ringway's?" asked Archy.

"You mean before I leave? I've thought of that. The idea might still work. I've got Clive Hutton's boy Rex as mate. He could take a boat like *White Wings* north, I think. And I've got his girl friend, too, Abe Harman's kid, Sally."

"She's good value," said Molly. "Rex is a bit wild for my liking. How old are the others?"

"The youngest is twelve. Average age ought to work out around fifteen, sixteen. The parents agree because they've no bloody alternative. Wouldn't you, if you had a kid?" He looked from one to the other, but none of them spoke.

"Please," said Kate firmly, "when can I get married?"

"It's not *when*, it's *if*," said Birdy. "I doubt whether you'd find a register office open. Anyhow, like I said, can't you just live together?"

"No, I want it done well," Kate said.

"If I have to, I'll marry them myself," said Molly, and she sounded as if she meant it.

"What about Father Gleason?" said Archy.

"He's dead, Arch," said Molly.

"Father Percival?" said Kate. "I know he's not in our parish, but that wouldn't matter."

Molly looked at her doubtfully. "I could ring him and see."

"None of my business," said Birdy. "The religion, I mean. But priests have got a bad name these days because they go about among people. I'd be careful, Katie, if I were you."

"But surely," she said, "we could find *someone* without it."

Birdy shrugged.

"I'm going to ring Father Percival," Molly said. "He's sensible, and if he can't do it himself he might know of someone who's safe."

She was away for some time. When she came back they all looked at her, waiting for her to speak. Finally she said, "Katie, if you want it written down somewhere, it'll have to be the register office. Father Percival hasn't got it but he expects it daily. His church is full of people with it. They've turned the pews around, seat front to seat front, and converted them into beds. But he says if we ring him, he'll give you his blessing over the phone. That goes for Mike, too," she added. "But that's all he can do."

Mike said, "Archy, where's the nearest register office?"

"I think I know," said Molly. "I'll go and look it up." When she came back she said, "It's not far. We'll all go in the big car. Birdy, you can give her away."

For a moment they thought Birdy was going to refuse. Finally he said, "Must go home first."

"Whatever for?" asked Kate.

"If you must know, for half a dozen bottles of champagne I've got stashed away. The *real* stuff, too," he grunted, getting to his feet, "vintage."

"You damned old hoarder," said Archy.

"Present from a grateful patient." Birdy grinned.

When they got to the register office they found it deserted, though the door was open. Whoever had been the last to leave had done so in a hurry. Ledgers, files, and forms lay scattered about on the counter, on tables behind, and in the smaller offices that led off the counter room. A red dog startled them by waking suddenly. He shot past them out into the street. The place smelled stale and hot, and blowflies buzzed against a windowpane.

"Don't let's all look in the same place," said Archy. "Let's split up. There'll be a bloody great book or a safe full of files somewhere."

"And the lines," said Kate. "The certificate. I want the lines."

Archy finally found the register and Michael the certificates. They stood with them at the counter. "Who's going to marry us?" said Kate.

"You'd better do it, Birdy," said Molly.

"I want it written down somewhere," said Kate.

"Who's going to give her away, then?" said Birdy. "Archy, you'd better. Come on, then, Mike. And you, Kate. Stand here. Together."

Birdy took a long time about it, filling in the entries carefully, using a pen from the desk and ink that had a flat metallic smell. The flies buzzed loudly against the glass. A car went by outside, and the red dog came back and stood in the doorway, looking in. Then it began to scratch itself.

"I don't know whether I've got this in the right order," said Birdy. "There's a bit to read."

He read it carefully and slowly, blinking a lot. Once he raised his voice when an army truck on heavy tires went by. Finally he said, "I suppose you're sort of married now." He looked up at Kate. "Here's the certificate." Then he added, "Slightly married." As Kate put out her hand it was shaking. Birdy shut the book and dropped the pen back into the plastic tray he'd taken it from. Archy cleared his throat. "For God's sake, Chooky, leave off howling, will you?"

That evening, after dinner, while they were sitting on the terrace having coffee, Julian rang Michael. The connection was bad and three times they were cut off. Finally, Mike came back. He did not sit down right away, but went to the edge of the terrace and stood with his hands out before him on the rail.

They stared at him, but none of them spoke. Finally, Kate got up and went and stood beside him. Still looking straight out before him, Michael said, "It's in the Institute now. They've shut off part of the building. Reece hopes — with luck he said — to be able to go on working . . . With *luck* . . ." He turned and faced them. "I'm beginning to wonder just what luck is," he said. "Once, I thought I knew. But can any of you tell me now?"

Four days later, at half past three in the afternoon, Archy got out of the car and went into the house through the kitchen door. Molly was at the sink, peeling potatoes. Archy stopped near the table, picked up a stainless steel kitchen knife, and stood looking at it, fiddling with it yet not really seeing it. He put it down, then slowly took off his jacket and dropped it on one of the kitchen chairs. Only then did he look at Molly. "I'm back early," he said, glancing up at the kitchen clock. Molly said nothing, just stood with the peeler in her hands looking at him. "They've shut the surgical wards," he said. "No more surgical admissions. Except for emergencies. If they can find someone to do them."

Molly turned off the tap. "That's sudden, isn't it?" she said. Then she dropped the peeler into the sink, crossed to the roller towel, and dried her hands, still looking at Archy, puzzled.

"I haven't been quite honest with you, Chooks," he said. "I haven't been telling you how bad it's getting. I told Birdy, too, not to let on." He looked at the knife he'd put down, picked it up again, and stared at it. "Today," he went on quietly, "I funked it."

"Funked what?"

"Seeing a patient."

"One of yours?"

He shook his head. "A new one. Query cancer of the bladder."

"I don't quite understand, Arch."

He looked up at her. "It's quite simple, I merely said I wouldn't see him."

"But why?"

"Because I knew where he'd come from. His wife rang me and

pleaded with me to see him. She lied about where he'd been, but I knew he'd come from a hospital out Parramatta way that was riddled with it. She was only doing her best. You can't blame her — I'd do the same. Actually, I don't know," he added, "whether I would or not. Don't let's talk about it. The fact is, I funked it. Christ, Chook!" He turned an anguished face to her. "You know how I've always felt about surgery . . . I've always regarded myself as having a skill I *must* use for the benefit of others . . ." His voice trailed off.

"I know all that, Arch." Standing beside his chair she pressed his head against her. "If anyone knows that, I do. And something else. Look at me." She put her hand under his chin and lifted his face. "I think you've done the right thing."

Suddenly, his face buried against her, Archy began to sob.

That evening Birdy came. They sat very quietly on the big balcony and listened while he told them that he was one day away — "One kid, a girl of fourteen, nice bright little thing with hair your color, Kate. Only one day away from going — we're just waiting to make sure she's clear . . . She's the last," he said. "The others are doing well on the boat. I'll get her down tomorrow night, then give myself three days shut up at home, and if I show no signs I'm off. If I get it, I've fixed it with the big chap, Rex, to slip moorings and have a go. They might make it. Any rate, it can't be worse than staying here. Did you know there was a battle today in William Street?" He looked around at them. "Bank, halfway down, a bunch of toughs raided it. Police turned up and it got worse. When I passed half an hour ago there were bodies still lying about." He fell silent, then said, "The violence is bloody. Stan Fellows rang me today. His wife's got it. He told me there'd been a pitched battle in some park out Manly way. A mob of people already camped there objected to others moving in. Shambles, he said. Police were called but didn't come. It's every man for himself now. Or very nearly."

"We heard," said Kate, "that an army truck full of bodies turned over at Bankstown. That was the day before yesterday. It's still there, just as it was after it turned over."

"What about the Islander, Arch?" said Molly. "Do you think it'll be all right? Someone might fly it away."

"I was thinking that, too. We'll go out in the morning and have a look."

"Birdy," said Molly, "have you got flour on *White Wings?*"

He nodded. "Half a ton of it. Why?"

Molly looked at Archy. "I've been thinking about flour. We can't take it in the plane, can we?"

He shook his head, "Not any real quantity, no."

"How are we going to make bread?" she said.

"I know how to make an oven out of stones and earth. For making bread," said Kate. "Tom showed me. He taught me lots of ways to cook and live in the bush."

Molly made a mental note that it was the very first time she'd heard Kate mention her dead husband in a normal conversation.

"I meant not having flour," she said. "You can make an oven all right, I know that, but what about the flour?"

"Chooks," said Archy, "we're going to try to find some island, or some beach, way up north, where there's tropical rain forest. There'll be breadfruit trees and yams and maybe casawa. Food like that." He took a deep breath, feeling the need to keep himself under control.

Molly said, "All I wanted to know is what do we do for carbohydrate, starch foods, bread substitute — call it what you like."

"We live off the land. Until we can plant our seeds. Christ, we've got enough seeds. Look, Molly," he said, his voice rasping, "others have cleared out, haven't they? And we can only suppose that they're surviving. They may not be. We don't know. I, too, am worried about what you call a bread substitute. But what the hell? What are we to do? Stay here until we catch it?"

"Not many people about here have caught it yet," put in Kate.

"How do you know?" Archy snapped. "With the houses shut up as they are, you'd never know what was going on inside."

Molly said, "I've never lived in the tropics. I wonder if I'll like it?"

"Probably," grunted Birdy. "Our thermal tolerance without clothes and the fact that we can't synthesize Vitamin D except in sunlight, or synthesize any ascorbic acid, probably means we're creatures, primarily, of a tropical environment." He grinned at Molly. "Our close cousins, the chimpanzee and the gorilla, even our more distant relatives, the orangutan and the gibbon, all lead us to believe we got to be human in a tropical environment. You'll like it all right." Then he added, "You'll bloody well have to."

"It's much the same with our parasitic diseases," said Michael. "There are a lot of them in the tropics. Which probably means they've had a long time to adapt themselves to feeling happy in a human host."

"So we get a whole lot of new tropical diseases, do we?" said Kate, and then the telephone rang. Archy got up and went inside to answer it. He was away a long time. When he came back he said, "That was Lew Strange — he's our next-door neighbor, Mike," he added by way of explanation. "Tina's got it, Molly."

"That's Lew's wife," said Kate to Michael. "And they've a girl, Eleanor. She's twelve or thirteen."

"How did Lew sound?" asked Molly.

"Poor bugger, half mad. You know what Tina's like. Now she's having hysterics. Lew and Eleanor haven't got it as yet, and Eleanor has shut herself up in her room."

"What did he want?" Molly asked.

"I don't know." Archy was silent, thinking. "Just to tell me, I suppose."

"To *warn* you," Birdy said.

Birdy didn't stay for dinner. Kate and Molly served it and the men helped them clear the table and stack the dishwasher.

At three o'clock the next morning the telephone rang. Molly woke before Archy and picked it up. At first, woken as she had been from a deep sleep, her whole being assaulted by the all-but-incomprehensible torrent of words that flowed from the telephone, Molly could make virtually nothing of it. One hand pressing the receiver to her ear, with the other she shook Archy to wake him.

"Who is it?" he asked.

"Eleanor," she said sideways to Archy, then back into the phone, "Eleanor, for heaven's sake, dear, get a hold of yourself. Try to calm down and tell me what has happened?"

Archy sat up and watched the hopelessness and the fear grow in Molly's face.

"What is it, Chooky?"

Molly dropped the receiver onto her lap. "Oh, God, Arch . . . Lew's shot Tina. Then turned the gun on himself." From the phone came a tiny chatter of desperate sound that crackled up at them.

Slowly Molly lifted the phone. Before she could speak there came Eleanor's frantic voice: "What shall I do, Mrs. Nolan? Oh, what shall I *do?*" The last sound was a long cry of despair.

She put the phone down again and looked at Archy. "God, Archy, what can we do for her?"

Archy gulped and said, "Nothing. Absolutely nothing at all."

"But she's alone in there with two bodies, Arch. She said he used a shotgun."

Memories of student days doing forensic medicine jumped before Archy. Of all things, a shotgun. He shook his head, trying to free himself from the ghastly picture.

"Chooky, we can do nothing. Talk to her. That's all. Here, give me the phone —"

"I can do it," said Molly. "Eleanor, listen, my dear. Are you listening?"

"Yes, Mrs. Nolan."

"Are you cold?"

"No."

"But you're shivering, I can hear it in your voice."

"I know, Mrs. Nolan, but I can't stop it. What shall I do? Daddy —"

"Now listen to me, dear — I'm going to see what I can do, so just hold on a moment . . ." Again, Molly put down the phone.

"I know," said Molly, "I'll ring Sister Philomena at the convent."

"But the Stranges weren't Catholics."

"That doesn't matter, I'm going to ring her. And if she can't help I'll ring the Salvation Army."

"What can they do?"

"They go," said Molly.

"Go? Oh, I see. You'd have to tell them that Tina had it."

"They've already got it at the convent."

When Molly finished telephoning she went and made tea, and they took it onto the balcony and drank it there, waiting for the dawn, their thoughts with the agony of the child next door who sat huddled on the front porch of her house, waiting for the novice Sister Philomena had told Molly she'd send as soon as it was light. In that time Molly prayed and remembered Saint Anthony: "Your life and your death are with your neighbor."

# 15 〰〰〰〰〰〰〰〰〰〰〰〰〰〰

"I just can't believe it! It's all so unreal! We've had this radio working for ten days now, and no matter what station I tune into I get practically the same thing." Steve had just turned the set off. "And I can tune into the whole goddamned world. This is a good set, and with that wire from the plane as an aerial around the room I can get all over. You've heard it. There seems no place at all where this disease hasn't struck, or is expected to. Maybe," he added after a moment, "we're the lucky ones."

"They'll get a cure for it," Elizabeth said.

"Well, maybe, but will they get it in time? That guy we heard from the U.S. just now wasn't exactly what you'd call a little ray of hope. Not by a long shot."

"It's as if," Steve said a few days later, "as if you and I are like an audience, sitting here insulated from the stage, watching the play, which is the world going bad."

"*Are* we insulated from it?"

"Well, those scientists and doctors and public announcements we hear all say it's spread by microscopic droplets in the breath and saliva of infected people. I can't see how it can come here."

"Unless they find us."

"Hell, they're not searching for us anymore. They're all too damn busy trying to hide from each other!"

One thing struck Steve at the time, though he did not comment on it. He noticed that though broadcast after broadcast spoke of vast numbers of people dying and often mentioned the famous by name, and though Elizabeth listened with him and sometimes commented that she knew some of those mentioned, never once did she admit the possibility that Julian might fall ill.

The day came when they heard for the first time a station making its final announcement. It was in Spanish, not a strong signal, and Steve guessed it was from somewhere in South America. "My Spanish isn't all that good," he muttered, concentrating hard on the distorted signal. "You know Spanish, honey?"

Elizabeth shook her head. "French and German only."

Carefully Steve homed in and held onto the signal. Then the voice stopped speaking and only the carrier wave remained. "Jesus," he said softly.

"What did they say?"

He switched the set off.

"If I got it right —" he interrupted himself. "Honey, we've got what, half a bottle of whiskey left?"

She nodded. "Nearly a bottle."

"Let's have a drink, then. The guy speaking was an engineer. He said that the station was going off the air because only he and a typist were left. He cracked up as he was speaking. He said his wife had died in his arms that morning. Jesus, I just can't *believe* all this stuff we're getting. I just can't believe it."

That evening they heard another transmitter announce that it was shutting down. This was in English, a Canadian station, the statement bald, unemotional, and brief. After it came the anthem. Some transmitters went off the air without any statement. Others played music: curious hodgepodge programs of classical music, pop, humor, soundtracks of musicals — tapes jumbled up in no order at all, as if an engineer was sitting in the control room putting anything on to keep the transmitter fed.

They heard scientists, doctors, priests, and politicians. Some stations played little but religious music, and the Vatican radio broadcast nothing but the continuous masses being said in Saint

[277]

Peter's in Rome. They heard three prime ministers and two presidents speak. They heard men with a shred of hope left, others in what Steve called "sheer blue funk." They heard grim snatches of talk in studios when a microphone had been left live. They heard radio amateurs saying good-bye to one another, and they got a lot of Morse, which Steve found difficult to follow.

The transmissions in English by the Voice of America, the Australian Broadcasting Commission, and the British Broadcasting Corporation gave Steve and Elizabeth most of what they learned. News bulletins were almost entirely concerned with the spread of the disease and its effects. Some people did not die directly of the disease. Some two hundred thousand died when a nuclear power station ran wild in Italy. More died when, either through accident or the design of some maniac, the germs causing plague, anthrax, and glanders escaped from a biological warfare laboratory in Tennessee. "And I thought," Steve said, "those bastards said they'd destroyed all that stuff." Infected with glanders, whole communities died in misery, ulcerating as foully as if they'd been the rabbits man had infected with myxomatosis. El Tor cholera swept through an Africa virtually overwhelmed by Ringway's and left great cities stinking centers of corruption in which only a few animals and plague-infested rats found sustenance.

Crops flourished and then went to seed. Grass crept from the verges onto the roads, and railway tracks grew red with rust. Summer lightning started fires that no one fought, and storms blew ships from their moorings and tore roofs from houses into which the rain ran unchecked.

On the day Steve could no longer raise New Zealand, he stripped more wire from one of the looms they'd brought from the crash and got Yehudi to climb with the end of it up into a big tree some seventy feet from the house. Though the new aerial increased the noise he received, it let him pull in weaker signals, and that night he heard stations in North America (an amateur in Entrance, Alberta, came in very strong), Brazil, Switzerland, and Holland (these in English) as well as the Australian news, the BBC, VOA, and South Africa. The broadcast from Cape Town was particularly grim. In a country with a medical service designed primarily to care for only the small white minority of the population, Ringway's disease was soon only one of many factors harassing a suddenly savagely depleted civil service. Carefully built-up and ruthlessly policed barriers between whites, blacks, and coloreds broke down literally overnight. Whites barricaded themselves in their houses and died there, burned to death, or were hacked down when they tried to run for it.

When Steve turned off the set at two o'clock that morning he said, "Isn't it extraordinary? We're listening to what would seem to be the end of human life on this planet, yet here we are, surrounded by people who know nothing of it, nor, I suppose, ever will. Because, as I figure it, they don't even know the rest of the world exists. They're so goddamned self-sufficient. All they need is one another and this bit of jungle. There must be a lesson in it somewhere."

"That news from England," Elizabeth said. "How does the BBC make up its news bulletins if they never go outside the building?"

"Telephones, honey. And they monitor other radio stations Same as VOA and the Australians are doing. But what gets me right here in this village is how *uninterested* these people are. Boar's Tusk, several of these people, have heard our radio and they just couldn't care less."

"But for heaven's sake, Steve, they can't understand what's being said!" she protested.

"What I mean is that they're not even interested in the thing itself, a little box like this radio being able to make all that noise and keep you and me so interested. You notice Yehudi today? He ignored it, yet he must have seen how *pleased* I was, how impressed I was by the effect he'd created just by hanging a bit of wire up into a tree. Maybe that's part of the lesson there is for us to learn from these people. While we so-called civilized races have been wasting our energies running up every new alley, these people have just kept their eye glued to the main chance: food, shelter, and, I guess, love."

"You're on dangerous ground," Elizabeth said. "These people could never produce a Beethoven or a Newton or a Shakespeare."

"Who said they couldn't? Maybe they have."

"Where is he, then?"

"What I'm trying to say —" Steve began, but she cut him short.

"I know what you're trying to say, Steve, but if their way of life is better than ours, then to achieve the kind of life they have we have to limit our aspirations."

"This is the argument that goes, it's better to be able to appreciate a Beethoven quartet — with all that means in terms of intellectual understanding and emotional suffering — than to be a human cabbage and know only that Beethoven was a German who wrote music. You, I take it, wouldn't want to be a cabbage?"

"Good God, no. Would you?"

"I guess I had no choice in the matter. The way I am, I suffer. But I still think there's some catch in life we haven't figured out yet, and that these pygmies have. It's as if they don't want to interfere with anything they don't absolutely have to. You notice how careful they are not to infringe on the jungle with their village any more than is necessary? It's as if cutting down trees is an act of violation for them. I bet the gods they have all live in trees, or streams, and maybe caves, and in the air and in plants. I think that if I could talk to them and tell them what this radio was they still wouldn't be impressed. I guess if we could tell them all about our world they'd spend most of their time saying so what? All the same," he went on more slowly, looking at the radio, "I'm sure glad you bought that set, honey. Imagine, without it, we'd be like the pygmies, knowing nothing about anything going on outside."

"In other words, we'd be happier than we are?"

"Now you're teasing me," he said, smiling. "You know very well what I mean."

Steve was soon so much better that the day came when Elizabeth suggested that they might try to walk slowly to the bald hill they'd seen on their way back from the crash. Steve was enthusiastic but said they'd better let Boar's Tusk know. They found him squatting under his house, making a wooden bowl, patiently chipping out the timber with a little stone adze, a greeny stone as smooth as glass and effectively sharp.

They were surprised at how quickly he understood what they

wanted to do. He wasn't, as Steve said, all that keen on the idea but he agreed. When they left the village the next morning at about nine, they noticed they were being followed. Elizabeth said, "There are about eight of them. Yehudi's with them."

"Yehudi's a man of some position, I guess," Steve said.

"Don't they trust us?" Elizabeth said.

"I don't think it's that. Maybe it's because they just want to make sure we don't come to any harm. Or maybe get lost."

The pygmies didn't follow them to the top of the hill but remained at the bottom of the fissure by which Steve and Elizabeth slowly wound their way up. As they'd guessed, the view was superb. But of the sea there was no sign, only range after range of mountains stretching to infinity. Just off the brow of the hill they found shade and a grassy patch, and there they stretched themselves and let the feeling that they were entirely on their own for the first time since the crash sink into them. They stayed until well after midday, and when they started down Elizabeth said, "Thank you, Steve, for that."

"Why thank me, honey?"

"Because I didn't ever think I'd be able to be really happy here. Now I feel it might be possible. I love Bald Hill. Somehow I feel it's our very own. Do let's come here often."

"Just as often as you like, love."

# *16* ~~~~~~~~~~~~~~~~~~~~~~~~~~~~~~~~~~

Miss Marler stood in the thin drizzle and watched the army truck pull away from the Institute. Under the tarpaulin was Julian's body, with three others. The lift hadn't been running for five weeks. She went slowly up the stairs, a frosting of rain on her hair and the thick wool of her cardigan.

She went into her office and sat on the camp bed to light a cigarette. She was the last one left in the section, though occasionally there came the sound of someone banging doors on the floor below. This was the porter's wife, whom hysteria and the fear of death had reduced to lunacy. Miss Marler smoked the cigarette through, stubbed it out, got up, and went into Julian's office. On Julian's bed, Edith, her large black cat, opened its eyes and stared at her. Then Edith stood, back arched, dropped her forequarters, stretched out her front legs, claws spread wide on the gray army blanket, and made a sound deep in her throat. As Miss Marler sat down in Julian's chair, Edith leaped from the bed and came to her, tail held high. Miss Marler patted her lap and the cat jumped lightly up onto it and began to purr, working her foreclaws in and out of the stuff of Miss Marler's skirt. Miss Marler decided she had much to be thankful for: her aged mother had had little strength to fight — she had gone in just under four days; Julian's long-drawn-out suffering was now over, and for Edith, the capsule Julian had given Miss Marler would make the end of life a process lasting no more than a second . . . But that was still days away, because as yet, Miss Marler told herself, she didn't feel too bad and her temperature was only ninety-nine . . . And she had two packets of candles left. She feared the dark loneliness of the nights more than anything.

Miss Marler looked up from Edith and stared at the top of Julian's desk, seeing nothing, conscious only of the feel of the fur under her hand. It was a cold day, and her heavy skirt and sweaters barely kept out the chill of the unheated building.

Then, on the top sheet of some papers on the blotter before her, words began to form themselves into a sentence . . .

"Miss Marler," she read — Julian's handwriting, but shaky, uneven on the page — "these are but notes and incomplete, but would you please type them up on the strongest paper you have and lock them in my safe with the Ringway file. With my heartfelt thanks for your friendship and all the help you have given me. Julian Reece."

She started, catching the reality, read it again, and then read on . . .

"Does man deserve his name: *Homo sapiens?* It was not given to him, he gave it to himself, in his arrogance imagining he was sapient. It was a fancied sagacity.

"Predictions are, of course, fallible, but the probability of disaster unless we changed our ways was so patently obvious that only a fool would have waited to be wise after the event.

"We elected the wrong leaders; we gave our future and that of our children to those who saw only good in the destruction and exploitation of our natural resources. We fell for the dangerous optimism of the ignorant, or worse, of the financially interested.

"Before this disease struck there were 3.6 billion people on the earth, most of them getting barely enough food to live on, housed appallingly and riddled with disease. Yet we allowed our politicians, economists, and businessmen to go on passing laws, inventing schemes and devil-take-the-hindmost-it-won't-be-me projects designed to increase 'productivity' and 'growth' and therefore to exacerbate what was already a virtually insoluble problem. To our leaders, survival of the species, conservation of the earth's resources, preservation of its environment, were of far less importance than what they saw as the deadly serious business of advantage for personal, political, or religious reasons.

"A hundred years ago man believed he could foresee something of his destiny. And it was good, so he thought. But we built on violence instead of justice and liberty, and reaped the harvest of tyranny. We believed we could bring happiness by industrial development; in the event, we brought misery and the physical corruption of our environment. We allowed our consciences to falter, then to die.

"We exhausted our resources, both spiritual and physical; religion ceased to offer consolation, our political systems gave no enlightenment. Suppression took the place of fulfillment. Not knowing what we wanted, what we *needed*, we were in ignorance of where we were going.

"Did man really desire freedom? Or was it slavery he was seeking? The politics he invented led men's leaders not to be lovers of men but seekers after power over them.

"Compassion, contemplation, love, became little more than words or at best words used without understanding. The soaring of the spirit that let man build Chartres Cathedral evaporated because we forgot what love and contemplation and compassion were about. In our blindness we lost sight of joy and found only the shadow of dissipation. We fell from the stars into the pit.

"As a scientist, I want to say that we distorted our knowledge, we offered it for sale on the altar of nationalism. Like the spirit of Chartres, the scientific conscience also died. We let our work serve the interests of power for the sake of power rather than serve the interests of humanity. If science can be called a search for truth, we were prepared to hide the truths we discovered through fear (in our jargon) of 'disclosing classified information' and being jailed for it. Or — worse — we allowed ourselves as scientists to cooperate with and to be dictated to by the political power seekers. In a world crying out for medicine, tools, housing, life itself, our greatest efforts went into inventing murder machines and the ways to tear our planet to pieces. Were we capable of developing a new morality? Our old moral values seemed incapable of spawning one. We knew the biosphere was One and

[284]

the species finite, yet somehow we seemed unable to grasp the enormity of our omission to put our knowledge to work. We ought to have renamed our planet *Torrey Canyon* because our course was as recklessly charted as was that ship's, and the ability to imagine what catastrophe could bring as limited as that of the master of that ship.

"In one sense, the emergence of the Ringway virus, far from being a calamity, may have been good. Those churchmen, who in the last months have been speaking of it as retribution for a Creation sadly managed by man may have some merit in their argument — whether one believes in an omnipotent God or not. That man was a bad manager is without doubt. Whether man will survive I cannot say; it may well be that some small, remotely placed communities will escape. Whether he will ever flourish again is also conjecture, but if he does then it may be that sufficient records of this time will remain for him to draw the lesson of survival. Put at its grimmest, the child Barbara Lambert (see Ringway file) may have been a benefactor in that the virus that developed in her body saved countless millions of people from dying in appalling misery and conflict from the year 2000 on through starvation caused by overpopulation and the social upheavals consequent upon it, and the inevitable shortages of resources capable of sustaining bearable life.

"There is this also: that in virtually wiping out man Ringway's disease removed him before he had quite destroyed the planet. The heritage we leave may be nothing to be proud of — we have been the poorest of caretakers — but we have not, as yet, done all the damage we were capable of.

"If man does survive and among his numbers there are Christians, will they question the sense of God's command in the Book of Genesis that 'man be fruitful and multiply and fill the earth and subdue it and have domination over every living thing'? It is in words as unheeding as these that so many men have sought to excuse man's savagery to the earth and the plants and the animals on it. Seeing no farther than his own uniqueness he has been blind to the uniqueness of every other living thing and enmeshed in his anthropocentric mania has actually convinced himself that he had a significance which gave him domination over every living thing. It is, incidentally, a claim he would find difficult to sustain to the satisfaction of those animals and plants his brutal dominion over has not yet wiped out.

"As I write this some ten thousand plants are facing extinction.

"Backed by big financial interests, the killing of animals for fun is thriving; in Italy alone three hundred million birds are slaughtered each year.

"Will a future and properly sapient man develop philosophies and ethics we should have discovered? Is it inherent in the makeup of our genus that the most successful of the religions we have invented should be based upon a God made in our own likeness? Are we inherently righteous and 'just'? Will future men regard the earth's resources as finite — which they are — or will they continue our blind squandering of them as if they had no end?

"Will there still be drug companies who spend more money on advertising their wares than on research?

"Is man capable of the realization that unless he can use again and again every particle of matter necessary for his survival then disaster is inevitable?

"Man is a recent accident of evolution. Must he be God's maddest experiment?

"We have been unable to learn that one of the necessities of survival is self-discipline. And the need for caution. Only the reckless play Russian roulette, not the brave. We allowed genetic engineering and molecular biology to reach a point where they were greater hazards to life than the hydrogen bomb — if that be possible. The common bacterium that lives in the human gut is a useful and common research tool, but the work that many scientists were doing was of such a nature that either by accident or design cancer-producing genes could be introduced into this bacterium. Once let loose, this very common bacterium could carry with it genes capable of bringing about almost any biological horror. A virus or bacteria so altered, if it escaped from a laboratory, could have inflicted on the world an epidemic of more than myxomatosis-size proportions. The fact that much of this work was being done under the cloak of military secrecy only makes our folly the more damnable.

"And folly is not too strong a word. Plutonium is a poison so dangerous that it is difficult to conceive why sane men would ever wish to make it. Yet not only did we make it, we lost a lot of it — because we know how many kilos of it we made, and how many kilos we can account for — and there is an alarmingly appreciable difference in the two amounts.

"But if these future communities are to be better caretakers of the planet than we have been, they will have to see a finer, brighter goal than we ever glimpsed. They will have to invent less anthropomorphic gods and different kinds of heroes, measure success and happiness by a different yardstick.

"The trivial will have to be recognized for what it is. They must see the danger of destroying vast forest areas — if these ever come again — just to make paper, that wonderful invention that we debased by using it in such enormous quantities for, mostly, the silliest and basest of purposes. Paper, the making of which alone accounted for five thousand tons of that deadly poison mercury, which we allowed to run into the oceans each year.

"Add to that" — Julian then had written, his hand by then so shaky that Miss Marler had difficulty in reading. "Add to that the insecticides, deadly killers, and some ten million tons of gasoline products deposited in the oceans every year, along with all the other chemical and organic pollutants we dumped, and we can realize just how carefully these future communities will have to tread if they are ever to see again the oceans — which cover seven tenths of the earth's surface — as the glorious creations and sources of life and life-giving processes (plankton, which makes the oxygen we breathe) they were before man joined the animal kingdom.

"New man, to survive, must see our virtues as his vices. He must regard 'growth' as the engine of destruction; 'increased productivity' as its handmaiden; must look with the gravest suspicion upon any product that means the use of irreplaceable substances.

"And work . . ."

Here Julian had stopped, his writing trickling away into a scrawl.

Then, farther down the page:

"Work must be spread evenly between all who can do it . . ."

On the next page Julian had written:

"Scenario for destruction, observed in expensive London restaurant (vignette). Plump woman with large steak (to provide which, an animal had to die) eating about one sixth of steak, then pushing remainder away. Same woman seen later leaving restaurant in leopard coat. Leopard killed by poacher? Then being driven off in one of three cars (owned by husband), any one of which cost enough money to sustain African (or any poverty-stricken) family for number of years.

"Cruelly, in our greed we drove to the very edge of extinction the whale, the largest animal ever to live on this planet, and a mammal, warm-blooded as we are, suckling its young as we do . . .

"Let those who will follow us not forget René Dumont's children of the backward countries who never attained their full promise, who died of kwashiorkor because the fish meal — from a seriously depleted ocean — that just might have saved them was fed to the chickens (battery bred and reared in misery) that were gorged by the rich."

Julian had then written: "Where to begin? The mind boggles, because power is in the hands of the privileged, whether capitalist or communist."

Then, on the next line:

"Ned Ludd was right. It was not he who was feeble-minded. His suspicions were so well founded. Start a Ned Ludd Society.

" 'What region of the earth is not full of our calamities?' "

Under that quotation was one word that Miss Marler stared at for a long time before she saw it was not Virgin, but Virgil.

# 17 〜〜〜〜〜〜〜〜〜〜〜〜〜〜

Archy sat in the Islander's left-hand seat, Michael in the copilot's with a map on his lap. At two hundred feet Archy selected flaps up and felt for the trim control. When he next looked at the altimeter he raised his hand above his head and switched off the auxiliary pump. Michael glanced sideways at him; Archy was definitely paler. As Archy set engine revolutions and manifold pressure to climb out at ninety-five knots with seventy-five percent power he moved uncomfortably in his seat. Molly was right behind Archy, and out of the corner of his left eye Michael saw Molly tense as she noticed Archy's movement. Kate was behind Michael, Crackers crouched at her feet, looking up at her with an expression that asked if all this was really necessary. Behind the empty seat was extra fuel in drums well lashed down and the gardening and carpentry tools and canned food and vegetable seeds and the medical supplies and instruments and clothes and candles, two good tents and other camping gear, and a rubber dinghy and hurricane lamps and kerosene and a shotgun.

"How do you feel, Archy?" Molly said.

"Tenderness," Archy said, trying to be funny, "in right iliac fossa." Then he said, "Seriously, Chooky, don't worry, I'm used to it. It'll go, it's just being aggravated by all the packing up. Besides, we've a doctor in the house, don't forget." He moved his right elbow, gently nudging Michael.

"That's right," Michael said, "and one who's desperately trying to remember all he can about McBurney's point."

"Now *there*," said Archy, "not being an epidemiologist, I can help."

"While under anesthetic, I suppose," said Molly angrily. "Talk about the shoemaker's children being poorly shod," she went on. "To think that you, Archy Nolan, should find yourself flying us all to . . . hell, to Kingdom Come, for all I know, with an attack of appendicitis —"

"Chronic," he put in.

"How the hell do you know when a chronic one isn't going to become acute? All we need now is a perforation and we'll be bloody lucky if we all don't die with you. Mike, can you land this airplane?"

Archy said, "Of course he can! And what's more he's going to begin flying it now," Archy went on. "Mike, stick your feet on the pedals and put one hand on the stick. Don't worry, Chooky," Archy said back over his shoulder, "this is a very beautiful plane, it hasn't one nasty bad habit. All right, Mike, she's yours. Just hold her there, ever so gently. Just try keeping her flying straight and level."

As Michael took control the Islander hiccuped slightly and Crackers put back his head, stared at the cabin roof, and let out a long-drawn-out howl.

"When," said Molly, "do you have to take your next tablet, Archy?"

"Not until this evening. Please," he went on, tension sharpening his voice, "do let me be, Molly. So I've a chronic appendicitis. And so it would seem now perhaps more uncomfortable than it's been in the past. So . . . so I'm sorry. Sorry for all of you, not just myself. But talking about it isn't going to reduce the inflammation. In the meantime, whether we make it or not, with this wind up his tail Birdy ought to have got quite a way up the coast — the same wind that is pushing him is pushing us, too. Everyone keep your eyes peeled for him. A big, lumpy boat, ketch-rigged."

Fifteen minutes later it was Kate on the starboard side who

picked it up. Then Molly got it. "About two o'clock, Arch," she said excitedly.

"He's well out," Archy said, picking up the small white dot, "if it is Birdy. Let's have a look. Mike, I'll take over."

Archy enriched the mixture for the descent and began a gentle bank to starboard, dropping at about five hundred feet a minute from the ten-thousand-foot altitude they'd been maintaining at fifty-nine percent power to give them the best economy of fuel. Archy had worked out that if this wind held, and they were burning about twenty-three gallons of fuel an hour, they could, with that particular plane's tankage, get more than a thousand miles before the need to refuel. It was a comforting thought. Now they had found Birdy's *White Wings*. As Archy turned out of the bank and saw that it was indeed her, he felt a stirring of the spirit that in some way he didn't understand seemed to indicate an omen rather good than bad. Though he also took notice that at virtually the same moment he felt what he decided could well be the first stirrings of colic in his right iliac fossa. Still, there was no nausea.

"Oh, doesn't she look *beautiful!*" cried Kate. "I had no idea she was such a lovely boat. And so big!"

The ketch was well down on her marks but making good speed under all plain sail. Archy let the Islander drop, coming up on the ketch's port quarter. He lowered flaps for reduced speed and at a hundred feet leveled off and swept by the stern of *White Wings* at about ninety miles an hour. They picked Birdy out easily, dumpy in white shorts and no shirt, standing with one hand grasping a weather mizzen shroud. With the other hand he was shading his eyes, looking up at them. A tall youngster was in the cockpit at the helm, others were forward. As the Islander flew past other children came up from below. Some of them waved, but Birdy didn't move except to turn his head, still shading his eyes, to keep the Islander in sight as Archy turned to port to begin the circuit that would bring him round for another run.

Ahead of the ketch Archy finished his turn and flew in parallel with the ketch's course. Archy, Michael, and the women waved. The children replied, but Birdy didn't move. His left hand remained on the shroud, his right flattened above his brows.

"Do you think he knows it's us?" Kate said.

"He knows," said Molly.

"But he's never seen the plane," Kate said.

"He knows all right," said Archy.

Kate was silent for a long moment, then she said, "Oh, I see," and sat there looking at Birdy, remembering the last words she'd heard him speak. "The Great Stoned Age," Birdy had said, and he banged the door of his car and drove off to the boat.

"We won't stay long," said Archy.

"Please, Arch," said Molly, "go around once more, will you?"

This time they thought Birdy nodded his head slowly, three or four times in an exaggerated kind of way. It was the only sign he gave. None of them in the Islander said anything until Archy had taken her up to ten thousand feet and settled her again at cruising power. Then Kate said, "But even with all those nice kids around him Birdy looked so lonely. He looked *so* lonely. Oh, but I do hope they'll be kind to him!"